Jesse Armstrong is the co-creator and writer of the BAFTA Award-winning *Peep Show*, as well as *Fresh Meat*, *Bad Sugar*, *Babylon* and, with Chris Morris, *Four Lions*. He was also co-writer of *The Thick of It* and the Oscar-nominated *In the Loop*, and wrote *The Entire History of You* for Charlie Brooker's *Black Mirror*.

Love, Sex and Other Foreign Policy Goals is his first novel.

'Within the first few sentences, *Love, Sex and Other Foreign Policy Goals* had me hooked ... combines the best of sitcom-style drama with just the right amount of gravity ... Armstrong's debut manages to be clever and fun while also retaining grittiness. I hope this is the first of many'

Independent

'A truly comic novel'

Esquire

'Armstrong at his comic best ... Armstrong's hilarious portrayal of flawed humanity wins it for me'

* * * * *Stylist*

JESSE ARMSTRONG

Love, Sex and Other Foreign Policy Goals

VINTAGE

1 3 5 7 9 10 8 6 4 2

Vintage,
20 Vauxhall Bridge Road,
London SW1V 2SA

Vintage is part of the Penguin Random House group of companies
whose addresses can be found at global.penguinrandomhouse.com.

Penguin
Random House
UK

First published by Vintage in 2016
First published in Great Britain by Jonathan Cape in 2015

www.vintage-books.co.uk

A CIP catalogue record for this book
is available from the British Library

ISBN 9780099578741

Printed and bound by Clays Ltd, St Ives plc
Typeset by Palimpsest Book Production Ltd, Falkirk, Stirlingshire

Penguin Random House is committed to a sustainable future for our
business, our readers and our planet. This book is made from Forest
Stewardship Council® certified paper.

MIX
Paper from
responsible sources
FSC
www.fsc.org   FSC® C018179

To my mother and father

SLOVENIA

HUNGARY

Zagreb

CROATIA

Velika
Kladusa

Bihac

R.Danube

BOSNIA-
HERZEGOVINA

SERBIA

N

Sarajevo

MONTENEGRO

A D R I A T I C   S E A

Former Yugoslavia
Summer, 1994

0   100 km

0   100 miles

Western Bosnia
Summer, 1994

CROATIA

Karlovac

REPUBLIC OF
SERBIAN KRAJINA

Internal conflict line

Velika
Kladusa

Cazin

*Internationally recognised border
between Bosnia-Herzegovina and Croatia*

Izacic

Bihac

N

0   20 km
0   20 miles

Territory held by the
Autonomous Province
of Western Bosnia

Territory held by the
5th Corps of the Army
of the Republic of
Bosnia-Herzegovina

Territory held by the
Bosnian-Serb Army

De facto borders and
front lines

Love, Sex and Other Foreign Policy Goals

Chapter 1

I was in London, and I think every other person in the room was posh. So posh, in fact, they never used the word. 'Posh', I clocked quickly, because I'm a fast study, is a little too close to the knuckle. 'Posh', it turns out, is actually rather common. 'Grand' and 'smart' are the words the posh use to describe houses and people and parties that are very posh. And if at those parties the posh ever meet an outsider who questions, even obliquely, the distribution of wealth and privilege from which the non-posh are excluded, they get ever so gently nailed forever as 'chippy', and that's a killer cobweb from which there is really no escape. Never be chippy around the posh. I got that fast too.

So, I was in a posh house in west London, and I could feel every single point at which my clothing was touching my body, and I couldn't imagine what in the whole wide fucking world I could possibly say to anyone.

We were all there in a sitting room up on the first floor, which struck me as a very sophisticated floor for a sitting room. It suggested that anything, really, could go anywhere and only the anxious bourgeoisie would feel required to have their sitting-around rooms at ground level.

The rough cotton of my shirt collar was chafing particularly. Taking a look in the large mirror over the mantelpiece, yes, I thought – for this encounter with Penny's family and close friends, for the Great Announcement, I had ended up choosing the sort of outfit a mother might pick for her seven-year-old to wear to a friend's wedding. M&S 'chino' trousers; a shirt checked with brown-and-red stripes that its manufacturers presumably hoped implied some sort of relationship with the countryside, and what it might be slightly grandiose to describe as a 'green sweater'.

Along the sides of the rectangular sitting room were sofas and comfortable chairs. A couple of low tables in the middle were stacked with champagne glasses. You could try to read the history of the rise and fall of the British Empire along the mantelshelf under the mirror: Indian jib jabs and silver candlesticks, Chinese pots and invites to American Embassy receptions. Underfoot, the rug over the carpet was red and Persian or similar, the pile so thick you felt a little unstable walking on it.

Actually, looking into the antique mirror, perhaps I looked more like a gawky cleric than a seven-year-old? The Doc Martens, poking out like a pair of regular-sized clown shoes, did very much give me the look of a once hip vicar who had undergone a crisis of faith and retired somewhere quiet to have a big think about everything.

Nearby, Penny's parents and younger brother, Von, were talking about an acquaintance's son who had been either promoted or mugged; it was hard for me to make out the concrete detail because I was preoccupied with trying not to fuck up the complicated manoeuvre I was engaged in: drinking from a glass. For some reason, taking a sip without chomping a bite out of the champagne flute like a loon or choking to death on the booze felt like it required all my powers of concentration. As her father moved round with

2

the bottle, topping guests up, I was actively 'planning' my next swallow. But it turns out swallowing is one of those things where too much planning is counterproductive. I spluttered a little and looked down at a side table.

Because all the while, as I tensed up ready for the announcement, there was, lying there like a time bomb on the table, my own personal problem. The humdinger, the shame-maker: The Gift. Back in the bookshop, it had all seemed quite amusing, after – what? – seven tours around the shop. Everything else seemed a little gauche. I wanted something playful. Not something obvious from the offer piles by the door, nor something classic and suggestive of the exam room. Nothing, for God's sake, from 'Humour'. Something a little bit tasty. Something unexpected.

Well, none of them would be expecting *this*. I could confidently predict that. For there, buried three gifts down, asymmetrically wrapped and poorly taped, was a hardback copy of *Elite Fighting Forces: Maximum Power* – a survey of various paramilitary commando units from around the globe and, furthermore, some cross-section diagrammatics of their key equipment and weaponry. This was what I was giving to win the heart of the young woman I believed I loved.

Penny stood and offered round the room a bowl of the jagged, lead-heavy crisps they liked – so expensive and painful to eat. She stood a head taller than her adoptive mother and father. A Nubian queen transplanted, she regarded her folks, as they rustled their fingertips in the snack bowl, with what looked to me a disdain so ingrained no one dared notice it.

The number of people in the room felt perfectly judged to make it unclear whether it was necessary to verbally excuse myself for a visit to the toilet. Can you, I wondered, just walk out of a room here, or is that in fact incredibly rude? Where, after all, are you going? Are you coming back? Perhaps not. Perhaps you have been grossly offended? Perhaps you're trying to steal something? But similarly, surely you don't normally, to everyone, state exactly where you're going each time you leave a room? Or do you? Is that exactly what you do? In the end I reversed out like I was at Versailles, or might have been stabbed in the back, laying down an additionally extended plasticised grin as covering fire.

In the toilet I splashed water onto my face, seeking comfort in the sort of thing someone might do in a film, like knocking back a Scotch in a bar after getting fired in the opening scene.

Elite Fighting Forces. In the shop it felt so obviously wrong as to be rather hilarious; the shiny cover shot of an SAS man crouching ready to shoot was an amusing counterpoint to the Nobel laureates and prizewinners. But isolated from its shop-mates I was pretty sure *Elite Fighting Forces* was going to look not hilariously, but slightly psychotically, misjudged.

'Gone to Ground?' a very thin man said in a cartoon speech bubble up on the toilet wall, unaware of a fat man, also in red hunting garb, hiding on the other side of a hedge. 'Gone to Ground?' When had it been produced – 1790? 1870? 1987? Product of the English Social Signifier Wall Coverings Company.

Splash.

But why had fatty gone to ground? What was he hiding from? Was this the *Cheers* of its day? But now the layers had built up so you couldn't see the joke? Presumably, fatty – like the fox – had gone to ground. But why? Why the fuck had fatty gone to ground? Was he looking for something? And then, as in the moments of mad allusive connection before sleep, for a beat it felt like the family – even fatty – knew I was hiding, and the cartoon was a rebuke to all the misplaced provincials who had

4

wandered into the house over the years and found themselves going to ground in the downstairs loo.

I was looking at my champagne glass thinking how wrong it had been to bring it with me (as if I was in a rough pub and someone might spike my pint), when it suddenly struck me that the length of my absence had probably crossed the point that implied defecation. What a horrible thing to do. To come to another person's house and then sneak away to a little room and do a huge shit.

I hurried to return, hoping to fit myself into a time frame that might simply have suggested a very long piss. But a spurt from the brass tap zoomed up the scalloped curve of the sink like an ambitious skateboarder and left my trousers looking urine-spattered. The solution, I decided, was to ensure the accident couldn't be misinterpreted. I flicked extra droplets quite liberally all over the area below the waistband. This was an unambiguous overspill, I wanted my trousers to announce. Not a urine situation.

In the sitting room, Penny oohed and aahed at every new present as if the person who'd given it had divined the true desire of her secret heart. The swathe of damp across my lap went unmentioned but not unnoticed as she claimed a set of expensive French art pencils were exactly what she'd been hoping for, dealt with an incredibly thick Norman Mailer book by swearing she had nearly bought it herself, and gobbled up a piece of sheer silk, wrapping it around her head and fingering the fabric with delight.

As she turned my package in her hands, I held for a moment a hope that God or elves might mean *Elite Fighting Forces* was a dream and beneath the wrapping would be a suitable book. But the truth was no book that shape and size could be suitable. A4 like a football annual. But thin. So cheaply, depressingly thin. As if even the people knocking out this man-crap had given up halfway through.

'Oh – wow. Thank you. Thank you, Andrew, so much!' she said, looking at it with a moment's hesitation.

'Yeah, it's supposed to be, I thought . . .'

'It's great!'

'It's just – stupid.'

'No, I'd like to know more about . . . Fighting Forces.'

And before I could interject, she took this treasure for a tour of the room. I wanted to make a public explanation, but an essay, maybe even a set of officially written histories, like those produced after the Second World War by each arm of the military, something like that would be needed to explain the cultural and economic factors that had led to this gift. Simon, my rival, and Cally, her best friend, gathered with an older couple in deliciously soft cashmere jumpers to take a careful look at *Elite Fighting Forces*. The last time anyone outside of an Oxfam shop would open its covers.

'It was supposed to be sort of – funny,' I said to her father.

'It's incredibly kind of you. Very nice of you to come. I'm Kenneth, wonderful to meet you.' The father extended his hand warmly. Admittedly, it didn't have quite the same warm effect as when we had been introduced standing in pretty much the same spot, in the same room, twenty-four hours earlier. But it was still nice. After all, I had the feeling that I was so insubstantial in Kenneth's estimation that up to eighteen or twenty visits might be necessary before I became fully visible. Up until then I would be a ghost who, if treated civilly and offered enough expensive crisps, might eventually fuck off. Kenneth looked like he'd met enough people now; he was basically full.

'And how do you know Penny?' he asked.

'From Manchester.'

'Ah. Yes. And what were you reading?'

'Oh, I wasn't at the university, actually.'

6

'Right?'

'I'm actually a construction worker,' I said. ('Like you might find in an American storybook or a pornographic video,' I didn't say.)

'Oh, right.'

'Yeah. I was thinking about going to university, but I'm sort of –'

'No, absolutely,' he said.

If our conversation was a cat, I had the feeling about now he'd have hit it with a spade, to put it out of its misery.

'Yeah,' I said.

When Penny first told me what her dad did I misheard lobbyist for 'hobbyist' and went on for several months thinking he was an attic Airfixer or annexe egg-cup potter. And even now, like a young child, I couldn't quite shake the conviction that my imagined version of him might turn out to have a basis in reality.

'And have you been busy at work, lately?' I asked.

He ignored this almost completely, giving just the husk of a laugh as he looked across the room.

'Huh, yeah. Nice champagne,' I offered, almost inaudibly, then a puckish variation: 'Champagne is nice.'

Kenneth walked away, leaving me alone to clench my buttocks five times in a row as self-sentenced punishment for general social crimes, before Penny arrived.

'Really, thanks, Andy.'

'It was meant to be –'

'It looks interesting.' She turned to an illustrated cross section of the outboard motor of a Special Boat Service dinghy.

What was worst was that in its flumping thud to the ground my gift seemed to have caused no surprise at all, as if any oddity I offered up would have been indulged: a chewed bone; broken biscuits. That, like a child wrapping his mother's hairbrush, I should be congratulated for offering anything at all.

'I thought it would be funny, Penny – look at these fucking beefcakes!'

She flicked her eyes over the photo as Cally and Simon joined us and she said, 'OK, listen, I'm going to do it now.'

'Shit, yeah?' said Cally.

'Maybe,' I said, 'we should wait till at least –'

'I think now is a good time,' said Simon.

'No,' I agreed, catching up, 'maybe, now is a good time. Is it? Would it be a good time, now?'

'Look, I've waited and delayed. I got you all here as support and I'm very grateful for you coming and I should have done it last night, and Shannon and everyone is going to be here tomorrow and we need the credit card. So I'm just going to fucking do it. But if it goes weird, will you help? Don't let me leave without saying it, all right?'

'*No pasarán*,' Simon said, clenching his fist playfully, and Penny did it back while I chuckled indulgently, like I knew what the hell they were on about.

Then Mrs Calman was upon us – 'We're thinking about just walking to the restaurant, is that all right?'

'Mum, there's something I need to tell you about the summer.'

'Oh, right?'

'I'm going to go. To Yugoslavia.'

'Oh. Your idea?'

'Yes. My idea. Our idea. We're all going.'

Simon and I smiled: it's going to be OK, *we're* on board.

'Well, let's talk about this later,' Mrs Calman said and gave a broad smile that tightened her mouth so her lipstick parted in places and revealed how white her lips were beneath.

8

'But I am going.'

'Look, let's not spoil this evening. Let's talk about it later.'

'Fine, but I am going.'

And through the mist, Kenneth, the imperial gunboat, came in to dock.

'What's this?'

'We'll talk about this later. I'll tell you later,' Mrs Calman said.

'I'm going to Bosnia, Dad.'

'No,' Kenneth said.

'I am.'

'No. No. No no no no. No,' Kenneth argued.

'Where? To do what?' Mrs Calman asked.

'I can't believe you'd just say no.'

'Well, if you just say you're going I'm just going to say no,' Kenneth said.

'Well, I am going. I've got a ticket.'

'Yes, well, I've got a chimney but it doesn't mean I'm a train.' I looked at the floor. 'Where? How? Why? No,' said Kenneth.

'This is bollocks,' Penny said and looked at Cally. They turned and walked out of the room and upstairs.

Simon and I, the men eager to take their daughter to be killed in a war zone, were left to explain things to the Calmans and the couple in cashmere jumpers.

'I think we just feel that at this moment, in this — era that, Bosnia, it's in Europe. And we have a responsibility to acknowledge that,' Simon said.

'I acknowledge that,' Kenneth said.

'We're hoping, there's a hope that . . .' Simon carried on.

'What are you actually doing?'

'We have a van,' I offered.

9

'Right. I believe they are already familiar with that technology in the Balkans.'

'And we're going to take the van and fill it with provisions, for people, refugees, and also, we're going to – we have a play to bring a message,' I said.

'Oh good!'

'But it won't be a one-way exchange. We'll also be there to listen,' said Simon, concerned, presumably, that Kenneth's objection was to any element of neo-imperialist condescension about the mission.

'Look. I am not letting my daughter drive into a civil war. I saw a man's hand get torn off by a drilling rig in Shetland. I've been to Islamabad, it's a shithole. My father was at Monte Cassino. I know all about this. I know a man who knows a lot more about this. I'm actually doing something on this, the firm is. I've been to Belgrade. In the seventies. So, no. All right? It's just a no, so will you please go upstairs and tell her that she will not be going.'

Chapter 2

The top part of the house was given over to Penny and Von. I reckoned that far under the sofas of the 'playroom' where our little mourning party gathered bits of Lego might still lie about. There was, after all, still one Babar the Elephant poster up on the wall. But in recent years the carpet had got pocked with little black burns where hot nibblets of hash had dropped from joints. Von, behind a pair of record decks, nodded his head out of rhythm with the music. Periodically he slid the cross-fader to bump two deep-house tracks seamfully into one another, looked up, bit his lip, and gave a little yeah-baby-I'm-on-it nod to the room.

Once Penny had got us all assembled – a mix of her London friends and some of the Peace Play Partnership – she retreated with Cally to her bedroom, visiting the playroom only periodically to smile at the pity of it all.

Sitting cross-legged by the wall, I wondered if maybe now I wasn't going to Bosnia? That would be a shame. I mean, mainly I liked the *idea* of going. I wasn't so sure about actually going. In a way I still didn't really believe we would actually go. Not us, physically. Though I did feel strongly that something should be done.

Most particularly, I felt this in relation to the fact that Helen hadn't been reading the papers or watching the news when it started happening. I was watching a lot of everything and I used to beat her over the head with it when she was groggy. 'We need to do something!' I'd say, and show her pictures of dead children when she sat quivering and pale, sipping at tea, dipping her lips like a fragile blue tit at the rim of one of our thick-sided mugs. At that time, I dare say, I had one of the most coherent foreign policies of anyone working on a building site in the Manchester area. I read the incoming reports with indignation. I had my favourites in the commentariat and on the world diplomatic scene, people who I thought of in some ways as my emissaries. It certainly made the news more exciting to have certain diplomats and particular ethnicities to root for.

Helen said I was overly emotional about it. She accused me during one row of having no inner resources – as though other people might be able to go off to the bathroom and dig some iron ore or diamonds out of their belly buttons. It's true I did like very much to be on the right side. And as an only child maybe I had grown up a bit milky and overly loved.

On her next progress through the room, Penny lingered a while and slid her back down the wall next to me. Her long legs, burnished with a patina of expensive oil or sheer good health, crooked up from her skirt and I looked over at Simon, twitchy, comically distant, two metres away on a beanbag.

'And guess what. To fucking cap it, they've said they won't put my play in the drama festival because of a stupid – thing.'

'Oh, shit, Pen. What thing?'

'A date thing. They got it late, the date was late. Because I've graduated. I sent it a bit late.'

'Oh. Right. God.'

'I feel — I feel almost censored.' I winced. She spotted it and winced too. 'I mean, I know that's disgusting when you think of real repression.'

'Yeah. But . . .' I said and couldn't think of anything more to offer.

'I should shut up.'

'No. Not at all.'

'The only effective censorship in late-capitalist nations is self-censorship.'

I agreed, strongly.

'But that's what I want to write. I want to write something — about all the things we don't even dare to think?'

'Yes. Yes. I know,' I said. 'What are they?'

'. . . I don't know,' she said and laughed.

I tried to think of something else true or real to say, but as I went grubbing around my consciousness I found myself barren. In fact, I wasn't sure I was even quite important enough to have a consciousness. Not a whole one. At least not yet, not a serious one. My feeling is, I'll think about that later — who I am. Internal conflicts, moral battles, soul quivers, deep depressions, raving happiness — they are all, like smart restaurants and Grand Prix racing, artichokes and the visual arts, not really *for* me.

'So what did my dad say, when I was gone?' Penny asked.

'It was tough. Me and Simon did our best.'

'Yes?' she said.

'He's a very determined person and it's easy to see how you could —' I flicked my eyes to Simon — 'crumble, but I think we — I — managed to keep up a pretty good front. I gave him the highlights, the social and economic and military sort of stuff and what our hopes and aims are, and I just tried to face the guy down. For what it's worth. God help me.'

13

'Look. Your old man's just a twat,' Simon said as he sat and joined us. For a moment there was a bristle. Then Penny looked at him and said, 'You know, he *is* a twat.'

'No. Yeah. Exactly. He is a bloody twat,' I said, with all the bravery of the guy who jostles out of the crowd to additionally knife the already dead dictator.

'Fuck it. I am going, now, to tell him. It is happening,' she said and gave a nod to Simon.

The problem with Simon, from my point of view, was that he was essentially me, only better. Any margin I could gain by playing up for Penny the exoticism of my normality was trumped by his. Simon was slim and aggressively Geordie – his family had actually been touched by the miners' strike. He had an omnivorous, serially monogamous intellect, becoming a fascinated expert in topic after topic: poetry, string theory, close-up magic, hypnosis, Middle Eastern cookery. He was, unfortunately, very interesting. He smoked roll-ups and sat around looking like he was thinking about things and, I felt, fucking up my chances of sticking around. I was pretty sure, after all, that metropolitan London accepted outsiders into the mix only drop by oily drop; not too many at once in case the mayonnaise might curdle.

Cally joined us as we headed down the creaky stairs. She was a great beauty, I suppose. Her face made up of protracted planes of flawless skin, stretched like canvas from her sharp cheekbones down to her chin. She clopped down the stairs at the rear like a happy heedless horse. The four of us arrived at the bedroom door. As in a farce, I felt the Calmans would surely be doing it doggy-style in bed, red-faced, when our deputation entered, but no. Kenneth was frowning, reading P. J. O'Rourke, and Mrs Calman *Wild Swans*.

'Hello. What the hell is this?'

'Dad, I *am* going. All right? That's what I've come to say. Bob is driving the minibus and we're going to Bosnia to stop that war.' We looked at her parents, old and corrupt in bed. Penny's face was set with determination, but as her words hung in the air she gave me the briefest glance and rolled her eyes, biting her lip at what she'd found herself saying. 'Doing whatever we can to stop the war.'

'Did you tell her?' Kenneth asked me and Simon, who both looked at the floor. 'I've seen a *hand come off*.'

'You've told me about the hand, Dad.'

'Once you've seen a hand come off, on the floor, and yes, now they could sew it back on, but – the human body is fragile. There are horrible things.'

'Exactly,' Penny said.

'The genie is out of the bottle. They need to see sense. It's dog eat dog out there. And it's right, none of those dogs is our dog.'

'So we let them eat each other, alive? The Serbs against the Muslims? It's not a dogfight. One of the dogs is a cat.'

'It's true, Mr Calman, it's really, more like a dog versus a cat, versus a chicken. Where the Serbs are –' I started, always eager to explain.

'It is not our business.'

'I'm sorry, Mr Calman, but if it's not our business, then whose business is it?' Kenneth looked at me. 'For – whither the human man – if we do not – aid our brothers in peril?'

There was a pause, during which people perhaps considered how wise I was.

'Where are you going to stay?' her mother asked.

'Shannon knows people.'

'Where?'

'Sarajevo.'

'Oh Jesus Christ,' said Kenneth.

'We'll just be using it as a base, taking my play to hot spots, to defuse things.'

'Oh, perfect, brilliant. Yes — go to the hot spots! This is a war, Penelope, a war.'

At that moment I followed Penny's eye to her father's clothes hanging over the back of a chair by the dresser. Poking out from inside his trousers were his crumpled pale blue underpants, the fabric worn a little thin, and the pathos of these creased man-pants seemed to undermine everything he said. Of course a man of such pants, with his sagging chest and his fuzz of grey hair curling out from the V of his pyjama top, would be scared.

Penny ended the interview by stating, 'I have a passport, I'm twenty-three years old. I can do whatever I want.' And then added, not entirely truthfully, 'We don't need your money. So I'm sorry if you're not going to support this, but we are leaving tomorrow.'

Chapter 3

'Where are you going, mate?'

Simon and I were billeted together that night in what the family referred to as 'Patty's Crap Room', on account of the large amount of crap that had been left in there by Patty, a departed au pair. There was a wide single bed and a two-seater sofa not long enough to sleep on. It was not made clear by Penny or anyone really what was expected in terms of our sleeping arrangements. My sense was that the family felt coming from the Welsh borders and Newcastle, from families of innkeepers and teachers, miners and so on, that Simon and I would probably be fine, somehow, in there, and there wasn't too much need for enquiry or direction. We'd agreed to share the bed and it had taken me some time to drop off. But now I'd jerked back alive.

'What?' Simon asked, easing the door open.

'Where are you going, mate?' I said again.

'Nowhere, mate.'

'Huh?'

'I'm just going for a leak.'

'Oh . . . did you not see? There's one in there. En suite.'

'. . . I'm actually going to see if Penny's OK, after everything. OK?'

17

'Oh . . . Shall I come?' I said.

'You're tired, get some rest.'

'OK. And . . . do you think you should – disturb her?' He didn't even think he had to reply to that and he began to push the door closed. 'Tell her I hope she's OK, from me!'

'Will do, pal!' Simon said softly, through the last disappearing crack.

Yes. That was going to be high on his list of priorities.

I tracked his steps until they disappeared out of range, and then – could I hear the knock? Could I hear the door crack? Was that the murmur of conversation? Or was it just the hiss of my ears listening in on themselves? Lying there, my monitoring felt effortful enough to burn calories, as if my hearing was now so sensitised that a pan dropped on a tile floor would blow my eardrums.

As the seconds he was absent became a minute, I began to investigate the new reality: Simon and Penny. The poet and the playwright. Two fresh graduates, magnetically pulled together. And as the minute turned into an unbelievable three, I thought I might be within my rights to simply march down and ask what the hell was going on? Then as three hit five, I started writing a bitter rant in my head, to be biroed out and left for her on the bed, full of nasty one-syllable words, criticism and emotional indignation.

I lived in that sour little pocket for quite a while. But then as seven minutes turned into eight, nine – I mellowed. This was the middle age of my despair and the passion of the three-minute hothead waned. Now I was sitting, like Old Father Time, knowing that ten and eleven and twelve minutes would all come and I would sit, grey-bearded on this rock, watching them all pass and smile at the passions of the human heart. I would leave no note, of course I wouldn't – too wise for that. I would just eat my toast in the morning, go to Bosnia with the gang, and be a simple soul, bandaging the feet of children, warriors, whosoever as might come to me, eating a little bread and soup in my simple dwelling – and if Simon was perchance shot in the head or nuts, I would be waiting. And when she came to me I would say, 'We had our moment, Penelope, 'tis passed now. I am happy with my book and my good soup.'

In fact, as I lay there, arms around the pillow, both ears doing their hard labour, I was aware that a part of me was willing my rival on. My heart beat so hard that to deny it the drama of defeat would be a little mean.

I imagined I would certainly be up all night. I took out my fat, battered copy of *War and Peace* and looked at the cover illustration of a grand ball. It would be impossible to sleep. And staying awake was necessary too: it would be rude to miss an appointment with my torturer when he returned. I was turning over whether I would bother to feign disinterest in the affair or allow myself to be frankly fascinated, when I dissolved into dreams of triumph and disaster during which my bed-mate returned scores of times with faces that morphed from dream to nightmare to primary-school teacher, landing up hard and cold at seven in the worst of all scenarios: he still wasn't back. Nothing has ever been quite so empty to me as Simon's half of the bed when I woke. No Cossack wife waving off a husband to Borodino ever missed her bed-mate half as much as I did then.

I sat up, and after considering and rejecting the idea of listening to my Serbo-Croat tapes on my Walkman, headed down to the little kitchenette on the floor below, where I toasted a heel of whitening wholemeal, leaving the untouched loaf fresh in its bag. The kettle boiled and in came the cleaner. She smiled and started to pull things out of the washing machine in a ropey-tangle. I hummed a little and turned to yesterday's paper on the countertop to mute the silence between us.

'You see that?' she asked. 'The girl?'

I smiled at her, which wasn't right apparently.

'The little girl who *stab* her mother?' she said and pointed to a story in the paper.

Now it clicked: the horrible and very popular trial of a child who'd murdered a parent. 'Who could do this?' she asked and I shook my head grimly. Indeed. Who? '*Who?*' she said again. I shook my head for all the pity in the world.

'A stab in the eye. Who could do that?'

Yes, the eye was definitely particularly bad; I really didn't know who could do it. Yet the cleaner was still looking to me as if I did but was unwilling to admit the answer.

'Who *could* do that?' I offered back in a move I thought might end the enquiry.

'She stabbed with scissors in the *eye* and then – all over.'

I really didn't see where to go other than further head shaking.

'The mother is asleep and she stabs with scissors? *Jesus Christ*. Scissors. *In the eye*?'

'I mean, who knows what the child must have gone through – to end up able to do such a thing,' I said, finally, in my surprising new role as counsel for the defence in the case of Good versus Evil.

'Jesus Christ! She is stabbed forty-three times all over!' she said, and Penny entered, passing the cleaner without a word as I seized up like something clockwork left to rust in the rain.

'Morning,' I said, trying to figure out how you generally look at someone.

'Morning,' she said and smiled and I began to plan, based on the smile, how we might have an affair behind Simon's back.

'I spoke to Shannon, about last night,' Penny said. 'I called her – Simon suggested it. She said, what she said was quite right actually. . .'

'Oh, OK?'

'. . . which was, no one wants us to go. No one. But we are going to go. I mean, like Simon said, Laurie Lee walked over the Pyrenees to get to the Spanish Civil War. I mean, for fuck's sake.'

'It's true,' I said. 'A lot of people don't want this play to happen. Which strongly suggests that it really needs to happen.'

'Yeah,' she said. 'I mean, not everything that someone wants not to happen needs to happen – but yeah.'

'No, yeah,' I conceded.

'I mean, why do you want to go, Andrew, apart from your dad's heritage and everything?' She leaned back on the counter as the cleaner departed.

'Me? Well, I just feel, as I think I've said before, that 1936, 1939, sometimes there comes a point, a moment, when you have to decide which side you're on. 1968,' I said, and then, '1976,' not entirely sure what precisely I was referring to, but confident there had been things to be for and against that year.

'No, I've been up all night and I just think, it's important to know why you're doing something.'

I nodded in agreement, my lip caught between my teeth. I eyed the sharp knives on the draining board and wondered which one of them I would use to cut my finger off if someone offered me a trade of one digit in return for the certainty that last night had been chaste between Penny and Simon.

'It's what I feel, Penny. It's what I feel. And – Simon, Simon, he helped you – through it last night? And . . . so on?'

'Uh-huh,' she said.

'That's nice. That's a nice thing.'

'Yeah. Good. So we're going, yes?'

'We ride at dawn. Fuck it, let's do it!'

'Great, well, Shannon's going to meet us with the van.'

'Wicked,' I said and clicked my fingers. Penny undid the seal at the top of the fresh bread and fingered her way down the slices, past the heel and a couple beyond, to pull out a perfect slice, and I wondered, if we really were going to leave today – to what I imagined would be certain death – how the hell exactly I'd got here. Which was the first domino starting the sequence that would end with me knocked into some trench in a provincial football stadium? Helen? The job? The fall?

Hospital. That was where you would say it had started. I'd ended up in hospital because of the final fall, but hospital was the link to Von. Our meeting in hospital: that was the silver thread that was going to lead to my death, when they traced it back – the tracers – if they could even be bothered.

Chapter 4

I was in a pre-med room getting dosed up before having my arm bones pinned back together, when Von was trolleyed in, legs jiggling on his wheelie stretcher. His first words to me were delivered straining like a mummy out of its sarcophagus, asking my advice as to whether he should admit to the nurse that it was taking much longer than he had expected for him to come down from a powerful Ecstasy tablet.

'Definitely yes,' I said. But Von got caught on a wave of euphoric abandon, one of the pill's last big beats of love, and as he grimaced through the final shudder of the previous night, he said, 'Fuck it, I'm not doing this all again. I'm gonna give it a go!'

I really thought that would be the last I ever saw of this son of Surrey or wherever – waggling some heavy-metal devil-horns back at me like he was in a video, not his actual life. He was wheeled off around the corner, so merry and high he would have raved on to the rhythm of a heart monitor if he'd heard one ping. But no, as it turned out, the downers fought the uppers sufficiently hard that they knocked out the big ox and he came round with his sinuses drained and all well.

We stayed on in the same recovery ward that night with an

old soldier guy who'd fought the Germans in Italy and seemed all charming and wily until he started to talk about how he'd 'do' our various nurses: this one in a cupboard; this one in a paddling pool; and one of them via a tabletop go-cart contraption of his own design – he had drawings – pulleys and spindles to be constructed so he could stay still at the table's edge while she was zoomed ecstatically in and out on his stationary member.

The old Lancashire geezer laughed and Von laughed back. He had the gift of being so totally comfortable with his privilege that everyone else was also put at ease. The next morning when the nurse brought a hand mirror so he could check out his swelling, it gave him visible pleasure to see himself again, that handsome blond best friend. His own countenance in that looking glass was a little pre-breakfast treat – a bump of coke, to put a zing in his day.

With his mild good manners and self-mocking benevolence, Von opened a little porthole and I climbed through and soon enough I was round for a smoke, and was unobjectionable enough to join his posse on nights out. I had no sense of how these rich Londoners regarded me – he lived with three big strong young southern men – whether they laughed about me, or tolerated me, or just watched me float past as they sat on the sofa, stoned and insensible. But with my building-site wages, I could stand a round and my tin usually had some weed in it, and anyway, in the end, the people who get to be in the gang, who are they but the ones who put in the hours? Plus, I realised, I had a certain cachet – not being a student, working on a building site. To them it was almost like I was someone 'real'.

His place was disgusting. A terraced house in Withington where they piled their washing-up in the bath and eventually started pissing on it. But it was still good to get out. I'd followed Helen from the Welsh borders to Manchester and at our place, by then, things were increasingly shitty. Helen worked night shifts at a bakery and I was on labourer's hours: early start, early finish. Often I'd come home after work to her waking and having a 5 p.m. breakfast, all woozy. I'd be knackered, my legs wobbling, my hair brittle with brick dust and cement, and my back aching for the plastic squeak of the avocado bathtub. I'd be ready to let the day sink away and be good to myself while she was looking through the binoculars of her false morning to all the troubles ahead.

We rarely shared a bed now and I would take my weekends on the weekend, while hers were Tuesday and Wednesday, so nothing matched and more and more she went clubbing alone. I tried not to think about where she spent the after-party hours before she came back home, fragile and asexual – a little nubbin on the settee, warm and vulnerable and drinking her tea with big eyes, backcombed hair wilting, hungry for cigarettes and gas fire. Those were our best times actually, when she was too queasy to talk and I could give her a cuddle and be forgiving of all because I could pretend there was nothing to forgive so long as she didn't tell me.

From my end, I tried to package up the stories of what I'd seen round at the student houses Von took me to, but they never landed. I couldn't quite describe how exotic they all smelt, how I'd seen such remarkable things: young people swaggering with such unwarranted confidence, people eating meals of extraordinary sophistication: a girl who ate a plump little steak, still red in the middle, with nothing but some lettuce leaves and olive oil – *Star Trek* food; glasses of wine that went undrunk as people left for the pub, the whole second half of a bottle sometimes that didn't get finished, just abandoned on a table and forgotten. I couldn't really frame all that. How I loved them, and hated them, with their electric toothbrushes in the bathroom, too lazy to waggle, grotesque and terrifying pretend little adults.

For a while I tried to include her – took her to the pub one terrible night with Von and his pals where she was so quiet and he was so loud. She didn't like them. Didn't like the look of them or the sound of them. They made her queasy and she felt, more-over, that her discomfort somehow, obscurely, was the price of their ease.

That night, as we listened to Von and his friends talking – about London and the people they knew and the rich thatch of connections that kept them warm and dry – I knew Helen well enough to feel the little spring of fury bubbling in her breast. My forehead grew hot, worrying that she was going to burst and accuse them of some unspecific social crime. But, instead, she went inward and dragged a torn beer mat along the grooves of the pub table. I smiled and nodded along with the conversa-tion, throwing glances like fishing nets at her, trying to pull her in, but she refused to be caught. When they went outside for a joint, I asked her outright, 'C'mon, Hel, what's the problem?'

She just looked at me and said, 'Oh, shut up, you rich fucking bastards.'

I shook my head, as if she had failed to live up to our credo of universal human commonality – speak as you find, and so on. But really I admired her a bit for the steely, almost sectarian, edge to her rejection.

So I stopped talking about them, started not to mention how often I climbed on the student buses and went down to the wide suburban streets of south Manchester to visit. Instead, when Helen came home knackered from work, in the grey mornings in the back kitchen where no sunlight ever made it, I'd throw her thoughts about my other obsession: my own personal foreign policy options.

She'd smoke cigarettes as I explained to her my idea of what I called FMI, 'forced mass intervention'. That was my Balkans policy and I had been refining it for some time – ever since I'd got back into current affairs.

*

For a while, when everything had been going well, I'd somewhat got out of history. I was nineteen, twenty, still living at home above the pub that my parents sometimes claimed, trying to drum up business, straddled the border – lounge in England, bar in Wales. It didn't. We were located across the river, on the dark north-facing side of the valley, the English hinterland of my Welsh town-village, Chirk. This was '89, '90, and everyone I knew had a car. We'd drive twenty miles deep into Wales, smoke a joint, and jump into pools where deep cold mountain rivers eddied. Then we'd go out and drink and then back to someone's place to talk and sleep like happy dogs wherever we lay.

One night I ended up in a sleeping bag next to Helen. She always watched everyone quietly with wide blue eyes. But that night I found out what she was thinking. She whispered funny generous things about our friends and we laughed. We cuddled chastely, from inside the double prophylactic bags, then got together properly the next week. We'd travelled to Stoke together, legs pressed up in the back of the same Honda Civic, and when we made love at her parents' place the next day it was buttery and gentle. She went to work and I stayed in her bed, up in the converted shed-barn behind the farm, so happy I did a bit of solo music-less dancing, threw myself back against the thick stone wall and shouted 'Fuck you!' merrily into the mirror.

Helen was hot. That is, it felt like her thermostat was broken.

She was so warm to the touch when we slept in the same bed I had to roll far from her radiating heat. She'd grown up on that farm. It was situated in the soft round end of a valley, a finger poked into the Welsh Hills, where the climate was equitable. Spring came early and summer lasted a long time. Her hippy parents had claimed the spot in the seventies. She had been friends with a boy from the hill farm up above. Like Heidi, from age four or five she'd climb the hill to go and see him. They played together every day for years until they moved on to certain naughty games in the hay barn and, caught by his mother, Eden got ended and she wasn't allowed to go round any more.

She told me that story a month after we'd got together. I liked her a lot. We hung out all the time, and in the end we called what we were in 'love' because we didn't really know what else it might be. It was certainly nice.

So around then, if I saw the news at all, it seemed natural to me that people would knock down walls and let noble old black gentlemen out of jail. History seemed to be getting on really well without any intervention from me.

Then things started to break up. Me and Helen seemed solid, but a couple of the older lads went to colleges and university and cities, then a couple more girls went to jobs or courses. But there were still three or four of us, including Helen, who were planning, getting our shit together, going in — when it suited us, but overall less and less — to the sixth-form college which was more of a hangout than a place of education. Those of us who remained in town would zoom up at weird times of the night to Sheffield and Leeds and Liverpool, to student-housing blocks, with our glamorous quantities of wage money fluttering at the lips of our wallets. Much better, it seemed sometimes, than actually attending. I read the *NME*, sitting out in the backshop of a low-price supermarket off across the border near Wrexham.

Helen leaving for university kicked off in earnest the evolution of my Balkan policy. I looked around one September and suddenly what everyone had joked hard and funny about all summer, how I'd be the last one left, how I should, finally, actually decide where I wanted to go, what I wanted to do, was suddenly, unamusingly, true. It had seemed unreal through August, but now Helen was in Manchester, her shared phone often engaged, her letters a page or two shorter than mine and my banged-out Mini was the only car left crawling the country lanes at night, looking for a spot to smoke a joint.

In my darkening mood, left alone in the sour-smelling supermarket, the siege of Vukovar started to seem like the sort of thing that would of course happen in the world. Mandela was out and the Berliners were free – but it was all so much more complicated than that. For the first time in my life I looked at my dad's *Express* in the morning. Then I started to buy my own *Independent*. Through the mornings I'd read a book – anything counter-cultural: Miller, Bukowski, Vonnegut, those lovely guys at first. Then my pal in Liverpool sent me his reading list and soon enough I found I was ahead of him. At the supermarket, hiding round the back, resting up on the soft bed of a pallet of nappies, I had a great deal more time for study than anyone starting at university, surrounded by lots of interesting and potentially naked fellow young people.

After fiction in the mornings, at lunch I'd go to this place, the European Delicatessen, where all the delights of the Continent were brought together for the enjoyment of the Welsh Marches. Quite the *Mitteleuropean* I'd feel as I ate an Edam and piccalilli and value-mayonnaise baguette, followed by a custard tart with a cup of tea and some modernist poetry spread across my lap. Through the afternoon I read non-fiction, theory, news magazines and the paper.

At first it was hard to know who to root for. Yugoslavia had seemed like a sort of fair-enough option to the stupid Left through the eighties. No one wanted to go the whole Stasi, but maybe a bit non-aligned and Yugoslav would be good? There was affection for that rambling nation; you could go there on holiday and if Tito and his partisans had murdered some tens of thousands or so in the mid-forties — well, in the arithmetic of the Second World War, you could round that down to nothing at all.

The Croats, I read, had a nasty, chequered little history to hide. Nevertheless, as their poor beautiful Vukovar was strafed, the first plank of my Balkan policy was laid down and it was this: don't bomb people. Do not blow human beings up. This led me, deductively, to support Vukovar against the Yugoslav National Army.

Round then, I asked Helen if I could come up and live with her, if she'd move out of her halls of residence and in with me? I made my request by letter, enclosing for comment, also, a long letter to the *New Statesman* on the situation in the Balkans. I called her up the next day to ask for her reaction. She told me my letter on current affairs was very powerful, but she hadn't been able to finish it in its entirety because she'd fallen asleep on it midway through, and her drool had made all the ink run. I laughed and asked if I could move in with her. She said no and I made out I was just very unhappy about all the conflict in the world.

I was going through a mildly pacifist stage anyway. The shop lads in the supermarket contained a mini-crew who were Wrexham Frontliners — a football-related organisation dedicated to talking about, at very great length, and occasionally doing, violence. Often they'd make jokes about how if I ever did a night shift with them they'd give me a Chelsea smile with a Stanley knife. I didn't find those jokes very funny. One of the lads, Neil, had gone to court for breaking a Scouser's leg with a fencing post at a pre-season friendly.

I could see why they hated the English: pretty, sandy, walled Chester, where I drove to buy jeans and records; pimply, correct Shrewsbury, up on its hill, gift-ribboned by the Severn below. Both were an affront to flat Wrexham, drab on its plain – I could see that. But it still seemed rather tough on me that I should feel a whirr of fear whenever I walked into the stockroom on a quiet night.

One on one, the Frontliners were fine. But in a group, if there were three or more, it could go dark. One time I wandered around into the backshop to find Neil's pal Sion pulling up his trousers after laying a shit on a flattened cardboard box. Then, as I tried to back away unnoticed, I got hauled into the circle and was invited to watch as he picked up the turd, munched it, and then offered me a bite. It was an inch from getting thrust in to my mouth before I realised it was Soreen Malt Loaf scrunched shit-shaped – we all laughed. But instead of making me part of the gang, it seemed I'd got my reaction wrong. That I was too disgusted by the crap-eating masquerade, all prim and uppity and English about faeces consumption.

A week later, I was drinking in Wrexham on a Friday night when I got spotted by the Frontliners as I nipped out of the pub to use the cashpoint. From the opposite side of the road they called me 'Bertie Woofter' and 'English Bridget', after the song 'Always Shit on the English side of the Bridge'. It all seemed quite matey in its aggression initially – I took a mock bow as they chanted 'cunt, cunt, cunt' and they all laughed at that. There were a couple of lads with them hanging back in the shadow of a passageway smoking, lads who weren't from the supermarket, and one of them chucked a two-pence coin over at me. As I read it, if I didn't respond I was inviting trouble, so I sang out a round of 'Does Your Sister Know You're Out Shagging Sheep?' With just me, against the seven of them, the insult felt humorously ironised by my physical inferiority. But I guess they felt it was insufficiently ironised, because a bunch of the lads darted for me. I turned and started running fast up Hope Street.

My pursuers were more pissed than me and one tripped and a couple lost heart. Soon I too was tired, and only Sion – the friendliest of them – was left chasing me. 'Andy!' he shouted.

'Why are they chasing me, Sion?' I asked, stopping up and drawing deep breaths.

But as I said it, he took my arms and buckled my knees from behind so I was low down when the others arrived. I didn't try to get away because it seemed like it might still be a joke if I treated it like one.

The biggest lad punched me. 'Oh aye, fucking yes!' someone said to him, but the punch came in at a weird angle so it didn't really land. I didn't look up at them or struggle; the whole incident was so degrading I didn't want to ennoble it with any form of resistance. I just wanted it over. Then three others came in close to give me knees in the face, more grinds than blows, but still the blood came from my nose, warm and worrying and fast.

Back at work that week, like a bit of shameful alley sex, we all pretended the assault hadn't happened. Sion made me a cup of tea on a tea run, but another lad asked me pretend-innocent how I'd fucked my nose up so that others could laugh. It wasn't the main reason I left for Manchester, but I didn't want to be around there any more. Helen had fallen out with the girls she was living with by then. She said she was happy to move in to the dark little place I found for us. Every other Saturday we could hear the groans from the Man City ground nearby and we watched the damp grow up the wall like an advancing army on a map.

Chapter 5

By the time I first met Penny, Helen had dropped out of her course, landed onto the night shift, and we were into our slump. I'd always known deep down that Helen sometimes fucked other people. When I rumbled her and we fell out, she said that she would 'try not to do it again', if she could, and she was very sorry that I was so sad. But there was this subtext that I was perhaps making a bit of a fuss about her simply being *very nice* to interesting and attractive people she met in nightclubs.

It was the day after our grim summit that I started falling over. The first time was on a patch of grease out the back of an Indian restaurant; then I walked into a lamp post and went over. The next time it just happened for almost no reason in the dark hallway that led to our internal front door. I began to feel a certain amount of respect for all the people I saw managing to stay upright all day. What skill, what judgement, to balance on just two legs!

The worst one, the last big fall, came as I was fingering the gritty residue at the bottom of the pockets of my ex-army great-coat. I was outside the Whitworth Gallery on my way to the building site, thinking unhappy Helen thoughts, hoping in my despondency I might look a little Ian Curtis, when I changed step to dodge an actual physical banana skin and hit some December black ice. I went over splat-flat and my palms went slap-smack on the pavement. There's probably nothing as funny as an apparently confident young man in an oversized coat hitting the deck, hard. That's definitely what quite a few school-kids and students nearby seemed to think. My teeth crunched, bottom set hard into top, and my arm throbbed as I lay there, wanting to cry. Making it up onto all fours, I did wonder if I might not give up walking altogether as simply too ambitious a form of locomotion.

There is a hospital right across the road from where I fell. But instead of feeling fortuitous, that was additionally insulting – like everyone but me knew I was going to go down. Hitting the button for the pelican crossing, my arm revealed itself to be newly rubbery. I couldn't get purchase to press in the infinite whorls of the cold, concave stainless-steel button. I had to ask an old woman to do it for me.

So that was how I met Von. And a few weeks later, his older sister.

*

The night I met Penny, Von warned me gravely that she was probably coming round, like she was some downer – an intellect who might X-ray us all and find us wanting. But when she came in – peck-pecking around at things, tall, as if, like a wading bird, her knees might bend backwards – and sat next to me on the settee, I breathed in her showered smell and my back tingled. It took me a while to get it straight that this tall beautiful black woman was the younger white boy's sister. I rolled my next joint tight with love, crumbled in extra bonus flakes of the soft hash that expanded as you scorched it, licked the Rizla with a dry tongue just wet enough on the tip to stick it, and got ready to pass it from my lips to hers like a kiss.

Her dark skin glowed caramel where the light from overhead hit her forehead and cheeks. I croaked, trying to let her know the joint was coming her way, but she didn't hear me and when I touched her arm gently she turned sharply as if I'd overstepped the mark. But then her lovely lips formed a soft billowing 'O' of comic admonishment and I laughed. She took the joint and passed it on beyond without honking on it.

Of course! Of course it wasn't cool and great and fascinating to smoke dope. It was boring and stupid and predictable and I wanted to renounce it right there! But that might look a little psychotic, as I blew out a fat stream of grey-white smoke? Besides, I couldn't frame the words correctly, partly because I was spiralling inwards, a little stoned. Finally I managed to ask what she was doing later – if she was going out, into town? She told me she was off to a meeting above a pub about Bosnia.

The news sobered me like she'd emptied a washing-up bowl of cold water over my head. I gabbled; I explained how I read the newspaper *every day*; I tried to frame how weird it was that she would say that; I laid out my own personal foreign policy, not as well as I would have liked, but the headlines. She asked what I thought was going to happen over there, as they headed towards the summer. I said I didn't really know, repeated some grim analysis I'd read. I couldn't believe my luck. It was as though I'd found another person at a party who liked exactly the same difficult-to-get-into indie band as me: Balkan Slaughter, now working on ideas for their surprisingly vibrant third album. I was all of a sudden in my element, the fug of hash around my brain cleared, and between us we churned up a hearty froth of indignation.

We left together, Penny linking her arm through mine like we were a country couple heading to the barn dance. We walked across the park to the bus stop under a row of great towering lime trees. I expressed my opinion that Europe stood on the precipice of a new age of barbarism, and I had never felt lighter or happier in my life.

Where I grew up was white. White as white Mother's Pride. But she was so extraordinary to me already – rich and London and bookish – that her skin colour was just a kicker. Before Penny, I think I'd harboured a fear that any individual person of colour might at any point in our relations request immediate verbal and/or financial recompense, from me personally, for the crimes of the British Empire and the transatlantic slave trade. But Penny, without knowing or trying, put me at my ease. Indeed, as we sat on the throbbing back seat of the bus talking fast and overlapping, it struck me that it was almost as though we were just two human beings.

The meeting was in a sour-smelling room above a pub on the Wilmslow Road. There were twenty or so students in there and ten or more local folk – including a pair of concerned middle-aged white women and a whole Asian family who ate flatbreads from tinfoil as they waited for things to start, the teenage daughter embarrassed by her parents. Shannon, the woman whom I was told had put up the posters, Sellotaped them to trees and lamp posts, pinned them through the student union, arrived late, like a rock star, breaking the terrible English silence and the feeling that was growing among us: that we had all, somehow, done something wrong without doing anything at all.

She strode up shouting 'Hi, hello!' in her friendly American way and everyone relaxed into the sense that yes, we were meant to be here and the start time was right and nothing odd or uncomfortable was going to happen. She made a little speech and then opened the floor for discussion. She had an excellent tone to her – made it possible to talk of heavy things with lightness, but without taking them lightly. She effortlessly occupied the role of leader, the fiery queen. Her American optimism was just the tart tang we needed for the litres of heavy, watery information we had imbibed about the Balkan situation. There was a solution. And we could help to achieve it. And therefore we should. Penny and I caught each other's eye and in our little twitches and laughs we could tell we were both enjoying her, and in that mutual enjoyment I felt a band snaking round us, pulling us together.

Shannon was a little older – maybe thirty or something, a bit of crinkle at the corners of her eyes. She wore a white vest that late-spring evening. Her arms were rich, nut-brown against it. Her face was sharp – a perky sniffing-out nose, hard high cheekbones and a jutting fuck-you chin. She looked ready for action. Ready to climb a tree, or down a drink; flat-chested and boyish, but also musky and alluring in her openness to the world. She retied her jumble of long brown curly hair often, and when she did so her vulnerable white underarms flashed to us like a swan offering its neck on a chopping block.

Sara, her minder and primary disciple, sat up at the front beside Shannon, nodding and making a note of things in a Woolworths value jotter as she spoke. Sara looked small, neat and studious. She eyed those of us who'd turned up suspiciously – with an air that there was probably something unwholesome about our attendance, something she was eventually going to tease out. As her orange Bic scratched, and her head jerked in concentration, she moved the clean, thin, blonde hair that fell often in front of her grey eyes with irritation, as though this distraction had never before tested her patience. Her timing was interesting: she'd not write for long periods as practical details were discussed, then when Shannon hit an aside such as 'war always hurts the weakest' she'd write intently.

Shannon's idea, when she eventually rolled it out, was that some of us – as many as could fit – should go to Bosnia, in a van. She knew how to get hold of the van via a man named Bob. We would load up this van and take it to Sarajevo. Bob, a rather round, older hippy, watched from his semi-detached position leaning against the wall at the back of the room.

'What?' he said, pretending he had been distracted rolling a cigarette. 'Sure thing. If that's what the lady says.' He took a sip of his pint of Guinness, looked down at his Mexican poncho and then back up and round the room with a rueful grin, making sure everyone had clocked the heart of gold he would have preferred to keep well hidden behind his 'gruff' exterior.

'He's a real "Bob",' Penny whispered, very close to my ear.

'Bob Classic,' I said back, hoping she'd say something else close and warm.

'Onomatopoeic Bob,' she said softly, and I was convinced I'd fallen quite strongly in love.

A huge amount of that first meeting centred around the van. The getting of the van, the fitting out of the van, the number of seats in the van, what could and could not be fitted into the van. It felt after a while as if getting the van to Bosnia was, itself, at some level, the central aim of the trip.

But beyond the van, and some supplies, Shannon's idea, she explained at the next meeting a month later, was to write and perform a play. A play that would transmit a 'mind virus', the primary symptom of which would be peace. 'Because peace can catch on just like war.' Sara wrote very deliberately at that point, not clocking that Shannon had said it with exaggerated gravity, mocking the idea just enough to make it plausible.

Shannon explained to us that we would zoom through the mountains, dropping our play like a good fart out the back of the van until – not this (but maybe this?) – the soldiers and the peasants and the intellectuals stopped for a moment in the presence of the majesty of the purity of youth bringing this simple strong idea to their mountain land with open hearts: peace.

We'd lost a lot of the folk by the time of that second meeting, the couple of middle-aged women, the Asian family, the freshers out looking for friends. But there were some additions. Cally, Penny's best friend, was with us. I tried not to resent her too much, sitting as an aggressively healthy barrier between us, shifting in her seat often, as I tried to catch Penny's eye. Also, from a defunct socialist international-relations society: Christian. Hard, compact and serious. He'd grown up around Camden, he told us afterwards, downstairs in the pub, like he was turning over a winning poker hand. His clear pretty eyes looked like they were scanning your clothes and haircut to check if you were any kind of threat. He was into critical theory and left-wing politics the same way he was into his button-down shirts and imported Adidas shell-toe trainers – because they made him invulnerable.

Penny was all lit up by the idea of the play. 'A *play*!' she said to Cally, who repeated it back to her over the pub table. Cally was a drama student and Penny, I knew, wanted to write plays, so they got quite excited together.

Of course, I was aware it was a little optimistic, Shannon's plan for the play, but up above the Hope and Hegemony, or whatever it was called, as that May day fizzed out, the clouds above just puffs of jokes about rain, I did think that maybe this gang could bring something good to the war – that perhaps stout heart and noble head were something in themselves?

*

'OK, you all know the situation, so the question now is, who's actually coming?'

When she finally popped the question, it felt like the previous twelve weeks of meetings had been a long set-up to the joke of non-intervention, and now the pictures of the dead Shannon passed around were the punchline. And you had to laugh. We were doing nothing while the strong massacred the weak. We could take food, we could take sustenance, but the best thing we could take, Shannon said, like Sontag taking *Godot* to Sarajevo, was something that announced clearly: we are people too and you are our brothers and sisters.

'Another's pain is not our own,' she said to those of us sitting in a circle at Penny and Cally's attic flat. We'd shifted there six or seven weeks in, once the hard core was set. It was ideal for me. I got to see Penny's kitchen; the poems on the fridge; the collection of single lost gloves she'd found and spray-mounted along the hallway wall. And sometimes, like some terrible freak, on my way to the bathroom, I'd poke my nose into her room and smell it: the delicious nothingy smell from her wide-open window, and scan the spines of her books, trying to remember an eyeful so I could read them and think of things to say.

'But what if it was?' Shannon went on. 'What if we could send feelers out around the globe – if we could all sense from afar at the end of these tendrils of feeling – every discomfort in the world? What if you shrivelled at every rape in China? What if no one could rest until everyone was content? That would be paradise, wouldn't it? That would be heaven on earth? If the web that held us all was infinitely closely woven, and if every person in the street would stop to catch you if you fell? So that's why we're going. We're going to say: another's pain is ours.'

Penny looked at me, too sombre to smile, and I nodded back at her. Maybe tonight I should finally try something?

'These evolutions of sympathy have been the leapfrogging of civilisation itself.' Shannon paused, taking a quick look at some biro on the back of a receipt. 'To feel common feeling, outside the family, the tribe, the clan, the region, the nation, across boundaries of colour and creed and gender and sexuality – that's been evolution as much as learning to make bronze and steel and atom bombs. In fact, it sometimes seems to me that maybe the two impulses are in a race? And we're going to see which outstrips the other? The push of the spear's point, or the rush and gush of the unstoppable water of fellow feeling, spilling through the gullies and the valleys out around the world, seeing what flames it can't quench?'

Sara didn't feel the need to write any of this down. She just looked round at us from Shannon's side and nodded like this was exactly how she would have put it, and now they were going to finally find out what kind of shitheads they were dealing with.

When Shannon popped the straight question, 'Who's coming to Bosnia?' Simon's hand was quickest to go up. This was his very first week of involvement, and I stared at him hard; as you would do at a man who has walked into Westminster Abbey by a side door during a coronation and casually put the crown on his own head.

41

Then Penny's hand went up — I didn't realise she was so set. Then another and another. And suddenly, in the space of a few seconds, I went from a man who was weighing up his options, to a man about to miss out on his dearest wish, which — I had just realised — was to take a peace play to Bosnia and extend the evolution of humanity to a new continuum.

But I got my hand up just a little too late. Beaten by a health-food cooperative worker named Kyrk. So as Shannon asked us the tie-breaker — why we wanted to come and what skills we could bring — I decided to roll out my trump card: my grand-father, and his special history.

'Look, I actually want to go because, my dad's dad, my grandpa, was a Yugoslav. Where I come from, a lot of Serbs came after the war, to the area, so it's quite personal and also, I speak it, Serbo-Croat. Because of my dad.'

'OK, fuck. Really?'

'I understand more than I speak,' I admitted

'But you can say things?' Sara asked.

'Yes. I can make myself understood,' I said.

'Kyrk?'

Kyrk looked afraid. 'I am able to — I know the edible mush-rooms. Many puffballs are edible.'

I could feel people smile.

And so, like a liberal Magnificent Seven of eight, saddling up to ride to the rescue of the peasants, the team was assembled: Shannon, our Lenin, our leader. Sara, her assistant, full of an unfriendly infinite pity for the world. Simon, my enemy, self-proclaimed 'poet', and soon to be author of a coruscating editor-ial for the university paper entitled 'Why We Go', which made Penny, and also, I'm ashamed to say, myself, shiver with the thrill of our moral superiority when we reread it. Cally, who

42

wore a face of sustained irony in the course of all our conversations – on any topic from international affairs to jam doughnuts – because, I suspected, she had no idea what in the world was serious and what was not. Christian, clever, clean, socialist, unsmiling, half with us, half hating us. Onomatopoeic Bob, our hippy van master. And finally Penny, who, it had been agreed, after Shannon read her unfinished script, *The Night Dog,* about a Border collie who comes to stay with a family and draws out their dark secrets (excellent, I had decided on a third reading), should author our peace play.

And couldn't Kyrk squeeze in too? Into a Kyrk-shaped jag, stuffed like a beanbag between the boxes in the back? Well, no. The belief that only eight could fit in the van, plus the aid, was a self-protecting mantra that Shannon and Sara, and eventually all of us, repeated in defence of the seriousness of the trip. That we would set off for a war zone in a thin-skinned rackety Ford? Fine. But that we would risk censure from the Belgian traffic police for driving over-capacity? That was too much.

Chapter 6

At the appointed meeting place, a residential car park near Regent's Park, I humped a bag of rice into the van. Bob had driven it down overnight – a modified blue Mark 2 Transit with a stubby, slightly apologetic nose. I knew the rice sack well. Accompanied by Penny, I had collected it along with three others when we spent a happy day kerb-crawling through Rusholme doling out the gang's aid budget – an envelope of twelve thinning tenners. The mass of rice shifted like unresponsive flesh beneath its plastic-fabric sacking, resistant to my attempts to dig finger-holds. Nearby, the string bags full of onions we'd bought way too early gave off a sweet stink from a single onion rotting in there somewhere.

Shannon, Sara and Christian joined us in the car park, having spent the night at Christian's place. Now they stood around a newspaper spread out on the van's bonnet as Christian made savage comments about the reports from the peace negotiations.

When they started discussing whether an intervention by NATO or a 'real socialist revolution' would best stop Serb aggression, I raised the flag for my own solution. The People's Conscript Force. 'A four-million-strong unarmed army which would march in and swamp ex-Yugoslavia with our common humanity.'

I couldn't really see a fault in it, rhetorically speaking. In practice? Well, I felt that so long as I stuck to it verbally, then there really wasn't much anyone could do to make me consider the practicalities.

'Revolution is impossible until it becomes inevitable,' Christian was saying. He said that a lot. It's a useful quote for almost any situation, since it can perhaps be best summarised as 'Things don't happen until they do'.

Simon helped me with the last onion bags, and when Shannon said the word, we climbed up into the van, looking solemnly at one another. The university kayak club were upgrading their 'minibus' in the autumn and Onomatopoeic Bob, who knew another hippy involved in the maintenance of the vehicle, had arranged for us to borrow it before it got part exchanged. Inside, three could ride up front with room for five more in the back on two rows of double seats and one person 'riding bitch', as Shannon called it, wedged onto a rice-and-rucksack throne among the provisions stacked at the back.

Cally sat next to Penny, and I managed to slide in behind on the back row, looking into the great thick mass of Cally's hair – fibrous and dense like coarse brown candyfloss. The engine shuddered up and I had a last panic as Christian climbed aboard and blocked me in: was I leaving to die in the Balkans?

I looked up front to Shannon behind the wheel, pulling her big shaggy cardigan close around herself even on this summer's day, and wondered if this was what people were like, who did things. Napoleon, Columbus, Hitler: actors who made their acting real. Was the cellar in Munich full of men sloshing their steins and saying, 'Yeah sure, whatever, mate. What did he say? Yeah, the fucking Jews, he's right, you know, mine's another massive lager,' who were then very surprised to find themselves, a couple of years later, marching into the Sudetenland and Austria and Yugoslavia? 'No, sure, Boney, let's march on Italy, Egypt, Prussia, why not? Russia? Fuck, yeah, sure thing! (Never gonna happen.)' Then freezing to death and mumbling under their breath, 'It fucking did happen.'

Bob looked hard at the road atlas. Next to him Sara picked cat hairs from Shannon's knitwear. At the back of the van Simon wiggled his bum, trying to make a suitable dent in a sack of rice. In the end, almost all the rucksacks had gone up on the roof rack under tarpaulin; there wasn't much soft material left for him to rest on and he sighed self-pityingly as he tried to rearrange a tin of ghee for an armrest.

As we made it into Camden, I tried to think straight for a moment about what the fuck I was actually doing. Did I want to go? Really? Well, yes, a bit. But why? I estimated that of my urge to go 51 per cent – the majority shareholding – was animal. Desire for Penny. Lust, and more than lust: to move eventually to a farm with her and grow potatoes and drink strong tea, that was the ultimate aim. Sex and conversation, and to sleep along the length of her dark-wood Norse-boat body from stern to prow.

Next, after Penny, was the humanitarian motive. The direct love of one's fellow man and outrage at slaughter on our own Continent. I was generous with myself and said 20 per cent of my urge to go was humanitarian, and looked to see if anyone objected, and since they didn't, I stuck at a fat fifth. Then, allied to the humanitarian motive, was the desire for praise for having had the humanitarian motive; the possibility that someone some- where might build a statue of me, or that I might be the subject of an inspiring assembly at my old secondary school. Being hard on myself now, that might equal 20 per cent too. After all, is there any charity without a PR plan? Without a logo? The truth is, action and display are part of the same movement.

The van seemed to be going round in a loop near Regent's Park.

Then there was the desire not to flake out, to follow through on a publicly stated aim. That was a hell of a lot when I actually considered it. But I said 5 per cent to make the maths work. Then, as we again passed the car park where we had started out ('because of the one-way system') I got down to the trace elements: lust for adventure, for seeing foreign skies, drinking their hard liquor: 1 per cent. Interest in local high-fat pastries: 1 per cent. Opportunity to read on the minibus: 1 per cent. And 1 per cent left for the carry-over, things I'd forgotten — possible role of peace play in preventing a second European holocaust, etc.

Even though Shannon wasn't concentrating — she was gabbling to Sara — she was a good driver, smooth on the gear changes and pigeon-vigilant at junctions, before pulling out with a frank American mixture of assertiveness and gratitude. Perhaps I could ask her to stop at the lights to go to buy rolling papers and never come back?

What made up this strong desire to stay behind? 40 per cent desire for physical safety: of a sphincter-loosen at the idea of actual guns and aid workers taken hostage and mortar shells falling like bad eggs on the food queues in Sarajevo; of not wanting to taste a bullet as it ripped through my cheek. Then there was fear of humiliation and failure in my pursuit of Penny. Say 20 per cent.

Ten per cent was the tug back to Helen, or at least home, for the loss of the little cuddle in the night. 20 per cent, a whole shocking 20 per cent, as I tried to be honest, was trepidation about physical discomfort during the trip; fear of uncomfortable sleeping arrangements in Sarajevo and anxiety about the quality of Balkan food. 5 per cent was fear of missing new cultural production, in particular new CDs. 4 per cent was 'professional' anxiety about what the fuck my life was going to look like when written down on a piece of paper if I didn't do something soon. And that left a 1 per cent for every miscellaneous desire to stay at home during wartime.

So those were the two 100 per cents that faced one another up. Fear versus Desire. But how big were they in comparison? I was fairly happy with the percentages but my ratios were harder to see. Was it 100 per cent of one blue whale of a desire to go versus 100 per cent of a single herring of a desire to stay?

We were progressing fast through the daytime streets of London now and we were definitely going the wrong way. Onomatopoeic Bob, the navigator, was mistrustful of state-sanctioned directions – 'They *want* us to go that way,' he kept muttering, looking from his London map to the road signs. He seemed to think that within the transport network were golden threads, ley lines of easy movement that the authorities took it upon themselves to disguise with their complicated architecture of signage. 'Yeah, they're trying to take us to Lewisham. They're trying to get us to fucking Lewisham,' he commented darkly as we headed further and further south-west, away from the Channel ports.

What I needed to do was to get my headphones on and pile into my tapes. But I wanted to catch anything Simon might call over to Penny. He was talking to her about his dissertation, going on about Wilfred Owen. 'His uncle played football for Wales, and when the English selectors declared he was in fact English, the guy went nuts and started getting drunk and arriving home waving a shotgun around. Wilfred's mother had to subdue him,' he explained. Penny was nodding, but I think he'd lost her. Wilfred Owen's *uncle*? That was a long way from the action. Too weary for *War and Peace,* I pulled the *Rough Guide to Yugoslavia* from my canvas shoulder bag.

'Happy holidays,' Christian said beside me.

It was true. The friendly blue book with its pastel picture of a Croatian coastal scene didn't match up with the Sarajevo we believed we were heading for: *an active and integrated culture that generates an exciting oriental feel.* History will tend to make an arsehole of you if you write a travel book for what turns into a war zone. Admittedly, there was mention of tension in the city: *was it right to build a new skiing facility in Sarajevo, a town with no skiing tradition?* I fingered the money belt strapped under my T-shirt. *Whether Sarajevo can continue to build on this burst of glory isn't clear, but one thing is certain: with its mix of styles and peoples . . . Sarajevo is the most fascinating city in Yugoslavia.*

'What are they using for money, do you think?' I asked Christian.

'The French soldiers in Sara buy a whore for two packets of Marlboro.'

Hmm. I looked thoughtful, and wondered, yeah, but what if I want some cheese? Would I have to go via cigarettes? Trade money for cigarettes and then . . . get a prostitute to use our allotted sex time to buy or . . . make, cheese?

'And how much is – a packet of cigarettes?'

'Whatever a man's willing to pay.'

I read on, looking for good 'cheap eats' in pre-war Sarajevo, cross-referencing them with a graphic I had from the *Independent* showing the worst spots for sniper deaths, so I could see where I might theoretically safely eat the best *burek,* the local *intestine-shaped pastries filled with a feta-like cheese or potato.*

'So, remind me, how exactly did you come to know the language?' Christian asked.

'What? Well, you know, actually, after the war, the Second

World War, a lot of Serbs, they came to live in the UK. Lots in Shropshire.'

'Yeah. OK. Right. Yeah, I've heard that.'

This seemed unlikely, since it was a lie.

'So your whole family speak it?'

'My gran and grandad – and my dad, he always spoke it to me, and round my nana and grandpaps.'

'I will not rest till we bathe in the Miljaka,' he said and looked past me out of the window. 'I will not rest till we bathe in the Miljaka,' he tried again – and this time I felt, well, I've let him know I'm definitely not interested in whatever he's saying, but it would be rude not to ask.

'How do you mean?'

'The Miljaka – that runs through Sarajevo.'

'Oh yeah. Right.'

'I want to get in it? Don't you want to get in it?'

'What, get in the river?'

Penny turned and said, 'I know what you mean. I've just got this urge to get in amongst it. Haven't you? To get at the heart of things?'

'This is the Spain of our generation,' Simon said from between the provisions. He'd got his feet up under him and his legs crossed, so he looked like a king-buddha on his sack of rice at the back. 'Laurie Lee walked over the Pyrenees to get to the Civil War. So we can take a minibus to Sarajevo for Christ's sakes, can't we?'

Fucking Laurie Lee. He was going to be the death of me.

*

It was in a motorway service station on the M20 that I got down to work. I'd been putting it off and off, hoping that some event

50

would intercede, that we wouldn't actually go, or some moment would arise when I could say, 'You know about me speaking Serbo-Croat, yeah? – well, that was actually a lie. My grandpa was just straight-up English and he had flat feet so he didn't even fight in the war, he worked in a cobbler's – where he possibly became interested in the human foot, because after the war he set up as a chiropodist, although interestingly he was never accredited to a professional body.' But there aren't many moments when you can drop those sentences into casual conversation.

So while the troupe assembled in a self-service cafe, I snuck off to a set of hard moulded-plastic orange seats near a nook of fruit machines and pulled on my Walkman headphones. I'd done good work on the cassette. 'Prince', it said on the adhesive label I'd stuck onto Side One of 'Colloquial Serbo-Croat', 'K-Klass' on the other.

The first section was a list of common vocabulary. I mouthed the words back and it was comforting. It reminded me of being in Manchester Central Library taking the cassettes out and sitting a while among the graduate students and old men and oddballs. I didn't know what the words meant, but as I repeated them now it felt possible I could busk my way through the next few weeks. *Dobar. Dan. Drago mi je.*

Then we got to the bit which had made me shut off the tape in the library. A conversation. A rattling market chat with nothing my ears could latch on to. As the gabble of consonants percussed shapelessly by, I felt angry. I needed help. I needed a way in. What the hell were they talking about? This is rude. Then, abruptly, it was over. There was a beep, a ping, and another long beep – signifying what? Should I repeat something? Take a drink of water? Write something down? Stab my forehead with a biro? I flicked through the inadequate leaflet of explanation.

Then another beep and the next conversation was starting and I didn't know what I was supposed to do. I felt like I was at a party and no one had shown me where the drinks were or said hello; instead everyone had in fact very much just started talking in rapid Serbo-Croat all around me.

I let the tape play on; a sullen student, starting to wallow in my incomprehension. I looked at the name of the author of the booklet and tape: Celia Hawkesworth. You're not going to be able to teach me Serbo-Croat, Celia Hawkesworth, I thought bitterly. I can tell. Your method is not very encouraging to the beginner, Celia Hawkesworth. I have no idea what anyone is saying and you're not giving me any help, *Celia Hawkesworth*.

The tape played on. I could still hear it but, haughtily, I was no longer listening. I would find a way. Soon I would let it drop, playfully, that I didn't know any Serbo-Croat, actually, and we'd all laugh at what a lovely rogue I was and everyone would grin.

The tape clicked off.

Chapter 7

At Dover, we huddled in the Transit waiting to board the ferry. The summer clouds dropped fat spots of rain that blotched the tarmac like splattering water balloons. Once the weather cleared, we squatted and paced by the van while Simon brought the news from his transistor radio that details of the new Contact Group Peace Plan for Bosnia had leaked to the media. Shannon, Christian and I all disliked the plan. Everyone who was an aficionado of the conflict did. It was the latest in the line of international mediation efforts: Carrington–Cutileiro, Vance–Owen, Owen–Stoltenberg. We all preferred for there to be Western intervention to save the Bosnian Muslims. Of course we all had our own separate reasons for disliking the plan and we all found each other's arguments slightly annoying

'It's nothing but Vance–Owen with a smiley face,' Christian said.

'Well, I don't know about that,' Shannon said.

'It starts from an invalid assumption,' I was starting to say when our attention was drawn to a Volvo stopping in the distance. At first it looked like holidaymakers arriving too fast and parking up at a skwiffy angle in the wrong place. But from out of the car stepped Von. He walked towards us over two hundred yards of wet Dover tarmac like Lawrence of Arabia. Penny couldn't believe it – that the family Volvo was down here. She climbed back into the minibus, thinking that something unimaginable was about to happen, that she might be grabbed by force.

When Von arrived, waving back to his dad in the car, he announced to the group that Penny was not going to be allowed to go unless he came too as her guardian. He presented the ultimatum with a straight face and a sense that, from his own point of view, he didn't give a toss whether he spent the next month under gunfire in Sarajevo or smoking weed in Hammersmith and wanking in his en suite shower room.

The first and most obvious solution was to say no, and just go. With Penny, without Von. But the threat they had sent him with, which he delivered as a fiendish kicker, was to cut off her credit card, the bubbling brook that lubricated the trip, fed by the unimaginably vast reservoir of cash that her parents kept, like hydroelectric potential, dammed up in Lloyds Bank. Shannon and Sara had grown used to easy access to Penny's card, swiped and imprinted and re-pocketed so often that little plastic filaments sometimes hung from it, shaved from the sides.

No, Penny's card would have to come, and if that meant pretty, funny, huge Von coming too, then so what? Except –

'Someone's got to stay behind. There's eight ferry tickets, there's only room for eight on the bus. That's all there is,' Shannon said, and a quiver of grim excitement ran through the group. For while no one wanted to be thrown out, here was drama that brought a bit of focus to a headachy evening by the great iron wall of the ferry. Someone was going to get eaten. But who?

Penny, safe now. Von, the wild card, the joker turned ace. Shannon, she got a bye, of course, and Sara too. Onomatopoeic Bob, with his screwdriver and road map, probably safe. Christian originally came from a separate Bosnian relief mission – 'Really,' he explained, 'technically, I'm an organisation, not an individual' – and therefore wasn't available for removal.

'It's between Cally, Simon and Andrew who stays behind,' Shannon said.

The three of us were being invited to scrabble for survival while the outsiders watched. We eyed each other, looked to our potential benefactors, and then Simon said, 'Listen, Cally should go to Bosnia,' and smiled at Penny, who smiled back.

I considered a veto but then agreed that of course she should go. 'Of course.' That's what I'd always intended.

I just hoped Simon would overdo the Christ act and say, 'Andrew, you should go' – because I fucking would, like *that*.

But no: 'I can . . . I have written pieces in support of our mission, obviously,' he offered.

'And I speak the language,' I countered, ashamed to be grappling in front of the gang, promising myself I'd dive hard back into Hawkesworth, soon, and looking at Penny and Von and Christian and Cally and thinking: how do you always stay out of the mud, you rich ones, how do you always escape the embarrassment?

'And my – poems? From the point of view of the popularising-of-the-message, I am able to offer that,' Simon said.

'Sure. That's very useful, Simon. Although, I do, myself, have a background in construction. I could help the folk we're going to aid actually, physically, rebuild their homes. Their shattered lives,' I said. Yes, so long as what Bosnia's refugees needed was a day labourer able to hide for eight hours at a stretch, lying among rolls of fibreglass loft insulation eating Cadbury's Dairy Milk by the square metre. Jesus, though, what indignity.

There was silent consideration before Von shouted out, 'What about a duel?!' and rooted in his bag. Shannon had been creating a short straw with matchsticks but as Von pulled out his two Nerf foam dart guns (essential items only in his luggage) the atmosphere by the van changed. The laughter suggested to everyone that yes, this is who we really were. Not old fucks who got too wound up over who would go on a peace mission, but funsters who could settle disputes with a raised eyebrow. Why shouldn't wars be fought with plastic and the Berlin Wall be reconstructed in foam? This is what we were all about!

So it was settled. Simon and I laughed and took up the children's blasters and giggled and goofed carefree to our friends as we each discreetly examined our weapons with minute attention. My spring loading felt rather slack. We joshed at Von as we took up positions, back to back.

'I'm Onegin!' Simon said and Penny and Christian laughed – and so I laughed too, though I had no idea what this meant. Von paced out what he, as owner of the munitions, estimated to be a reasonable size for the field of honour.

'The gauntlet has been thrown!' I said.

'I demand satisfaction!' said Simon.

'Who shoots first?' Shannon asked.

'Me. I'm a fookin' stoodent. He's a townie,' Simon suggested, smiling but not joking.

'All right, you bag o' shite!' I replied.

I offered my opponent good luck and Cally dropped a sheet of kitchen roll to signal that the paces should begin.

In nearby estate cars families getting away before the school holidays looked on and smiled. My heart tick-tocked and my head was fuzzy with fear and desire. I could kill my rival and have unlimited access to Penny; off, out there, under gunfire, under canvas, huddled close in a ditch, tending a crying child – it was all possible. The glorious boring hours would stretch on and on. We might see horrible things which would bond us in complicated ways. I reached the sweatshirt lying on the tarmac that marked the end of my walk and turned. I could see the glint of real loathing in Simon's eye as he extended his arm and took a second before the foam dart darted. I was not permitted by the code of honour to dodge. I must take the punishment beyond first blood, to the death. But as it flew its metres, I saw the tail fin swagger and the dart nipped past to my right, where, losing velocity, it floated to the ground.

I let Simon sweat as a mocking 'woo!' went up from the little Colosseum of gloating patricians who circled us, unable to imagine the turmoil in the gladiators' hearts. Then, with a dry mouth, I squeezed off the click of my gun and my dart popped into a nice parabola. Not such a brave shot, without so much drive, but my God – I'd estimated right – what accuracy! It arced through the air and everyone could see where it was going. At the last instant there was a brush of wind. Would it take it over him? Too high? No! My dart was finding its mark regardless. There, coming almost to rest – yes, as he saw there was no escape, Simon sloped his scalp so that it came in, *landing* right on top of his fucking head!

People giggled. Simon did not even have the compensation of a flesh wound. He had lost in a fight to the death by getting big laughs, and as he wanted to cry for his forfeited life, he had to turn to the gang and pretend to chortle with them, balancing the orange thing on top of his head of shaggy black poet hair and then shaking it off into his palm with a mock bow. I had never known success so complete. To have won while Simon lost, and publicly, crushingly; to be victorious and magnanimous at once, how unbelievably sweet. Last night's possible tumble and the hope, the fear, the worry, all became insignificant, for while Penny was not jumping with joy at his imminent departure, she was not weeping either. The cleavage was made, the break was clean, and if they had had one night together on the eve of departure, then it could become to 'Penny & Andrew' an amusingly sour starter to the delicious main course we would enjoy in the killing fields of the Balkans.

As everyone poured out of their vehicles and bumped and nudged up through the throbbing innards of the ship, I considered the new make-up of our group. A poet down. A lunk up. It didn't feel great. And yet, Von's high spirits and charm were compensation. He apologised again and again until it became a joke. He asked, playing up the moron, where Bosnia was and whose side we were on. Beneath his pretend stupidity, he hid his real ignorance, and in our recapitulation of the Bosnian Muslims' suffering at the hands of Milosevic and Karadzic we re-enforced our serious sense of ourselves. We were on a ship going to Europe to help stop a war.

I watched the holidaymakers bubble out from the stairways leading from the car decks, something heart-rending in the men of each family leading the way, checking the deck plan and memorising their stairwell colour and number and letter.

Bob bustled ahead and found a corner spot where we could all sit together. He waved his arm towards us urgently, so we'd hurry and join him before he had to fight off the uninterested crowds. I looked at Penny and we shook our heads a little. Caring about things that didn't need to be cared about — that's what seemed to characterise getting old. It crept in. Where you're going to sit. The location of small objects — little bits of paper. I'd seen it happen to relations. An ever growing army of unimportant things took on shadowy importance until it all overwhelmed you and you came to think everything mattered: and then you died.

We ate in the family lounge from Shannon's Co-op supermarket supplies: soft white baps that split in our hands, splatted with fat curlicues of butter, slices of Spanish onion and wedges of Cheshire cheese too crumbly to support themselves. It might have been the best thing I have ever eaten. We looked around at people picking at bowls of overpriced thick, hardening chips and silently reproached them with our good sense, our foresight and our benevolent vigour.

Chapter 8

There were no clear plans about the sleeping arrangements over 'in Europe'. Shannon had tried to keep things realistic, but when we'd talked about what would happen once we were on the Continent it was discussed as though we would be in a new realm, among a time of gifts where, who knew, maybe we'd make it into the Ardennes to sleep with a woodcutter or a charcoal-burner or an old woman with a cottage built of caramels?

Where we in fact found ourselves that first night was pulled up outside a French service station. Onomatopoeic Bob had little time for the motorways and road markings of Europe, so it had taken us some hours to escape Calais and its hinterland, following the minor roads Bob found more to his taste.

I couldn't sleep on the parked-up minibus. I was worried I would fart or dribble in my sleep. Christian, irritatingly, slept soundly next to me as I looked at his white, white skin and imagined I could see the hairs pushing out of the follicles before my eyes. I watched the side of Penny's face lit orange by the sodium lights until I was bored of my own yearning and climbed out of the van, through the car park and into the bright white of the service station.

My single sausage looked dry and unpromising in an unbuttered bun on its white plate. I walked, my legs still gurgling under me from the ferry, and sat in the atrium to watch the truckers come and go, then opened up *War and Peace*. Heavy going: Pierre was involved in the internal politics of the Freemasons. I flicked between the pages of the novel and my biroed aide-memoire of who everyone was inside the front cover. Helene. Yes. Helene. I knew her. I wondered for a while if I was more stupid-clever Helene, looking for social advance. Or nice Pierre, lucky in my duel. Or in fact neither, just some nameless serf in the background of a less well-remembered scene. I looked at the cover illustration hard and felt very tired. The night-shift catering staff stood in the doorway of the kitchens, willing the trickle of incomers to stop entirely.

Sara didn't see me when she arrived. She was focused on the beverage woman as she held a styrofoam cup under a nozzle, as if she might get bilked on the deal, lose a few drops in a hot-choc heist. Sara was small and neat and self-contained. She was wearing her favourite white denim jacket and a white T-shirt under it, and white cotton trousers, all of it still immaculately clean. It looked like it cost her money to smile. While I had ambled back and forth considering all the products available before making my bad choice, she made the purchase of her hot chocolate look like the only sensible choice in the world. Her mouth chewed on itself in concentration as she watched the lid going on and the drink hitting the tray. Everything about her suggested she took her life extremely seriously. Her tray, was it clean? Her drink, was it full? Her change, was it correct? In her every move she was alert to someone trying to give her less than she was owed. I thought about bowing my head down in my book but she clocked me, so I waved her over.

61

'Can't sleep?'

'I'm actually doing security watch,' she said.

'Oh, OK? Do you want me to do a turn?'

'Yeah? You?'

'Yeah. Sure. What does it involve?'

'Can I ask you a question, Andrew?' she said, sitting and looking directly at me.

'Yes,' I said, which I guess is the answer people want when they use that self-dramatising preamble.

'Why do you want to go to Sarajevo?'

'Oh, OK. Well, I want to help. I mean, I think that as well as the practical help we can give with the food and the supplies and the – message of the play – I guess – in another way I want to go merely to register a certain common humanity with –'

'Uh-huh,' she said, cutting me off. 'And can I ask you another question? Would you mind stopping all the staring at Shannon? It's rude and it's actually a bit weird.'

'I'm sorry? What do you –'

'It's obvious what you want to do to her and she's not interested. We're an item.'

'God, I'm sorry.'

Sara was an actor. We'd all had to go out and see her on a peace play bonding-and-inspiration evening in a Movement Piece about the pharmaceuticals industry, in which it was rumoured several cast members got naked. To everyone's eventual disappointment, they in fact did. For about a quarter of an hour Sara and two male cast members lay on separate lab tables in a gesture possibly symbolic of the way the big drug companies treat their subjects. Also, possibly in a gesture symbolic of the director's desire to see if he could cause enough of a sensation that a reviewer from a national paper might come in to watch the show. However boring it was, Sara's willingness to lie there never-theless marked her out as the Real Deal in terms of artistic commitment. It was that night Shannon publicly confirmed their relationship, by giving Sara a long, long kiss of congratula-tion when we all went down to acclaim her in the large photo-copying cupboard that served as the dressing room.

'You know, I don't think I do stare at her.'

'Well, you definitely do. Whenever she says anything.'

'OK.' I sat for a moment and looked at my sausage. 'You don't think you could be confusing me *looking* at her with me *staring* at her, do you?'

'Everyone wants a piece of her, fair enough. Penny, you, Bob. I've had a lot of things taken away from me in my life, but not this one. Do you get it?'

'Yes.'

'Do you promise to leave her alone?'

'OK. Yes. Absolutely.' It didn't seem to be a huge concession, like Poland renouncing territorial claims on Wyoming.

'OK. Good.'

There was then a period when I found it very hard to think of anything to say.

'I can do a security watch if you like?' I said finally.

'Thank you, but Bob and Shannon and I have agreed a rota.'

I took a bite out of the meal which I was now very unhungry for. The bun caked against the roof of my mouth and the sausage bounced about like a fucked-out squash ball.

*

Nothing grinds out the romance of travel for an English person like the rainy fields of northern France. That sour-mouthed morning, I had to look at my map to summon any thrill at all for being abroad. 'Artois. Picardy,' I said to myself, trying to jazz up the whitening humps of land that swelled beside the motorway like a much less interesting England. The red-roofed houses looked prim and unwelcoming. Thinking of the war dead ought to have ennobled the land, but I felt sure wherever I looked was just a patch of backstage nothing rather than glamorous former battlefield.

Shannon, though, was high with being on the road – and she started to sing a song loudly with everyone repeating her lines after her. 'Oh Jehovah, I am dying!'

Everyone: 'Oh Jehovah, I am dying!'

Shannon: 'Please put the cat on the table.'

Everyone: 'Please put the cat on the table.'

Shannon: 'If it's eaten, we are beaten, by a once and future king!'

Everyone (growing triumphant): 'If it's eaten, we are beaten, by a once and future king!'

Looking at her singing, abandoned, almost free-associating, I could see what Sara was so eager to protect. For although she could get insistent and prickly on the topic of the murder of innocent families in the former Yugoslavia, she did also have this demonic streak of pure fun. She felt things deeply: joy, pain, the suffering of others, and once you'd been around it you wanted to plug into her vital force.

Shannon: 'I don't know, but I've been told, Shannon Vanzetti's growing old!'

Everyone: 'I don't know but I've been told, Shannon Vanzetti's growing old!'

Shannon: 'If I get shot, gotta call me a medic, shoot me full of that funky anaesthetic!'

Everyone: 'If I get shot, gotta call me a medic, shoot me full of that funky anaesthetic!'

Perhaps I did love her and Sara knew me better than myself?

Living with Shannon, what would that be like? A lot of brown rice and weeping and laughing; a kitchen tabletop slopped with tea and milk and the coarse grains of demerara sugar, and probably homeless people brought home for supper occasionally. The parts didn't really fit together – I could see myself coming into the kitchen in a denim shirt to a fug of smoke and chat and laying a beetroot from the garden on the table, but I didn't look happy. Plus, of course, she seemed to like women more than men. No, Penny was the one for me, with her shelves and shelves of novels and, I imagined, her many, many drawers of clean underwear. For want of a better plan, I playfully tugged on a braid of her hair. She looked round and I said how sorry I was that Simon had got bumped and she said it was OK, warmly, and I said, 'But on the other hand, you know, fuck him. He was a dick.' And she laughed at my brutality.

'I'm only joking, obviously,' I said.

'Freud said there's no such thing as a joke.'

'Yeah, but Freud was depressed. I think he'd just watched *Police Academy 3: Back in Training*,' I said, and we smiled in a way I hoped might be conspiratorial.

Chapter 9

How long does it take to drive to the Balkans? In my head, I'd always assumed we'd somehow be on the road for a week. A week-ish. A day for the crossing, then France, Belgium, Germany, Austria, Slovenia; it had to be a day per country, surely, given what a ramshackle outfit we were? Then there would be break-downs, probably, and garage stops. That's what my revision time-table was based on: a fat week of eight-hour minibus days listening to my Serbo-Croat tapes; that would get me some-where. So as Shannon drove on, I gave myself the morning off to watch the big and little nations out of the window. We flew high on elevated motorways through Belgium, which seemed, at a speeding hazy distance, to be a land of shallow industrial hollows, filled with grey Lego.

Crossing into Holland, Christian fell asleep on my shoulder. He wasn't heavy, but small and compact, a tight little package, as if his body had been oven-shrunk onto his bones. Though he was thoroughly well connected – his parents government lawyers or university teachers or both – he'd gone to a comprehensive school in north London, so he would sometimes roll his eyes at the things Penny and Cally said. But then, as often as not, he knew the party or the people or the club they were talking about and would join in the chat, sniffy, pissy and dismissive. I knew he wouldn't like to wake resting on me – it was a sign of a certain weakness – so I let him loll there, his dribble dampening my shoulder.

'Maastricht,' Onomatopoeic Bob said to no one and shook his head and laughed a little laugh that begged someone to ask him what he was laughing about. But we all punished him by leaving him hanging.

Maastricht. The name resonated like a boring Austerlitz. John Major's Waterloo. It made me smile. Had Simon been here, he would have rolled out the sophisticated-sounding theory that the UK had supported the recognition of independent Croatia as a bargaining chip to ensure that British workers wouldn't get generous European Union job protection. I could see, if you had a certain slant of mind, it made a nice conspiracy: that the smashing of Yugoslavia had taken place on the backs of British workers. But I didn't buy it. And that Simon wasn't here to say it made me happy.

What was surprising to me was how quickly Germany went. I mean, Germany is a considerable nation, any geographical or historical analysis would confirm that. But we seemed to eat up the fucker like it was nothing at all. We hugged the slow lane, yes, but Onomatopoeic Bob was becoming depressed and acquiescent about the route. For a while he continued to claim that a lot of times there were 'less famous' roads that took you just as quickly as the motorway, but increasingly he just muttered his dissenting addendums once Shannon was rolling us up a slip road to the autobahn.

So Cologne, Bonn, Nuremberg – all these big guys came and went so fast I couldn't believe it. Up in its north-west corner,

Germany felt gristly with life – rich with tissue and organs and nerves all twisted up around the arterial Rhine. Aachen, Dortmund, right down to Frankfurt: there was really no relief from this great length of heart and brain and muscle, pumping money and cars and tin-openers out and round the whole of Europe.

It seemed rude to race past them. Cologne Cathedral? Bonn, so recently a capital? Surely worth an hour? Frankfurt! Were we not going to linger for *Frankfurt*? I was in a state of anxious stasis. I knew theoretically I needed to get some Serbo-Croat into my head, that the available hours were drifting past, but in every actual minute I found something new to look at out of the window.

Plus, while I knew that there could be repercussions, embarrassments about my lie, they weren't very clearly delineated. I hadn't broken any law; surely there would be a pretty wide margin for obfuscation if the moment of truth ever came? Even with just the *dobár* and *dan* I already had in the locker I'd be able to kerfuffle and exclaim at how much I'd forgotten, wouldn't I?

'What about a proper lunch?' Shannon asked the van in Bavaria. It was only three roundabouts off the motorway before we were among the big Alpine chalets surrounded by their geometric woodpiles and mountain pastures so verdant in the summer sunshine they made you want to laugh. We rumbled along hedgeless roads, whose unbordered curves made them feel toytown. A strip of grey painted on the green.

The restaurant we chose was a walkers' place, but with an area for boots to be taken off at the door and net curtains and carpet thick enough to give it a shush-dickhead-you're-in-my-front-room-now atmosphere. We were seated in the middle of the room. The waiter viewed the ordering process as a negotiation whereby we'd start out with a proposition and after some frowning he would write down what he felt was an appropriate compromise. A company of middle-aged walkers smiled at us benevolently. I tried hard not to look at Shannon at all. But not looking at her seemed to involve quite a lot of checking where she was and every time I did, Sara clocked me and I could see her suspicions confirmed.

'So, the question is,' Shannon started, summoning the meeting to order as the water glasses clinked down, 'whether we go in under the radar, or over the radar?'

'Under,' Onomatopoeic Bob stated with great certainty.

A large amount of meat was delivered to the table.

'The pros are that under the radar we have greater flexibility, we're free agents. We owe no one anything and we keep out of all the bullshit,' Shannon said.

'And the cons?' Penny asked.

'The argument against going in under the radar,' Christian said, 'is that it's impossible and will never happen.'

'We're not talking about actual *radar* radars, are we? There are no radars?' Von asked.

'Well, that's not true actually, Christian,' Sara said, staring him down and ignoring Von. 'Apparently a band got in to Sarajevo over Mount Igman and played a gig about three weeks ago with no official crossing papers.'

'Right. And how do you know this?' Christian asked.

'My friend told me.'

'Yeah, well, that may be right, that probably is right, but think: how many borders are we going to try to cross? How many checkpoints? All the European Union and the national borders — the militias, it's a fucking mess. Maybe it's possible under the radar. *Maybe*. But if we're going to do this thing why don't we do it for real? What are we sacred of? People go through. Convoys go through. The UN.'

'The UN,' said Onomatopoeic Bob and laughed. 'Yeah, right. Murderers.'

'Well, not quite murderers,' I said.

'What do you call someone who kills someone?'

'They don't actually, do they – kill anyone?' Von asked.

'What do you call someone who lets someone else be killed?' Onomatopoeic Bob said.

'I don't know, a . . . naughty bystander?' I said.

'OK, you call them naughty bystanders. I call them murderers.'

'Well, they aren't,' I muttered, as I chewed on the soft-rope iron taste of the overcooked beef.

'We should be official,' Christian said. 'It's a war zone. You don't want to fuck around with that. Some bunch of militia? At midnight? In the middle of the countryside?' I chewed and chewed but, like a bit of carpet edge, the piece of meat in my mouth was amenable to being moved around, but had no interest whatsoever in disintegrating.

'Our dad said he has an embassy contact in Zagreb we should check in with? To help,' Penny said.

'What, Dirty Ronnie?' Von asked.

'Ronald Hatch. He's a – I don't know what it's called. Not the ambassador but like a . . .'

'I think he is the ambassador?' Von said.

'No, he's not. He's something.'

'Maybe. He's definitely something.'

'Is it worth at least investigating?' I asked, trying to generate enough saliva to sail the beef down on a wave.

'I don't want to kowtow to anyone,' Bob said. 'This mouth don't suck no pinstriped cock.'

'I guess we wouldn't want to suck cock, we'd just – see what the procedure is . . . theoretically, and if it's too much bullshit we could always back off?' I said.

'I don't want to put my dick in their hands,' Bob said, switching cocks.

'Would you object to filling in a form?' Christian asked.

'No, I'll fill in a form, obviously,' he said, and looked around the group. 'I'm just saying, Shannon, this group is non-aligned and, you know, we're . . . human to human. A lot of the bullshit down there is because of "Oh, we're UN", "We're Serb", "I'm a Bosnian", "I'm a Yugoslav", "I'm a green", "I'm a black", "I'm a yellow banana with a tank". I'm just saying, we're all just people regardless of colour or creed and we shouldn't forget that.' He smiled simperingly at Penny, who looked away.

I moved on to a piece of coarse white meat. Chicken? Or turkey? Chicken, I reckoned, dense and flavourless, like a wodge of newspaper print wrapping a sponge that had been soaked in slightly savoury water.

'OK. Official route or unofficial. Shall we vote?' Shannon asked.

'I don't think we should vote,' Onomatopoeic Bob said. 'People will just do what they think. I think we should just see what happens.'

'Who thinks we should vote?' Shannon asked and everyone but Onomatopoeic Bob put their hand up.

'I did not vote,' Onomatopoeic Bob noted.

'You abstained,' Christian said.

'No. I just wasn't involved.'

'OK,' Shannon said. 'The proposition I'm suggesting is we go to Zagreb –'

'Where the man who isn't an ambassador is,' said Cally.

'And we just – we don't push it and we play it cool but we see

71

what the situation is with the authorities and if it doesn't feel like it's going to compromise us, we go down the official route?'

'Yes, I think we should check out the possibilities,' Onomatopoeic Bob said, like that had been his view all along. Then we took another vote, which was unanimous.

An hour later, the bill was much on my mind. Von started its aggressive inflation with the first round of tall brown bottles of Bavarian lager, then he upped it again with a schnapps order and I wondered at his sublime equanimity at the spending of money. It's quite a skill, spending, I think, and probably quite distinct from having the resources to pay. Sure, they're related, but the ease that comes from years and years of successfully satisfied financial transactions, once you've got it, the lack of fear or kerfuffle about a bill, it is unrelated to money. He's not scared, I thought. If he couldn't pay he would be sure that some way to sort things out could be found. That the crunch would be funny when they said 'Give me' and he said 'I haven't got'. And if the bill was going to eat up his last D-mark then he'd pay that too, content that something would come along. Wealth probably warms you twice. Once with the raw power of the money and once with the layer of fat it leaves you with, blubbering you from abrasions.

'So how's the play coming along, Penny?' Sara asked.

She smiled serenely. 'Oh, good, very good.'

'And can you give us an insight?' Sara asked.

'It is what it is,' Penny said. 'It takes the sort of themes we've talked about and gives them a twist and a punch. I hope.'

From those early table beers the afternoon soon crackled into fragments. Shannon went with Sara, walking to the edge of the conifer limits of the restaurant compound, talking intently.

'Here you go, man, have another one, I'm buying rounds,' Von said and handed me a bottle of beer in a little anteroom bar. The proprietor regarded us coolly. He seemed to accept that it was his job to provide us with beverages when asked, but he was not about to pretend he liked it, selling all this product.

Christian was encouraging Von to have a chaser. They were forging an alliance, north London meets west London. Handsome meets handsome.

'I once shat myself after drinking too much Pernod, so it gives me the heebie-jeebies,' Von said. Pretending to display a degree of weakness was one of his ways of making friends.

'Put an egg in it. Pernod and egg,' Christian said; he kept a tighter ship but could see the attractions of Von. 'A Pernod and egg white and a Tia Maria and milk, please?' The owner said he had no such items in his compact sitting-room bar, intended for the consumption of a little white wine before dinner. Then Von asked for twelve whisky and Cokes – playing a game of trying to provoke him into either liking him or barring us all. Von wanted a climax to the afternoon, hugs all round or bolted doors. I snaked out to the loos, where Cally and Penny were having a smoke by the back door. Onomatopoeic Bob had skinned up a little soldier of grass and Golden Virginia.

'Is that going to be OK?' I asked, nodding to his tin, packed with a Ziploc bag of weed.

'I've got a place I put it,' he said, and pointedly passed the joint the other way. I looked back into the restaurant, thinking that the owner had probably never smelt a joint. After the number went round a couple of times, Cally and Onomatopoeic Bob went in to Von and it was me and Penny alone. I wobbled on my heels.

When you think you're in love with someone your dials get

thrown so far off it's a joke. A stolen glance feels like a long stare, and a long stare can feel ridiculously brief. You don't really know how close to stand or when to talk or when to stop, or certainly what's reasonable to claim in terms of attention, because you're an unfillable hole, you'll take whatever they'll give.

'You are a cool person,' I said. Urgh.

'Thank you,' she said. It wasn't quite 'So are you.'

'Yeah,' I said.

'The thing about me,' she continued, 'is I'm just like a potato.'

'Uh-huh, right!' I said and looked at her for a moment. 'How do you mean?'

'I'm just there, you know, like a potato. I'm not — I'm just what I am.'

'Oh. OK?' I said.

I'd been troubled ever since the night we met, going to see Shannon talk, that I'd somehow always missed the moment, that the previous minute was always the one when I should have acted — to show or tell her I liked her very much. I'd been living with a secret and it had turned pale and sickly under its rock. I'd got all twisted up around ideas of furtiveness and tactics. For a second, pissed and calm, this felt like a moment where maybe, in the Bavarian sun, I could just lean forward and kiss her and set everything right.

But I guess she could tell. Like a cow sitting down before the rain, or a pig facing slaughter: something in the air — the milli-seconds of pause I left, or how I licked my lips — told her where I was going and she headed it off by saying, 'You know I'm in trouble?'

I asked how and why, and she said that she had strong, strong feelings for Shannon.

'She's so — I don't know. I just feel things for her.'

74

'Oh God. Yes. Yes. I can see. God, totally. I can see that.'

'Yeah?'

'Oh yeah. To tell you the truth, Penny . . . me too.'

'You too?'

'Yes.'

What an incredibly clever move! A chess move. Now we'd shared our feelings, it would be a little duplicitous for Penny to act without letting me know.

'Fuck. Really?' she said and I nodded soulfully.

But I guess, as I thought about it, you would also have to say it was additionally a pretty stupid move.

'She's a really great person, isn't she? Such passionate engagement with people and issues,' I was saying, boring myself, when Von appeared and wordlessly took the nub of the roach and honked it out.

'I'm collecting for the bar bill.'

'Oh, I thought – didn't we pay in the restaurant?'

'Yeah, this is for the bar bill. For what we've had in there after lunch, matey.'

As Von had downed more and more of the brown bottles and encouraged us all to join in, it had definitely felt like he was buying. But, as I pulled up my checked shirt and dipped into my money belt, this wasn't, so far as I could see, an implication that could be resurrected into a form of words that wouldn't blow the atmosphere.

'Cheers, bossman,' he said, rubbing my notes together as he headed back in.

'I thought he was buying them in the bar?' Penny said.

'Yes! I did think he seemed to be suggesting that, didn't he?'

'I don't know how much cash he's got with him, but he will spend it all. Then he'll spend yours.'

'Right, but the card?'

'That's for me. He doesn't have a card. Mum thinks the credit card might stop me getting raped.'

'Oh, he doesn't have a card, of his own?'

'I mean, I hope if we meet rapists, they have a credit card machine.'

'Yeah,' I said, a little stoned, wanting to join the joke but feeling I could easily go wrong.

She looked through to her brother at the bar. 'Everyone's corrupted by money, Andrew. But you have to be careful of the rich, because they know exactly how fucking nice it is.'

Chapter 10

Back on the bus, Shannon pulled onto the road as I practised looking at her longingly. There was a mean-spirited flavour abroad as we tried to settle into the uncomfortably right-angled seats. The beer turned sour on our tongues.

'The problem is the news media overcomplicate it because of their own interests,' Onomatopoeic Bob said, over his shoulder, from up front. He was angling for an argument about the war.

'Which are?' Penny asked.

'Look, Penelope, TV has one aim. Ratings, correct?'

'Er, well . . .' I said.

'Yes or no, they want people to watch?' Onomatopoeic Bob went on.

'Yes,' Christian admitted.

'And does war make good television or not?'

'You think, what, they're overcomplicating the picture to prolong the war, to increase their viewing figures?' asked Penny.

'I'm just a guy who can see something, I'm not saying what it is, but it's interesting what shape it is.'

'We were pretty quick into Kuwait, that's all I'll say,' Christian added. 'That would be my message to the Bosnian Muslims — find oil in Sarajevo and fucking quick.'

'The weapons traders won't let this war end. This is their honeypot,' Sara said.

'That's true,' said Onomatopoeic Bob. 'The gun runners always win.'

We hadn't actually talked much about the war for a while, not in a concentrated way. The weeks after the first meeting, we'd sit around the dark varnished tables of an empty high-ceilinged pub in Didsbury and get competitive over how sick the war was making us. It was the marketplace bombing in Sarajevo in February that kicked us, like NATO, into action. The next meeting was held at Penny's — and Shannon brought a scrapbook of horrible pictures from all the national newspapers and we handed it round, trying to give the correct amount of reverent silence to each photograph before turning the page. Both were horrible though: not looking at the pictures enough, like everyone else I knew did, and looking at the pictures too much, like most of the peace play troupe did.

For just how long should you look at a picture of a dead child? I would never have boasted about this to anyone out loud, but I did think I knew just about exactly the right length of time. I wouldn't have wanted to put a figure on it, but somewhere between disregard and fetishisation is a sweet spot of appropriate reverence. I suppose that's what I felt I had a good handle on: the proportionate response to the war.

But now, a bit drunk, people were unlocking the strong feelings that in the general run of things didn't get an opportunity for airing. Now they lit their opinions like magnesium sparklers for the sheer enjoyment of seeing their words shimmer.

'I did hear from my father that to sort the whole thing out and impose a fair deal needed forty thousand troops,' Penny said.

'Right? Yes?' Christian said.

'Or four — was it four hundred thousand?' She looked at Cally.

'Er — it was — I don't know. But it was really, really surprising and bad actually. And interesting,' Cally said, with one of those trademark mushy nursery sentences, delivered with a slight scowl in an attempt to make it fit for public consumption.

'Anyway, whichever it is, it's double what the British Army actually is,' Penny said.

'I think it will come soon,' Shannon said. 'It will have to — we'll send in the soldiers. I mean, what are the US and the UK armies for? All these tanks sitting in Germany in the middle of fields and there's men and women dying, buildings getting dynamited.'

'If we've got them, send them in,' Bob said.

'Bit of argy-bargy. We like a bit of that. Send in the Inter City Firm. The Headhunters!' Von said.

'The British Establishment would never risk a white soldier for the life of a Muslim child,' Sara said.

I knew a couple of lads who'd joined up as squaddies after school. One who was so struck with the military he used to go jogging round Chirk — up to the castle and back with a rucksack half filled with house bricks. He didn't have a particular admission requirement in mind, it was more like a declaration of intent, his twilight laps of the new estate. I never liked the kid. Long face, thin unkind lips. Nor his mate in joining up, Geraint. But still, thinking it might be their slim white limbs, their soft PE-shower bellies that took the bullets, I felt queasy cheering them in.

'I suppose the legitimate question is, what peace would they enforce?' I said.

'What peace would they enforce?' Onomatopoeic Bob said,

but mimicking me in a wheedling high voice. There is probably no feat of rhetorical brilliance in the history of human debate which can survive the funny-voice treatment.

'Look, there are people dying, Andrew. We have an army. Send the army to stop the children dying. It's not hard?' said Shannon.

I didn't like any of it. I didn't like the lack of attention that almost everyone gave to the people dying. I didn't like Shannon's ease with putting young men's bodies into the gunfire. I didn't like the simple solutions of idealists and I didn't like the obfuscating overcomplication of cynics. I was a connoisseur of the conflict and all gross solutions offended my refined understanding of the subtleties of the situation.

Scraping along the main roads at the bottom of Germany, the evening closed the day off and we simmered down from our alcohol boil, moaning for frequent piss stops. Onomatopoeic Bob had to hide his surprise when a number of attempted right turns into Austria found a river in the way. We finally discovered a route over at the border town of Braunau am Inn. There we parked up on the outskirts at eleven or so, many already asleep, the rest of us trying to curl comfy on the plastic-covered seats we were growing to hate.

The next morning, I walked into town to look for a croissant. The sun was bright and my hangover not terrible. I had a maths problem running in my head, along the lines of: if Shannon loves Sara and Sara loves Shannon, and Penny loves Shannon and Andrew loves Penny and Penny might like Simon, who thankfully has been subtracted, then what the fuck does that equal? It was a problem that needed simplification, but I didn't know what to divide it by. One of the issues was that I didn't really totally believe in lesbians. I mean I thought, like vampires, they were a fun idea, but they weren't much in evidence on the Welsh borders. Sara and Shannon acted like a couple, but I knew they'd both had boyfriends and of course Shannon just seemed built for worship – like a great cathedral you had to admire. So Penny's feelings for Shannon I hoped might just be admiration so overheated she'd mistaken it for the horn, and when it actually came to *doing something*, she might find that, like wanking over a picture of Mahatma Gandhi, it proved hard to translate one strong feeling into another.

The morning was clear and the hanging baskets along the main street were still dripping from an early watering. Having successfully bought a creased and sugary morning pastry with German marks and a smile of apology, I felt optimistic about the language issue. '*Dobar dan. Oprostite, govorite li engleski?*' I said to myself, sitting in the first shy heat of a summer's day, flicking through my guidebook on a bench, as the tape played.

I read my guidebook's paragraph on the history and cultural highlights of Braunau am Inn as an old man walked past – and felt an embarrassed flush zoom through my whole body, popping up bright into my face. I shut the book sharply: We had, it seemed, entered Austria via the town of Hitler's birth. I smiled at the old gentleman with his loaf of rye bread in hand and he smiled back.

The pastry was dry in my mouth. I sat a little longer and watched the townspeople as they climbed onto their morning mopeds, drove their VWs and BMWs and even their Peugeots through the streets. I was full of a boundless patronising pity, which, if I was honest, masked quite a bit of revulsion. How could they forget where they were? How could they possibly remember?

I supposed that there was, really, no reason not to live here. Except maybe, wouldn't you rather live anywhere else? In the whole world? Then again – shouldn't we all perhaps move here, squash out the stink with normality? Was it quiet heroism to buy your bread in the street where a tyrant was born? Could your walk to the bakery beat down, step by step, the shadow of history? Especially if you got a doner from the Turkish place on the corner?

Guidebook in lap, I felt hugely self-conscious. Who came to this town for its history? What monsters they must have hosted. And what did they say at tourist information? Market this, you poor fucker: 'We do have one claim to fame, but it's a rather unusual one . . .' 'No, we have no statue of our most famous son, actually . . .' I walked back to the van concocting a cover story that it was impossible to imagine any local demanding.

'*Why are you here?*'

'I am merely visiting the towns possessing the churches with the highest spires in Austria! Yours is third tallest. Look, my guidebook says so! Congratulations. I had to come!'

At the van, I aimed to keep my discovery a secret and usher us out of town as quickly as possible. But I was so hungry for a connection that, as she spat toothpaste into the storm drain at the edge of our car park, I was tempted into sharing my piquant little nugget with Penny. It filtered out from there.

It was a nightmare for me, the reaction of the group. I would describe it as frank, uncomplicated curiosity. Most of the gang wanted, if you can believe it, to go and take a look at the Hitler house. Why? Well, because it was 'interesting'. Of course it was interesting! It was *too* interesting. And the way they talked on the way down to Salzburger Vorstadt 15! Saying his name out loud! I followed at the back of the crowd looking only at the pavement and humming in an attempt to drown out the words of my companions. Von asked the way with the phrase '*War ist Hitler's haus please danke?*' A young woman in jeans and white trainers and a New Order (not *here*!) T-shirt pointed the way in a manner I found utterly unreadable.

Salzburger Vorstadt 15 looked long and non-domestic from outside. It had been a hotel or lodging house when he was born, apparently. In front of the house there was a stone with an inscription. As we looked dumbly down at it, a woman walked past and muttered something which sounded critical. I found that quite a relief. This was all horrible, the whole situation, so I was glad for the group to be able to see themselves through the townsfolk's eyes: beery Britishers, paying homage, or worse, to Hitler's birthplace.

Onomatopoeic Bob took the lead in making our sentiment clear. He moved forward and with a decent swing, kicked the Hitler stone, espadrille on granite, and looked back at us like he'd taken a bullet for the team.

'Fuck him,' he said. 'This is where this whole mess started, right here.'

'Fuck him,' Von said and kicked the stone too.

Another man passed us by with a look of busy bourgeois indifference. Penny and Cally kicked the stone one after another. Then I kicked it, feeling it was now *what we did*, but a little harder, because the impacts had been growing softer as the original gesture got shrouded in the mists of time, becoming merely symbolic. I was something of a revivalist. My toe stung in my Doc Martens as Sara read out from my guidebook that 'the material for the memorial stone against war and fascism came from Mauthausen concentration camp'. At that point I stopped still. I looked over at a passing hausfrau. She was shaking her head. I smiled, then, unsure of my next move, kissed my fingers and touched them to the stone, hoping that maybe the kick and the kiss, taken together, might express both my negative assessment of Hitler's career and my approval for the sentiments of the stone.

Chapter 11

From Braunau we headed to Salzburg, narrowly avoiding an Onomatopoeic Bob-advised double-dip into Germany at Berchtesgaden. As we made it across the tail of tadpole Austria, the Catholic spires shot up from the heart of every town, most of them spindly and straight like dongs, others onion-domed at the summit, even more like dongs.

A couple of days into the drive, the boundaries of my person were dissolving. But I wasn't shrinking, shrivelling into my seat – I was expanding ever so slightly. It felt to me by then that the borders of my being were coterminous with the edges of my 'bit' of the van, in such a way that a nudge of Christian's Adidas shoulder bag a few centimetres into my footwell felt like a thumb pressed on my windpipe.

The natural border of our territories went down the middle of our two-man seat, where the plastic seat covering puckered into a cleft and shredded like elephant skin. That division was clear. But our conflict was kindled by the fact that down the middle of the seat back in front of us there was a moulded plastic imitation of a seam. Because of the arrangement of the seats, this seam didn't align with the crease in our own seat, it was in fact a couple of inches to the left, in his favour.

The scene was therefore set for a bitter turf war – each of us seeing it as too trivial, too important, to raise verbally. In a series of tit-for-tat raids he shuffled his bag over into my area, theoretically unconsciously, and I nudged it back, as if without noticing. Then I sent my actual foot in – an inch or two over the legitimate boundary, just as an initial bid, so that later I could compromise at a fair point. I kept my foot there for several hundred kilometres of Austria, while my heart beat hard.

Christian kept his eyes down on the collection of short stories he was reading and periodically underlining with a knowing smile. The volume was *A Suitcase Between Friends* by Douglas Hurd, the Foreign Secretary. Penny's father had given it to her and she had passed it on to Christian. It was signed in the front by Hurd: 'With affection and admiration to "Good Old Ken"', followed by an exclamation mark and question mark which hinted at some manner of interesting or boring relationship.

As we made our way towards Slovenia, Christian's delight increased steadily. He started to laugh as he read. That is always irritating. 'What's so fucking funny, *friend*?' you want to ask of this person off on their own, having a good time with an author right in front of your face while you're trying to mind your own business among all the horror in the world. He banged a fist into the seat in front of him. 'Oh man, *this is it*!' he said and crossed his legs with merry abandon.

It wasn't that he was actually enjoying the book. More that he felt he had found in the collection the ultimate testament to the utility of his chosen field of study – critical theory.

'There is so much in here! He's saying so much!' he said to

me, but aimed it over for Penny and Cally's benefit, as he double-, triple-underlined and shook his head.

This deconstruction was what his course of study had been preparing him for. A man had written a story and he was going to take it apart sentence by sentence and dissolve it in his proving fluids, and, in a subsequent analysis of its constituent elements, utterly fuck the author.

'Is that what it's about – fucking the author?'

'No – what? That's incredibly reductive,' Christian said and made his counter-attack by jutting his desert boot right up against my Doc Martens.

He told us that though he actually felt quite sorry for the Foreign Secretary, he *was* going to destroy him. The arsehole had broken cover – out from all the speeches and the declarations of what he thought he thought. Now he'd accidentally strayed into Christian's field of fire and the poor Foreign Secretary had *no fucking idea* what weapons were going to be brought to bear.

He soon finished the second short story of the day and looked exhausted, as if he'd been making love for twelve hours straight. He moved his foot away from mine entirely, in what I took to be a tactical feint, and sighed.

'So. My God. Amazing. "The Summer House".'

'OK? Interesting story?'

'So. He's written this sort of "tale" about a Serb living next door to a Croat – in Bosnia.' He smiled to himself at the threadbare obviousness of the conceit and I smiled back, because I am something of a spineless shit. 'And they build this summer house, together in their gardens, but of course they do! Then off somewhere, a Croat rapes a Serb soldier's sister, and in retaliation the Serb mortar-bombs our Croat's house and he dies – in the *shared summer house!*'

86

'OK?' I smiled.

'It's so obvious! It's like – it's like a fairy tale about a shopping trip, where a man just goes to the shop and buys some tuna and comes home. That's it. The story is just what it is. It lies there like a piece of cheese in a fucking vacuum pack.'

'Not good?'

'Oh no, it's *brilliant*. It's written in this sort of "prose" that's like, if he had a job doing the descriptions for the toys in the Littlewoods catalogue, he'd get fired, first day. But it's when you dig down – I mean, he's the *Foreign Secretary*, and he's written a story which exposes his view precisely: he's a sad wise observer watching an unavoidable pub fight with his gin and tonic from the window of his club. It's moral equivalency writ large. Or writ shit.' He laughed. 'His other one is a sort of fantasy about a *fictional Foreign Secretary*. And guess what this hero does? He turns a party conference debate the way of intervention in a foreign war. Yeah?'

'Yeah?' I said.

'It's like the Grand Wizard of the Ku Klux Klan had written *To Kill a Mockingbird*. It's an alternative reality where he's a *good man*. It's extraordinary. Did you read it, Penny?'

'Yeah. I thought it was interesting,' she said.

'Yeah? Interesting how?' he prickled.

'Well, I'm not sure it's totally fantasy fulfilment, is it?'

'Well, it's an alternative reality, where he's good?'

'Yes, but it ends, after the Foreign Secretary has ordered champagne in his suite, to toast his success in arguing for intervention, with the news that his wife's brother has been shot?'

'Exactly! In Madeupstania, where the conflict is meant to be happening!'

'Yeah,' Penny said. 'But that's saying: there are costs associated with the solution of military intervention. Yes?'

'Correct. Illustrating that — to the folks with chopped cock for brains.' Christian's mind was working fast, wriggling away from his initial position.

'So, it's not a fantasy of his good self, it's a warning about what would happen if we did go in? Right?'

'Oh sure,' said Christian, bristling. 'It's multiple, of course it is. You defer one vain justification for non-intervention and there'll be another one along in a minute!' He wrinkled his shoulders and shuffled and then added, 'Andy, is it OK if you move your foot over so I can just put my bag like that? I think we both might be more comfortable, yeah, mate?'

I was speechless at his audacity.

'Oh, of course, totally, I'm sorry,' I said, eventually, my tone indicating to all, I think, that I was teetering on the edge of devastating sarcasm.

*

Outside the van, the pitch of the roofs was becoming decidedly Alpine. Widely obtuse, they overshot the walls by a metre or so front and back, ready for snow. It hurt me how well organised everything was. The roads, the system of payment at the motorway service station, the log piles. I felt we were being continually silently reproached for the relatively shitty disorder of the United Kingdom, our turbulent temporariness. That feeling about everywhere I'd ever worked and every institution I'd ever passed through — that the system had recently changed and no one quite knew how it worked yet and soon it would change again so why bother getting too involved?

We were into Slovenia by late afternoon. Slovenia. How very weird it felt to be looking for *Slovenia* on a map bought from a

European service station. The world was being remade – we had grown up with East and West German football teams and the Iron Curtain that made everything to the east just counties of red Russia, where everywhere from Vladivostok to Prague had a Yuri Gagarin Street. To be looking now at Slovenian border guards, with their cutely differentiated uniforms, their flag – searching a bit unsuccessfully for some new spin on three stripes of white, red and blue – it all suggested a return to before the First World War, when the modern was newly modern.

The whole thing was exciting, to see these names bristling back onto the map: Croatia, Slovenia. What next? Would dragons return? Might Assyria or Rome spring back up like a trodden rake, alert and twangy, looking for fun? And of course, at the back of the palate, Bosnia, Serbia and so on also tasted of a return to catastrophe, to triggers and dominoes and Great Powers getting sucked down the vortex by small war on the heel of small war.

As we approached the border I had an excuse ready. Nevertheless I built up a prickle of sweat on my palms and my head movements became stiff and self-conscious. But as we were processed through the border I was not called upon to explain that Slovenian is actually quite a separate language from Serbo-Croat. There was almost no verbal interaction required and I walked out of the little Portakabin smiling, feeling light and airy. It was stupid of course, I knew that, and my stomach still gnawed deep down, because soon we would be in Croatia, only one little country between us and that border – but when you're looking at a death sentence, every hour's reprieve feels sweet.

So – we were in. Looking at the dream face of the break-up of the oddball six-way boho Yugo marriage. Here in Slovenia the kids were doing fine and the Croats could come to Christmas lunch and there might be joshing about how rich the Slovenes were and how fierce the Croats came on, but no one would shout or break a plate. The whole place, with its name — the sort of thing an American arts student, or a weary foreign secretary, might make up for a central European state in a story — felt magical, an alternative reality.

Once through to the other side of the border, the very first woodpile announced a new world: all stacked and fallen, then jumbled back up in a muddled heap. The breeze blocks of a farmhouse unrendered. In a factoryish yard, propane gas canisters the length of torpedoes jostled in a crate at wild angles, and at the fringe certain ones lay on the ground, the fallen pickup sticks.

'Look at that. As soon as we're over the border,' I said to Penny and nodded to the wonky logs. 'Yeah? Did you see the ones in Austria?'

'Huh?' she said, mildly interested. 'My dad would say that was because the Communist Party has robbed them all of the urge to keep neat log piles.'

'Yeah. Right!' I said and shook my head.

'What is it, then?' Christian asked, spotting an opportunity to get his nose in. '"The Slovenes are an untidy people"? Is that in your guidebook? From 1910? "Narrow of forehead and thick of brow, not to be trusted"?'

I flushed and hid my eyes from Penny. 'No — I'm not saying, race . . . or — but what about culture and —'

'The colonised Slovene? The subservient, surly Slav, yeah?' Christian said.

Sometimes that's what it seemed intellectuals specialised in, taking things you said that were just things and turning them into accusations. Making the normal horrible.

Sara turned round too now. 'What about your value judgement, Andrew – why is a tidy pile better than an untidy pile?'

'Well, the tidy pile is – it's – it's easier to get the logs out and, in a messy one, the ones that are outside the pile, they're not covered from the rain?'

'Does it matter?'

'Well, it matters if you're making a fire.'

'Why do you automatically assume they're going to use the wood to make a fire?' Sara asked.

'Because . . . they definitely are?'

'They probably are, Sara,' even Onomatopoeic Bob conceded.

'. . . What if they carve the logs? Huh? And wet logs, for a reason you can't even imagine, are better than dry ones?'

I left it a moment and then said, 'No. I guess if they carve the logs and, for a reason I can't even imagine, wet ones are better than dry ones, then I guess it's good to have an untidy log pile. You're right.' But once Sara had turned back to the front, Penny looked over and gave me a delicious wink.

We drove with the front windows down and the sliding back windows open, so a rush of air made the afternoon tumbling and fresh. The country we passed through was green and crushable like a chlorophyll berry and raked with rivers. I nuzzled the window and dozed, and noticed, when I woke now and again, that in Slovenia, actually, the post-border crossing mess was the exception, possibly the only untidy log pile in the whole country.

'Why couldn't it all be like this?' Onomatopoeic Bob said from up front. 'Let a man be what he wants to be.'

'There wasn't even a fight here, was there?' said Cally.

'A little – ten, twelve dead. Nothing really,' Christian said.

We travelled in a fog of ignorance. I was interested in where we were but Onomatopoeic Bob would not relinquish the map, so as I dozed I dream-plotted our progress by road signs. Much of the time we seemed to follow a broad river which I thought I might claim to an interested observer was the Danube, but at times it narrowed into not much more than a fat stream and I thought I was overdramatising. But then it would widen and go an exciting chemical-clear blue-green over white stone and I wondered if I wasn't expecting too much of the Danube.

We skirted Ljubljana and made it to the Croatian border at the town of Obrezje as the light was dimming. We pulled up at one of the four kiosks dotted across the lanes of the motorway. Shannon looked over to me like now the linguist might be needed. But in fact, entry was easy. The guard took our bundle of passports, thick and blue, and looked in at us through the windows. 'Why would it be a problem to come into our country?' the prickly border post seemed to ask. 'Yes, we have a flag and uniforms, and indeed ample stationary supplies like any other nation, and why wouldn't we? We're interested why you would think there is anything at all different about Croatia, which is just a perfectly legitimate country like any other country, or isn't it? Is that what you're saying?'

As the van made its way down the broad concrete taper and back onto the highway to Zagreb, I felt I had banked my first piece of credible real estate from the trip. 'I went to Croatia during the war,' I could truthfully say now, and I rolled it around my head, trying it out on teachers from school, regulars from the pub, watching their reactions and trying to look back at myself, ennobled, in their eyes.

In Croatia we were close to the war. But not yet *in* the war. I surveyed the countryside closely, thinking that maybe I might clock somewhere a burnt-out house. It's not a great feeling, looking for a burnt-out house. It raises the question of why exactly you want to see one. I consoled myself that I would have preferred that there weren't any burnt houses at all. But since there were, somewhere, I thought it was important to see them. Still, feeling you're on a kind of arson safari is uncomfortable. Because if a burnt-out house is the most common piece of big game you're trying to tick off, what is the highest value trophy you could spot? Is that what you've come looking to take home: sight of a dead child? A memory that you won't roll out for just anyone; but late at night, after some spirits, if someone deserves it, if they really want to get into it, you'd have that in the locker?

Chapter 12

It was drizzling slightly as we made it through the post-war suburbs of Zagreb and into the soft Habsburg honey centre. A couple of miles out west of the main square we found an oblong park that looked a little like a military parade ground, bound on its two long sides by turn-of-the-century apartment blocks. At its far end was a car park serving modern apartments, which, with its green apron before it, had enough of the feel of a camp-site for us to park up. As night fell, Onomatopoeic Bob laid out some rugs and started to tie an awning from the van while Shannon went off with Penny to buy food. I was chosen, due to my language abilities, as the one to 'make contact with the UN in the first instance'.

How do you 'make contact with the United Nations'? Yell 'Boutros-Boutros Ghali' in the street three times and try to summon the Secretary General like a genie? I stood in a call box near the city's central Jelacic Square and fed coins into the slot by the receiver cradle. Von held the aggressively hydraulic door open with a shoulder and looked bored and encouraging at the same time as, to my surprise, I got an immediate answer from the pre-war British Consulate number listed in my guidebook. The Consulate gave me a number for the UN which led to an immovably French response. When I spoke English at them repeatedly I was transferred, via a lengthy and unpromising series of click click clicks, to a woman who spoke a little English.

'Oh, hello? Hi, yes, we are a group and we wish to enquire how to get the ability to cross from Croatia into Bosnia, to go on then to Sarajevo?' I said, my diction going second-language in sympathy.

'There are briefings daily at Ilica barracks,' said the woman's voice, in an accent which, like the flavour of a cheap sweet without its wrapper, was hard to place. 'What is the nature of your visit?'

'An independent – humanitarian mission. Primarily, we wish to enter to – to – to – make a performance to promote the peace,' I said, adding the definite article to make it sound more definite.

'This is not possible at this time.'

'OK,' I said, then looking at Von, 'Might it be possible. Please?'

'It is not possible,' she said and put her phone down.

'I understand,' I said, to no one. 'Do you know at all when it may be possible?'

So there it was. It was not possible. I had always thought it might not be possible. 'It's not possible,' I said and Von shrugged and started to walk off, but not back towards the van: off up towards the square.

Von did love a treat. He made this little drink fun by inflating how illicit it was, implying that we were stealing time from somewhere. We sat under an awning outside a bar by the cathedral, up past the illegal money changers, and listened to the Sunday-evening bells toll, feeling naughty and bonded. On the quiet pavements young men and women started to hurry to

Mass. People you would never see going to church in England: kids in thin sportswear, girls in short skirts, shouldering together under a buckled extendable umbrella.

Von chugged down his second tall glass of beer and asked if I'd like an Ecstasy tablet.

'Er – I don't think so, no.'

'No?' he said queryingly, like I'd turned down a wine gum.

'Have you even got one?' I said.

'Yeah. I've got about a hundred,' he said, 'so no one'd be losing out.'

'Von,' I started, 'are you not worried about smuggling such a large amount of drugs?'

'It's only a hundred. It's not a thousand,' he said, winning the argument to his mind. 'Look at them all go, Andrew. She's fit as fuck – why does she even need to go to church?' He was looking at a girl in a black zipper top with raven hair who wobbled on the cobbles. He nodded to the young man at the table next to us. 'She fell the right way off the fuck-fuck cart?' I expected the guy to be offended, or be the girl's brother or father or something, but Von's antennae hadn't let him down and soon 'Vlado' had joined our round. He was Aussie-Croatian, in the country 'taking a look' at the situation. He wore what looked like genuine Ray-Bans and a Dynamo Zagreb tracksuit over a pink Lacoste shirt.

'They love it here,' he explained about the churchgoing. 'Fucking mad for it. The Chetniks and the Muslims are all cutting each other's throats for God, but these are the only pricks who actually *go*.'

Vlado explained that he was not a nationalist, like some of the fucking nutters you got. He was just here to help. Von told him that he was with some hippies and we wanted for the Serbs to stop 'battering the Bosnians in the arse'. Vlado laughed and they did a man-shake.

'The thing about your Serb is — and I've got tons of mates who are Serbo — but, mate, and they'd say this themselves, the guys aren't even Slavs. They're Turks who got out of bed the wrong fucking side. They're wackas, mate.'

'Yeah? So where would a guy go to get cunted in Zagreb?' Von asked sweetly. 'What about coke — can you get a bit of chang in this town? Or some cuddly sluts? Are there any cuddly sluts available, for handjobs?'

Vlado's mate let Von hoover a line of something in the bogs but Von thought it was mostly ascorbic acid. We ended up watching highlights of Friday's Russia–Sweden World Cup game, with Von wincing the powder down the back of his neck and Vlado accompanying each of the Swedish goals with a 'Fuck *you*'. We all got caught up in the good mood in the bar and stamped our feet along to the merry-sounding songs.

Vlado wobbled with us home to the van. The streets were totally quiet by midnight and Zagreb felt like a provincial town trying to fill a capital's boots.

'So. OK. Who do you want, Andy?' Von asked as we zigzagged down the pavement. 'Can I have Cally? And Shannon?' he said.

'What — this is, for — what?' I asked.

'I'm just saying, so we don't waste spade work. I don't want to be all nice round Cally and find you've been pulling the same shit? Because the thing is, I really want to get a suck job off of Cally.'

'She is nice.'

'But I don't really like her?'

'Oh. Oh dear. Right,' I said.

'I mean, I do, a bit. I don't hate her. She just bores me. But cos she's matey with Penny . . . It's a bit — I don't want to get all snarled up with her?'

'Of course.'

'And I have my own particular tastes — you know, for what to do.'

'Right? As in?'

'What I like in the way of dirt. Private shit,' he said, ending enquiry.

'Oh?'

'And I don't want to get into all that with my sister. But it's a hard one, cos I don't want to miss out on a suck job, obviously.'

'Obviously. That would be horrible,' I said.

We were now on the main drag of Ilica Street. Beautiful buildings painted in chocolates and faded ice-cream yellows lined the streets, the stucco pitted and pocked where bits had flaked like psoriasis plaques. As Von considered the geometry of his suck-job situation, I asked Vlado about the chequered shield on the Croatian flags the whole city had gone bat-shit for. It was like I had pushed a drawing pin into his flesh. He got animated and explained that anyone who said it was fascist was factually incorrect, because the shield on the new flag had actually been specifically altered so as *not* to be offensive, since the Ustasha version started with a *white* square in the top left-hand corner of the shield, while President Doctor Tudjman had insisted the new country's started with a *red* check in the top left-hand corner. 'Everyone comes after Croatia for fascism. Why? Why the fuck?' he asked. 'Why? No reason. Why?'

'Right,' I said, thinking after the fourth 'why' he might be sounding a note of irony. 'Not the quarter of a million killed at Jasenovac?'

'Yeah,' he laughed, 'sure, and the rest! Half a million, one million, three million! I'm sure, like, where did they hide the bodies? Yeah, that happened, for sure!' He laughed and Von laughed and I smiled too, because even though I thought I knew what he was implying about the concentration camp, he had, all told, bought us a lot of bottles of beer.

We hugged farewell to Vlado at the van, which, we noticed, had been spray-painted with a logo in our absence. 'Peace War!' it now said on the outside, in a poorly executed graffiti script that made it look like we were some unfilmed offshoot of a now cancelled youth television show.

Chapter 13

The Ilica barracks, which hosted the daily aid-organisation briefings to which we were not invited, were a little further west, at
an old Yugoslav National Army complex on a crossroads.

Inside the buildings, what struck me was the huge amount
of admin involved in overseeing the conflict. A war does create
an extraordinary amount of *fuss*. We progressed down many long
corridors following A4 printed 'Briefing' signs which had each
letter jiggling in a different jaunty colour.

When we reached the briefing room ours was by far the largest
group. Towards the front two young women with United Nations
High Commission for Refugees (UNHCR) passes were chatting. A
couple of African guys in suits stood at the back. A nervous young
man approached. 'I'm new, I'm Cafod. Who are you?' he asked.

'Hi, Cafod, I'm Andrew,' I said and Christian laughed.

'CAFOD – Catholic Agency for – what is it – Overseas
Dicking?' Christian said.

'Ha! "Development",' the young man said, unsure whether he
should protest and defend the charity's brand values. 'I'm new.'

'We're new too. A peace play,' I said.

'Yeah, I'm not actually a Catholic,' he said, eager to confess.

'That's OK, we're not really that peaceful,' Sara said.

The briefing was largely incomprehensible. A Danish officer in an impressively soft, freshly laundered uniform gave a list of map coordinates where gunfire had been reported. There was discussion of the movement in the 'ICL' ('Internal Confrontation Line,' Cafod whispered to me), an itemising of sections of road that were likely to be closed today and tomorrow, all of it hilariously over-detailed for us, as though we had turned up for our first biology lesson and been directed straight into a case conference on an imminent piece of open-heart surgery.

At the end, as the Dane started to shuffle his papers, Shannon brushed all her hair back and, unashamed of her ignorance, asked, 'This is our first briefing. Is it safe, in general, to go to Sarajevo? And what route would you suggest?'

The Dane didn't allow himself a smile.

'Yes, it is generally safe. Up until the point a bullet goes through you. At which point it is no longer safe.'

'We are the Peace Play Partnership going to Sarajevo – which road do you suggest?' Shannon persisted.

The officer consulted a list, then looked up and gave us his undivided attention for the three seconds he felt we were worth. 'You are not going to Sarajevo, madam. You have not UN crossing permissions. The Croats won't let you out, the Serbs in the RSK won't let you in. Also the Bosnian authorities won't let you in. Go home.'

'Thank you. We will be leaving for Sarajevo tomorrow,' Shannon said.

'Then good luck, and we shall make reservations for body bags and repatriation of remains.'

Shannon led us back towards the van at a hell of a pace, her arms chugging angrily at her sides. Then, like a steam engine fed overly combustible material, having spluttered and zoomed, she slowed to a halt on the pavement outside a cheap luggage shop. At first she said we would leave right away, straight for Sarajevo. Then she said maybe we would drive into the UN complex with our provisions and pour cooking oil over the very clean Dane. But in the end she agreed with Penny that we should check out what assistance we might get from Dirty Ron Hatch and the British Embassy before driving for the border.

*

While the afternoon was still hot, Penny and I pulled down our bags from the roof rack to hunt out our smartest clothes: hers a red cotton summer dress, me a crumpled shirt and my smart 'party' trousers, whose inner seams zip-zapped against each other as I walked. Penny had procured for herself and Von an invitation to a teatime reception that afternoon hosted by the Zagreb 'Friends of the British Embassy'. Cally and I were to be their guests.

The four of us made quick progress through the nineteenth-century part of the city to the Ante Topic Mimara Museum. From outside, the building looked like a slightly less ugly Buckingham Palace. Inside, it felt like the sheer volume of space ennobled us, refined our vanned-up, penned-in sensibilities. We clipped through gilt passageways with the sensation that our interactions were now somehow more elevated and subtle.

When we reached the high-ceilinged gallery where people were drinking white wine on the British government coin, all the little circles of talk were closed to us, so we plucked bunches of brimming, top-heavy wine glasses and turned to the walls to look at the paintings. I gravitated towards a horrible picture labelled as a Rubens. A woman (Mary? Probably. Usually) was surrounded by cherubs packed into the painting like fat prawns.

'I like this one,' I offered and Penny looked sceptically at it before taking me to one of some oysters that I really did like. Although if asked why, I think the most honest response would have been that I liked it because it looked almost exactly like some oysters.

'You know, these are mostly botch jobs and fakes.'

We turned and Penny gave the man a kiss on the cheek. It was Ronald. He didn't look dirty at all. He looked patrician and, more than anything else, clean. The flesh of his neck, though loose, was pulled taut by the cuff of a clean white shirt collar, buttoned tight with a nice lilac tie set off by a light grey suit. His long face managed to look at once noble, stoic and preposterous, like he was a bloodhound dancing on its hind legs at a circus.

'Yes, they can't admit it,' he went on, taking a look around, 'but there's probably only one or two pieces in this whole place that are competently restored and genuine. The best pieces are all the looted ones.'

'Really?' Penny asked as I looked at Ronnie and he nodded swiftly at me.

'He turned up – this "Ante Topic Mimara" – in Munich, end of the war, at the Allied Art Collection point, papers in hand, saying he was the head of the Yugoslav Restitution Commission. He didn't manage to claim much at first. But he found an accomplice, a young German art historian, and she gave him enough information on what was unassigned to manufacture Yugoslav claims. One hundred and sixty-six masterpieces of European art were loaded onto trucks and simply driven to Belgrade.'

He stooped in at the painting. I looked at Penny. She raised her eyebrows to say, 'He talks too much,' and I smiled to say, 'I like it!' because I could tell she did too.

'Later, he and that young art historian married and she now

lives in a castle in Salzburg that he bought with the proceeds of selling the Bury St Edmunds cross to the New York Met. Have you seen it?' he asked me out of nowhere, like a teacher checking to see if everyone is paying attention. 'It's incredibly beautiful and rather anti-Semitic,' he said.

'Like your mother,' I said and looked at Penny, hoping this might be a zinger, but suddenly unsure as to whether Penny might, in fact, be Jewish. She smiled and Ronnie decided to take me for Dorothy Parker in a crumpled Next shirt rather than something more unpleasant.

'No one knows where he got the cross. Indeed, no one knows who he was, really. He may have been the young man who stole the ivory from Zagreb Cathedral in the twenties and sold it to Cleveland, Ohio.'

I guess what was dirty about Ron was that, like a bad friend, he didn't take care of us. After that first exchange he mingled, brutally. Leaving me and Penny conferring. Maybe this was all we were going to get of him? What if he slipped away with the King of Romania and a janissary and a flamenco dancer and we never got to make our request for help? Eventually Penny chased after him and asked how he thought we might get to Sarajevo. He deflected the question with an offer for 'one of you nice couples' to join him for dinner with some other guests. Penny and I said farewell to Cally and Von, who winked at me lasciviously like he'd dodged a bullet, and we followed Ronnie to a nearby hotel.

Ongoing renovation meant that the handsome art deco private dining room was divided in two by a large plastic sheet, secured with beige fabric tape to the walls, ceiling and floor. Ronnie complained to a manager, but there was nothing to be done apparently, and we all settled down as Ronnie made jokes about the partition of Yugoslavia and our plasticised Iron Curtain.

He placed me and Penny amid the other six diners like cooling rods in a reactor. The hub of the event appeared to be a lithe young man with a perm and a quick smile who carefully shook each person's hand and thanked us for coming, while Ronnie, at his side, whispered a briefing about each guest into his ear.

Among the most voluble diners were an American academic with a great bulbous nose honking red with a danger warning and a trim acerbic ex-Conservative MP, who started the conversation by inviting general career overviews of Nixon, who had died a month or two back.

'Of course, his greatest crime for liberals was ending Vietnam, the exquisite wound they liked to prod. They couldn't forgive him that,' the ex-MP said, kicking things off.

My brain froze. What did I think of Nixon? Nixon. Bad? Nixon was . . . bad? That was as far as I was getting.

'He was a certain kind of genius,' the academic said, a smile playing around his lips. 'He was, as Melville said of the Nantucketeers, "a Quaker with a vengeance". His loyalty was his downfall.'

I looked at Penny to see if she thought we needed to say anything.

'His only real demerit, with hindsight, was that he acquiesced to the final severing of the dollar relationship with the gold standard,' offered Mark, a Canadian banker in his late twenties with a serious, beaky look.

As the conversation developed, it seemed there were a number of things that were commonplace truths for the group that I was not aware were generally accepted: that the First and Second World Wars were the same war; that both were a disastrous error for the West (but probably the Second more than the First); that Nixon was a great guy; that civilisation as a going concern would end within the next hundred years – indeed, that it sort of already had.

Professor America took an optimistic view. He believed that

105

monkeys might survive the coming resources/nuclear crash and, 'with a fair wind', they might be capable, within less than ten million years, of evolving back into a form of humanity.

The ex-MP demurred: 'Only lice, and molluscs, will persist.'

The first course was presented on a silver salver, pink gelatinous rolls filled with a white mousse and a sprig of green on top. We were invited to serve ourselves as a waiter offered us the tray. I took two of the little things, put one on a piece of baguette and scoffed it whole.

'Delicious,' I said and Penny looked at me with widening eyes. The salver had finished its journey round the table and it was now clear there was one starter each. I began to scoop my additional roll onto my fork to offer across the table when Penny put her hand firmly on my arm. The waiters conferred in the corner as my fellow diners studiously ignored my greed. Then, after a brief agonising delay, a single additional starter emerged from the kitchen. Ronnie took a nudge from the permed guest of honour and led the conversation to the situation in the Balkans.

'I think the Clintonistas are going to tire of Yugoslavia as a bedroom in which to demonstrate their ardour,' Professor America said, bringing news, it was implied, from Washington. 'I think Lift and Strike will wither on the vine, in the long run.' He presented himself, mournfully, deprecatingly, as super-liberal and had a habit of saying he was 'very worried' about issues that he then framed dismissively in a way that suggested he didn't give a solitary shit.

'The US has often been bilked by its Anglophile presidents. That's why we ended up in two world wars,' he said.

'Halifax's sole mistake in public life was to believe Churchill would fail more quickly than he did,' the ex-MP countered – or added – I wasn't sure which.

'But then the worst president we ever suffered, of course, was Lincoln. At least that imp Milosevic has a hope of keeping his republic together. Lincoln had no hope. His success was dumb luck.'

'If Halifax could have made a decent peace with a trustworthy National Socialist, then there could have been a British imperial Indian summer of extraordinary capital accumulation.'

'He had a quasi-mystical view of the Union out of all proportion with reality. Milosevic is a Girl Scout compared to Lincoln in terms of his commitment to keeping his nation intact.'

'If you quantified it in terms of loss of global authority, territory and capital reserves, there is a strong argument Churchill should have been hanged for treason,' the MP said, relishing the ruffle in the room.

'The road from Appomattox leads directly to the Watergate Hotel,' the professor said.

'What about the – Jews and the slaves?' Penny piped up, and some of the adults smiled at her like a child in the room had asked if she could marry her mother when she grew up.

'I'm very much afraid that Churchill was an anti-Semite and Lincoln was a racist,' the professor explained.

'I don't accept those terms,' Ronnie said with an irritating smile.

'But – they . . .' Penny started.

'Churchill did nothing about the Holocaust and I think the worst thing that has ever happened to the African American community was the Emancipation Proclamation. An internal revolt would have produced a different America,' the professor said.

'Could the US afford it? A Balkan deployment?' Ronnie asked.

'The global reserve nation can afford anything it likes,' said the banker.

'But the thing about the Clintonistas is they don't understand war. They weren't forged in it, so they fear it too much,' the professor said.

'A coward is much more likely than a bully to get into a fight,' the ex-MP warned, and everyone nodded at the wisdom, including myself − although I was pretty sure this definitely wasn't true. 'But, as regards intervention, the UK's pragmatic check will hold, I think. Thank God.' He smiled at the man in the perm and then at Penny. 'Give my very best wishes to your father, won't you?' he said.

Quite early, at eight or so, the coffees over, Ronnie guided the permed host to a corner meeting with the ex-MP and an older man who had said almost nothing through dinner. There was a good deal of clasping of forearms, hard jokes and laughing. Ronnie walked away with a look that said his work was done. Penny and I were marooned, the ones no one needed to seduce, until Ronnie guided us to the door and brought the permed man over to say farewell.

'Your father's work on behalf of Yugoslavia is very much appreciated. Would you tell him "The Group of Industrialists" send their thanks,' he said to Penny.

Then Ronnie smiled at us as if we'd done a good job and pulled from his jacket pocket an ungummed cheap white envelope which contained a thick, folded piece of paper bearing the UK coat of arms and offering a few paragraphs of assurances of the 'allow the bearer pass without let or hindrance' variety − with Penny's and Von's names and 'Charity' in bold type.

'You should go in through UN Sector North, OK? North.' He kissed Penny on the cheek, took me in one last cool time, smiled a lips-but-no-eyes smile and made it clear it was time for us to fuck off.

Chapter 14

Outside, running on white wine for blood, the pavement bounced up to meet my feet and one question went round and round my head like a novelty hit. Did she like me? Well. She'd let me stay at her house. That was a foothold. She didn't *hate* me. It implied safe-haven rights, at least. That if I took a leathering, or my leg was damaged by a Land Rover mounting a kerb or some other weird urban mishap, I could go to her door in Hammersmith and legitimately claim a phone call, a toilet visit and a glass of water. But it was quite a leap from that to imagine her letting me put part of me *inside* her.

We walked around the proud pimple of the National Theatre and down towards the railway station, and talked for a while, drunk and fast, about Shannon. Shannon and Sara, what Shannon was like, what she was really like, what she seemed like, what we liked most about her and what we liked even more than that. Our boozy chat went along fine, but I felt like I was stealing my electricity from next door. I could always get us sparked up talking about Shannon. She pulsed energy. What was harder was making heat by just rubbing ourselves together.

Our arms brushed from time to time, a little tacky from the

sweat cooked up by the evening, and we took a detour through the botanic gardens. It was nearing nine and they were closing up, but sprinklers still spurted into the air, looping splutters of water like lazy tracer bullets. The broken-down glass houses glittered. I looked at Penny's smooth coffee-coloured skin as she debated for us the odds of successfully making it into Bosnia. Or was it coffee? I guess all skin is coffee-coloured. It depends on how much milk you put in. It was lovely – that was the thing. And those soft un-lipsticked lips, the vertical gullies washed with a dye of red wine. Her hair a mass of slightly unfurled braids. Dark brown eyes with a lively zip which twitched about looking out for the new. Jesus, how I wanted to lie down on the grass with her.

If you find someone intimidating you're sometimes told it helps to think about them standing before you naked. I swallowed, dry-mouthed. That didn't apply in this case. Instead, I told myself, searching for composure, that her face was really only a collection of features, when you thought about it. She, in common with Mr Potato Head, was in possession of a pair of ears, eyes and lips, etc. Perhaps it was even possible to imagine that somewhere in the world there were men who weren't my rivals? Dolts who would rather pursue some big blonde?

'So can I ask. Dirty Ron . . .?'

'Ronnie? He was just someone who was around. There are always people around. Ambassadors and ministers and . . . you know?'

'Yeah. God, right,' I said, then thought I'd better add, 'I mean, I have absolutely no idea what that would be like.'

'All right! Sorry – Little Andy from the slums!' she said merrily.

'No – just . . . I just don't. I'm not being –'

'It's OK. No. My house is just very social. I've been having this

110

feeling, actually, ever since I went to Manchester, that when I come home – that I'm – imposing.'

'Uh-huh. Because . . .'

She picked up a piece of wood, bone-dry and crumbly from the path, and threw it underarm towards a rubbish bin.

'It's a feeling around the house that's crystallised something I think I've felt all my life. That I'm this really really really well-liked guest. Loved. That I can do almost anything. But in the end, if I'm too irritating or troublesome, someone might ask me to leave. And inside, I think I've always felt a certain amount of – gratitude. I had a cat that used to shit all over the place and I felt just . . . terrible. Von, his dog, well, that was just fine, chewing the shit out of my mum's expensive shoes. But my cat, you know, that felt like a problem? Von was never grateful. He pretended to be, but he wasn't. And for a while – fourteen, fifteen – I pretended not to be, but really I always was. And he never was. He just says words.'

I felt so far out of my depth that the best thing I could do was furrow my brow deep enough to plant beetroot and nod. But after a while my silence became noticeable.

'It's difficult. Parents are – it's a difficult relationship – even when . . . you know?' I observed. 'But yours, that's – it doesn't sound good?'

'My grandmother once offered me two hundred pounds to lose half a stone. I think her dead husband might have supported Mosley. But Granny was a very committed Christian. So is my mother.'

'Hmm,' I offered.

'They're good people. They are.'

Something about the way my face was going made her repeat it a few more times until I had to say, 'No, I think they are.'

'But their approach to dealing with having a black daughter was to pretend they hadn't noticed. I think that really was just the most – gracious – and enlightened way they could imagine of interacting. They never told me anything about where I came from, or who, and I got the strong feeling it would be rather rude to ask. So I used to look – in my dad's study there was this big multi-volume set, *Peoples of All Nations*, from before the First World War, people from Papua New Guinea with their dongs out. That sort of thing. And I used to look at the pictures of Africans and I'd try to figure out who I was, where my people came from.'

'Ohhh. That's not right,' I said firmly.

We walked into an area where long-stemmed white tobacco flowers surrounded a frothy carpet of blue periwinklish stuff. Above us the wide arms of a copper beech made a grotto of a bend in the path. The air was gold and summer held still; calm, clear, soft and ebbing. Penny let her arm form a loop I passed mine through and we walked the path among the flowers.

I was stuck on a cusp. An extra act, a further shove just outside the comfy, was needed to get me over the edge. Up ahead, there was an expanse of raked, open sandy ground. A single eucalyptus trunk thrust up from it. Our grotto loop was about to end: we were leaving heaven. All things must pass and I shouldn't let this, so I angled Penny round with my arm and leaned in to suggest that, if I was allowed, I would kiss her.

I would like to write a small companion volume on the kiss. Maybe three. The Circumstances, The Aftermath and a brief hundred pages on The Kiss itself. To condense brutally, what can I say? It was nice. It was soft. If something is able to be both all-consuming and ever so slightly perfunctory, it was the kiss. For while it was a proper kiss, not some goodnight bullshit, when it started to break, she gently eased me back so we were marching again two abreast — and we just walked on as I wondered if round Hammersmith and Notting Hill people did a lot of kissing, a lot of fucking too maybe, and so you could kiss someone pretty hard in a botanical garden and it needn't mean much.

I wanted to say, 'We did just have a kiss, you know. That happened, may I record?'

'So. Shannon is thinking of breaking up with Sara,' Penny said, instead.

'Oh God. Really?'

She had taken Penny for a gritty coffee last night while Von and I were drinking and told her all about it. 'Apparently, Sara's possessive and has a diminished libido.'

'What's Shannon going to do?'

'I don't know. Do you want to toss a coin for her?' Penny smiled.

'Oh, I — you know. You go first!' I said. 'I'll wait in the queue.'

'Do you think we'll do any good, Andrew? My dad said on the phone all we were was a vanity project.' I was still stuck two conversations back, thinking about the kiss. 'Can you think of one single piece of art that has ever changed anything?' she asked.

'Well.' I turned to look at her dead straight. Lining up for another kiss. It wasn't going to work. 'Penny,' I said, 'art works below that level. You're doing something else — it's about — possibilities, not direction, isn't it? Otherwise it would be propaganda, wouldn't it?'

'Karadzic is a poet, you know?' she said, and walked on.

'Hm. Like Simon,' I said and looked up into the darkening sky innocently.

An alley cat skipped across our path and Penny stopped and just pointed.

'Fuck me. Yeah? A cat?'

'Oh wow, right?' I said.

'Just after I told you – about my cat? Yeah?'

'Yeah. OK, yeah, I see,' I said.

Penny did tend to see a world bursting with signs and symbols, congruencies and connections. I liked that about her – that when you were in her company you passed through streets pulsing with meaning. As we watched the alley cat sniff at a rubbish bin she started to speak for a while about cats. Cats in ancient Egypt and witches and their familiars; shape-shifting; the cat through time; medieval mass cat burning and Christian belief; the domestic cat; the cats of Norse gods; lucky oriental cats; the Cheshire cat; T. S. Eliot and Catwoman; cats in Freud; and all her grandmother's cats.

But to me, I'm afraid, it was still, basically, a cat. All the other stuff, it's interesting, but is it, really, anything to do with an actual, everyday, shitting-in-the-litter-tray cat?

I wondered, as she talked more, if maybe human brains weren't just too good. Over-spec; swollen to a capacity which once would have calculated how much forest you needed to clear to grow x amount of corn to make it through winter. But like a sci-fi super-computer, the unforeseen consequence of building such an impressive tool is that in its off hours it will tend to create such things as Catwoman and Christianity.

As we made it out of the gardens, and Penny started to tell me about Ceridwen the Welsh goddess and her white messenger cats, we heard a shout from a hotel terrace. 'Celery!' Von shouted in a sing-song voice. He was sitting with Cally, both of them slumped with lager.

'Celery?' I asked.

'Celery, celery. If she don't come, got to tickle her bum, with a lump of celery!' he sang.

They'd been drinking hard the whole time we'd been at our dinner and now their thoughts and words looped out in that boring, lunging stream of consciousness where everything, for the drunk, is urgent and interconnected. We sat down with them. The girls huddled up for a conference as Von said into my ear, way too loud but, just, I think, inaudible to Cally and Penny, 'She gave me a fucking handy in the lav.'

'Oh – right, good,' I said, trying to make out he might be talking art history or foreign policy.

'She's a slut. She wanted me to do it to her, stick it right in, in the bogs.' Penny looked over at me enquiringly

'Uh-huh. It was a lovely dinner, thank you,' I said nice and loud.

Cally whispered and wobbled into Penny's ear. Penny laughed and smiled and patted her friend's hand in response, but when she looked over at me she dropped a delicious wink and I felt that this little coupling might represent a tactical advance for me. By handjobbing Penny's brother, Cally had inadvertently cut off a supply route of intimacy, and I was more than ready to step in and airlift alternative emotional support.

'She grabbed my fingers and tried to get them up her. I hardly touched her and she came like a fucking train,' Von continued.

'Uh-huh. OK,' I said. Then, for the benefit of the group: 'Oh, we talked a lot about, you know, the current situation, Lift and Strike and so on.'

'Can you smell? Smell that.' He waved his fingers under my nose and I tried to ease his hand down quickly and unobtrusively.

'OK!' I said and looked at Penny, hoping the credit card would cover the long, thin, ticker tape of a bill.

*

It was a hot night. While me and Von and Christian lay on foam pads underneath the plastic sheeting Onomatopoeic Bob had

115

hooked up, the rest of them slept in the van with the doors open. What woke us at three or so, I thought, was the soft smack of some great squat pheasant-like bird landing on the awning, thudding the middle down like an unrisen cake. But soon another bird plopped, and another – the rigging wilted, and I realised they weren't birds but house bricks, and the muddle of laughs I could hear was the gang of seven or eight lads lobbing them. They shouted loudly, pissed, and ready for a fight, ready for anything bad, but still ever so slightly embarrassed to be waking us. What they wanted was a confrontation, it seemed, not just to smash our heads in while we slept.

Von fronted it up like a caterpillar, standing in his sleeping bag, wanting to know what the fuck was going on? Christian and I started to retreat to the van immediately, tugging Von by the shoulders of his unbuttoned corduroy shirt. And once he was certain we would restrain him, he became ever more belligerent. 'Fuck *you*!' he shouted at them, in their light blue jeans, clean-shaven like a boy band.

We managed to pull him inside and rolled the side door shut hard, violently waking Shannon and Sara; their annoyance with us clambering in got wrapped up with surprise as the van began to rock. There were streetlamp-lit faces looking in and jeering, three or four on each side. The pitching of the van became alarming very quickly as the faces started to chant, 'Bleiberg! Bleiberg! Bleiberg! Bleiberg! Bleiberg!'

'What are they *saying*, Andy?' Cally asked me, rearing up from one of the double seats.

'Bleiberg! Bleiberg! Bleiberg!' they shouted.

'They're not happy,' I said. Everyone seemed to find this translation rather impressive.

'Tell them to stop. Tell them, Andy!' Shannon shouted.

It was an emergency situation. As everyone looked at me, I shouted back. '*Laku noć, gospodine popovicu! Laku noć, gospodine popovicu!*'

It sounded decent and I was pleased with my pronunciation. The rocking abated slightly. So I gave one more. '*Laku noć, gospodine popovicu!*' I said commandingly. (Full translation: 'Goodnight, Mr Popovich!')

The phrase did seem to have a calming effect. Then I saw the pale face of our friend Vlado, slamming a fist against the window and shouting 'Bad Blue Boys!' in English with a snarl. I responded once more: '*Laku noć, gospodine popovicu!*'

'Bad Blue Boys will fuck you up!' one of Vlado's companions added.

'Mate, what the fuck, mate?' Von asked, but Vlado had disappeared.

As we all peered out, like tourists, watching for what was going to happen next in the aquarium of the night, we saw he had in fact retreated just a few yards. He was handing his buddy a length of scaffolding pole and the kid started to run at us, a mini Lancelot.

'Come on,' said Onomatopoeic Bob, 'there's more of us – let's get out!'

'Let's fucking have them!' Von said.

'No,' Shannon said. 'We're not fighting.'

The scaffolding pole clanked into our side. That was enough for Onomatopoeic Bob, who went for the door handle to lead a countercharge as Von tooled up with a long-handled socket set.

'No!' said Shannon and pushed Onomatopoeic Bob away from the side door. 'Fucking no, do you hear me? Anything, anything else. Show them what bullshit this is. Show them anything. Show them our asses. But no fighting.'

I was not sure about the wisdom, either tactically or in terms of the semiotics, of showing the aggressors our buttocks. But in the absence of another plan, the arse riposte became the working proposition.

Sara and Von unbuckled almost immediately. There were a lot of drawstrings around, pyjamas and so on, which made things easier, so on a rough count of three, as I once more shouted 'Goodnight, Mr Popovich!', between ten and sixteen buttocks hit the glass of the van and formed a force field of arse that we hoped would change the dynamic of the night.

It was impossible to know whether it was the massed bottoms, or a break while reinforcements were called in, but there was a definite lull in hostilities after the butt parade. We conferred quickly. The decision: to pull out. Me and Christian wrestled in the awning, and all the other stuff from outside, while the rest of the team prepared the van for the highway. And so, under enemy fire, we pulled out of Zagreb, heading for Bosnia through the bristling night.

Chapter 15

Before we left, everyone had told us that if we did drive to Sarajevo, the wise route went through Split on the coast. Then you could enter Bosnia through the British United Nations Protection Force sector, and that — as well as feeling a little cosier, maybe offering a look at a *Daily Mirror* and a Marmite swap — meant not travelling across too much Bosnian-Serb territory. From there, you could get pretty close to Sarajevo through Croat and Bosnian government-controlled land before climbing to the city on 'back roads' over Mount Igman.

But that was thousands of miles of detour. So it didn't take much for Penny to persuade the group we should follow Ronnie's advice, ignore the war, trust the road map and drive directly at our aim, heading south for the uninviting blood blister of the Krajina.

'It's inside the Croatian nation,' Christian explained to Von, 'but Serbs have been there for centuries, in the majority. They got relocated. "Krajina" is border. Border between the East and the West. It was the bulwark, the groyne, to stop the Ottomans. This side Croatia and the Hapsburgs; the other, the Turks. The Serbs were the tough motherfuckers they shipped in to stop the Muslims coming for us in the night.' Von nodded slowly but I don't think anything was going in. 'When Tudjman took Croatia independent, the Krajina Serbs got scared, and they started off this whole shooting match by carving out their own little statelet.'

'What a fucking mess!' Von said and closed his eyes to ensure the end of the history lesson.

The tyres hissed on the empty road. I thought of the kiss and for a moment my belly fluttered and a frog of excitement beat so hard in my mouth it was almost fit to pop, its innards all tubey and disgusting.

'So in the Krajina, the Serbs . . .? Are the Krajina Serbs, are they – the, in this case . . .?' Cally stumbled, searching, I think, for a sophisticated synonym for 'the goodies' – 'Is their claim legitimate?'

'Well, I don't know?' Christian said. 'They got hyped up by Belgrade. But – you know, they think a million Serbs had their throats cut in World War Two by the Ustasha, so they're worried. Since the end of '91, they've had their own Republic of Serb Krajina with the UN holding the rope on the borders.'

The roads knotted up round the small city of Karlovac, where fat gas holders loomed above us. In the darkness we couldn't see much else. The highway was empty mostly. Occasionally, we clocked our brother, sister vehicles: a white UN truck and then a convoy of Croatian army trucks – their speed through the moonlight making them feel ghostly, secret and sinister.

A little after four in the morning, we hit the first checkpoint into the Republic of Serb Krajina. The crossing outside the little town of Turanj, manned by Croat police. We stopped near a set of four fuel tanker trucks in a bleak road siding. Shannon parked and invited me up to the front row, ready to deploy my linguistic skills to argue us in. Once I'd clambered over to make a four,

Sara watched disapprovingly the spot where my thigh couldn't help meeting Shannon's. I was careful to look back at Penny as if I was a cat getting the cream.

The border guards were two guys, one slim and wry-looking, the other guileless and grinning, popping up at our window like a border-guard dolphin. I waved cheerily, '*Dobar dan!*' To my relief they answered in English.

'How many bombs have you in your car?' the wry one asked.

'Ah?' I asked.

'How many bombs, how many pistols, how many guns and how many radar?'

'Er — none,' I said.

'How many none?'

'Zero — none,' I said.

'Good,' the wry one said. 'Now we look to see if you lie and for executions of lying.' But when he pulled a finger-gun he smiled and I laughed and felt that I was kind of doing very decent translating.

Nevertheless, as Onomatopoeic Bob and I walked round to open up the back of the van, I did wonder how much there was between us and a summary execution. Would that make the papers? A front page? Or just a couple of paragraphs in the *Independent*, and maybe months later on a Sunday a photo of our parents holding up pictures of us as kids in a 'Tragedy in Bosnia' investigation special? 'Could the authorities have done more to safeguard this idealistic group of youngsters?' Yes. Yes, I thought, maybe they could have, actually?

The border cops looked at the sacks of rice and other provisions while I looked at Von, wondering where he had hidden his one hundred Ecstasy tablets.

'To where are you going?' the wry cop asked.

'To — to Sarajevo,' I said.

'This is not possible,' the other one said, still smiling broadly.

'We have permissions,' I said, and pulled out our sheaf of papers, none of which was a permission.

'This is not a road for Sarajevo.'

'We're going this way, the quick way, through UNPROFOR North sector,' I explained.

They looked at each other wearily; there was so much they could explain, but it was all too difficult. Instead, they checked our passports and just waved us through, saying they'd see us in an hour or two when we were sent back by the UN.

Fifty metres or so on, the next checkpoint was more homespun. Von sighed deeply: 'Another one?' Christian taunted him, saying by his estimate we'd have to make it through up to fourteen different national, regional, splinter-state, UN, militia and customs checkpoints before we even got close to Sarajevo.

There was no hut or shed at the roadside; the road was just blocked by a few trucks. There were some cars parked up with tents and chairs and dead oil-drum fires, and everywhere banners and painted slogans and the *sahovnica* chequered chessboard flag. It looked quite pleasant by the cars. Old men sat in their open hatchbacks, a Thermos of something warming and throaty getting passed around.

'What's going on?' Penny asked. I peered at a banner dry-plastered across a lorry's beak and pretended to read.

'Croat refugees – pushed out from Serb Krajina, complaining. They want to be allowed back to their homes. This is a blockade, it's unofficial.'

'Well, let's ignore it?' Von said.

'Yeah, but if they shoot at us, it doesn't really matter if the bullets are official or unofficial when they go through you?' Bob said. In the back, Von flapped his hand to us, making the sign for yap yap yap, oh fuck off.

An old woman with a clipboard approached us speaking German, which Christian knew, so he talked to her. To pass beyond this troop of grannies and grumpy dads it seemed they needed to be treated with a respect inversely proportional to that demanded by their appearance. They wanted to know why we had not faxed through in advance a request for a crossing permission?

'Because we didn't know you even existed, let alone that you might have a fax machine, which is probably "plugged in" to a gap in the plasterwork,' Christian said to us quietly in English as he rustled for our papers.

The head border-granny was content to allow us to progress as long as we promised to telephone before we tried to come back through, and let her biro her initials in each of our passports. Assisted by two attack-grandpas in tracksuits and baseball caps, she also required the freedom to poke our rice sacks with an umbrella and unscrew the ghee lids to sniff at the contents. But when she encountered the tin seals under the plastic screw tops, she didn't make us break them. A certain level of inconvenience had to be generated in honour of the war, it seemed, but it wasn't like they wanted to be dicks about it.

Next up, on the very edge of town, was the UN, the peace-keeping insulation around the disputed Serb Krajina. We cantered towards them, a colt growing cocky at the jumps. A group of Polish peacekeepers manned the barrier. A disused garage, the two wrecked pumps sticking up like tombstones under the canopy shelter, was home to a cluster of armoured personnel carriers and a Portakabin border office. The Poles also cast doubt on our route, smiling laconically and offering the girls cigarettes while an officer informed us briskly, in good English, that we were absolutely forbidden entry. It was too late; we needed UN-accredited identity cards; it was the wrong road; our vehicle was not suitable; it could lose him his job. Goodnight, goodbye, go home.

At this point, where I would have readied the van for a U-turn, Penny bolstered us with her trump card: her sense of metropolitan entitlement. She poked her head forward to shout after the officer that of course we must be let in. He said no again, and she said yes again. His blank refusal was so irritating to her that she extemporised a false version of history so forcefully she sounded like she believed it herself. We had gone to the barracks on Ilica – of course we had. We had attended a briefing with the Danish Officer, 'Petersboden', who had assured us, *himself*, in *precise terms*, that while our UN passes were in the process of being issued, we would not be prevented from crossing in the meantime.

Shannon waved our sheaf of papers. Penny unfolded the Dirty Ron letter to its full extent and pointed at the United Kingdom coat of arms and mentioned Douglas Hurd and NATO and said she would be making calls about how we had been treated.

The officer went back to the Portakabin. Maybe he made some calls, or maybe he adjusted his balls and read the paper, but at some point he made a calculation and a soldier was sent out to us, nodding us through with a head movement so subtle it hardly happened.

We then crossed into a no-man's-land. The road trundled over a maze of little streams and rivers that glistened black and silver in the dark. We had left Croatia proper and were heading for the Republic of Serb Krajina, the little puppet nation kicking inside its host state like the world's most unfriendly foetus. In the van, everything was tight and still. We were going in, to meet the Serbs, the butchers of Bosnia and the tormenters of Sarajevo, and we carried in all of us this feeling that when we hit their checkpoint we'd be looking at something evil. But if I could stand up to them, if I could speak to them, if I could just somehow get us through, I felt surely Penny might kiss me again, and then again and again and perhaps, after a while, it would be rude for her to stop, and she'd be mine.

Chapter 16

The arc lights at the checkpoint into the Republic were intensely bright. Two cars waited ahead of us, engines off, queuing before a closed barrier gate. The first car contained an EU monitor from Denmark. He told us he'd been there since 6 p.m., that there were only two soldiers guarding the post and everyone was going to have to wait till the morning when 'the commander' returned. Along the side of the road there ran a thin marker-wire from which, at irregular intervals, hung skull and crossbones signs and UN warnings in many languages of landmines beyond.

I climbed out for a walk and a flick through the pamphlet that accompanied my language tape. Slowly, early morning hardened and the town of Turanj solidified out of the haze. The place was utterly fucked.

The area had seen heavy fighting, as they said in news reports. It had seen heavy fighting – and heavy fighting had poked its fucking eyes out. As the buildings became visible, they formed the kind of landscape you might come across in a nightmare, logical for moments but when you tried to look at it all together, it made no sense. The walls of houses started out confident from their corners and then fell away in crazy jags, smashed-tooth edges, with buckled, red-tiled roofs lying broken-backed inside. All the glass was gone pretty much, some of it replaced by plastic sheets. Everywhere the houses' render was pitted with scatters of inverted-nipple bullet marks.

I headed back to the van and tried to sleep.

Penny announced the death sentence.

'Andrew? Andy – will you talk to the border guy? He's here. Andy?'

As I pulled myself upright, Shannon offered me our collection of papers and shouted to the big man outside, flanked by two young women in dirty purple camouflage, 'He's coming. He'll speak with you now.'

So this was it, my stumble of death. I don't much like confrontation and I don't much like authority in displeasure and I don't much like being misunderstood, so as I high-stepped through the tangle of limbs in the back of the van and clambered over to the front-bench seat, I didn't much like anything about my situation. And when Penny smiled and gave a heart-breakingly supportive jaunty wink, I had a moment of everything zooming into a sudden omnifocus. The world felt crushingly vivid –

Outside, wisps of grey dust swirl up from the rip in the pile of cement sacks stacked beside the checkpoint hut. The hut is a shipping container just the same as the one where I would eat lunch back at the building site. The Serb commander has one of those aggressively bald heads that makes you think of the skull below, the skim of skin a shoddy cover story for the facts beneath. He raises an eyebrow and I roll out my prepared phrase trying to machine-gun it off as confidently as possible.

'*Dobar dan. Govorite li engleski molim?*'

He looks stern, says something incomprehensible in Serbo-Croat.

'*Can we talk in private, please?*' I say in Serbo-Croat, my other prepared phrase, and nod for us to talk away from the van. He does not say yes or no but looks at me. I say it again and he moves back maybe a centimetre.

I manage to get out of the van. I angle my body so my friends can't see my mouth. I ask again if he speaks English and he says no. Then I simply say, 'Sarajevo. Please?' He says no. I say it again. He says lots of things I don't understand, but ultimately, no, and marches back towards the window of the van.

As I follow him back Penny and the rest are looking out of the windows at me, their champion. The commander looks at me to deliver the bad news. I tell them he's refusing to let us through. Shannon wants me to persuade him.

'It'll be no use,' I explain. 'He says – he says that the fighting in central Bosnia is too heavy.' This might well be the sort of thing he would have said. I look at him and nod.

'Tell him we're a peaceful student project,' Shannon says. I gird myself as he comes closer. I look to the floor – I try to flex my brain as if it is a muscle and some bit of knowledge might pop out of its folds. Help me, Celia Hawkesworth, help me! But there is nothing, so eventually I screw up my pride until it is nothing at all and make up a phrase: '*Prokcsim estudentisch nu sommint.*'

He looks, surprisingly, not at all bewildered and replies with a stream of Serb that is not comprehensible to me.

'He, um, he says – this is not possible, unfortunately.'

'Tell him we must go, it's important,' Penny calls over and I nod seriously and then, digging my fingernails into my palms, dive in, again with my ching-chong Serbo-Croat: '*Istus muchovich jancka. Importo. Prosvich va.*'

Remarkably, the commander doesn't look like a man who is being insulted with a meaningless version of his own language, and I wonder if perhaps, by magic, I might be speaking Serbo-Croat? Hawkesworth, you witch!

His next stream of Serbo-Croat is still not comprehensible to me. So perhaps I can speak it, but I definitely can't understand it. 'It's still a very firm no,' I say. 'He says we are insulting him a little.' I throw that in for spice.

'Show him the permissions again and say we insist.'

I proffer the permissions and he takes in the crests but doesn't look interested or take hold of them.

'Read them out to him!'

I fear that my madey-uppy language will not be fit for the task, so I say (though he has said nothing new), 'We must go now, he says, or he will be forced to move us off the road.'

'Tell him to go fuck himself!' Sara says suddenly.

'I'm not saying that.'

'Fuck you!' Sara shouts over as Shannon starts to wind up the window and the rest of the gang remonstrate with her.

'Fuck you,' the commander says back in English and I feel a twinge of annoyance at having become redundant in the exchange. He reaches his hand out and I fail to understand for a moment and then realise what he wants and pass him our bundle of passports and papers.

He spent a good twenty minutes in his shipping container with our passports.

'What do you think he's doing?' Cally asked me, the resident expert on this gentleman and his temperament.

'Probably burning them,' I said darkly, knowledgeably.

When he returned to hand back the papers he said something slowly in Serbian. I looked at him. Then he said it again very, very slowly.

'Something something something *levo* something something,' he repeated and asked if I understood.

'*Da. Oui. Jah.* Yes,' I said.

One of the purple-camouflaged border-guard girls walked a BMX bike round to the front of the van then jumped on.

The van all looked at me. '*Levo*' meant, I was pretty sure, left.

'He says . . . go left.'

The road ahead was straight.

'What does he mean?' Penny asked.

'I don't know, Penny. I asked and he just said, "Go left."'

'Well, ask him again.'

'. . . I did, he just − look, it's a subtle thing − but I think too much . . . questioning might have a bad reaction.' Penny looked at me and nodded. Not sceptical, but intrigued.

'He says we must − go left.'

The girl soldier on the BMX kicked off and Shannon looked at me. 'Shall we follow her?' she asked.

'Yes,' I said and looked straight ahead resolutely. Shannon started up the van. I had no idea if we were about to roll into a minefield or be shot up in a hail of bullets. Although, I consoled myself, in either of these eventualities, my friends would never discover I couldn't in fact speak Serbo-Croat, which would be a bonus.

We followed the cyclist as she wobbled her weight from side to side, standing on the pedals for two hundred metres or so until the road forked. She peeled off to the left and gestured with her arm to the right-hand fork. Shannon looked at me. 'Left,' I said and she turned the wheel to continue following the bike. The militia cyclist looked over her shoulder, saw us still on her tail and skidded her bike to the ground. Shannon pulled sharply to a stop.

Quite slowly, so we could see exactly what was happening,

130

the girl in purple undid the popper on her white leather waist holster and pulled out a handgun.

'*Ne levo, ne levo,*' she said as she came towards the window, waving the gun casually side to side, the barrel drooping under the weight of its own seriousness.

'Left?' I said in English.

'*Ne levo.* Not left,' she said.

Shannon went into reverse.

'Ah, *not* left,' I said, nodding sagely, like this was an easy mistake to make. '*Not* left.'

'Not left?' Shannon said, looking at me.

'Yeah, not left.'

'Otherwise known as right?'

'Yes. Not left, right. That's correct. Right is correct,' I said and looked ahead as though calm and concentration were necessary.

The bike guard watched Shannon pull back and then, catching the weapon a couple of times on the lip of her holster, put the gun away safely.

'What the fuck is going on?' asked Von. Cally was sitting in front of him and took one of his hands to comfort him and reassure herself.

Back where the road forked, we headed right. 'Is this OK?' Penny asked.

I looked out of the window at a bank of spindly green trees on the roadside, squinted my eyes, and pretended to consider something. 'I *think* it's OK,' I said. Around the next corner, concrete motorway reservation barriers painted red and white and topped with barbed wire were positioned across the road, forcing us to turn into the car park of a small football club.

As we crossed the large rectangle of sandy dirt, a pair of Republic of Serb Krajina militia guys stopped their game of dice and pointed for us to park up behind the clubhouse. We could see the pitch beyond, lush and unused, the grass still watered and growing high; around it ran a scaffold rail and on one side a mini stand formed of two rows of benches under a little plastic lip of an awning, with the breeze-block club house behind.

We got out. It all looked fucking worrying to be honest. Football stadium and militia. Shannon and I tried to talk to the dice guys but they weren't interested – they just stayed in their two plastic stacking chairs either side of an ammunition box and carried on their game. Von started to throw rocks loudly at a can. I do this sort of thing wherever I go, he was announcing: I'd play hopscotch in the torture chamber.

'How long do we stay here?' Cally asked me, brimming with a sense of her value and vulnerability.

'As long as it takes,' Shannon cut in. Tanned and fearless, she was the other way – meeting the world with a frankness which seemed to drain away the possibility of complicated horrors.

Then there was a rumble like an earth tremor and a six-lorry train of tanker wagons crossed the car park. The militia guys saluted them as they passed and got a nod from a pair of soldiers in red berets who travelled in a Cherokee jeep at the front of the convoy. Once they had passed, a civilian car appeared. I recognised it as one that had waited out the night at the checkpoint behind us. The owner, bearded and tense, sat in the back, while the baldy-headed commander from the checkpoint sat up front with one of the girls in purple, who drove across the car park unnecessarily fast. She and the commander got out.

'Who speak Serbian?' the girl asked us, in English. Shannon and Penny looked at me.

'Er, I can,' I said.

'Tell what he says,' she said to me, pointing at the commander.

132

He looked at me sideways, slightly uncomfortable, having had, I guess, a certain amount of experience of my translation skills.

He said a long sentence in Serbian. I looked at the peace-play bunch. They stood in a line. I counted the number of weapons I could see. Four: one rifle each for the militia guys; a side arm for the young woman in purple and one for the commander. I looked at Penny. She looked at me expectantly, waiting for the translation. Were we being informed that we were about to be machine-gunned? Or being told to leave immediately? Or advance to Sarajevo and collect two hundred marks?

'Say,' the bald commander told me in English.

'I cannot say,' I said.

'Say!' he said.

'What is it?' Penny asked. 'Is it bad?'

'I – I don't know. I can't say.'

'What? Say!' the Serbian said.

'I cannot say!'

'Why can't you say, Andy? Is it really bad?'

'I can't say. I'm – I'm not sure I can speak Serbian,' I said, then stumbled a simplified version in Serbo-Croat.

'*What?*' Shannon said.

'Andy?' Penny asked.

'Why you said it, you can say?' the border-guard girl asked.

Why indeed I said it, I could say?

'Look, everyone, I'm sorry but my Serbian is not as good as I thought. This is a difficult dialect.'

'What do you mean?' Shannon asked.

'I'm sorry. It's – gone,' I said.

'Where's it – gone – Andy?' Penny asked.

'Fuck me! *Andrew*,' Von said, almost triumphantly, thrilling to the drama of it all.

'I don't know. I'm sort of — looking, in my head, but I guess, I've not got as much there as I thought I did. I think lots has changed. Has lots changed?' I asked the female guard in English. She looked at me blankly and I felt like a small fish flapping on the quayside, gulping down the terrible air while everyone watched me dying.

Just then the man in the back of the car said, 'I speak some English.' He was allowed out to come and join us. He had a thick, strong, brown bear's body and a big face — a head like a medicine ball, with a poesy of wet pink lips hiding in the middle of his glossy beard. His eyes were small, deep black drill-holes in balsa wood, widely spaced above humps of cheek. The whole effect gave the sense of something secure to hold on to, though he must only have been in his mid-twenties.

Everyone looked at him as he said something to the guards in their own language and they spoke back.

'They want to search your van,' he explained.

The dice-playing militiamen were summoned to pull every-thing out from the back, and all the rucksacks down from the roof rack, and laid their haul on the dirt of the sand-and-gravel car park. They stuck lengths of bendy plastic into the bags of rice, jiggled the onion bags, smelt the bleach, even touched a finger onto a rag that they dipped in there. They took off the little metal inner caps from the big tins of ghee and tasted that too.

And while they did all this, the others gathered round me.

'What is going on, Andrew?' Sara asked in a calm, measured way that didn't necessarily preclude moving on shortly to the twisting of a corkscrew into my eye.

'I suppose I might have exaggerated? I didn't think I had, but it looks like maybe I have? I wish I hadn't. And I didn't — in my mind. But it turns out, in my mouth — there isn't as much

134

Serbo-Croat as I thought was in my brain. I'm sorry. Maybe more will come back?'

'Yeah, maybe,' Penny said and turned and walked away.

'Penny!'

The commander said something to the bearded guy and he reported back:

'They want the girls to go into the bathroom in the sports centre and the boys to walk back to the command post.'

'Why?' Shannon asked.

'He says – for searching, but –' and here he lowered his voice – 'I don't know if you should do this?'

'Tell him we will be searched here. The women can do the women, the men the men,' Shannon said. The commander acquiesced without acknowledging any acquiescence and we lined up on either side of the van.

'I'm Juso,' the bearded man said, as he lined up next to me.

'Is this going to be OK, mate?' Christian asked him.

'They're just country fucks, you know?' Juso said.

'Hey, Andrew!' Von shouted as one of the dice players approached him, and chucked me a matchbox. I caught it one-handed and Von smiled at me and raised his eyebrows as if we were starting out on some fun routine we had previously outlined. There was no rattle to the box, and as soon as I poked it open and saw the wedge of cling film I knew it was the pills. By then the militia guy was nearly upon me, so as casually as I could, I tucked it into my waistband. This was not a good joke.

As the search came up the line towards me, I was almost willing to step forward, hand Von back the package and take the repercussions, just to get out of the conspiracy.

But when he finally reached me, the militiaman found the whole search beneath him. He ran his hands down my sides and round my back carelessly and fast, as though frisking me too thoroughly would demean him.

'I was just splitting the risk,' Von said to me coolly afterwards when I marched up to him and asked what the fuck he thought he was doing with the pills.

'What if they'd shot me?'

'They're not going to shoot us, Andrew, we're from London.'

'I'm not from London,' I said.

'Still, it's all fine, so shush up and give me back my pills and stop having such a white-out, you lying little cunt.'

To shut me up, he gave me a bear hug and lifted me off the ground like we were having a joke about it all, but squeezing me hard, pressing his forearms uncomfortably into my kidneys. To my shame, once I was back on the ground I looked down, shook my head and laughed as if there was something amusing about this crazy caper and that all in all he'd been a pretty good guy.

'I guess we got the pills in,' I said, smiling insinuatingly.

'Exactly.' And he gave me the reassuring grin of a mobster taking his first monthly protection payment.

Just then Juso came over with his slow, rocking animal walk and reported that the commander 'says you are not welcome to enter'. And with that, the commander waved gaily as he and the girl headed back on foot to their border post and the militia guys went back to their game of dice.

The sun beat down hard on the crappy car park. Our little purgatory. I was an outcast, a liar, and as I walked away from Von, looking for a friend, my companions all angled their backs and made out they hadn't quite seen me.

Chapter 17

Juso squatted low, his great shoulders drawn up round his heavy head, and scratched in the dirt with a stick. He gave Shannon his assessment of the situation: we wouldn't be going anywhere without handing over money and goods.

'They're peasants. For everything they want something.'

He was being held up too, while they looked at his papers and made some phone calls. He was a Yugoslav, he said, born in Belgrade to a Croat mother, Serb father. He'd gone to school in Ljubljana, Slovenia, but now the family home was in Banja Luka, in the heart of Serb Bosnia. The way he told us all this was precise – like the speech a politician has prepared to give in answer to a difficult question he knows will come up in a radio interview. He had been living in Germany since he was eighteen – ten years working for a car-components firm and going to night school – but now he was coming back. His brother had been made to fight. He'd hidden from the Serb militia successfully for a year but a neighbour informed on him and he'd been jailed and then released direct onto the front line at Gorazde. Their mother's anger at the neighbours had eaten her up, Juso said, till the cancer in her stomach laid her out dead. So now he was heading home to help arrange for the disposal of her apartment and effects.

'But if you had to say, what you are, Serb or Croat?' Von said.

'I wouldn't say,' Juso said.

'Nice,' Von said. 'Good man, good on you. But if you *had* to?'

'I'm Yugoslav.'

Sara jumped in with the view that we should stand fast and hand over nothing.

'What if we're still here in a week?' Christian asked.

'If we're here for a week it's our problem. If we're here for a year, it's his problem,' Sara said.

'What do you think we'd have to give him to get through, Juso?' Shannon asked, giving him that lovely full attention that made you feel you should weigh your words grain by grain because they would all be individually appreciated.

'I don't know. Something. You need to give him something to show he can take something, you know?'

'Let's give them something and get going?' Penny said.

Shannon nodded. Von pinged a pebble, hard, with a stubbed toe punt towards the militia. Of course Penny would think nothing of giving away the lot. She had been taught by life that in the end there would always be more of everything.

'I think, we give him whatever the fuck he asks in return for free passage. It's shit or broke time,' I said. It was the opposite of how I felt, but I was trying to make myself ingratiatingly in tune with the mood of the group.

Christian looked at me as if he was surprised I thought I even had dispensation to speak. No one responded, and Penny didn't even give me a glance.

*

Eventually, the commander returned. Even in the direct, unshielded sunlight of the car park, his bald head stayed white and dry like something shocking and organic you might find in a sandpit. We made our offer of a certain amount of goods, but in reply he told us he'd talked to 'Bosses – lots of bosses, big bosses' and we could leave immediately. So long as we headed towards Bihac in western Bosnia and took the road through the town of Velika Kladusa.

Christian's reaction, when we circled up to discuss, was that we had hit pay dirt. Bihac: it was, if anything, in worse shape than Sarajevo.

'Since May '93 there are six UN Safe Areas for Muslims surrounded by Serbs in Bosnia. In the east, Srebrenica, Sarajevo, Tuzla, Gorazde and Zepa, and in the west, just Bihac.'

'And what – I mean, I know – but say again, what is a Safe Area?' Von asked.

'A Safe Area is the United Nations designation for a place under particularly heavy bombardment,' Christian said, and Bob laughed.

It pissed me off, that people made a comedy out of this paradox. The Safe Areas were only funny if you figured you knew the answer. Then maybe the 'UN-protected' towns getting all bombed up was a sort of black comedy. But you could only laugh, I thought, if you knew absolutely nothing at all, or if you knew absolutely everything. But to pretend that the joke in itself made you clever? That seemed a bit much.

They talked over the Bihac offer for some time. But everyone was a little reluctant to give up on Sarajevo. That was the place that our mothers and fathers had heard of, where Sontag had gone. Whatever the indie glamour of cold-shouldering the major label, Bihac felt a little diminishing.

'Baudrillard considers missions to Sarajevo nothing but "life-lines along which we suck the energy of their distress",' Christian said.

That hung in the air for a while.

'And you think Bihac is better?' I asked. He ignored me.

'And do you do whatever Baudrillard says?' Onomatopoeic Bob asked.

'I'm not saying that Bihac is necessarily better. All I'm saying is that Sarajevo is hyperreal and media-saturated. Maybe it'd be good for us to go to somewhere more authentic. Baudrillard says that really we're jealous of them in Sarajevo, that we're the ones that are dead, and they are alive.'

'Except the ones who are, actually dead? They're the *most* dead? Yeah?'

Christian looked at Von hard, trying to make out if he was being stupid or clever.

We continued our discussions. Meanwhile the militia guys carted away half our relief aid – two of our four sacks of rice, four of onions, a good deal of bleach and several kilograms of ghee.

'Hey!' we said, high-pitched, as we stood stock-still, making dead sure our body language couldn't prompt the raising of a muzzle.

'Was that the deal?' Bob asked.

'We didn't make a deal,' Sara said. 'Hey!'

Shannon sat on one of the squat 15-kilo tins of ghee while Sara tried to mount a departing rice sack. The militia guys picked it up and let her slide off as they carried it towards the clubhouse. She remounted like a child trying to get a last go on a funfair ride, finally hopping off just before the sack disappeared inside the football pavilion's fire door with its ripped Juventus poster.

Eventually, the commander gave a thumbs up from a long

way off, signalling his pillaging of the van was at an end. As we watched our provisions depart, Juso also said goodbye. He would not be travelling any further. At least not yet. He explained they were trying to sting him for Deutschmarks he couldn't afford, but he believed if he stuck out a few more hours or days, sooner or later they would tire and let him pass.

It was only after Penny offered to pay Juso's way in return for some guide and translating duties, and he immediately accepted, that I wondered if this wasn't what he'd had in mind all along. The swift and businesslike way he strode over to hand the militiamen the money (out of our sight) suggested that our offer had been at least pre-considered, if not engineered.

Maybe I was being paranoid. The whole stop, the 'big bosses' intervention and the diversion to Bihac had put me in a state ripe for the consideration of plots and intrigue. Dirty Ron and his directive to travel in through the Northern UN Sector; this commander here and his insistence we head for Bihac by way of Velika Kladusa. I wondered, as we jockeyed to reboard the van, if somehow Kenneth or someone might not be steering us from afar? I tried to piece it together and while it seemed unlikely our bald commander had a hotline to Hammersmith . . . I did find it all quite pleasant to think about. It's relaxing, I suppose, a conspiracy. The idea that someone, somewhere, is paying attention. The Jews, the Masons, the Establishment. It's very appealing that the hidden hand at least might have a clue what the fuck is going on. And then if you clock it – well, that's almost perfect. The world is under control and you know how. Everything is tidy.

Cally took a spot next to Von and he mouthed up to me as I climbed on board, 'She's cock-hungry!' Cally's move meant that Penny was free and I slid in beside her. We were such a long way from the kiss now it felt a different world. She looked at me briefly as I sat down but then turned to look out of the window and sighed very slightly. My tummy gnawed. Hungry and desperate.

'Penny. I just wanted to say, about the language thing.'

'Yes?'

'I'm really sorry.'

'It's fine,' she said, still looking out of the window, unwilling to give me even the negotiable foothold of some anger.

'The truth is – the truth is, I don't really know any Serbo-Croat. None.'

She turned to me sharply and snapped, 'Then why did you say you did?' She'd fallen into my trap! Even if it was a trap which had required me to throw myself onto a sharpened stake as bait.

'I think – I wanted to come very much – and at that meeting, I didn't realise it would be a big deal. I wanted to come a lot,' I said and looked at her meaningfully.

'Yeah, OK, fine.' She crossed her leg, nudging me quite hard. But even a kicking is a form of attention.

*

At least we had Juso's Polo to follow. We weren't going entirely naked into the internationally unrecognised Republic of Serb Krajina. The countryside we travelled through was not what I think of as border country. Where I come from, Wales ends like a wave crashing onto the Shropshire and Cheshire plains. An invitation to the hillbillies to roll down and steal from the fat of the land. Here in Serb-populated Croatia, for many centuries the last shoulder of Christendom holding the door shut, the country was light and airy – a succession of Surrey commons, the trees birch and alder and other spriggy things with widely spaced boughs, letting the light breeze through to the straw-coloured high-growing grasses below. The country-side was not too serious, the houses stationed clear and bold like salt and pepper pots, Tupperware cubes, proud on a shaken picnic blanket.

For the most part, the houses and cafes we saw by the road were not war-torn. Many road signs and barns were painted with the same nationalist symbol: four Ss painted as Cyrillic Cs arranged symmetrically around a central cross. *Samo Sloga Srbina Spasava* – Only Unity can Save the Serbs – but everything was prim and well tended.

Then, in the second or third hamlet we drove through, among the country farms that stood abutting the road in their generous pockets of land, we passed one house that was all burnt out. One black tooth in a mouth. And as I looked at it, and then, after, once we'd passed by, looked back towards it as it slipped out of view, it felt much sadder and harder to understand than I had expected. Any number of things might have brought it to this derelict state. But most probably just one thing. The single family shut out. The child in the corner of the playground. A night; a warning; a brick through the window, a shit on the doorstep, a look away in the morning and then, what? You go? Pack up the car with no one asking you what's happening or where you're going? Or worse. You wait it out, see how bad it might get? In your bed, then sitting on the stair steps till 3 a.m., looking for a nozzle that might poke in, or a petrol puddle to spread under the door, and it doesn't come and it doesn't come for a week, a month, but how long can you wait, do you think, till your half-friend tells you really, now really, the time has come and you've got to go, things have got just too bad?

Chapter 18

Onomatopoeic Bob took the wheel as we got close to the Bosnian border. He drove dangerously, optimistically, throwing the van at the world and trusting it would catch us, grating the vehicle into the bends, daring us to flinch. But the roads were largely empty as we chased to keep up with Juso. An EU Toyota Land Cruiser. A short convoy of Nepalese UN armoured personnel carriers. Just a couple of the home-grown boxy white Zastava Ficas; of the few cars we saw running, most were actually BMWs and Mercedes.

'Will you be OK? A Serb in Bosnia?' Penny asked Juso when we stopped for a coffee and sour-cheese *burek* lunch. The cafe owner was professionally sociable, happy to leave his regular customers grumbling as he attended to our orders and made out all was possible, even sandwiches (off menu), 'hot milk', 'English tea', 'dry meats', 'festival of apple fruit'.

Juso said that his understanding was that the people over the border were good people and he should be safe. Shannon looked at Juso and smiled, and explained that we were very grateful but she really didn't think that it was wise, his coming into Bosnia with us. Then, most unexpectedly, Sara said she thought that

Juso probably knew pretty well what was safe and what wasn't safe and that if he wanted to come then why shouldn't he?

The gang quietened and watched. Shannon said calmly that maybe in fact Sara was right, if Juso was happy to come, of course we would be happy to have him. Juso smiled his slow smile at Shannon and nodded. Sara got up fast and uncarefully, knocking her coffee onto her pastry and dousing its brown greaseproof-paper wrapper.

'Are you OK?' I asked as she looked around unhappily.

'Shut up, you fucking – monolinguist.' She marched off towards the toilet and banged the swollen door loudly three or four times to pull it into its frame.

*

After the triple-lock to get into the Krajina, leaving was surprisingly easy. There was a UN post but the Republic of Serb Krajina and the Bosnian border points were just yards apart and seemed to have very cordial relations. The RSK had been pre-warned about us, apparently, and happily passed us on to the Bosnians. The Bosnian guards were neat and tidy and wore a uniform with a crest – the fleur-de-lis shield with a ring of writing around it. A big solid hunk of a man greeted Onomatopoeic Bob with a firm handshake, taking our driver to be the boss. Juso did some explaining, and the handshake came also for Shannon and then, as we got out of the van, each of us received a big manly grip and a look into the eyes.

It didn't feel odd at the time. We were good folk who had travelled hundreds of miles and were now finally reaching our destination, and it was nice but natural for this man to acknowledge that. Juso explained the route prescribed to us by the

145

militiamen. The guard and Juso conferred a little longer. Juso said the guard was asking if we would stop up in Velika Kladusa, as the road to Bihac was dangerous and we would need to 'make talks' to see if it was possible to get there. We said we would. I was very happy to do so – indeed, a little of me wondered if we need go any further; couldn't we dump our remaining cargo here, just over the border on the first deprived child we saw, learn our lines, perform Penny's play and zoom home to be interviewed at Dover by someone from *Channel 4 News* about the horrors we had seen?

*

I think it's possible my generation – that is, the handful of people I met at school and in clubs and on sofas who I ever talked to about anything – grew up always looking out for the opposite. Always ready to spot an irony, a twist. Expecting, almost, every park tramp to be a professor fallen on hard times, every lollipop lady to be an ex-ballerina. So when we saw things plain before our faces it jarred and made us laugh. I knew, of course, Bosnia was Muslim, but I guess inside I thought, 'Yeah, but really, it's probably just the same.' After all, everything is more complicated than it sounds. There are probably more churches there than mosques or some mad thing, because of the screwy subtleties of history, etc.

So, when we crested the hill above Velika Kladusa and the bowl of countryside below was suddenly studded with a dozen minarets, it made me want to laugh. To see the actual mosques scattered across the countryside of rural Europe – as if Church Stretton had one and Ellesmere and Whitchurch, so alien and yet so natural, as if snowdrops poked through all plucky in August – it was just so very . . . straightforward.

After that first mosque-gasp, our arrival into Velika Kladusa was anticlimactic. I guess we thought news of our coming might have filtered through from the border, that there could have been a reception committee. But there were no children singing songs, or fire hoses spraying arcs, or municipal politicians waving us in. There was nothing. We rolled into the place slowly, people checking our vehicle out with the level of additional interest they might have spared for, say, an ice-cream van.

Rounding a street corner into the heart of town, we passed a small construction site and then a big supermarket. 'Agrokomerc' it said out front, bold in tomato red. The central square sloped down from this Agrokomerc, a rectangular patch of dry brown grass, tree-fringed, with roads down either side and a couple banded across the middle. There were little shops set back across tan concrete pavements, and cafes with sun-faded ice-cream posters. At the top of the gently sloping square stood a Red Star war memorial, and halfway up on the right, a municipal building with a flag at full mast.

Juso stopped up nearby. We drove a loop of the square looking for somewhere more ceremonious to disembark, but came back round to park next to him by some municipal bins.

We spilled onto the pavement and Shannon took an exaggerated breath, as if this was the air she had always been seeking. Onomatopoeic Bob went one better and knelt and kissed the pavement. An old gentleman with white hair and a short-sleeved shirt passed us by, his thick forearms veiny with the weight of shopping bags full of fresh produce. He got hit with seven or eight *Dobar dan*s and smiled incuriously back. We skittered there on the pavement trying not to be at all affronted by the total lack of interest from those we had come to aid. Somebody needed to do something to stop a sense of futility setting in. Shannon led the way, taking us up a side street and into a bar.

147

It was dark in there. The side facing the street was all glass – but dark, smoked glass, so when one of the many men huddled round the high bar checked out a passer-by they had the furtive look of a punter at some one-way-mirror joint. The marble-effect flooring of the bar receded far back, into cool sparse expanses where sporadic plastic ferns on plastic Doric pedestals tried to make things less desolate. Von ordered a round of huge beers for everyone – even me – while Juso and Shannon went back to the building with the flag 'to tell someone we've arrived'.

'There you go, Monolanguage,' he said as he gave me my chilly litre.

The only indication I could make out that the bar was within a war zone was their use of UHT milk. Everything else on offer spoke of a well-supplied establishment. This wasn't exactly the sort of horror story I had thought I'd be bringing back from Bosnia: 'You know, they have to use UHT milk in their coffee over there? Horrible – I mean, they do that a lot in Europe anyway. But *also* several of the ice-cream products pictured on the posters outside stores are for product lines that are in fact no longer available. That is the sort of hell we are talking about.'

Now we were among those we had come to save and entertain, we were a bit shy; newly minted superheroes worried about climbing into our costumes and shouting our noble aims. Everywhere around us were men. Proper, shaved and stubbly, moustached and sceptical men. It's a prejudice of mine not to really trust men. Serious men, standing or sitting together, smoking and talking quietly – I've never really wanted to know what they're saying, because rarely in my experience is it nice.

I stayed close to the heart of our troupe waiting at the high, sugar-scattered marble bar counter. But at the fringes of the group, some fraternisation took place. Von swapped Deutschmarks for tokens for the pinball machine and lost lives at a prodigious rate. Penny chatted with a guy in a fresh white shirt who smiled and eyed her and Sara with the love–hate eyes of the bar Lothario.

Shannon and Juso arrived back with information: that the town's head man, Fikret Abdic – aka 'Babo' – was out at a chicken-feed factory, but that we should await his arrival to talk about getting to Bihac. This talk, it had been implied, might take a while. Sara, meanwhile, had arranged with Hasim (the guy in the white shirt) for us to view a set of flats where we might stay the night. I preferred the sound of the uncomfy hotel at the top of the square, but Shannon treated Sara with exaggerated gratitude, like she was drawing out a four-year-old who has recently had a tantrum.

The flats were down at the bottom of the town, where it petered out into dusty roads and a stream before a bank rose sharply up to a castle which overlooked the town.

'The family had to go away,' Hasim said as we all arrived at the building. He was mostly bald on top, but he wore a ponytail, and the stringy black strands that made it all the way, valiantly, from front to rear provided a little crown-cover. Below the flats, at ground level, there was a bakery and next door a hardware shop full of rotavators and string and coal scuttles. Up above, two flats opened onto a central vestibule. Hasim unlocked them swiftly with a twist of a Yale key and a kick of his foot to open the flush white doors. In the showcase apartment all nine of us pushed into the narrow hallway. A low pile of children's clothes was stacked on a side table by a telephone, coats on the hooks, drawings on the fridge. I asked Juso to double-check that we weren't being offered cohabitation with a family.

'No no, empty empty,' Hasim said, peering in businesslike

fashion down Penny's silky top as she squeezed past him in the doorway. 'My friends go,' he assured us.

'We're here to try to help about the war,' Shannon explained, as we assembled in the vestibule to begin the negotiations.

'Yes,' Hasim said, looking at the floor.

'We hope to perform a play in Bihac and perhaps here?' Sara said.

Hasim said nothing at all. Perhaps due to a total lack of interest in our project or perhaps because he was worried a conversation about our honourable motives might be the preamble to us asking for some special arrangement regarding the rental fee. He opened at a straight-faced hundred marks per night per person. When we were disbelieving, he hid behind the language barrier and ducked down to say, in fact, per flat. But when we murmured between ourselves and shook our heads to one another, he recalibrated again to say that was for all of us, for both flats. Shannon consulted Penny, who consulted Von.

Hasim went into one of the flats and turned on a tap to demonstrate the availability of water. He turned on a TV to heavy static and the possibility that somewhere, in moments of the electric fizz, a human being was represented. He sat on a sofa and put the children's clothes from the hall into a carrier bag. When the hemming and hawing was coming to a crescendo and Penny was saying maybe the hotel at the top of town would be better, Hasim pushed the point and unclipped two keys from his Holsten Pils key ring, handed them over and said we could pay whatever we could afford. He *wanted* us to stay. As we took the keys and thanked him, he said one hundred marks again. I looked at Shannon to see if she would say anything but she just took the keys.

*

Von gripped the windscreen wipers, hopped onto the Transit's stubby bonnet and climbed up onto the roof, from where he beat his chest and shouted 'Von! Von! Von! Von!' down the street, then untied the tarpaulin over the rucksacks and chucked them down. Von took the big flat to the rear, along with Christian, Penny, Cally, Sara and Shannon. I was still being shunned, it seemed, sent off with Onomatopoeic Bob and Juso into the smaller flat across the hall.

It felt a little like the end of the party as I closed our door. I tried to summon up some little society out of our gang of offcuts by pacing the kitchen and making some jokes about a pot of indistinct pickle in the fridge. But I know that I am insufficient material to start a party.

I attempted a difficult shit, overly aware of people walking the corridor outside. With nothing doing, I undressed and stood in the chocolate bathtub and pulled the curtain across. The water dribbled out of the shower head as if to say, Look, after pumping me up this high, you can't exactly expect me to be *rushing* to get back down again, can you? I didn't even pull myself off – I couldn't bear the sadness of no longer having that little pleasure to look forward to.

I ran my hand down the pile of towels folded up on a corner shelf, alien in mysterious ways. How well you know the towels of home. This one threadbare and greying, this one bought on holiday for too much, the subject of a row or a bit of gay abandon. The new towel thick with a peach synthetic nap, bought as a lunge towards a new life, when all towels might be this way. Where had they gone, the owners of these towels? I wished them well, as I pushed their unabsorbent fluff up and under.

*

'Hey hey hey! I've come to seek asylum in the cool flat!' I said across the way, trying to hide from pathos in plain sight.

Christian looked at me evenly. 'Hail the monolinguist,' he said. 'We're actually doing some writing.'

'Nice nice nice. I can write up some of my trip diary,' I said, pretending his discouragement was an invitation.

In the front room of the apartment, Penny sat on a leather couch, covered in a red velveteen throw. Christian had made a kitchen tray into his desk on a big soft armchair. Von sat cross-legged, very close to the TV, with a white, vaguely medical, earpiece plugged into one ear, watching *Santa Barbara* with his hands pressed together, his fingertips touching his lips in deep meditative concentration. Out of the window two kids wheeled bikes past. Rich smells from the bakery and a sewer mingled in the room and for the first time I felt in my bones that now we were nearer the Mediterranean than the North Sea.

Penny looked me over and raised her A4 binder to keep the contents private.

'How's the play coming along?' I asked after an interval of silence.

'Good,' she said.

'Is everyone still pissed off about the language thing?' I asked.

'Language disguises thought. So at least you're probably a very clear Serb-Croat thinker,' Christian said and laughed.

'Heh,' I said.

'Wittgenstein,' he said.

'Sorry?' I said.

'It's fine. It's OK. It's a shame, but we're here. It's all right,' Penny said and shifted over on the settee so that I could go next to her.

I found my diary hard going. It ended up largely a list of meals and condiments. In the kitchen, making us tea, I asked Christian about his work. He wasn't writing yet, he explained: he was thinking. Making character sketches. And plot drawings. He had formed the conviction that if he could physically represent the relationships in his proposed work in a sufficiently detailed diagram of the correct 'emotional proportions', he would have basically cracked it. He was, he said, pretty confident that his idea for a book would be better than most of these novels that 'people put out'. Partly, he explained, because of the inevitable coarseness — all the little bits that must be left out — of actual written books. His, he explained, would be infinitely subtle, infinitely allusive, infinitely capacious — but actually rather slim and spare. He went on talking about how great his book was going to be even as Penny amended her play and I tried again on my diary. Occasionally he looked over at me as I wrote, like I was jerking off in public, or clobbering pieces of tree together with a mallet and six-inch nails while he was trying to figure out how to inlay walnut in the delicate patterns of a bureau.

Back on my thin mattress over its wire rack, I listened to 'Love Will Tear Us Apart' loud on my Walkman. But it didn't give me the jolt of heart-tug and longing it used to. So I found myself imagining it being played at my funeral to see if that kicked the old soul-buzz into action. It did a little, and as I imagined Penny and Helen smiling bravely by my coffin, as Ian Curtis sang, I must have drifted off.

Chapter 19

In the morning, a young man came to call for us, saying that 'Babo', the town boss, would see us at the Cafe International. Mohammed, the messenger, led the way, preferring to travel by foot, it turned out, once we were all in the van. We drove next to him, kerb-crawling the half-kilometre to the cafe. Though the situation was odd, Mohammed made it feel OK. He was thin and rangy, his muscly arms hanging loose from his shoulders like a puppet's. He wore combat trousers and a dirty white vest and beaten-down Nikes. His little beard and red-veined eyeballs and slow conspiratorial smile made us feel we'd maybe found one of our own. Once we were on the straight road into town, he dropped back behind us, pulled a long stalk of cow parsley out of a bit of urban hedge and whipped the back of the creeping van like it was a slow heifer. Shannon and Penny leaned out of the window and laughed.

The cafe was near the central square. On the pavement terrace, middle-aged men played cards with unfamiliar markings: the outer fringes of the royal court. At the door were armed men, some with the same crests we'd seen at the border and one with a red beret. Mohammed held up an arm of warning when we went to enter, so we idled on the pavement until, after a wait that had just started to become uncomfortably long, one of Babo's adjuncts came out.

'You know Babo?' the man asked. He was a big man, but one who wasn't comfy taking up all his space. Maybe a caretaker or a primary-school teacher before the war.

'We understand he is the man we need to ask to get permission to go to Bihac and perform our play?' Shannon said.

'You have brought food for us?' he asked.

'We want to bring it where it is needed,' Shannon said, trying not to look too pointedly at the big dishes of breakfast stew and side plates of chips which were just then being delivered to the card players outside. The big man in his loose suit headed back in and a new wait began. After a few minutes Von grew bored and went to stand on the tired brown grass of the main square. He kicked a ball listlessly with some fifteen-year olds, flicking it for keepy-ups and booting it far away when he lost control, then smiling a good deal too much at one of the boys' insufficiently older sister in her turquoise T-shirt and white shorts.

I liked Babo as soon as I saw him ambling out to greet us. From afar he was a regulation Yugoslav bureaucrat, his face a dab of watery pink paint above a grey suit. But as he approached he shrugged off his jacket, slung it over his shoulder revealing a short-sleeved shirt, and when he got close you could see that in his podgy, milk-pudding face, half Milosovic, half Ken Clarke, were set the most swift-moving little grey-blue eyes. Their velocity and vitality mocked the big bulb of fat that swelled over his belt and made you think of a very quick-minded beast hiding deep at the back of a cave.

He shook all our hands one by one in a way which was proper,

155

even over-formal, but with a smile that suggested we all knew this solemn dance was nothing but a prelude to the flowering of the true connection that existed between us all.

'Hello, hello, and welcome. We understand you have supplies for us?' he said.

'Er, well.' Shannon looked around. It seemed rude to say no. 'Yes, we, do – but also, is Bihac in need of supplies?'

Babo stepped back to excuse himself and look at an important piece of paper handed to him by an assistant – he said something to Mohammed, who stepped forward to explain.

'They have supplies in Bihac due to the United Nations.'

'Oh . . .'

'But we would be very grateful,' Mohammed said. Then Babo returned his attention to us and made a face to indicate that the piece of paper he'd been forced to look at was some piece of piffling bullshit.

'We wish to perform a play to promote peace,' Shannon explained.

'We are very in favour of peace,' Babo said.

'We are in favour of peace too. Very much.'

'Very much so,' said Babo and we all smiled at each other.

'So is there a venue that would be suitable for our play – a small theatre or a hall or so on?'

'Yes, good. We have peace. So, we wonder . . . We are concerned that a play about peace could disrupt peace. Too much peace, you know?' Babo said, and laughed.

'It's just about peace?' Shannon said.

'And some other themes,' Penny couldn't help but mention.

'How many other themes?' Babo's big uncomfortable adjunct asked. Shannon looked at Penny.

'Er – how many? I'd say about . . .' Penny looked uncomfortable too; she would have liked to laugh and say you couldn't possibly say.

'Three. Or four?' she said.

'That is too many themes,' Babo said and held the moment for almost the perfect length of time before letting his smile come so we could all laugh.

'Listen. It's fine, of course it is, but first, can we look at it?' Babo asked.

'Well, that would be great. Penny?' Shannon asked. Penny nodded assent. 'And afterwards, we would hope to take it to Bihac? We understand you might help?'

'Yes, to Bihac is not possible.'

'Why not? We're in Bosnia and –'

'Due to the conflict. It is sad. It is a very complicated situation. I must go but we can explain. I am so pleased to meet you and honoured you have come and we wish you every success!' And Babo was off, to a waiting Mercedes, which did a three-point turn and was chased up the hill by two jeeps and a bunch of other cars.

Mohammed talked to one of Babo's guys and it seemed that the idea was for Penny to take her play to present to Babo the next morning, up in his castle, the one overlooking the town. Meanwhile, the guy with the red beret went towards our van and opened the back.

'Hey!' Onomatopoeic Bob shouted and started to walk towards him.

'Hey!' Shannon said.

'What's . . .?' Penny said and looked at me.

From out of a nearby car two more red berets with an invulnerable look about them walked hard and fast towards Onomatopoeic Bob, as if they might not stop when they reached him but just sweep him away between them. But they did stop and made a physical barrier as the first beret swung out onto the road the supplies that remained in the back of the van.

Shannon shouted over, asking him to stop until we talked with Babo, but he didn't even look in her direction.

'They're taking our stuff. That is so flagrant!'

I looked at Penny and shook my head. But instead of joining me in a lament at our misfortune she puckered her lips, which I took to mean that it would be great to have someone who spoke Serbo-Croat right now.

'Now look. Seriously, guys. Yeah?' I found myself saying, striding up to the two big lunks blocking Onomatopoeic Bob from the van. 'Yeah. Come on, that's aid, for the Safe Area?'

The awkward adjunct came over, moving his big frame jerkily, like a reanimated corpse.

'We need it for babies. For sick and dying babies. OK? Thank you,' he said and bowed slightly to our group. Then he said something to the guys unloading our van, who laughed a raw hard laugh that didn't sound like it was connected to infant mortality. The two red berets bristled up an extra half-inch at Onomatopoeic Bob and me.

'Well. If it's for babies? Yeah?' And I looked back at Shannon and Penny and shouted, 'But we trust you will distribute these items equitably!'

*

After we had, depending on how you looked at it, either delivered aid to sick babies or suffered a brutal theft, Mohammed took us for an apologetic coffee at another bar at the top of the square, next to the Agrokomerc supermarket. 'You see, we are in a unique situation here,' he explained. 'Surrounded by Croatia, and by Serbs, so we need more than anyone to have peace and prosperity. This is a very well-functioning area with good relations. Since the war came we have made special arrangements for peace.'

'We are in favour of peace,' Sara reconfirmed.

'But the government in Sarajevo, they want to be the big guys, yes? They didn't like our peace. They said, "No peace." They said we must have war.'

'But the Serbs, they want the war? Yes?' Onomatopoeic Bob asked.

'You have some crazy guys everywhere, right? Sure. But here, sure, we are Muslim, but it's Yugoslavia, you know, why make wars when you can make peace and work and sell? Babo has kept things good.'

'OK?'

'Yeah, so down in Bihac these hardline war guys, crazy guys really, very strong on jihad, yes? They are like, "No peace. War, war! You must have war, war is fun, war is great."' He jumped around, doing his impression of the war-crazy Bihac faction, his lose limbs bouncing and jangling comically until we all laughed. 'So in the end we say, "Fine, whatever, guys, have war, we'll have peace."'

'Jesus,' Onomatopoeic Bob said.

'So we have our peace. Look around you, everything is good. But the Bihac guys want us to fight everybody, but we don't, so we have some problems with them and that is our situation.'

Once Mohammed departed, we wandered back to the bar from last night, where the unfriendly atmosphere was now familiar and even comforting. Penny bought us all a sugary breakfast of small airlinish croissants in tight inflated plastic packs, very small bottles of rehydrated orange juice concentrate with 'properté de la armée française' on the labels, and milky lukewarm instant coffee.

I noticed that, unlike with all other customers, the proprietor put Penny's change on the counter, not in her hand.

'Yeah, I think he thinks not only is black skin disgusting, but also that it's catching,' she said. I shook my head sadly. Still, I hoped I wasn't expected to actually *do* anything. I felt I was a strident anti-racist. But on the strict unspoken understanding that this attitude should never cost me personally any degree of diminution of status, freedom or prospect. Indeed, feeling overall that being so forward-thinking I might be due some kind of benefit from society at large for my unnaturally swollen tolerance glands.

I sat, gripping my seat edges on a coffee buzz, giving the owner occasional hard Paddington Bear stares when he wasn't looking, and not knowing quite what we were doing or how we fitted in. Von bought a round of beer after the last coffee was gone and from then on the place became our hub for the day. Shannon took a spot at the head of one of the tables and talked politics with Juso, as Von encouraged Cally to come and marvel at him racking up points on the pinball machine.

Sara said she thought there were actually 'bigger fish to fry' and got Onomatopoeic Bob to agree to drive her round town looking for the supplies we had 'so foolishly let go' in case we could claw some back. Something about her disgruntled, distracted air made me think Penny might join in. So I volunteered too. But instead she announced she was heading back to the flats to make finishing touches to the peace play and I was stuck with Onomatopoeic Bob and Sara.

Beyond the central rectangular square, in the opposite direction to our flats, the town dipped away to an industrial area. A coach park, a little stadium and light industrial areas jostled with the big barbed-wire-fringed compound over which the UN flag flew. Somewhere down there, I guessed, was where our aid had disappeared, but I had no intention of facing down the red berets, so didn't mention it. By the time we returned to the bar empty-handed everything had gone fuzzy. Afternoon barrelled into evening and people retired for woozy naps and hunted out fatty baked goods.

I lay on the settee in Penny and Von's apartment watching Tudjman, the Croatian president, on TV and tried to explain to Von again what had happened in the former Yugoslavia. He seemed to have got it finally locked. There were obviously finesses I wanted to make to his understanding, subtleties and ambiguities to be teased and further explicated. But at least he appeared to finally be solid on the Serbs, the Croats and the Bosniaks, and the way they descended in that same order in terms of their magnitude of blame for the current situation. He pulled Cally's hand a long way up his thigh and said, 'Look at that fucking dick.'

Tudjman stood, dressed in a double-breasted grey suit, speaking to a younger suited man at the head of a set of marble stairs. He looked peeved and constipated behind the pink murderer's tint of his steel-frame glasses. Von got up and offered his hand to pull Cally from the settee. He took a last commanding look at the TV, shook his head and said, 'That fucking bastard, when will he be satisfied?' in a way that made me suspect he believed he was watching Milosevic, without giving away enough to allow me to actually correct him.

As Von and Cally went into her room it became obvious the walls were so thin that we were going to be silent partners in their humping. It felt, in fact, as if we could hear the very slide of fabric as their layers came off, but maybe it was just the scrape of the steel feet of the bed on tile and the bangs of the mattress base against the wall that we heard, and we filled in the rest.

I looked at Penny, and raised my eyebrows, hoping that there might conceivably be something darkly erotic about watching Balkan politics on TV through the noise of her brother's sexual activity. But she kept her eyes firmly on her marking-up of her play.

'Can I show you something?' she asked eventually.

'Well, sure,' I said. She closed up her file and passed it to me.

'I just want someone to have a look for me, if I'm going to have to tell Babo about it? I'm not sure – how much more it needs, lots or a little or – I'm just, I've looked at it too much, I think.' I smiled reassuringly.

'Penny. I'm sure it's amazing.'

'I could say loads about – where the bits are that need more and what I'm thinking. But just to say, before you read – just keep in mind one thing: Petar is not – Petar could have Matilda's lines and the whole section that starts in the country kitchen, to the end, could be first – that's all. Basically you could reverse the scenes. Like a palindrome. Is one idea. It's based on *Ulysses*, structurally. There's lots of concerns, but I want them to just – drift, to infuse. I don't want people to even be aware. I've said too much. OK?'

'OK,' I said and opened the folder with great reverence while Penny went to the kitchen to fetch some beer and avoided bearing witness to that intimate moment when the reader lowers themselves like a swimmer into the pool of the writer's world.

It took me a few minutes to clock what was going on in the play. It was biroed up and there were many crossings-out. But as I read, intensely focused, flicking back to reread sections and then forward to move on again, slowly but surely an overpowering aesthetic realisation began to make itself force-fully known to me:

It was shit.

It was total horseshit. It didn't really make any sense and when it did it was thunderingly obvious or complicatedly bad. I started to leaf through the pages quickly, noticing that I was growing more and more excited. Penny came back in and sat, attempting nonchalance on the easy chair, tucking her legs under her and sipping from a beer as she read *Black Lamb and Grey Falcon*.

Next door the slips and slides and laughs of foreplay were giving way to the steady knock-knocking of some endgame sexual contact.

After an odd, jarring start, the play quickly seemed to lose all connection to the reality it had never sufficiently established. The narrative jumped away – to different characters, elsewhere, several times – then circled back to the original characters doing things which seemed confusingly disconnected from their initial actions. The character dialogue was a mix of 'common speech' – such as has never been heard – and meandering political declamations, but all at the emotional pitch of a dirge. I hunted through them, these speeches, sniffing for where 'Maya's' feelings might be Penny's own, hoping to find a key to unlock her personal passions in the mechanism of the piece. But increasingly I concluded that there really wasn't that much of her in there. She truly had tried to imagine how a young Bosnian woman raised on a farm might feel about the sale of a favoured bullock. And she went on about that cow for pages and pages and pages.

The tapping went fast and woodpeckerish next door, and then it was over.

After half an hour or so Penny went to the kitchen again and when she returned she hung around the doorway, unable to bear my silence any longer. She stood there looking at me until I couldn't prolong any more this delicious period when she was entirely focused on me and I still had every card in my hand. I was aware that as soon as I said anything at all I would begin to lose my allure. But still. Ultimately you must act and lose, I suppose, and try, in your losing, to win a little back.

'Well, it's amazing, obviously,' I said, and she breathed out dramatically and came to sit next to me.

I understood now why she'd asked me to read it and not Christian or Shannon. Not because she was dimly aware of how bad it was. Presumably, like any artist who's started with high hopes on a sketch or a short story or picking out a tune on an acoustic guitar, she half hated it and then half wondered in the night if she wasn't the world's greatest genius. If maybe, even in its very faults, her work didn't somehow maybe outline the shadowy reality of the subtlest emanation of humanity's true shape.

No, she'd chosen me not just because she was aware I liked her very much and she would receive a glob of honey in any cup I gave her to drink, but also because she had overreached and that in me she recognised a fellow prevaricator. The play, by any honest estimation, was at best half finished. After a certain time it simply petered out into a series of lined A4 sheets with 'ideas for scenes' and things like 'Petar confronts Maya about the money, angrily' and 'Colin tells Hetty about his dream – she reacts'. 'Bomb hits marketplace – woman tells about dead children (Heartbreaking?)'.

I told her in the end that I wanted to sleep on it. I took a gulp of red wine as though I might have been deeply affected by the action of the play, and asked for time to consider the work's depths, in this way securing an invitation up to Babo's castle with her in the morning – so we could talk more on the expedition.

Chapter 20

'Look, the truth is I think it needs a lot of work . . .'

'A lot?' she said.

The walk was turning out to be a hard climb and we'd let Juso and Shannon break off ahead so we could talk.

'Let me finish. Of course it does, all great work does. Indeed all great works always remain, in a way, unfinished, don't they?' She looked at me and I teetered on the edge of credibility. 'But the essentials are there. I just think rather than reading it out to him, you should sketch the idea?'

'Yeah? Yeah,' she said, then: 'Yeah?'

We had decided to make the trip on foot rather than take the van, because from down below it looked like the castle was close. But the road out of the village had whispered along the valley floor like smoke, and now, as we snaked up the S-bends towards the circular castle walls, we were late and Penny was growing anxious.

'Just tell him the basic structure – that's simple,' I said. 'Right?' And I wondered if it was possible to love someone and also quite enjoy torturing them, because this question, I could see, made her stomach flip.

'Well,' she started, rehearsing, 'it's a story about the war and how families – about how a single family and other people around the farm – react, and the war is symbolised, by a – by the coming, advent of the army, to the town, but they want to sell their house or cow – that shifts, maybe too much? But they need to sell one, to be able to – to move away from the war or army (war would be too direct), but because of their ethnicity, the other people – the bad people – or are they? – swindle our original people out of their cow. And the army make the war, we discover, for their own ends, or so it seems. And then there's the indeterminate shelling. That we don't know where it's coming from.'

'I like that – that's a great detail,' I said.

'Thank you. Yeah, so then there's the ideas about the dreams and the counter-dream and it ends. I'm not sure right now, between you and me, how it ends? . . . I mean, it feels very hard to precis?'

'Sure, but the story of *Macbeth* would be hard to precis, wouldn't it?'

'Um . . . not really,' she said.

'No, sure. But I guess one thing you could do – is, for this meeting, simplify?'

'Yeah. I guess. I suppose the thing is – and I wouldn't say this to anyone but you – but the play is almost too complex to just be able to say what it's about?'

'Completely. I get it. Absolutely.'

'But what could I say it's about?' she asked.

'I think it might be a good idea – to have a dummy version to outline, for him?'

'What – a simplified version?'

'Sure, or even just a very basic – an idea, it may seem a bit pathetic, but something with a clear set of characters and an ending?'

166

'God,' she said. 'Yeah. Right. The dummy version. Maybe that would be good? I hate talking about my actual thing anyway.' She looked thoughtful. 'But what could it be? Shit. Shit.'

Having worked on the play for around six months, she now had, I guess, twelve minutes or so to come up with a rival, superior version. She looked at the road surface and frowned.

'I had an idea once for a thing you could do, someone could do, about the war,' I said.

'Yeah?'

'Yeah. About a . . . a village under threat, who hold hands – and stop a glacier. It seems crazy, but it works – they stop the glacier. It would be sort of magical?'

'Hmm. Not to be rude but it sounds a bit – not corny.'

'No, sure, sure, it's from – it's a riff on –'

'No, go on, how would it work?'

'It's fine, forget it. It's simplistic,' I said. I was much happier talking about her terrible ideas than my own. 'It's totally crummy, you're right.'

'It isn't. It sounds great. Just a little trite?'

'Sure. Go on about how to explain your play then, Penny?' I looked at her mildly.

We walked in silence for a while. The castle, coming into clearer view now, was the size and shape of pictures you saw of Elizabethan theatres. Round and stony outside, with a tower in the keep and one above the main gated entrance. The day's heat was just starting to make itself apparent through the morning's cool, the sweaty shoulder starting to grime the shirt.

'It needs to be amazing, is the thing,' Penny said.

'It should be incredible,' I agreed.

'It should be something where people just see it and . . . like – did you ever see *Platoon* or *The Killing Fields*?'

167

'Simple, but universal. A fable.'

'Exactly. So when people see it, they're like — "Fuck."'

It was then that I reminded her of the plot of Douglas Hurd's 'The Summer House'.

'I met him once at my dad's friend's. He was actually very nice.'

'Exactly, he probably won't sue you!' I said.

'I could subvert it. Ironise it,' she said. 'But the essentials. The shared house, destroyed. It's quite powerful, isn't it?'

'It does have a sort of mythic resonance.'

We were starting to really sweat as we finally passed an old woman in a peasant headscarf and long grubby skirts. We'd been gaining on her for ten minutes as she marched, huffing and stopping, slowly up the hill. She refused to smile as we overtook her. Outside a farm, on a bend a little further up, there stood one of the stone outbuildings with ventilating slats for drying animal feed, which we'd discovered were common hereabouts. Inside, we could make out heads of maize lying in a jumble as each little sweetcorn shrivelled in on itself.

A UN Land Cruiser whined in a low gear as it approached and hooted hello. Our jeans, our well-fed haunches and stumbling city walk must have marked us out as non-locals. The vehicle pulled up beside Juso and Shannon. When we caught up the French soldiers invited the four of us to take a ride to the top with them. It was like that in a war zone, I noticed: a kind of reverse triage prioritised those in least need, as though people could only really bear to help those who didn't much need it.

The driver had thick black hair, wet from the shower or greased back, and peered over his wheel like a pensioner in a county town. His companion, crew cut and English-speaking, let his bicep bulge big from a green T-shirt as he gripped onto the hand-strap above the front door. They were impressed we had an audience with Babo. They were talking ceasefire agreements with a subordinate military commander somewhere up there. But when Shannon expressed some approbation for Babo's fondness for peace, the front-seat passenger made the French pouf of disbelief.

'Babo is a crook,' the strong-armed passenger said, addressing himself to Shannon in the rear-view mirror.

'Yeah?' she said. And I felt my stomach shift uneasily.

'He's a smuggler. Fighting his own. Muslim on Muslim.'

'He won elections. Right?' Juso said.

'Oh sure,' the soldier said and, getting a fix on Juso, clammed up.

'But, he seemed a nice guy?' Shannon said.

'He is a nice guy. He is. If you're his buddy. This town is full of dentists and doctors and − foot doctors − what do you call them?'

'Chiropodists?'

'Exactly. Chiropodists. Something like five chiropodists and three vets and − everything is here. He found the best doctors in Yugoslavia and paid them two thousand marks a month to come to Velika Kladusa. But in Bihac, they're dying. From the Serbs of course, but also from Babo's fighters. Muslim on Muslim. A fucked-up civil war inside this whole shitty civil war.'

With a final flourish of acceleration, the Land Cruiser reached the Frenchmen's destination, a flat-roofed concrete bunker that looked like the lavatory block at a safari park. Outside, a huddle of Babo's soldiers waited for the French deputation.

'Could we get to Bihac, do you think?' Penny asked.

'Not with us. Unless you have blue cards?'

'No. No we don't,' Shannon admitted.

169

'Then, nothing gets to Bihac,' said the passenger, as he swung out, 'unless Babo says so.'

*

We walked the final hundred metres up to the castle, past artillery pieces dug into neat sandbagged redoubts and a red-and-white-striped vehicle barrier. The castle's double doors were made from hard new brown wood like a suburban front door, but fitted into an old stone doorway topped with an ogee arch.

'What do you reckon?' Penny asked. 'Is that true, Juso, about Babo?'

'It depends how you see everything,' he said, into his beard.

'But Muslim fighting Muslim?' Penny asked.

'Sure, maybe, I don't know, but if someone says you must fight – must you fight? Can you fight to not fight?'

'Uh-huh?'

'Everyone says the French love the Serbs too much anyway and they like to smuggle a little brandy. So. I don't know anything. I'm just a guy. The Republic of Me. I don't give a fuck.' He marched a little ahead of us, combing his black hair with his fingers, annoyed at being the reference book we turned to but then also queried.

Though there was much activity back down at the concrete military bunker, to greet the arrival of the French, no one was coming in or out of the castle doors, so I knocked with a knuckle rap.

'Oh *Igor*?' Shannon said and the gang chuckled.

Around one of the artillery pieces, I noticed four men smoking while one did some sort of maintenance work. Here it was: my first look at the war and it looked like nothing at all. Like these guns would never really be fired, and if they were, it would all be quite clean and clear. You just loaded your guns up and sent the shells over as your message to explode forthrightly on the other lot.

We waited a long while. Eventually a catering worker looked out from a window. I caught his attention and he waved us down to a side fire exit. A message got passed through and soon we were being led along corridors, like those of a meeting centre, then up to the main courtyard of the castle. All around the cobbled, well-swept keep, catering supplies and other stuff was boxed up on pallets. We followed a young woman into a part of the castle where there were offices and meeting rooms. Babo, we learned, was in fact busy. But one of his guys was there to greet us in a large room at the top of a turret. Milan. He was too fat for any real soldiering, but nevertheless he wore XXL camouflage fatigues and a red unit badge with a picture of Popeye the sailor man on his shoulder. After greeting us, Milan moved away from his desk, dodging the great many pieces of paper spread across the floor, before lowering himself uncomfortably onto a squat leather settee and inviting us to sit.

The decoration of the place was as though Barratt Homes had been asked to make some improvements to a medieval castle. The windows were wide and high in brown metal frames, but the ceiling (polystyrene tiles) was a little too low for the room to feel grand. There were some prints of wild birds on the wall, a number of coffee tables with gilt frames supporting glass tops. The carpet was blue and new. All over it, walked-upon fibres rubbed up into wispy balls and the whole room had a fresh-carpet chemical-clean smell.

Penny licked her lips and her solemn eyes swept the room

171

nervously. She was dressed all in black. A black polo neck and black jeans. I felt a thud of regret at ever having wished her anything other than pure simple success. The papers in her hand shook. I gave her a thumbs up, a wink. She nodded back to me, serious and ready. She explained to Milan she would give a quick overview of the play we had in mind and then fill in the detail. But after just the initial sketch of the 'The Summer House' – the two government officials of different ethnicities, the joint endeavour ruined by a bombardment – Babo's stand-in interrupted to say he thought it sounded good, very good.

I smiled at Penny, who smiled back, wide and massively relieved.

'Really?' she asked.

'Yes,' he said.

Penny smiled at me again and I shook a tiny happy fist at my side. But before we could squeeze any more praise out of him for Douglas Hurd's idea, he moved on to the meat and drink of the meeting.

Yes, yes, it all sounded good. He liked the play a lot, great, yes. Take it to Bihac by all means, with Babo's blessing. Maybe it will encourage in them peace? We could tell the world on our return that Babo had sent a peace play to Bihac to plead, argue, beseech. Milan explained that Babo had received certain requests and communications and in return had given certain undertakings, and was in theory willing to let us through with blessings. But, we would need protection and, though neither the town authorities (the forces of 'the Autonomous Province of Western Bosnia') nor the UN could provide it, Babo knew there were mercenaries in the area. They might be willing to protect us – if we so wished – for a price. Milan could direct us to them if we would agree also to carry a message and some items through to a certain official in Bihac?

'What sort of message. What items?' Shannon wanted to know.

The answer was soothing but unspecific. Shannon looked to us and back to him in a way which didn't rule out the idea in principle, and therefore quickly allowed it to become a fact. Milan explained that the mercenaries were camped out beyond the town near a river and, since the road was mined, the safest way to reach them and seek their help was via dinghy.

A few minutes later, we were standing in the courtyard like kids waiting for a PE lesson. From a kitchen outlet fan came the sharp tang of burnt garlic. We heard some shouting and utensil-banging from within, but when we looked at Juso for a transla-tion he said it was just hungry soldiers, complaining about late breakfast. Soon enough two canoes were brought up – balanced one on each shoulder by a young soldier and Mohammed, his marionette legs looking like they might buckle under him. He offered to drive us back down the hill, with the canoes roped to the top of a Zastava.

Mohammed freewheeled down from the castle to save fuel. The car hissed past pasture meadows, all the windows down, filling the car with the rush of clean air and the sound of birdsong and the first individual chirrups of grasshoppers. From the curving road we looked down on Velika and beyond to the fat bowl of good country all around, safe and green in the summer sun.

*

Back at the flats, we made it upstairs to be greeted by the homely stink of dope. Throaty laughs made the four of us cracking the door open feel like outsiders. A few extra beanbags and kids' chairs had been dragged into Penny's flat and the living room had become the hub for a morning smoke-up. At first it looked like the room was full of people we didn't know, but actually it was just the regular faces, Onomatopoeic Bob and Sara, Von, Cally and Christian, augmented by a Belgian guy from a United Nations High Commission for Refugees deputation and a young woman from the Spanish European Community Monitoring Mission. 'The Europeans' had heard about us on the town grapevine and had come to check us out.

'You should hear what they're saying about Babo!' Sara announced as we entered, rather pleased to be the bearer of bad news.

But Shannon nodded that Mohammed was about to come up and join us and simply said, 'Later. Us too.' Sara looked chastised and when passed the joint suddenly declared that actually, she didn't think it was cool getting high when people were dying, and left for a lie-down. Shannon followed her out, trying to massage her shoulders through her seersucker shirt, but Sara wrinkled from her touch.

The Europeans looked slightly alarmed by our arrival, like we might be the adults in the situation. It's true we were full of brisk walking and morning air, and we had a plan. But soon Penny went from standing hands on hips and telling everybody about the castle and Babo and Milan, to taking a hit of the joint and sliding down onto the couch with Juso and Mohammed, and as we talked and laughed the room took on the feel of an ad hoc youth parliament.

Alazne, the Spanish woman, talked about the foolishness of our parents' generation, the ones who had started the war and who refused to come in and stop it. She had a short button nose and long earlobes. Very long. In fact. Fuck. Were they stretching before my stoned eyes? To her the future was simple: 'Little countries, little places. Little towns and restaurants and shops.

Not so much the big ones.' It all sounded fine and good. The future would be Bosnia and Euskadi and the Republic of Wales and Flanders and, why not – if they wanted – the Autonomous Province of Western Bosnia? The economies of the future, Alazne explained, would be little artisan cheeses, transported to and fro, by big airships, leased out from co-ops. All perhaps to be flown by handsome, wholesome young women with perky breasts and ears like basset hounds.

'Just a question, guys,' Penny said. 'But do you think the UN would escort us down to Bihac?'

'For why?' Alazne asked.

'To take aid,' Penny said.

'Although we don't have any aid. Any more,' Onomatopoeic Bob mentioned.

'Sure, but we are an aid mission,' Penny said. 'We *were* an aid mission.'

'Uh-huh?' the Belgian guy said.

'But now we want to take a play,' Penny said.

'To promote the peace,' I explained.

'Er – you can ask, but the French – the French are the garrison here. They are busy. There's a lot of fighting around the pocket.'

'The pocket?' Von said.

'The Bihac pocket – it's surrounded,' Christian explained.

'Do you have UN authorisation to enter the pocket?' the Belgian asked.

'Yes,' Bob said.

'Sort of,' Sara explained.

'No,' Christian elaborated.

The Belgian guy and Alazne looked at one another. Then Alazne said, 'To be honest with you, I think, maybe but, really, no. I don't think without aid and without crossing permissions

175

or authorisations. No. You can ask for the help of the town but . . .' She looked at Mohammed, who was apparently absorbed in using one of his fingernails to skim out little curlicues of detritus from the nails of the other hand. 'Well, you can just see.'

'Then I guess it's the mercenaries,' Penny said.

There was a boom in the distance, which I took to be a quarrying blast – I'd heard them often growing up. But the way Alazne looked up made me wonder. I didn't want to be the gauche one, so I raised my eyebrows at Von.

'Was that a fucking bomb?' he asked.

'Artillery. I think they're doing bullshit. Range-finding. Almost practice, but I should go.' Alazne stood. So did the Belgian, but as he did, he wobbled between the couch and a comfy seat. The colour dropped out of his thin face, his eyes fluttered and he shuddered back to the floor, just missing a litre bottle of Karlovac lager.

'Take care, my friend,' Mohammed said. 'You don't want to make a Martinovic.' Across the room, Juso bristled.

'What's that?' Juso said, in fast like a blade. The Belgian took a sip of water and opened and closed his eyes.

'I'm sorry,' Mohammed said and flicked away a little ball of fingernail dirt with his thumb. I could feel the tension in the room and grinned benignly around, hoping to help it pass; but Von looked between Juso and Mohammed like a bad umpire and, spotting and enjoying the friction, said, 'Aye aye? What's that?'

'I was joking about something,' Mohammed said down to the carpet.

'What though?' Von asked.

'Shall I make some tea? Who wants tea?' I said, but stayed sitting there.

'It's a guy who was assaulted in Kosovo – it wasn't so funny

176

maybe,' Juso explained and I thought I could feel the Serb in him bristle, however high above the conflict he felt he floated. His little eyes shrunk further – black peas receding far into his whiskery white-plasticine face.

'Yes, well, maybe,' Mohammed said. 'We don't know. No one knows.'

Our Belgian friend tried to stand up again, straightened himself and strode out of the room with the exaggerated poise of someone who feels they are in fact walking on the moon. In the kitchen, I heard water run for a very long time.

'Doctors from Slovenia and Croatia and Macedonia as well as Serbia agreed he could not have got it there himself. OK?' Juso said.

'Sure, man. Brotherhood and unity.' Mohammed waved peace fingers.

'What happened, Juso?' Von asked.

'Look, it's kind of how the war started. It's bullshit of course, what's happened afterwards, but the start of it was horrible,' Juso said.

'He was a Serb farmer,' Mohammed told us. 'Djorje Martinovic. It was maybe the first thing to piss off the Serbs. Before Milosevic, before anything, in '84, '85. The story is that he was – excuse me, ladies – fucked in the ass with a bottle, by Kosovars.'

'That's what happened,' Juso said.

'If you believe the revolving presidency of the executive council of government doctors.' Mohammed smiled.

'It doesn't sound that funny?' Onomatopoeic Bob said to Mohammed.

'No, but there is the possibility, you see, that actually, that he wasn't raped but that he was trying to –' Mohammed made the jerk-off mime – 'sitting on a bottle. This is very much a possibility

177

and he made up the story because it is not such a cool thing, jerking off with a bottle up your ass.'

Suddenly Juso was standing up. The big body he ordinarily kept curled in on itself unfurled and he picked up the Karlovac bottle and prodded it at Mohammed. 'How does a guy get that, *the fucking wide end* you see, up his ass? Ah? How does that happen?'

'I don't know, man.'

'You think you could get a bottle up there? Yeah?' Juso said and shook the bottle at me. My sphincter tightened; it did look very wide. 'And anyway, why? *Why* would he? And how could you? Do that, to yourself?'

'Well, as suggested, by the investigation, it could be that he put it on a stick and sat on it?' Juso looked dubious but Mohammed continued. 'I don't know! Apparently he was a farmer, apparently they say he did this kind of thing? Apparently you can do it. Maybe he had lots of practice?'

'Why would a Serb do that?' Juso asked.

'Why would anyone do that?' Mohammed replied.

'Look, all kinds of things — a guinea pig, whatever. Guys dressing up as babies. Ladyboys. Feet. In the earholes. Yeah, sure. But that, I don't see it. No way,' Juso said.

'Sure, I don't know. It's just what they say.'

Juso put the bottle down on the coffee table.

'It's fine. It's cool. Who knows. It's just not so funny because Serbs have been impaled in Kosovo many times in history.' With that, he crossed the floor, claimed again from the door that it was all cool, and went out, shouting to Shannon, and for our benefit, that he was going to examine the canoes and check the hulls were sound. Because soon we should leave, to see the soldiers, the mercenaries — our protectors for the journey south.

Chapter 21

In the early afternoon Mohammed drove us down to a spot where we could launch the canoes. An oval shelf of pebble shouldered out of the river, which flowed as wide as a football pitch. We waded out to the pebbles and positioned the two canoes ready to go, their back halves scratching on the stones, their prows wobbling and alive in the current. The craft had come, apparently, from a former youth camp near Bihac and had Communist Pioneer logos stencilled on the hulls.

Juso, Sara, Shannon and Penny took their places in one – their combined weight pushing the boat into a gritty gutter, so that the rest of us had to shove hard to get it roaring with a plastic-on-gravel grind out into the water. Then we climbed into the other boat and shuffled off inelegantly, levering the craft forward with our hands. They were the high command vessel. We, the muscle, followed.

We only needed to paddle gently as the water narrowed to a tennis-court span and the fat current carried us along the green throat of the river. The riverbanks grew steeper and steeper so that eventually little clay-and-pebble metre-high cliffs ran to either side of us, topped with thick grasses, thin pale-leafed trees and woody plants.

In front of me, Von's thick neck with its golden curls looked reassuring and solid in the sunlight. I had a sudden urge to kiss it. Perhaps making out to Penny that the object of my obsession was not her or even Shannon, but her brother – that could be a handy subversion. The complication might somehow make things simpler between us and in a night of weeping on about my lust for Von, I could more easily slip into bed with her? Also, maybe I'd like it? I urged myself on to imagine slipping a hand round Von's waist, to the fat root of his dong. Maybe it would be nice with a bloke? Watching TV in bed and not trying so much? I urged a gay boner into shape, but nothing came off. Though, to be honest, I wasn't sure how much I was cheering it on and how much holding it back.

We'd zoomed ahead of the others and now, behind us, Juso laughed at something Shannon said. Then I heard a big splash. At first I thought it was just horseplay – the slap of oar on water and splatter. But when Von flattened his paddle against the flow, we spun round to clock the action: Sara was trying to get out of the other canoe. Shannon was gripping her arm and the boat was listing violently. Juso and Penny yelled at her to sit back down.

'I've had enough, OK? I've had e-fucking-nuff. I don't want to be a cog in this machine. I don't want to see all the little fucking looks, all right?'

Sara finally levered herself out. And as she plopped into the water it became clear the bottom of the river was actually stand-able.

'I am not blind,' she said, waist-high in the water. 'And I am not deaf and I know what's going on.'

'Sara?' Shannon said. 'What the fuck? Nothing is going on.'

'It is going on.'

'Nothing has happened.'

'You're doing your thing on him, Shannon, you fucking are.'

'You sound really crazy, Sara, you know that? You need to have a breathe and think what this is about for you. You're under a lot of pressure and I want you to think clearly about what is real, OK?'

As Sara waded off towards the riverbank the water rose, up to her armpits now, and though she stood easily, she stumbled as she moved, all creased brow and determination.

'What do you think is going on? Sara? Seriously? Ah?'

'You're . . . making him like you,' she said. It was a losing argument in every respect, except for the fact that it was true. Shannon could easily make you like her. By shining her strong beam on you so you were fully illuminated and your every move was made to feel silvery and fascinating. Like a secret dope plant, you grew big and vivid in her warmth, feeding on the artificially nutritious conditions.

'I'm fucking – out of here,' Sara said, dropping her feet away and starting to swim back to Velika against the current. She got nowhere – staying resolutely still next to Shannon's canoe, until once again she stood. Shannon dipped her head to Sara's ear and said something. Then Sara swam downstream towards us.

Like a hard-heart after the *Titanic*, I worried that her grabbing at our boat might capsize us, but she seemed happy to just float, her hand on our stern. She grimaced and shrugged when we asked if she was OK, then dipped her face down into the cold water to escape the world, before coming up with a flurry of thoughts. 'When is he even getting to his mother's? What do we know about him? Hasn't he missed, somewhere along the line, her funeral? Maybe he cuts babies' throats. Maybe that's what he does for a living?'

'Sara . . .' Onomatopoeic Bob said.

'We don't know. He's a Serb. Isn't he?'

'Are you sure something's going on, Sara?' Onomatopoeic Bob asked.

'Yes yes fucking yes. Or it will, or it has. I don't know. Blahdy blah. Yes no. Whatever. I know when something's changed. He's getting her treatment. I know you all want to fuck her.'

It was hard to say whether contradicting her would be soothing or infuriating. So I just said, 'We all know you're together. Everyone does.'

'It's just, you can't make a team out of one. You can't play tug-o-war on your own, pulling on just one end of the rope. If you give and give and give, you feel empty.'

It was true, I thought. Love is hard to do on your own, without encouragement. You can keep up interest for a certain amount of time; that's nice. That's romantic. But at a certain point a solo lovist becomes a unicyclist: proud, determined, even brave, but not entirely a serious proposition.

In the other canoe, Juso was asking disingenuously for a trans-lation of the situation, shaking his head and making out he was innocently, foreignly, baffled at the crazy happenings among his anglophone friends. And all the while, he moved closer to Shannon.

Beside us, Sara dipped her face down again and stayed under water so long this time I wondered if she wasn't trying to kill herself. But as she bubbled up, her wet face blank and chewy with grief, from the valley walls came the thud and whoosh of an explosion or an impact. Something warrish, for sure. But what? It felt like it was ahead of us. But as soon as the sound was over, it was gone, and the only coordinates left were in our memory.

'What the *fuck* was that?' I said.

'I don't know – where did it come from? What was it? Was it a bomb?' Onomatopoeic Bob said.

'Shannon?' I shouted over.

'I don't know,' she shouted back as her canoe paddled towards ours.

I noticed that all of us were looking at Juso now. The Balkan might be acquainted with the secrets of the bomb more than us.

'OK. We go back,' said Onomatopoeic Bob authoritatively.

'You think it came from ahead?' Shannon said as they pulled up next to us.

'Yes,' he said. 'I don't know.'

Chapter 22

I think the main reason we carried on was that when we stopped paddling, the river's flow continued to take us downstream. It was the path of least resistance. All action was risky with decision; if we went with the flow, at least the universe wouldn't punish us for a choice. But, as we drifted on down the river, the two canoes close, Sara between us like a corpse, one hand on each hull, I did have a strong sense that my actions might not be entirely explicable to an outsider.

– Why did you continue down the river into the hands of the death squad even after you'd heard the explosion?

– I don't know, Your Honour. Er, I can only apologise.

When we made it round the next bend in the river we were confronted with three men in camouflage, waist-deep in the water. They were laughing and picking dead and stunned fish from the river's skim, throwing some to shore and some at each other. Smaller dead fish, like little floating Roman coins, eddied all around.

'Catch this, you fucking seal!' one of the soldiers said as he spun a small trouty fish by the tail and another lad jumped in the air and gnashed at it as it passed. English speakers. Dynamite fishing. The Mercenaries.

They must have had some advance warning from Babo, because they didn't look too surprised when we shouted hello. The fourth of them, the guy catching the fish on the shore, clonking them with a little mallet and sticking them in a plastic bag, called out to us.

'So glad you could join us. Shall we put the jolly fucking kettle on?'

*

Bev, the fish killer, led us up to their camp. I walked right behind him. He had a convincing soldiering gait and thick muscled arms, but his bottom was wide and unglamorous inside his combat trousers and his khaki T-shirt rode up when he lifted his arms, showing wobbles of fat around his kidneys. The back of his neck bubbled with painful-looking spots boiling under the skin.

'Nearly there,' he said after we'd walked for four or five minutes. The top of his head was flattened off and his short brow came down in corrugated ridges. There was something eager to please in him which I recognised and liked, though I think he knew it was in him too, and didn't think it befitted his role – so he followed his encouragement up by mumbling 'You lazy cunts', as though to himself, but loud enough for us to hear.

Their camp was a handful of civilian tents clustered around a permanent fire. There was a separate cooking-and-washing area formed from a set of water butts and a standpipe outside the ruins of a farmhouse. Nearby, some rows of low-growing cherry tomatoes and a tangle of pepper and aubergine plants made up the remains of a masonry-strewn vegetable garden.

Bev introduced us to the other mercenaries as they returned to the camp to dry themselves by the open fire. 'That's Jonno.

185

He's hard as nails and a bastard with it.' Jonno was younger than the other men, in his early twenties and pale-skinned, not sunburnt like Bev and the others. He looked pleased to be informed what sort of person he was.

'OK,' said Shannon.

'Mad Mike. He's loco. We call him El Loco.'

'Does he prefer El Loco or Mad Mike, in general?' Onomatopoeic Bob asked.

'Hey,' Mike said, and as he warmed his wet legs he began to slide pieces of metal in and out of a machine gun in a way which could conceivably not have been solely for our benefit.

'Call him whatever you fucking like, he won't do what you ask unless there's a bottle of beer or a fifty-dollar bill in it for him,' Bev explained. 'And that's Chapstick. You'll get used to the nicknames. He fucking loves his ChapStick.'

'Nice,' Von said as Chapstick, on cue, applied some ChapStick to his unblistered lips.

'And are you the commanding officer?' Shannon asked.

'No, love,' Bev said, raising the eyebrows on his boxy head.

'Can we talk to the commanding officer?'

'The CO's in his cave, but if we brew up, you can tell me what we can do you for. Sound fucking scrumptious?'

Jonno produced a large, crushed box of Tetley tea bags wrapped in many layers of cling film from out of his rucksack. You could see his muscles coiled tight around his bones like a soldier's, but his face hadn't yet learned impassivity.

Von looked at the fresh box and Jonno's pale face and asked, 'How long have you been here, Jonno mate?'

'Long enough to know a tit from a teapot,' Bev answered, as Jonno peeled away the layers of cling film like a field dressing. Bev tapped out some little spoonfuls of instant coffee from a tin.

The mugs he made for me, Sara and himself were so stingy with the Nescafé that his economy destroyed its own purpose; he might make his stash last forever, but he'd never taste coffee again.

Shannon asked the soldiers if they'd been involved in any fighting locally. No one seemed to want to answer. Eventually Bev said that things were quiet in the surrounding area right now. Chapstick and Mad Mike had fought with the HVO, the Croat Army, in an international division, but a couple of months back had become irritated at the lack of action.

'The Croats were knobheads anyway,' Chapstick explained. 'We wanted to help the Mozzies. On raghead protection, aren't we? They're the ones getting pasted. Done up the wrong 'un.'

Bev and the CO, meanwhile, had apparently seen action together near Travnik in central Bosnia the previous year, while Jonno, the youngster, claimed to have been 'all over the shop'.

'I'm here for the craic,' he said. 'I don't give a fuck.' Bev nodded like the kid was getting his lines right and spilled the collection of river fish onto the grass. He and the others began trying to gut them with knives longer than the fish. Chapstick sat on his combat helmet, onto which he had penned, like a Vietnam guy: 'War is Swell' and 'Kill them all & let Bod sort them out'.

'And – with your, your captain – is this all of you?' Christian asked.

'It's enough, mate,' Bev said.

'Sure. I was just asking.'

'And who's actually paying you, as of now?' Shannon asked.

'We're awaiting the mission. Could be the locals, your lot. Could be another crew. Whatever, guns for hire. That's the game. If you don't like the game, don't sit down at the fucking table.'

Bev glanced round at the other mercenaries and smiled, and they laughed, although there was no humorous element to his observation.

If you're a mercenary but you're not getting paid, what exactly are you? I wondered. Is it better to be paid to kill people, or not? Paying for it is horrible, but I guess we do like people to take money for what they do. It makes it less like dressing-up.

'Fucking logistics, isn't it? We've got a whole posse a hundred clicks from here. Fucking Aussies, some Boers, Polacks, fucking liquorice allsorts. But movement is difficult. We're trying to RV, rendezvous.'

'We wouldn't even actually be here, but the bus didn't go to where we wanted to go,' Jonno said and Bev looked at him sharply.

'The bus never goes where you want it to go,' said Mike.

'Uh-huh. Tell me about it,' said Von.

As I finished my watery coffee I felt a shift in my guts. A half-week's worth of carbs coming loose and bearing down like a carrier bag full of pebbles. I asked where the latrine was and Bev laughed like I'd asked for a dry martini.

'Oh, the "latrine". It is situated to the left of the rose garden, adjacent to the gymnasium, sir.' He got big laughs for this. 'In the fucking woods, pal.' He pointed vaguely and chucked me a 'shit roll'.

I marched away fast, over a little access track for the ruined farm and towards the copse that was the suggested site for my necessary activity. But I fancied it was potentially still within earshot of the fire, so I ducked under a boundary wire, over a ridged hump, and reached the edge of a conifer plantation. Once in there, I crushed back some bracken to make my toilet, thinking about snakes, and mites and things that swim up your

188

cock or drop from trees. I crouched and tried to push what felt like an entire length of Scots pine out of my body, all the while plagued by thoughts of that poor farmer, possibly raped with a bottle, or possibly just a man whose cover-up for his embarrassing wanking preference ended up as a vivid paragraph in the manifesto of a group of nationalist intellectuals.

It was as I started walking back towards the camp that I saw two of the mercenaries eyeing me, Bev and a new one (the commanding officer?). They looked serious.

'Stop. Stop right there!' Bev said.

'Why?'

'Because you've walked into a fucking minefield, dickhead.' This was the CO. He immediately started to massage his temples like I was a problem he'd been dealing with for hours.

I stopped stock-still. 'Are you serious?'

'I told you to shit in the fucking woods,' Bev said. 'What are you, the fucking Pope?'

'Where is it? Really? Is this serious?' Penny and Shannon and the rest were starting to join the men now.

'Yes we are serious. Don't fucking move.'

'Where's the minefield – who? What's? What do –' I said.

'Just stop still,' Bev said.

'I am. I'm still!' I felt suddenly extraordinarily irritated at the idea of minefields. It was just so *dangerous* to bury bombs where people might walk. 'Whose minefield is it?'

'The lot who were here before us – the town mob. It was a training camp. They mined the perimeter, they said.'

'Why didn't you tell me!'

'I told you to shit *in the woods*. Why did you go a fucking mile off?'

'I didn't know which woods!'

189

But in fact the designated shitting copse was right there, obvious and distinct, and added to my current humiliation I was also revealed as someone with an unmanly need to shit far from civilisation.

'Is there not a map — of the mines?' I asked.

'What are we going to do?' Shannon asked.

'Listen, to be honest, the other mob were jokers,' Bev said. 'There's probably only twenty MURDs in the whole field. There might not be any?'

The fact that, as well as being a man standing in the middle of a minefield, I might also be a man not standing in the middle of a minefield, I didn't find all that reassuring.

'Do you think?' I asked.

'Fair dos, there probably is some. But not many, hardly any,' said Bev.

'It only takes one,' the CO said. Which had also occurred to me. I took him in for a moment. Grey crew cut, a chewy, bovine, mouth. He looked around slowly, a sort of esteem Hoover canvassing every nook and cranny for endorsement.

'What am I going to do?' I asked.

'All right. Fucking hell. Hold on. I'll get the mine detector. Don't move.' And I admit I did feel a minute's slight relief before Bev came back holding a broken swingball set and rotated the metal section so the tennis ball looped around his head. 'All fucking clear, mate!' he said and laughed raucously at his own joke.

'For fuck's sake.'

'Nah, you're just gonna have to come for it, matey.'

'No,' I said instinctively. 'There has to be another way.'

'Er — metal detector. No. Trained dog. No,' Bev said.

'Can't you *get* a metal detector?'

190

'Where from, mate?'

I wanted to say, 'From anywhere.' From the Littlewoods catalogue, mailed to Vienna; Penny can drive to pick it up, poste restante, and come back with it. And if it takes a week – so be it. Throw me fish. Raw fish. Actually, cook it, with a little salt, and lemon. I can wait.

But as I surveyed the faces down below, they suggested – even in their supportive, anxious glances – that the fetching of a metal detector was an essentially impossible task. Penny, like the rest of the gang, looked horrified by my situation – but also somewhat resigned to it.

'C'mon, mate,' Bev said.

It seemed I was about to lose my life because taking the action necessary to safeguard it would just be such a colossal *hassle*.

'You get so many false positives with a detector, anyway,' the CO said.

False positives didn't bother me so much. 'What if I step on a correct positive?'

'It doesn't even pick up some,' Bev said. Which probably clinched it. 'Some of these mines don't even show up.'

I stood for a long time while people asked various supportive and niggling questions.

'Can you remember what way you walked out?'

'Can you see your footsteps?'

'Why did you go so far?'

'C'mon, mate,' Bev shouted again after a while. 'Or it'll get dark. Then you won't be able to see a fucking thing.'

I sat down carefully, 'to think' for a while, and asked as many useful questions as I could about mines and what they might look like and whether I might not be able to use the toilet roll as a mine-clearance device in some way. To which Bev gave a number of sarcastic replies and told me that yes, shit roll would work as a 'magic carpet', and if I only stepped on a mine briefly it would not detonate, which I was certain was a joke. As Juso and Christian drifted back to the fire, I was considering simply refusing to move. That if I lay down and stayed the night, then everyone might see that I at least took my life seriously and might go to hunt out a metal detector, or requisition the items necessary to build what I had started to design in my head: a highly manoeuvrable small dirigible with a rope ladder that could hover above me until I climbed to safety.

In the end, the strongest impulse motivating my Walk of Death was the sense that people were waiting for a show that was late starting. I stood up and, trying not to sound reproachful, announced that, all right, I was coming back and to make ready the preparations in case there was a need to evacuate me as a medical emergency.

Here was a moment. A moment of life or death. Or also, of walking across a patch of nothing-dirt carrying a toilet roll. Then, before I took the first step, something I would never have normally done seemed suddenly possible in this extra, super-oxygenated pocket of life. I looked up and shouted, 'I like you, Penny!' and took the step.

If there had been an explosion then, the scene might have ended well. As it was, with no explosion, she was left to smile and say, 'Oh.' And, 'Thank you!'

Then, like a man tripping in the street and attempting to cover it by incorporating subsequent fake stumbles into his walk, I followed up my shout by adding, 'I like you too, Christian! And Sara and Shannon! I like you all!' They called back, after a beat, that they liked me too. I looked at Penny and the way she smiled, revealing no teeth and then looking at the ground, improved my situation a little, in that I now actively wanted to die.

My outbound tracks were not visible; the ground was miserly underfoot – dust over rock with just a few spidering clumps of grass. Sometimes I thought I saw a footprint; sometimes, often, I thought I could maybe, just maybe, spot a telltale divot of something buried, but then played mind games between myself and the mine-laying intelligence; perhaps the divot might be a ruse to head me onto a better hidden bomb?

There was something incredibly undramatic about each step. I never really expected the earth to blow under me; it was always the step-after-the-step I feared, not the step itself, because the notion that putting my foot down could kill me seemed so very mad. Initially, I high-stepped, like the red-coated soldiers on the edge of a cereal bowl I remembered from childhood. (Please don't let that and everything else about me get blown to bits.) Eventually, however, I stopped the high steps and went – twelve or so paces in – for a more insouciant gait, something that, while not quite normal, tried to make out I wasn't so fussed about losing my legs.

In a film there would have been a red line, and once I stepped over it, sweating, I'd have been in the clear. But in reality the end of the ordeal was gradual and unsatisfying – each step I took seemed to make it increasingly unlikely that I would be blown up. Once back in among the group, everyone patted me on the back and Shannon squeezed my hand and Penny kissed me on the cheek and we headed back to the camp. But as we walked, I still felt in the ground for the hard nub of something military. Killed by a mine right after making it out of the minefield, that was just the kind of joke wars liked to play, I thought.

'That was grim. Are you OK?' Penny asked, falling into step

beside me. For once, I wasn't so desperate to spend time with her, not after my unilateral declaration of like.

'Yeah, good,' I said. Then, 'Sorry.'

'It's OK,' she said. Perhaps I was something of a hero? A bog-roll-carrying hero.

'Yeah. That was weird. I know. I just wanted to say that. About the liking.'

'It's fine,' she said.

'But, yeah. I do like you.'

We arrived back to the camp and she didn't say anything more in reply and I was left with the uneasy feeling that, like the mines, my declaration had somehow failed to go off.

Chapter 23

Round the fire, as the afternoon started to click and buzz about us, the CO pulled out a bottle of the local plum brandy, slivovitz, and some washed-out plastic yogurt pots to drink from. His face was full of an effortful melancholy, like someone had drawn a sad face on a cauliflower. He must have been forty or more and wore British Army camouflage, while the other mercenaries had a collection of weird odds and sods. His pronounced overbite sent his lower jaw jutting out like a battering ram and meant his sentences got all spliced up with spittle.

'Do you mind me asking,' Sara asked him, once we were all sitting back round the fire, 'do you mind me asking what you actually think about the war?'

'It's bollocks, isn't it?' Bev said, looking round at Chapstick and Jonno and Mad Mike and finally the CO, who remained impassive.

'I wish I wasn't here,' Chapstick said. 'But no one else is sorting it out, so it's muggins's turn, isn't it? Buggins here.'

'But you'd rather not be here?' Sara went on.

'Oh no, I love it, don't I? Living in a fucking tent using a hose pipe for a shower, what do you think?' Chapstick got laughs for this from his fellow soldiers and also smiles from Von, Christian and me who found ourselves involuntarily drawn into the alliance of men. But not Juso. He was staying quiet – although he whispered something into Shannon's ear.

'But you could go home?' Onomatopoeic Bob said.

'They don't want to go home, do they?' said Sara. 'They like it here, killing people.'

'Sara, we are here asking our friends for a favour.' Shannon held her gaze. Sara's lip quivered, on the brink of saying something beyond the pale of normal human interaction, until, unwilling to lose face, she just made a little noise that signalled disgust with the world and in particular its most corrupt invention: all of us.

Even the soldiers seemed a bit embarrassed. Bev looked into the flame appearing and disappearing under the aluminium kettle and said, 'You all live safe in your houses, but who's keeping you safe? Fuckers like me?'

'And what if you went home?' Sara asked.

'And leave it to someone else? Some poor other fucker? No thank you, that's not my game.'

Sara stood up and stared down towards the river.

'End of the day, I don't give a fuck, to be honest with you. They're all Russians to me. The lot of them. It's their bed they've shat, so they can roll around in it,' said Chapstick.

'I'm all about the money,' said Jonno.

Juso looked at Shannon and smiled secretly from within his big beard, as though something had been confirmed. Bev clocked this and poked at the fire with a twig. 'The money we're on, we'd be crazy to do it for the money,' he said.

'So look,' Shannon interrupted, 'what we want is an escort to go down to Bihac.'

'What about the the Knobheads? The Helmets?' Bev asked.

'The UN?'

'Yeah?'

'We're not accredited. We don't have the blue cards. They say they can't take us, so we wondered if you might escort us?'

'I bet you fucking wonder,' Bev said and all the mercenaries looked at the CO, who seemed not to have heard.

Then, without looking up, the CO said, 'It's not easy. It's dangerous. There's fighting. Bihac ragheads versus Babo's ragheads. Never mind the fucking Serbs. Nasty. And you lot are what we call fuckslops.'

'I mean, you are mercenaries. Presumably, you've been through fighting before?' Shannon asked, innocently.

The kettle was boiling now, the steam hissing out into the warm air.

'Oh, we've seen fighting, love,' Bev said. No one wanted tea. We all sipped at our yogurt pots of spirits periodically.

'Yeah?' Sara said and raised her eyebrows just a bit too high.

Bev leapt at the little hint of mockery. 'Men, made to eat fucking grenades and run at their own families? Yeah?'

'Jesus,' Onomatopoeic Bob said, like he'd panned a nugget of gold that could now be carried back home. The rest of the gang went silent and reverent. Even Sara bowed her head.

'Sorry — they *swallowed* grenades?' I asked.

'You don't forget that.' For want of anything else to do with the hot water, Bev washed out his and Mad Mike's yogurt pots, as though sterilising them, before filling them up for their next dram.

'Wow. How?' I asked, widening my eyes.

'Fucking stuffed them.'

'Yeah? A *whole grenade*?'

197

'With lubricant,' Bev offered.

'And how did they pull the pins?'

'Look, pal, human bombs. You wouldn't ask that if you'd been there, OK?' That was no doubt true. 'Long fuckin' delay.'

There was a wobble in the air. After a while, Bev said to the CO, 'Show them.'

The CO looked into the embers, then intently at the backs of his pasty hands, as if he hoped the strong black hairs there were aerials which could send out terse communications without the need for him to speak. 'No,' he said after a long pause.

'Go on,' Bev said.

'No, shut it,' said the CO.

'What is it?' asked Sara.

'Show them, sir.'

'I'm not showing them.' The CO got up.

'Look, what the fuck have you got?' said Sara.

'He's got a bit of somebody,' said Jonno.

It sounded pathetic like that, so after a beat, having wandered over towards his 'cave' – a slightly larger Halfords trademarked tent set away from the others – the CO said, 'I have an ear.' But that also sounded rather small somehow, so he came back and stood above us and looked into the flames a while and added, 'To remind me of the chaos.'

'Oh, right,' said Penny. 'Yeah, I have a Filofax to remind me of the chaos.'

'Shut the fuck up,' Bev said and started to whittle on a piece of wood with his fish-gutting knife.

'Don't talk to her like that, you arsehole,' I found myself saying, and Bev sprung to his feet to tower over me.

'C'mon, hey, let's all just shush,' Shannon said, looking at the handgun the CO had pulled gently from his webbing belt.

'Oh yeah, blah blah fucking blah, then a gun ends the conversation. Brilliant,' Sara said. 'Fucking brilliant. The man with the gun ends the conversation.'

'What are you doing here, anyway? Ah? Getting your noses wet and your fingers red. You don't know the first thing about a combat situation,' the CO said.

'Yeah I do,' Sara said. 'I know the first thing about a combat situation – the kids get killed and the women get raped. I know the first fucking thing all right.'

'No. The first thing is the men fight and the men get killed,' the CO said.

'Yeah, and you fucking love it,' Sara said.

'I do not fucking love it.'

'Course you do, you all do. Look at you, looking at your fucking gun. You're pathetic. It's a fucking pipe with a clicker on it and it pings and out come little cocks and it makes you all think you're so fucking important. Well, it's boring.'

'You can't understand killing, until you've seen killing,' the CO said, putting his pistol down.

After a beat Penny said, 'Well, yes, you can.'

'You can fucking shut your cakehole, little Lady Fauntleroy. How did you get here – in your fucking Jag?'

Penny looked at me and raised her eyebrows. I looked at the men and their guns and took a breath.

'C'mon now,' I said.

'Come on now what, you *prick*?' said Bev.

'C'mon now . . .' *Feel the noize*? *Dance everybody*? *Touch me, babe*? 'C'mon now. Yeah?' I said.

'Look, if you've got a problem, come and tell me, don't snivel like a quim,' Bev said, letting his long knife catch the sunlight so the reflection zinged into my eyes.

199

The CO put his hand on Bev's arm.

'It's OK. It's OK,' Shannon said and tried to shift the balance of the afternoon. 'You are a group of warrior men. We haven't seen the things you've seen. For our reality, peace is the thing, but we can't know your reality, we just have to accept it, but what we're here to do is, as another tribe, to ask your tribe for help?'

She said more soothing things to the men, words that were not so important in themselves but the tone and pitch of which lulled them. She explained how we were aiming to take a play to Bihac to spread peace and also hinted that the money we were carrying was not insubstantial.

The CO said they would have to think about it and he and his soldiers retreated to his aluminium-framed cave.

When they came back, they stated their price for escorting us. Three hundred marks. Plus a number of self-aggrandising provisos: that we would travel the journey in silence, 'for security reasons'; that the mercenaries would travel in separate vehicles, and that they would take us to Bihac town limits and no further. Shannon bargained them down a few marks and shook the CO's hand as he looked at his watch, like he had a busy afternoon in store. It was decided that we would rendezvous in town the morning after next. The junior mercenaries walked us down to the river to push us off – roughly, in big unfriendly zooms.

'Oh yeah. Oh fuck yes,' Bev said and then shouted to us as we floated out of earshot, 'Don't do anything I wouldn't do!' as a sort of meaningless all-purpose upper-hand-grabbing almost-joke.

Paddling back, the river water splashed in and made my jeans squeaky and cold, while the back of my neck, in the August sun, felt like a clothes iron was being pressed against it. We didn't talk much. I considered whether I was suffering some form of shock from my mine ordeal, but couldn't really find a way to claim I was. Looking across to the other boat, I frequently met Sara's gaze and she smiled at me for the first time in a while. I smiled back, both of us obscurely disgraced.

Then, in an eddy, up close to the riverbank, we saw something. It took a moment to work it out, but snarled up among some yellowing sheet plastic and a bobbing blue bleach bottle, there was also a corpse. A woman, jammed up so that she jarred against the sides of a little inlet, the debris around her surrounded by a scum of opaque bubbles.

While we stopped and looked, both canoes started to drift backwards with the river's flow. Eventually Shannon said something and we started up again. Our paddles dipped in with little distinct plops afterwards. It was difficult making headway against the big push of the river. Then we began to discuss what it had been like for each of us, when we had first seen the body, and whether it was slightly before or after another person had seen it and what we had first thought it was and what we had then thought it was and when we'd realised what it really was.

Then after that it went quite quiet, and that flurry of discussion felt like a party compared to what we were left with, each thinking about a dead woman in silence. For a while I tried to play detective and wondered if she might not perhaps be something less obvious than a dead body in a war – a fisherwoman who'd stumbled, or was she pushed?

We'd most likely passed it on the way downstream as we'd chatted and laughed and Sara cried. Sara pointed this out. At first I refused to accept it and said it must have happened while we were at the camp. But thinking about it, the way it was stuck in its bit of river, like a huge Poohstick jammed out of the game, the body must have been there for days. It made me feel giddy, teetering on the edge of something bottomless, to have been so oblivious. But you can't know everything, I guess – some secret thing will always be out of sight waiting to prove you stupid.

Chapter 24

We had forty-eight hours to wait before we took the long dangerous road south across the internal conflict line to Bihac. Shannon intended for us to use this period to finally rehearse the play. Once upon a time, the plan had been that we would 'workshop' in Sarajevo, so that the locals had a chance to 'engage with the piece'. I didn't really know what this meant. I assumed it meant more than watching, but less than actually being in it, and didn't see quite what room there was between these two poles. The planned workshop had meant we'd never got ourselves too hung up on boring old rehearsal. But now that we knew how hard it was going to be to physically get into a Safe Area, Shannon worried that our stay there might have to be brief. We would need to be ready to put on the play quickly, 'like theatrical commandos'.

So with no indoor space available, and in a nod to the workshop idea, she scheduled a rehearsal period the following day out in Velika's main square. Penny smiled and said that would be fine: we'd start with a read-through and from there she'd want to keep the text 'flexible and open'. But as we walked up to the usual bar that night, she was worried. 'Do you think it's ready?' she asked.

'It could be readier,' I said.

'Readier and steadier. I'm going to stay up all night and rewrite it.' Or indeed write it, I thought.

'Do you want help?'

'Sure. If you like. Thanks.' She stopped to get something down in her notebook and smiled, to let me know she was brimming with material.

In the bar, things went well. We found a good spot across from the pinball machine and the owner brought us lager in stemmed glasses and a meagre one-nut-deep scattering of complimentary peanuts in a clean Heineken ashtray. It was dark in our air-conditioned corner and I shivered in my baggy khaki shorts as she talked in general terms about things she thought her play should be like. 'Like Friel's *Translations*?'

'Yes!' I said, in total ignorance. My reading at the University of Supermarket had been wide, but, like Offa's Dyke, there were huge gaps in the edifice.

'Like *Catch-22*?' I said.

'Yes. Like – like Evelyn Waugh mixed with Walt Whitman!' she said enthusiastically.

'Umm. God? Yeah!'

The general principles were actually fun to discuss. She rather liked being hard on her old self as she sipped the frothy heads off the Karlovac lagers with limitless ambition for her new self. It was engaging to see such enthusiasm, although the realisation that everything you wrote yesterday was total shit seemed not entirely compatible with the expectation that everything you wrote tonight was going to be utter perfection.

Nevertheless, we went back to the flat on our three or four beers high and buzzing. The process started out with Penny writing and passing me pages as she went. Initially, we discussed them, I made suggestions and she rewrote accordingly. But slowly she started to nod for me to make the agreed amendments myself.

'This is fun? Isn't this fun?' she said as we got to page five of the hundred needed.

'This is fun,' I said.

'I mean, it's obviously going to be terrible. But right now I feel hugely optimistic!' she scrunched up the page she'd just written and popped it in her mouth and then spat it in the bin. We both laughed.

She did seem to be remarkably relaxed about my level of liking for her. If someone had told me they liked me like I'd told her, it would have cramped me up and made me all jerky and unusual. But I suppose she was more used to people liking her than I was. Perhaps, in fact, she was more likeable.

Getting down to the writing, a sense of freedom coursed through me. It was because I felt that 'I' wasn't really writing. All the bits that were trite and overly neat, boring, flat or clichéd, I put down to 'her'. Then every four or five pages I smuggled in something which I thought of as worthy of myself (though often, when I read these bits back, I decided they were actually still more 'hers' than mine). We followed the Castle Plan, largely, the one we'd sketched on our walk to Babo's based on the Foreign Secretary's short story.

When I passed my pages back to Penny, sometimes I saw her nod and smile, or look over at me with something like admiration. Other times, her pencil went to work and she passed back a further improvement. Unswallowable gobbets of plot or difficult changes of character trajectory, we erased by tackling head on. We worked well together. I could hear how people talked and she was not afraid to guess or make up how they felt.

And as the hours went on, I couldn't help feel that our

collaboration was proof of a greater potential compatibility. Because it was a little sexual, the tussle. Sometimes when I'd rewrite her and she'd rewrite me back, we'd create a scrawly little tangle over which one of us had to relent. But the hour tended to massage out the knots. Two, three o'clock concentrated the mind. Powered by slivovitz and instant coffee and water and crackers, I shuddered with caffeine, and as the morning approached I relented here and there. Or we came back to some great divergence of opinion an hour after it happened and could no longer remember which side of the argument we had each manned.

We finished our draft at four and read it back silently, Penny sitting at the table on a stool, me standing at her shoulder. I leaned against her back, a mini-spooning after the dry hump of the writing. She wore a thin sheer-cotton top and I could feel her body's warmth through it. At five, we finished reading, smiled in satisfaction at having brought an artefact into the world and went to separate beds for a couple of hours before rehearsals.

*

At seven I woke to her knocking on my door. She'd just read it all over again and wanted to talk outside.

'I'm not sure, Andy.'

'What?'

'I wonder if we should go back to my original version?'

'What the – the . . .'

She leafed through her file.

'I mean, I like what we've done with my stuff. I do.'

'Look, it's a basis for discussion,' I said, a panicked swell rising.

'Or we could just do exercises. Tell them ideas and devise something?'

I'd been suckered. Lured, into creative engagement. More than that: Borislav and Mr Tomic, how would they fare without us? Trapped in a limbo, in a war which, worse than never ending, never even started. We needed to help them, to coax them into life and let them suffer a little, to show the world the meaning of pain.

'I just feel. I like what we did last night. I do. But is it trite? Is it too straightforward, and didactic? Is it intelligent enough?' she said.

What I heard was: 'I like you, Andrew, but are you intelligent enough? Are you just a man from a building site who has read off a layer of Penguins and now you think you're fucking *it*?'

'Sure. Sure, absolutely. I share your concerns. I think our new version may very well be truly very terrible. Awful,' I said.

'Well . . .' she started to object.

'But your older work, which I think of as the frame, the drive, that still exists? Right? That's in the bank. Look, we've stayed up all night – shall we just give our new one a go?'

She looked at me for quite a long time. 'Yes. You know, I am grateful for this, Andy. I'm sorry if I'm freaking out? Am I freaking out?'

*

The arrangement was for Mohammed to help us sort out the logistics of rehearsals: copying the play and warding off locals to set up our rehearsal space. After breakfasting on hard baguette and thin strawberry jam we met him outside the flats. He was smoking a Drina. He offered the pack to Penny and me. I took one. His relationship to Babo – and Babo's relationship to the world – might have been obscure; and how he got these Drinas,

207

who knew? Still, you don't have to offer a couple of your last ciggies to anyone. He pulled out a lighter. I imagine that tearing a strip of woodchip wallpaper from the most neglected room of a Blackpool boarding house, filling it with workshop shavings and dead woodlice, would taste something like the hairy fume of inhaling one of those wartime fags.

At the newsagent's, giddy from the tobacco, I leaned for relief on the huge grey photocopier. Mohammed was doubtful it would work, but it did. It chugged lugubriously, one of the few machines in the world that looks the correct size and seriousness for the magic it can do, sliding our warm copies into its out-tray and stapling them too.

With lengths of synthetic orange twine and some tent pegs discovered in our apartments, Mohammed and Onomatopoeic Bob marked out a rehearsal space on the parched grass of the town's central square. Shannon was provided with a plastic director's chair from the unfriendly bar. Cally sat cross-legged and read her photocopy, mouthing to herself and rocking back and forth from the hinge of her hips.

She was sitting next to Von with a thumb hooked into the back pocket of his jeans, but eventually he asserted his independence, going off and buying a sugared waffle from a cafe and sitting a way off, making out he was reading the copy of *The Magus* which he pulled out at times of stress and looked at hard. He'd had it at hospital when I first met him. The leather Winston Churchill bookmark had not advanced noticeably through the pages in the six months since.

'I thought it was very proficient,' Christian said, approaching Penny and me with his script. 'I think this is something I can be involved in.'

'Oh. Thank you,' Penny said, shooting me a look.

'Yeah. I can see what you were trying to do.' This, I happened to know, was actually high praise. Christian also felt he had a fix on what Pynchon had been attempting, what Flaubert had wanted to pull off and what Joyce had been aiming for.

Cally and Christian were to be the two leads – the Serb and Croat neighbours. Through the first act they would build their summer house together, while Bob, Shannon and Sara (as husband, wife and daughter) fleshed out our scenes of tender antebellum Balkan domesticity. Von – an incredibly poor actor – was the rueful wise apple who cast a jaundiced eye over proceedings, half professor, half narrator. Penny and I, meanwhile, were bloodthirsty soldiers who, rather brilliantly (perhaps), were sometimes Serb, sometimes Croat. But always boozy and swaggering.

The sun sawed at us. As it headed towards eleven, Shannon called her players into a tight circle on the wiry brown grass. Penny and I smiled at one another and she reached for my hand and gave it one brief damp squeeze.

There was an especially nightmarish quality about hearing the play read so soon after its writing. Words and phrases I had thought we'd bettered came tumbling out of other people's mouths shamingly raw. Self-consciously tantalising plot threads were revealed in the bald sun to have no conclusion. Sometimes I chased the text ahead, looking for the next glob of drama, the next bit that might work. But as I flicked forward in the script, these dashes felt like races into a desert. So I'd return hoping for relief in the present – urging the cast to knit something decent from the depressingly insubstantial, yet still surprisingly coarse, thread Penny and I had spun.

However, as we came to the end, and a feeling of nausea swung my tummy, it became apparent that the group rather liked it. It had lasted about the right length of time. It started with a situation, things changed, it ended, it appeared to investigate some feelings. God knows, maybe it even did?

Or perhaps that is all art is: pretending. And I had peeked behind the curtain? If you make people up, say they feel a certain way, then some folk, some dupes, sometimes believe you? When it finished and we clapped ourselves heartily, I think it was the happiest the group had been since above the pub in Manchester. People already had the feeling that their lines were theirs alone, tangible. So that when we discussed changing them, there was a reticence, a tug back for something about to be lost.

I leaned over and squeezed Penny's knee. She kissed me on the cheek. Shannon thanked her, and Penny said that I had helped her; indeed, that I had written most of this draft. It sounded, the way she said it, like of course she had done it all, especially when she added another 'No, really, he did'. The group clapped me lightly and I smiled and raised an arm of acknowledgement. The dependable accomplice, a playwright's Tubacca.

We broke for Shannon to do some 'small group work' with Cally and Christian. Penny listened from the side, biro in mouth, waist hipped out, her forehead scrunched and thoughtful. I found it powerfully alluring. It reminded me of how rousing I used to find it to watch Helen dance long ago from the balcony of a club: someone utterly absorbed in something else, entirely whole and completely unrequiring of me.

*

A little later, I sipped a very low-quality coffee, sitting at the foot of the Red Star war memorial, watching scenes being rehearsed

210

with a satisfaction permitted by the fact that they were beyond earshot. Von had gone off once again to try to make contact with his dad and report on our progress and plans. But however many Deutschmarks he gave to Hasim and however long he spent in his 'office' he could never get an international line. He came back pissed off, and went to listen to techno very loud on his Walkman, lying flat out under a plane tree. That was when Mohammed caught me with the letter.

'Will you give this to Penny when she is finished?'

'Thanks, Mohammed. Of course, man. Great. Did you see the play?'

'Yeah.'

'Yeah?' I said.

'Yeah,' he said.

'Thank you,' I said.

'Yeah no – I like you guys.'

'OK? Thanks.'

'Yeah, I liked the – the words. There were some good – you know, like when the guy said: "No – no fucking way." I liked that. Strong.'

I wasn't sure who'd said such a thing.

'You're good people, coming here, you know, some people don't like it so much, they think English – Americans – no. But I think – yes.'

'Well, I like being here. I like it here. I love the pastries. And the sun. Obviously we have also the sun in our nation, but not so much as . . .'

I wasn't concentrating. My heart was quivering its beat, pulsing out to fingers which fibrillated as they held the envelope. I knew the writing, I thought. And there it was: Simon's address written in spider-quick biro on the back.

211

Mohammed retreated, saying he would see me later, yes, for the handover, of Babo's package? I hardly listened as I nodded yes.

I walked over to a park bench to make my decision. The only possible reason not to open the envelope was that it was the wrong thing to do. But if I didn't? I couldn't see that anyone would ever know I'd done the right thing. Whereas the wrong thing? No one would ever know I had done that either, and it would be much more . . . interesting. Besides, the airmail gum barely tacked the envelope flap down. It was stuck with the adhesion of the driest desert lips closed before a kiss. It was so very simple to untack it. If a rip had been required, then maybe not. That would have felt violent. But this little finger sliding under and gently along? Almost tender.

I scanned the letter to the end without really connecting the sentences, racing ahead to the next paragraph, looking for the emotional protein.

Dear Penny

I don't know how to say what I want to say. I tried to say it so many ways. I must have written this fucking letter a hundred times, a thousand counting the unfin-ished drafts in my head. But I can't seem to get it straight in prose, so, forgive me. I've taken the cowardly (brave?) option and composed a small something for you. That last night at your home, I felt very close to you. Anyway, before I betray myself, I'm going to stop and simply say: read the enclosed, read by lamplight, read by gaslight, but read in the full light of knowing this is how I feel.

Avec un certain regard,
Simon

On a separate sheet, there it was. He had only gone and written her a fucking poem. A carefully targeted, emotion-tipped arrow. This was nuclear escalation. What could I possibly do to respond to a *poem*? Paint her a picture? Write her a symphony? Choreograph a dance? I unfolded the A4 and my first hope was that it would be so overreachingly erudite as to be unintelligible. Just plain clunky would also be great: too truthful, blunt and fat-fingered — that would surely fuck him.

But when I read it, it was horrible. It opened with this:

> When the War with the Robots comes
> I would like it recorded
> that I never much liked the humans anyway
> But I do like you.

And then it got better. And better. It was short, sweet, direct, and touching. Ironised enough to protect itself and its author, open enough to lay himself bare. It was, I thought, as I read it a fourth time, pretty much invulnerable. A sweet cherishing love poem straight from the heart. Fuck. It was so fucking lovely it almost persuaded me I should leave them to it; that I wasn't worthy of the love affair I had wandered into.

Penny looked up towards me from the rehearsal area, in her shirtsleeves, offering a wave and a thumbs up. I waved back.

Some things that you do which are terrible don't feel so bad at the time. This one did. I crumpled the poem. Then thought better of it. And instead ripped it across and across and across, carefully but with a heavy heart, as if I were tearing up some instruction booklet necessary to my own safe functioning. I did it deliberately and quickly, and scattered it in three separate municipal waste bins. Then I sought out a piece of notepaper and a pen from our unfriendly bar.

I could pocket the letter, and make a whole night's work of my shitty smear, but then there would be the danger that Mohammed might mention the letter's arrival to Penny and reveal me? So I found another bench a good distance from her and the troupe and settled down to work, quickly; roughing out a couple of drafts, before putting together the final version in careful anonymous block capitals, to ensure it wasn't obviously in a different hand to the letter.

Before the final fold into the envelope, I read it back one last time:

How like the summer hours are thee?
Sighted, clothe-clad, sad and yes, to me,
Not mad, but glad-ening,
To my very core, my swelling 'root',
That once would have wished to find a 'route' into you
I wanted, 'tis true, to make a love so savage,

My nights were filled with dreams of havage.

But I must give my 'root', sad to say, 'the boot'.
For while your mind is so teeming –
With little thoughts, like clever fish
Of which you are rightly proud,
I must off to wrestle the Whale of Truth.

See, I must plash on, to the mountain far,
on my lonely journey, whale at my back, staff in hand,
A monk of the mind, unrooted, pushing onwards,

To the grand summit, the high peak of human
endeavour: the sea.

& I cannot carry you on my shoulders there, dear,
I am weighted enough with: my
Talent, my whale, my knapsack and blank road map in
    hand.
They make for a heavy load, and believe
Me, if I could
But make room for you, strapped to my whale of
    endeavour,
Clasped in my knapsack of gathering fame,
With my crampons and trunks,
So I would!

Oh, to share a tent with you, and to whisper sweet
Words and push my sea urchin into the clam of
    yourself under the stars
But it cannot be!
I must climb the highest peak,
Alone, save for my whale, and staff
Farewell, then, small fish I never caught,
I shall fire my harpoon tonight to nought!

I laughed like a villain as I read the last lines over, then went
back and entitled it 'The Fish and the Whale'. I slipped it back
in with its letter and licked the remaining gum enough to tack
down the flap.

When rehearsal broke, I gave it to Cally to deliver into Penny's
hand. Then I sat as if reading *War and Peace*. But the words were
hard on the page, entirely resistant to my eye. I watched Penny

open the envelope, wander to a spot on the grass and read. The first time she attended to the pages so briefly I hardly believed she'd read them. One scan of the letter – I felt irritated at her on Simon's behalf – then a quick read of the poem. If her face betrayed anything, it was bemusement. She tucked everything away in the envelope and into her back jeans pocket. Then, a couple of seconds later she pulled it all out again and read it over more carefully. My skin prickled, feeling she might turn to me and, like in a horror film, issue a finger-pointing, curdling denunciation across the park. But no, it went away into her pocket again, and as she headed off to talk to Shannon I felt like the constellations were aligning. My covert operations were preparing the way for my gathering forces – ready for the big push.

Chapter 25

That afternoon we packed up from the flats and Penny paid ponytailed Hasim with a folded bundle of marks. I was watching him count them seriously on the bonnet of his Mercedes, scared that I would be asked for a further contribution out of my thinning money belt, when Mohammed showed up and asked if he could speak to me. He led me off, asking how things had been going and what I thought of Velika. We were a little way out of town and walking along the riverbank when he got down to the matter in hand. There was a shift in the atmosphere, like a dense cloud looming across the sun on a bright afternoon. Things felt cooler and flatter. He explained to me about the package for Bihac.

Babo did not want to trust the women, Mohammed said. He did not trust the hairy driver, Onomatopoeic Bob. But they liked the look of me. Mohammed was checking I could be trusted. With an attaché case. It would come from Babo, to be delivered, so ran the precise instructions, only into the hand of Hamdo Abdic, commander of the 502nd Brigade of the 5th Corps of the Bosnian Army in Bihac. Did I think I could be trusted to deliver it? Would I accept the consequences if it did not make it through?

'I think you can trust me, yeah?'

'Yeah?'

'Yeah, I think I'm the sort of person who tries to do what he says he's going to do.'

I liked talking about myself like this, as if I was merely an extremely well-informed observer. It made me feel more substantial, a less wobbly entity.

'I tend to come through, for a friend,' I noted. 'But why does Babo want to send something to Bihac, to the 5th Corps – aren't they the enemy? Aren't you fighting those guys, to stay out of the war?'

'Don't worry. Yeah? We are all Bosnians. There are links. It is complicated. Don't worry. Yes?'

'Yes.'

'Good,' Mohammed said. 'If you make it through, *straight* to Abdic.'

'*If*? "If" we make it through?'

'I'm sure you will, but if you do.'

'Well, OK. Yes of course. "If" though?'

'OK, *when* you make it through. You should. You will,' he said.

'No, sure, I'd be pleased to – and if there's anything else I can . . . I mean, Mohammed, is that like a 98 per cent chance of a safe passage, or more of a 51 per cent likelihood?'

Mohammed laughed and patted me on the back. 'You will be fine. I promise.' That was reassuring. It would have been more reassuring if he was an omnipotent God, not a man in a pair of knock-off Levi's and an 'Indiana Yacht Club Superior Nautical' T-shirt. But still.

'Would you think of coming? Of going, Mohammed?'

He laughed again. 'They would kill me.'

'Yeah?'

Mohammed's jeans were thick enough to protect him from the thorns and nettles that grew at the sides of the path. In my khaki shorts, I was more of an Edwardian lady picking my way through behind him, stumbling to keep up as he talked over his shoulder.

'Yes. Yes. I was in the army. I was in the 504 from Cazin, but after – when there was a ceasefire with the Serbs in '93 – we all thought, well, we've done it, we have peace and we came over. Babo signed for peace, with Karadzic. Everyone – everyone wanted to come over to Babo.' Mohammed stopped in a little clearing under some willowy treelets and let me take the lead as the path led up away from the stream.

'But not everyone did?' I asked, stamping my feet hard on the ground in a way I had once been told would scare off snakes.

'No. The crazy ones. And the politicians, they stayed, and some of the units of the 5th down there, they are crazy or scared. They would shoot you for coming over. In Bihac the government is strong, you know. It's a big city town. But everyone wants to come to Babo. Have you seen the doctors we have here? The cheese? We have everything. Why do they want to have nothing?'

I smiled, though he couldn't see my face, and nodded with exaggerated dips of my head. 'But the Serbs, can you trust them?' I asked.

'Everything can be OK with Serbs. Everyone thinks the Serbs are the bad ones but let me tell you a story. Before the war, our neighbours were good ones. The only problems were with the other side, they were the ones who let thistle and weeds grow and the seed blows – you know? And they were Muslim. Well, not real Muslim, but the father was. He was different. He was from Kosovo originally but – his wife. You see, I am not Bosniak at all. I come from Bulgaria. A real Turk.'

I think he could sense this wasn't coming over to me as compelling.

'Look, you know about the Ustasha? You know about Pavelic, the Croat bossman, the Poglavnik and the barrel of eyeballs he kept, in the Second World War? On his desk? He ate them like oysters. Serb eyeballs. It's complicated. You know there was a Muslim SS regiment? Yes? So, do we have clean hands? Does anyone? No. Fine. So if a man comes to my house and gives me a loaf of bread, he is my friend. If a man comes to my house and he kills my chicken, he is not my friend. After that then, maybe, "Is he Serb, is he this, is he that?" You understand? Right now, in Bihac, my Muslim friend from before would kill me. But here my Serb enemy keeps me safe. So. Yeah?'

'OK? Yeah. No — I get it. Just people, take them as they all are, if you can?' I said, like a slightly mistranslated greetings card.

'Exactly. Yes,' he said enthusiastically. '"Just people, take them as they all are, if you can."' Then he tapped me on the shoulder and we both stopped. He smiled widely and said, 'Except the Russians. They're just motherfuckers.' And we both laughed a nice, naughty, complicated laugh.

We'd been walking for a while, on the path that rose up from the river and back to the road, when we saw a worrying flash of synthetic colour across the other side of the river. Like a soldier, Mohammed ducked down, and I copied him, keeping low. We crawled down into a little hollow and then up the other side to its brow to get a view across. I was up close to Mohammed's body — he smelt of fresh sweat and tobacco and the sharp chemical citrus odour of cheap soap. He levered himself up on one of his sinewy brown arms and didn't duck down.

Shannon was down there directing. Mohammed looked at me and I looked at him. This was obviously something we

220

shouldn't watch. On the other hand, it was quite interesting. She was directing sexual activity. Only slowly did the phrase 'threesome' come to mind. What it looked like, if you didn't glamorise it with a name, was something more lumpy: a twosome, plus another. Or maybe, three interrelated onesomes.

Watching made me feel a little religious, or at least socially conservative. It suddenly occurred to me quite forcefully that two was a good number for sex, even that it was, perhaps, the 'natural' number.

Three did not look like it worked so well; it was too many, by a factor of one. Because while they tried, with Shannon lying back and Juso rubbing his beard into the beard between her legs, lapping like a cat, and Sara kneeling at his side trying to reach under and milk him cow-wise, it didn't seem to quite fit. There was lots of organisation necessary when they shifted position. In fact, it looked like a further additional person was required, really, solely to be across the logistics. In their absence, Shannon was Napoleon, getting the baggage train in order and checking the supply lines before Sara now lay back and Shannon rolled up on top, sliding a hand under her, and Juso, the spare sticklebrick, arranged himself side-on, trying to get his member into some friction-providing crevice.

Then he moved away and, considering the problem architecturally, chose to lie for a while on Shannon's back; not looking, it seemed, to go up the bum, but to ride the groove of her buttocks. But the weight was clearly uncomfortable for Sara down at the bottom, and besides, the people-pile was unsteady and short-limbed Juso was having to strain his legs and arms like a human table to stay up top. After a while he climbed off, retreated and knelt uncomfortably, his kneecaps arrowing into the ground, and wanked generally – towards the scene from offstage, like a porno linesman.

'So. What's in there — the attaché case I'm taking to Bihac?' I asked.

Mohammed looked at me. We were both embarrassed to still be there, half watching. He said he didn't know and nodded his head for us to leave.

We retreated quickly and as we made it up to the path back towards town I asked him what he *thought* might be in the attaché case. A dissonance entered our communication. He didn't lie, I don't think. It was just that suddenly we were calling out to one another over or round some rock of circumstance that was too obvious or important for him to explain or address.

'Nothing. I don't know. Important things, but papers or so, I guess?'

I was left ignorant and dissatisfied, uncertain even what it was I didn't understand. And apprehensive too, in case, like a frightened teenager waving down as he grips the cold steel of the pylon, my eagerness to make a friend had led me far beyond my nature.

Chapter 26

When I woke, early – before seven – the mercenaries' two Toyota jeeps were already idling, their diesel fumes chugging black and casually wasteful outside. The two vehicles, borrowed from Babo, were to drive in front and behind as protection vehicles for the van.

Bev hooted jauntily outside the apartments despite the hour. None of the mercenaries deigned to get out. Through the window I could see they all carried guns, at once tools and props; both serious and frivolous, threatening and protective. All the peace-play troupe made it up and out without central planning or chivvying – even Von. He and Cally had shared a bed for three nights now and had a bit of the couple's self-bubbling disregard for the group. Von's small Berghaus rucksack bulged – prolapsing out of the drawstring top were some of the apartment towels.

Juso said his farewells. I watched from the pavement as he kissed Shannon and then Sara too. He was red around his deep-set eyes and so was Sara. They'd all stayed up late drinking, playing gin rummy and swilling out the taste of one another with slivovitz. Juso pressed something into Shannon's hand,

and something else into Sara's. Only Shannon was dry-eyed and clear.

'Good night?' I asked Von.

He, Cally and Onomatopoeic Bob had gone drinking in the unfriendly bar, where they'd got taken up as heroes, emissaries of reasonableness to the savage south, and been bought many rounds of booze.

'Umm,' he said. 'You?'

'Yeah.' Penny and I had spent the evening going through the notes harvested from the day's rehearsal. She had them all recorded in a thick black notebook like a policeman's. Most were little changes we implemented right away. But as we went through the selection of bigger questions, we started striking down one by one the tantalising new directions proposed during the day. Each, as we got to it, seemed to wilt under examination; to become a suitable case for dismissal. Sometimes Penny drew a line through the new idea. Sometimes she just undid it with a big fat question mark. Or wrote: 'Further discussion.'

'I'm not quite sure they totally understand what they're meant to be saying,' she said a couple of times, puzzling over some dick's query from the rehearsal process, before writing in 'No action required' or 'Try it again and see how it feels'. Soon enough we had dispensed with the lot and changed only a word or two.

'Are those from the flats, Von?' I asked as he tried to stuff in the towel that bulged from his bag, pulling out a Nerf gun to make room.

'I need to finish that shit,' Von said.

'I'm sorry?'

'Cally. Bullet in the head, I reckon.' He nodded at her. She looked very fine, standing on the road in the morning sun, her thick hair hanging luxuriantly, shot through with sunlight as

224

she talked to Penny – their friendship looking appealingly full of complicated intimacies.

'Yeah, today's the day. I'm out of there. I need to keep my options open.'

'Yeah?'

'Yeah. You don't want to eat the same sausage every day, do you? That would be mad.'

'We *are* heading into a war zone, Von?'

'Yeah, but she's not exactly going to get killed, is she?'

'It's just not a great time – to – end something, is it?'

'I don't know. I kind of like her, but she's not a Bond Girl. She's barely an eight. That's not good. What if I get stuck with an eight? She's not far from a seven. I'd be a laughing stock. Plus –' he looked around furtively, and began to whisper – 'she wanted me to put it in.'

'Right? You mean . . .'

'I don't put it in,' he explained.

'You don't put it in?'

'No, I don't put it in.'

'Right? Why – not?'

'It's not my bag. I don't play that weak.'

'How do you mean?'

'It's dirty. I've never put it in. Aids? Yeah? Suck jobs, handjobs. Sweet. Do you put it in?'

'Er, well, yeah. When I – yes. When it's . . . polite.'

'Yeah, well, I don't put it in. It's my choice.'

'No, sure,' I said, suddenly alive to the suggestion that I was somehow seeking jurisdiction over his complicated sexuality, forcing him to accept the culturally hegemonic demand that he *put it in* somewhere he didn't want to. 'But – is that – how does she . . . is that OK, by her?'

225

Before he could answer, and just as Shannon was chivvying the troupe to saddle up and depart, a Mercedes came past slowly, shuffling us all off the road and pulling up beyond. It was Mohammed with the case for me and a letter from Babo for any roadblocks and checkpoints we might encounter. I took them and clasped hands with my friend.

'As well,' Mohammed said quickly, 'tonight I hear in Bihac town they are showing *The Three Amigos*?'

'Oh?' I said. 'And?'

'And?' he asked.

'And – what?'

'I thought you should know.'

'Right – is it dangerous – should we not . . .?'

'No, you should go.'

I nodded, serious. 'And the man – will I see the guy there, to make contact?'

'No, just, it's with – Mexicans and cowboys?'

'Yes, I know.'

'My friend told me, they said on Bihac radio?'

'Oh, OK – oh, right. Thank you.' Mohammed walked away, leaving me feeling I was in danger of becoming too wary to enjoy the simple pleasures in life: Chevy Chase and the flowers in the hedgerow.

Just then Bev jumped out of his jeep and announced that the CO thought one mercenary should travel with us, and he was taking a seat up front, in case of 'bullshit'.

'What kind of bullshit?' I asked.

'Your kind of bullshit. Wagons roll!' he shouted.

We all climbed in. Shannon and Onomatopoeic Bob joined Bev up front, with Bob taking the wheel. Before the van door swung shut, Shannon gave Juso a last quick dab of a kiss on the cheek. They said nothing. But, oh, his face. As Sara sat behind Shannon and rested a hand on her shoulder, I looked at Juso and wondered how do we have the balls, all of us, to walk around with our faces, these great meat plates, every thought baldly plastered across them? He looked so forlorn. It's indecent, really, that we go about with these beacons stuck permanently on, flashing out everything to the whole world.

Whatever re-alignment or catharsis the three of them had been looking for down by the river hadn't come out right. Sara put her arm round Shannon's neck from behind. We pulled away, following the kick of the front Toyota.

*

When you break up there are a lot of different departures, but usually one solidifies in memory as the archetypal essence of the whole fucking mess. Somehow with me and Helen, it ended with her leaving at night in a taxicab. I was the one who was going to leave our rented flat first, so she could stay and pack up before returning to the borderlands, back to her mum and dad's place at the end of the valley. But that night, she was going over to her friend Yvette's, leaving me behind to put my stuff into cardboard boxes. We'd parted hard during various arguments. Some days she left for work with things so gloomy and oppressive that the weight pushed me small all day, till she came back to our little house to find it pressurised like a diving bell. But of all our various endings, that taxi departure felt like the one. It cost money, and also it was done without emotion.

Penny had kicked it off, though I don't think she knew it. After a big peace-play meeting, we'd driven to Rusholme together to buy relief supplies in the Indian supermarkets. We prodded sceptically at various sacks of rice, and I ended up sluttishly spilling my feelings about Helen and the whole situation: her probable, well, definite, infidelities, the ways we didn't match up quite right (I didn't mention the ways we did, as I looked up from under my indie-boy fringe, like Princess Diana). I felt, as we walked back to her Fiat Panda, like I'd gone over the top; slit the belly of a ewe and let the whole disgusting mess of the thing disgorge in front of her. But she didn't seem to take it that way. She took it in her stride and didn't say anything dramatic like 'Leave her' or 'Why do you put up with that?'; the only thing she did to express any opinion at all, as I recall, was to make a face at one point.

Right after I'd laid it all out and said, 'Ah well, maybe that's just what I have to put up with?' – that's when she did it: she made a curl of her lip and I felt a crack zigzag through me. It wasn't a big intervention – I'm not sure she knew she'd made it (though she definitely did) – but it was enough. At once I saw it all through her eyes, with a bit of perspective. A definitive declaration – I was being fucked over. And in addition, wasn't I also getting a hint that I shouldn't be treated this way? That *someone else* wouldn't do this to me?

*

As the van farted off Sara massaged Shannon's shoulders and the two of them looked only forward. They started to discuss how well everything was going and how amazing we all were and how everything was so exciting in a kind of balming call-and-response chant.

The road out of Velika Kladusa was flat and wide. White vehicles from the French UN garrison buzzed past us a couple of times like hover vehicles from *Star Wars*, inhabiting a cleaner parallel reality. At the very edge of town there was a vast and churning cement works where men seemed to work still. The compound next to it was a big Agrokomerc food-processing plant. It featured a central tower, an oblong of narrow steel-framed windows extending up many storeys against a grey, rendered exterior. It all looked New Dealish and socialist-honourable. Then, as the commercial stuff receded, we rolled down into a happy valley of fat cows and sheep.

I looked at the briefcase at my feet. And then, with an almost physical convulsion, the fear that had been abstract for the last day suddenly flipped itself into a solid realisation: it was a bomb. It was clearly a total fucking bomb.

The best — almost the only — defence against concluding that it was a bomb was that no one else had suggested it might be. Everyone knew I'd been asked to make this delivery. I'd told them and no one had raised a fear. They'd all seen it arrive and me carry it aboard. Perhaps it was too obvious? To send your enemy a bomb with a timer, or a switch set off by opening or some such — that was too much like a child's game. No one would actually attempt it, would they?

Surely it was too risky? What if it was set off accidentally by a jolt in the van, or poor manufacture? How could Babo trust we wouldn't check? Unless, of course, he considered us to be what we certainly were: entirely expendable.

The more I considered The Case of the Case Between My Legs, the more it seemed that there could be no very good reason for thinking it was anything other than a bomb. It ballooned down there in the footwell, filling my consciousness. It tick-tocked its silence, and my intimate relation to its hard edges, its cheap lock,

made me nauseous. Every glance down I blinked into my last
ever look, the blast triggered by a little road bump. Using my
calves, I cushioned the bomb with all my concentration. But I
said nothing. I had accepted the item, therefore I swallowed up
the fear for the gang. I was a little Jesus. So that my friends could
chat and buzz, I suffered the agonies on my plastic-seat cross,
nailed to the spot with a stupid smile across my face.

*

I'd noticed the twang in Bev's accent at the river camp, but
hadn't chosen to explore it. Up in the north English-Welsh
Marches the pitch of accent gets squeezed four ways: from the
south, swelling it up, comes something West Country, slow and
rural; from the east, the Midlands, a doltish murmur; from the
west, a Welsh rhythm that's made hard under the pressure from
above: Merseyside and the black rock of Corwen and Ruthin
pushing down. So it pops up, this dialect bubble, as something
you might name Hard-Country-Lilting-Stupid.

Bev had it. And in the corners of my mouth, so did I. Enough
for Bev to ask me as we settled into the drive, 'Where you from,
mate, by the way?'

'Chirk way.'

'Yeah, I thought you sounded like a twat,' he said affection-
ately. 'Who do you know? Do you know any lads?'

'Just – not really.'

'I'm Shrewsbury. I was EBF,' he said.

'Oh. Right.' The English Border Front.

'Right. I was. But I changed my firm in the end.'

'How come?'

'Fucking – just my mum went to live somewhere else from

my old fucking man, so I ended up Llangollen, Wrexham Frontline?'

'Oh, right,' I stuttered. 'Yes. I worked outside Wrexham for a bit, in Gwersyllt, the supermarket, night shifts. Stock lad?'

'Then you'll know fucking, Sion and Neil?'

'Er? No? Maybe? I think I –?' Sion had held, while Neil screwed his knee in my face.

'Yeah. Wankers.'

I laughed, non-committal.

'Fucking hell. How did you end up here, you sheep-shagger?'

'I met these lot in Manchester,' I said.

'Student?'

'These are, yeah. I was working on building, fucking, yuppie flats.'

'All right, and what are you, a chippie, a brickie?'

'No – fucking, general. I mixed the muck. But – good money up there.' I could feel Penny regarding me. 'Fucking good, great fucking – independent arts scene and that,' I continued.

'Tidy,' he said.

'Tidy,' I agreed.

As we drove on in silence, I wondered whether Bev might be someone I could confide in about the briefcase? His big shoulders under his black T-shirt spoke of a bull's power packed into a human's skin. Just looking at the red swelling spots across his neck you could feel their angry tautness, the pressure of the pus mantel beneath. He might be acquainted with explosives, able to think straight about life and death. But also . . . he might go wrong. Some men you can't ask for advice safely, not real advice, because they can't live in ambiguity. They can't not know – even when they don't know – for even a breath. They leap on a solution too quickly and then get tied up, confused between their advice and themselves, and their whole aim becomes having their counsel taken up. Any consideration or hesitation is taken as rebuke. So if I asked and he said we must throw the briefcase out of the window, that is what we would have to do, or else turn the situation into a trial of wills. And that would, in turn, colour his every other decision, and we might end up being made to drive into an ammunition dump, on fire, to be taught an obscure lesson about trusting his wisdom.

The valley we travelled was shallow and a stream ran beside the road for the miles before we hit the small town of Mala Kladusa. The blacked-out burnt-through houses started to appear only gradually, an infection that took hold slowly the further we got from Velika.

Most of the houses were the square, red-brick, almost Alpine villa-farms, large, simple Playmobil designs. Between two of these, up a little drive, we saw a smaller bungalow – a flat-roofed oddity, burnt and empty and turned into an X-ray of its own structure. The back wall was knocked down, so, as we travelled past, for a moment you could squint right through from its missing front door to violent, green nettles growing behind. On the road nearby, a group of four male pensioners stood looking seriously at a piece of engine lying black and oily in the centre of their huddle as they encouraged a boy of twelve or so to investigate it with a stick. Which one of you bastards burnt your neighbour out? I wondered – wanting to let rip the accelerator on revulsion, at the same time as pushing the brake down hard on a quick judgement. Everything is complicated. Everything is simple. It depends how far away you stand, I suppose.

A little later, out of nowhere, Bev said, 'Yeah, a direct hit from a shell will basically turn you inside out.' This seemed to be a perfectly acceptable opening conversational gambit to him. 'Your lungs, your guts, your intestines, still full of shit, burst inside out.'

'Oh. Right,' I said. 'Yeah?'

'Yeah,' he said, 'yeah. It's like a fucking fig or a watermelon, smushed up.' Christian and Penny glanced at me.

'Hmm. That's quite a thing,' I said, looking at Penny, trying to broaden this disgusting discussion to the floor for input.

Then, as we rode up towards the small settlement of Pecigrad, Bev announced we were about to hit 'sniper alley'.

'Sniper alley?' asked Onomatopoeic Bob.

'Yeah, this is the main road. This is what it's all about – they've moved up and down here like a whore's drawers,' said Bev, relishing the fear that rippled through the van.

'But they – they wouldn't hit us on purpose, would they? I mean, sniper alley, actual, proper sniper alley is in Sarajevo, isn't it?' I said.

'They popped a UN Frog,' Bev said.

'They killed a peacekeeper?' Shannon asked.

'Yup. In March. Fuck knows what they didn't like about him.'

'Will they shoot at us?' Von said. 'Who would shoot at us?'

'Oh yeah, fuck yeah. The Serbs on a recce. The 5th Corps have been known to have a pop. Babo's Velika mob, practice. Fun.'

We all looked at one another, I guess checking if we were ready for this, if this was what we'd come for, to run this gauntlet. But Shannon didn't look back, or across at Bob, who kept glancing at her. So eventually we all looked ahead too.

The 5th Corps, the Bosnian Army unit left in Bihac and the surrounding pocket of land, was comprised of seven to ten thousand men, according to Bev. He sketched out how the 5th Corps faced Bosnian Serb forces to the east and south, Krajinan Serb forces to the west and Babo's Velika Kladusa Autonomous Province forces to the north.

'It doesn't sound good,' said Penny.

'They're fucked, to be honest, love,' said Bev. 'They should get into bed with Babo, I reckon. Most of them want to.'

As Bev talked snipers, I slid myself down in my seat in what I hoped was an unobtrusive fashion. There is no shame in being afraid of death, I don't think, but there is somehow a shame in being amateurish about it. Fine to wear body armour, shaming to be found to have packed your chest, as I had that morning, with the last couple of *Independents* pulled from your blue ruck-sack. Similarly there is no shame in saying, 'Everyone lie on the floor, get down,' as Bev did eventually, but that premature selfish slide hurt me in Penny's eyes, I reckoned. She looked over and smiled quizzically at my slump, then got it, tapped Cally on the leg, and did likewise.

As we made it through Pecigrad there was a gunshot. It didn't hit us. It may not even have been aimed at us. We might easily have not realised it was gunfire without Bev. Inside the van it sounded like a distant pop, rather jolly, and then we heard the whizz of an irate insect on the pop's tail. By then we had all been lying across the van's floor for some time, in a pattern I dubbed 'crazy herringbone'. Von was on top of me, his belly across my bum, making me feel protected, the bottom child in a fight-cuddle-scrum. Christian's white Reeboks were near enough to my face that I could see the Union Jack stitched into the tongue in minute detail. Penny's face had ended up close enough to mine that I turned my hot breath away from her in case it wasn't fresh. My cheek lay flat on the cool briefcase as I supported it from underneath. If it blew now, it would take me head first.

'Bob, you are OK driving, aren't you? Bob?' Shannon asked.

'Pull over, mate, if you need to,' I shouted up.

But he said nothing, and we trucked on, listening for the next pop and whizz.

I did truly believe that it was important that something was done – about the situation, about Bosnia. That was the prayer I said to myself to remind me why I was lying there. I was even willing to say I would, theoretically, lay down my life. The problem was that before I did any definitive laying down, I would prefer to see all the facts and figures laid out. Because if by some dash across a checkpoint I could get three thousand, or even just three hundred, women and children to safety, if I could shield the last infantryman as he planted the final flag of multi-ethnic victory, then yes – I was willing to let my brain say, at least – I would make the sacrifice. But getting my throat shot out by a sniper on my way to see *The Three Amigos* badly dubbed at an open-air screening? That wasn't really for me. And nor was going out here, sweating and smelling on the bottom of Christian's trainer the remnants of what I thought might be good old British dog shit.

There was another pop and Cally made an odd noise that it took me a beat to clock as fear. From on top of me, Von stretched his arm out and his big soft hand took hers. And Penny raised her head to peck a kiss down on my cheek because I think I too might have made a little whimper.

Soon, the light coming into the van altered, Onomatopoeic Bob chugged us back a couple of gears and we rose out of the most exposed part of the road.

'Should be all right now,' Bev said and I didn't have the heart to overly query the qualifications around this reassurance. Instead we all shuffled back upright, to see a temporary roadblock of tyres and planks and barbed wire ahead.

'They haven't got time to be fucking around, these are front-line boys,' Bev explained.

As our convoy pulled up, the soldiers, all smoking cigarettes, looked in at each vehicle cool and hard, making out they were predators and we were prey. Beside the roadblock a tape player rested on top of a metal saw bench, blowing battery-powered Bruce Springsteen into the summer morning. A few of the soldiers wore uniforms bearing the crossed-sword badge of Babo's Autonomous Province. One man, despite the growing heat, had a long coat that looked Second World War, Russian. He was short and the coat went all the way to the floor so he resembled an undersized wizard. I sensed, hoped, that they cared a bit too much for their rough look to be real killers. And yet – this supposed, I guess, there was something somehow authentic about a killer.

In the car ahead of us, the CO said something to the lead roadblock officer. It didn't look like a difficult negotiation; it seemed they had received advance warning of our convoy and we got waved through without offering our papers. As we filed through the soldiers stared in hard and frank at the women. Shannon stared right back.

It was just a kilometre or two until we reached the hamlet of Skokovi, where we would pass though the mirror to the other side, into the pocket of territory protected by the Army of Bosnia-Herzegovina.

'It's changed hands three or four times,' Bev said as we arrived.

Skokovi was the most brutally and recently fucked of any village we'd seen. The houses were all burnt out entirely and what remained of the blackened masonry was badly shot up. The tarmac was chewed with bomb, mortar and grenade craters and caterpillar-track indentations. The houses that you could tell were once houses had ended up as open-sided sheep pens or cowsheds. The single remaining staircase, as on a stage set, led nowhere. All over the place, interior decoration, wallpaper and woodworked details never intended for exposure to the elements were forced to make new accommodations.

At the outer edge of the village was a UN armoured personnel carrier. We stopped up. They looked at us, waiting for a question, and we looked at them, expecting to be challenged. But as Shannon stepped off to demand free passage it became clear that they had no mandate to check our progress. The lack of intercession left me feeling mournful: the authorities were no longer interested in safeguarding our well-being; we were outside the pale, swimming free. This was a land beyond jurisdiction, where no papers obtained.

Bev got us all to lie on the floor of the van once again as we exited Skokovi. I tried to position myself so my head would be near Penny's again, in case more kisses of reassurance were available; or so that I could ask to marry her if I was hit in the belly by a sniper's bullet. Onomatopoeic Bob, the captain of the ship, could officiate, and maybe then I might pull through against the odds and we'd still be married and we could tell our kids how it happened on the deck of a Transit in Bosnia. But this time I was late down and my groin ended up between Von's spread legs. My head was on the small of Christian's back and Penny was a way off, nearer the back doors.

The van bumped onto bad road, and I clutched the briefcase tight, hoping very hard that it wouldn't blow. For a half-kilometre or so, I pretty much equally prayed the vibrations didn't shake the blood into my bone so that I ended up with a hard-on rubbing against Von's legs. Even in a battle zone he wouldn't observe any decorum about not mentioning it and in a flash I imagined my embarrassing hard-on both remarked upon, revealed, and then, immediately after, blown clean off, twirling through the summer air like a cheerleader's baton.

Once we were back on smoother road, there was a murmur from the front and the van halted. We sat back up in the seats to see the first glimmer of the Bosnian state embodied by a man with no left eye, a decent military uniform and a purple Miami Dolphins baseball cap. Even I recognised that the weapon he carried was not quite of the modern era.

'What is that gun?' I asked Bev.

'Second World War,' Bev said, and some additional information about calibres and so on.

While Shannon focused on talking to Miami Dolphins in broken English about the transformative possibilities of theatre, suddenly, from out of their jeeps, front and back, the mercenaries were on the floor, pulled and forced down onto the road, spread-eagled, their guns kicked, swivelling and skittering on the tarmac, while all around them Bosnian soldiers shouted unfriendly instructions very loud and very fast.

Chapter 27

Bev had no weapon visible, so he was left in the van with us while the CO, Jonno, Chapstick and Mad Mike were patted down and had all their small items confiscated.

Shannon tried to explain that they were just guarding us during our journey. To which Miami Dolphins replied, 'It's OK. It's OK. We don't shoot them now.' Which I hoped was intended to be more reassuring than it sounded. There were three Bosnian soldiers at the front jeep, four at the back one. The ones at the front got the CO and Jonno to crawl on their hands and knees towards Mad Mike and Chapstick by the back jeep. I smiled supportively at them as they passed, but the CO didn't care to look up. All four of them were then ordered to roll and shuffle like seals on a beach till they were in a line.

'Is it OK?' I asked Bev.

'No,' he said.

Miami Dolphins was clearly not the commanding officer. The top guy seemed to be a man in a soft beret and aviators. He looked lean and engaged and, unlike a lot of the soldiers we'd seen around, as though he might be quite good at war. While he asked questions of the mercenaries on the floor, he constantly

surveyed the scene up and down the road. He soaked up everything and emanated a deep knowledge that the circumstances
of any one second could be vastly different to those of the
previous. He said something final to one of his soldiers, a gentle-
faced man, a baker without hat or bread, and stepped aside to
consult with Miami Dolphins.

The baker and a troop of six other soldiers got the mercenaries
to their feet and marched them to the side of the road towards
some birch trees. The guy in aviators supervised the collection
of the weapons left on the road.

If I was one of the soldiers in the baker's squad and he said
'the big man says shoot them, shoot this scum' or something,
I wouldn't want to. I'd hate to. God knows what nightmares
you'd suffer after. But honestly, in the moment? Wouldn't it be
simpler, less fuss, to squeeze the finger a few times and hope you
didn't get the burial detail? Wouldn't it be a bit self-regarding to
refuse; almost like suggesting everyone else enjoyed it? Of course
they didn't. It was a job to be done and to excuse yourself would
be pernickety. To privilege your own purity over the dirty job
in hand, it would make you look like you thought you were
some small-time saint.

'Are they — are they going to be OK? They're our friends,'
Shannon said out of the window to Miami Dolphins. He glanced
at the guy with the shades, who came over to us. He let us know
the order of priorities by handing Miami Dolphins a length of
hosepipe, which he took down to the back of the van, where he
removed the petrol cap and fed the pipe down into the tank.

'Umm . . .?' Shannon said.

'I am Ejup,' said the boss. 'Those men will not be hurt. They
will be sent back. We are taking their weapons and vehicles. You
are the Americans on a peace mission, yes?'

'British. And American. And we are bringing a theatrical piece to change the situation here?'

'Yes. You have word from Babo?'

Shannon looked back at me.

'Yes. Yes, I have something for – for the commander,' I said, passing forward our letter and holding tight my case, rather reluctant to give up the bomb for the moment.

'Is he taking all our gas?' Shannon asked. The man in the Dolphins cap had just, to the amusement of a couple of buddies, got a mouthful of diesel as he started the siphoning.

'We need diesel. You will have enough to make it to Bihac. The rest we need.'

When he had sucked enough of our juice to fill three old motor-oil containers, Miami Dolphins held the hose high to stop the fuel coming and Ejup waved for us to depart.

Shannon looked at Bev to see what he made of it. 'I think we go, shall we go?' she said.

Bev held quiet for a long beat. I feared he was going to say something like 'You take the big guy! I'll handle the other three.' But he had no plan, no secret man knowledge, and he just squinted through the birch trees to where his friends were lined up and said, 'I hope they'll be all right.'

'They'll be all right,' Bob offered.

And then there was a burst of gunfire, close and loud. In the van we all ducked and Ejup waved us off. Bob put his foot down. As we looked back we saw the mercenaries run out of the wood and back up the road towards Pecigrad and Velika Kladusa.

'Are they . . .?' I asked.

'I don't think . . . I think it's warning shots?' Bev said.

'Is it?' Shannon said.

'If they were going to do something, they'd wait for us to go.

241

Wouldn't they?' I said, not wanting a war crime. As I counted up, it looked like three, then four − definitely all four I was pretty sure − made it to the road. They ran, stumbling, away. Bob calmed the pace as we humped over the hill and began to wind down through fine trees on a steady steepish descent towards the largest town before Bihac: Cazin.

*

As we drove south, I could almost sense that under our wheels we rode on the threadbare last matting of a state. This thing we kick against, that stops us burning down bus shelters and paves the roads, it is indeed woven of perishable vegetation, and here it had almost worn through. I looked back to where the road-block was no longer visible and realised that I strongly believed in the state. The warm milky cowish ride on the great beast which hardly minds who it is carrying; and in its vast disinterest leaves room for its citizens to thrive, the birds on its back peck-pecking as it trucks on down the road it lays before itself. Without the state, everything is just men by the road with guns telling you to do things.

We skirted Cazin. In the suburbs children behind low wire fences waved at us as we passed. Inside this, the Bosnian government-controlled area, time had ticked back. For lack of fuel, things had gone from the car to the horse, the handcart, the repurposed shopping trolley. There were no more checkpoints but everywhere you could tell we were near war. There were men in fatigues, bunched mostly, but also singly. Bristly things were all around. Not just the spikes of guns, but radio masts, metal spikes at unfriendly angles, the iron core visible within rent concrete.

We crossed the dipping plateau through a pressing heat. The cloud cover was total, lying in long white-grey ridges, chunky beneath; a thick duvet trapping the air above the land and cooking it hotter and hotter.

'Are you OK?' Shannon asked Bev again as we approached an impressive castle. Ostrozac, my guidebook said. Its buckled towers and broken skirting walls might have been hit by this or any number of previous wars.

'Yeah. Yeah. I made a tactical decision to let the situation play out,' he said.

'And what do you think we should do about you?' Shannon said. Bev shifted in his seat.

'I'll look after you,' he said. It was one of those shoves too far people under pressure make. Until quite recently he had been our protector. Now, with his gun in his waist belt, he was a cargo that endangered us.

'It feels like we might be safer without you, actually. But if you'd like, we'll take you in to Bihac?' said Shannon, the Plain Dealer.

Bev squirmed, all English and affronted. 'Those hills are full of Serbs, to be fair,' he said, nodding to the other side of the gorge we were descending. But none of us in the van felt his side arm offered us much protection. 'Look, I'll ride you into Bihac, make sure you're OK, then see where we're at, but right now you need to hit the deck quick fast for snipers?' We responded, but a little slower this time, like workers in an office who have seen too many fire alarms that month. The road swished back and forth and by the time we reached the Una River at the valley's floor and Bev said we could sit up again, I felt motion-sick and resentful. All that scunning around on the floor for nothing. Not a single shot.

The narrow valley bottom we travelled was only wide enough for a three-ply of road, railway and river. We passed a large and disused hotel complex on the riverbank, built for Communist fun. You could imagine fat bureaucrats hitting forehands on the red-clay tennis courts, thunking through the ball with heavy Warsaw Pact alloy rackets, their pioneer kids off singing songs of brotherhood and unity in the woods. Soon the hills parted around us and we travelled on to a plain that ended in new hills and, just before them, Bihac.

As we arrived in the suburbs, past compounds of non-functioning light industry, the noise of a loud fart ripped through the van. Von, headphones on and oblivious, wantonly eating up Duracells to loudly power his Doors tape, smiled, eyes closed, presumably believing he'd slipped one out unnoticed. His sister tapped his arm sharply to let him know we had all heard and he offered an unembarrassed 'Apologies. I thought I'd got away with it!'

The northern side of the town, where we came in, was furthest from the Bosnian Serb lines. Their forces cupped the town in an unfriendly hand from below. To the west and north-east, these Serb lines joined up with the border of their allies in Serb Krajina. With the Autonomous forces of Babo to the north, enemy positions surrounded the whole pocket one way or another. On a map, it looked rather perverse of the Bihacists to hold out. A child colouring in would certainly crayon over the edges of the pocket; it should really be the same colour as the surrounding territory, that would be much simpler.

The damage was light and sporadic as we passed through the northern streets – shells and mortars had popped holes in the concrete only here and there. But even undamaged areas showed the secondary infection of the conflict. Trees were cut down to stumps; gate posts and fence posts had also gone for firewood, leaving their wire fences sagging.

For the want of other suggestions, we headed to the hotel on the river recommended in my guidebook. Following the advice of a pre-war guidebook felt certain to lead us to some irony – a death pit or an amputation hospital that had overtaken the tourist spot. Before we got there, as in a dream, a municipal policeman waved us down at a flat dusty crossroads and in English told us we were the peace mission. Yes, we said, we are. He said we should proceed to the Park Hotel 'to meet with the rest of your team'. We explained that we were all on the van, but the policeman quickly lost interest, going to admonish the owner of a Polo who was blasting his horn behind our stopped vehicle. Bob drove on as Sara worried out loud that perhaps we'd been beaten into town by another theatrical collective hoping to bring peace to the region.

As ever, there were no welcome signs or children with flags, but arrival at the hotel felt like our most successful arrival yet. It was a low clumpy white building just outside the little kernel of the old town, set a way back from the broad beautiful Una River. The flat green-grassed land it stood on felt spongy with the possibility of damp.

Inside, there was even a reservation made for us, by 'Fikret Abdic' – Babo's proper name. They were trying to kill each other – the two pockets – but still accepting each other's hotel reservations. The receptionist spoke no English, but she smiled at us encouragingly and handed out keys with a certain flourish, like each new key was a further embellishment on an initial magic trick. As we signed in, a butterfly of hope started to flutter. *They were all double rooms.* Shannon and Sara took the first one, Sara fussily signing and depositing a passport while Shannon surveyed the lobby.

It was covered in a thin, hard-worn carpet, more lino-with-a-nap than carpet, and this stuff continued up the walls, where there hung lots of brown and green linear minimalist paintings. 'A Luxury Hotel' was the line it was trying to sell – you could see from the cream leather armchairs and settees dotted around the reception area. Their scalloped backs made them look theoretically sumptuous, but when I tried to sit, they were slidey, impervious to humanity and slightly off scale, really more suited to a doll's house for three-quarter-sized manikins.

Von signed him and Cally up for a room while giving me a sly glance to underscore that this was absolutely the last time he would be indulging her. The wheel of possibilities spun, but I didn't have to actually do anything. Mine and Penny's work together on the play had bonded us in the eyes of the group, so they arranged themselves around us. Christian and Onomatopoeic Bob took a room while Bev, smoking out of the front doorway, keeping an eye on the pistol he'd left on the bus, was billeted alone.

Penny signed us in, and I felt, giving my date of birth and handing her my passport out of my money belt, that this was a little like our secular marriage. My guts filled with popping, elevating bubbles at the hundred little intimacies to come: the washbags hung together, the shared shower room, the end-of-night reviews of the behaviour of our friends and enemies. I could look at her while she slept! That clean, clear, serious kaleidoscope of a face that I could never somehow quite fully understand – I'd have time to study it while she was unconscious. Not on a chair right by her. Nothing odd. But little glances, small crumbs to be broken off chunk by chunk from the huge treat I'd been granted. Yes, I was a happy man, even before I fingered the corner of the vast unimaginable hope that *something* would happen.

Then I saw him. And everything turned to fear and shit.

All at once he was among us. The murmur of a cheer went up and I had to join the rest in exclaiming how! and what! and wow!

'Simon!' Penny said and held his shoulders like he was the marvel of the ages. 'Fucking — *Simon?*'

Chapter 28

'How the fuck?' Shannon asked.

Onomatopoeic Bob embraced him as though they were old mates. Christian too. And shamingly, since he was the centre of the action, I too tried to get some allure to rub off by giving him a man-clasp of happy seriousness. I looked him in the eye like we'd had our differences but here we were, engaged in something bigger than both of us, and slapped him on the back. Before retreating, I made sure to place the briefcase down at his feet.

Simon kissed Penny on the cheek and then did the same, slightly more perfunctorily, to Sara and Shannon and Cally, and even to Bob, right onto his reddish bristles. Everyone asked all the questions again and he, well showered, clean and adjusted to the altitude, waited for the giddiness to die down. He invited us through to the bar where he calmly walked *behind* the bar and slid open a metal fridge door to pull out many beers. It was as though he actually owned the place; even the Deutschmarks he pushed into a tin after he'd counted out the beers looked like an after-thought.

As he opened the beer caps, we laid our bags in a pile. I retrieved the briefcase and pushed it into the centre of the impact-cushioning heap. Then we sat around him on angular dark wood chairs ready for our audience with the hero.

'So how the hell did you make it, man?' Onomatopoeic Bob asked.

'How long have you been here?' Shannon asked.

'So,' he said. 'Yeah. OK, after we got split at – what, Dover, so, yeah. I just thought for a while and I went back to London – this is what, this is only like, ten days ago? God, it feels – anyway – I was low – I sent a letter through . . . I don't know if that . . .' Penny nodded that it had indeed made it through, and then as he held her eye for a beat, she dropped his gaze flat. 'Um. What – er, yeah, where was I? – so, yeah, so I basically had a very big think about what I was going to do?'

'You wrestled with the thought-whale?' Penny said wryly.

'Er – I guess, you could say I . . .?' Simon wrinkled his brow. I looked at the floor and hoped he wouldn't ask what the fuck she was talking about.

'Yeah, then I thought, fuck it – and by then, I'd talked to your folks, Penny, and they'd spoken to a guy in Zagreb and he said you would be going to this place Velika Kladusa, and I just thought, fuck it.'

'Ronnie did . . .' Penny said. 'He told you we'd be going to Velika?'

'But . . .' Shannon started to say, 'we didn't know, did we, till . . . later?'

She and Penny looked at one another

'Yeah. He said Velika,' Simon said. 'So, I thought I'd come up through here and go up there and I flew to Split and then there's a British garrison there and they got me over the border and most people head for Sarajevo from there but I got a ride with some UNHCR folks. Sort of: Livno, Bosansko Grahovo, Tito's cave, then came out through the Krajina and in at the Izacic crossing?'

'OK. That works,' said Onomatopoeic Bob, generously, a map open on his lap.

'Yeah,' said Simon. 'And I've been here a few days, and it's a sort of a living nightmare and it seems someone dies almost every day, sometimes more. But the spirit of the place is remarkable. And how about you guys?'

After we'd told him about Croatia and Zagreb and the retreat under attack, the border crossings, Babo and his castle, the mercenaries and my minefield humiliation (this last in perhaps too great detail), people exclaimed the last 'fuck's and 'shit, man's and finished their beers. Then everyone but me smiled round at one another, pleased at this reuniting of the tribe.

*

Penny stayed downstairs while I took our bags up to the room. It was narrow and uncomfortable, the two single beds lined up against one of the walls, a narrow walkable area beside them and then a zone of jutting laminate-topped chipboard desk and wardrobe all built in together. A fluorescent tube buzzed above behind thick, ridged plastic. The small wall-to-ceiling tiled bathroom had a deep background odour of chemical-swilled waste that emanated from the dark corners beyond the lavatory. It was the most unerotic set-up imaginable.

Once I'd laid out our bags, I went back to the gang to explain that I needed to make good on my promised handover to Hamdo Abdic, the 5th Corps commander.

'What is it?' Simon asked

'I don't know,' I said.

'Right?' he said, sceptically.

'It's a briefcase,' I explained.

'Sure, but what's in it?' he asked again.

'It's private,' I said.

'Right,' he said and looked at me like I was definitely a dick-head.

'I don't know exactly what's in it. It comes from Babo. Fikret Abdic in Velika.'

'Ugh. Him,' Simon said.

'He was pretty good to us, actually,' Penny said.

'Well, they don't like him here.'

'He's actually created something pretty interesting up there,' Onomatopoeic Bob said.

'Yeah, well, it looks different from down here. Serbs on all sides. Dwindling ammunition. The pocket is on the verge of collapse and Babo collaborates with the enemy.'

Shannon talked about how multi-ethnic it seemed to be up in Velika and how wide was the availability of doctors, chiropodists and cheese, and how Babo had secured us passage south. Simon said nothing in response, but sighed heavily and let us know how deeply he was intertwined with the complexities of everyday life in Bosnia by telling us where we could buy chewing gum, tampons and bottled water, if we needed them; who Shannon should see at the town council offices about where best to stage our play; and suggested I start my search for Hamdo Abdic at a command post near the bridge.

I tried to trick Penny into agreeing to come with me. I claimed that I was rather scared of going alone, which was also in fact true. She looked at me. Men assume, on the whole, that women like men who are fearless, and I think that's probably right. But if you've no hope of success in pulling off the rooster-strut, there is always the geek gambit: the bid for intimacy out of an apparently frank admission of weakness. If it was a chess opening, I'd say it left you in fearful danger later in the game, but upfront it has a decent chance of at least getting things going.

As we approached the soldiers at the bridge, the Una River ran wide beneath. Aquamarine, churning around small green islands. I told Penny the story I'd read some days ago in my guidebook, that apparently it was called the Una because a Roman legionary on first seeing it had declared it the best, 'the Numero Uno River'. I'd been storing this up, a nut to roll out at a suitable moment, but now that I did, it seemed rather unlikely and not especially interesting.

'But, yeah, it's beautiful. It's a beautiful river,' I said.

'Yes,' she said.

How rich with fascinating insights and complex emotions I felt, but how poverty-stricken I seemed to be in terms of things I actually had to say.

The militia at the bridge did not speak English and my pronunciation of 'Hamdo Abdic' caused confusion. But as we persisted with our questions the two soldier guys got the idea that we weren't going to simply fuck off, so consulted a third guy who made some radio contact and told us in French to wait.

We stood smiling beside them for several minutes, but it soon became apparent this might be one of those waits that lasts hours not minutes, and we couldn't keep up our initial level of silent goodwill indefinitely, so retreated to sit on some sandbags piled up at the approach to the bridge.

'What do you think is in there?' Penny asked, looking at the briefcase I laid carefully behind the sandbags.

'Papers?'

'Why don't you look?'

'It would be rude to look. Don't you think?'

'That's very scrupulous of you, Andrew.'

'Yes,' I said. She was smiling playfully, but I couldn't really join in for fear she might next insist teasingly that we open the case, which would indeed be bonding, unless it exploded, and we were both blown to pieces, which wouldn't. 'I think that trust — especially to those we don't know — is something like the glue of humanity, don't you?' I said, and winced.

'Yeah?'

'I don't know,' I said. 'I'm such a dickhead.'

'Yeah?'

'I don't know, I say these things, but, I don't know. What does anything mean?'

She looked at me, trying to guess, I think, whether I was having a nervous breakdown. For my part, I was trying to grope towards some true expression, but also hoping I could stir up enough sympathy and confusion that I could admit to my poem treachery before it came to light. Maybe even mumble or cry enough to pass it off as confused passion rather than calculated duplicity?

'Why do you even hang round with me, ever?' I asked.

'Oh, I don't know. You're interesting. You're different,' she said.

Different. I was 'different'. That was something to work with. Different. Deviation from the mean. But, in which direction? Towards the oddballs and the Sasquatches and the men who keep their piss in jars and write equations with lumps of coal on their bedsit walls? Or towards the brilliant, the other-worldly, the Bowies and the Rimbauds and the people who reject bourgeois convention by fucking really really well for hours at a time?

Just then a Suzuki jeep arrived and an old driver in a dirty cream cardigan got out and waved to us. The army guys at the bridge instructed us to jump in and soon we were in the back seat. I tried to cushion the briefcase between my legs as we zoomed across the bridge and then veered right immediately afterwards, to the south.

'Are we going to the front?' I asked Penny, and then again, too quietly, the man in the cardigan.

'Are we going to the front?' Penny asked me.

'I think we are going towards the front,' I said.

'Hamdo?' the man in the cardigan asked.

'Hamdo Abdic,' I confirmed.

'Hamdo,' he said.

'Do you think Hamdo will be at the front?' Penny asked.

'Are you OK going to the front?' I asked her.

'No,' she said but smiled yes.

'That's exactly how I feel,' I said and I took her hand and she gave a companionable squeeze, and it felt natural and good. But when the moment came for a break and she started to withdraw, I gave an additional clutch and left my hand there damp around hers for what felt just a little too long.

It was a short drive till we were well past the outskirts and into a reedy suburb that petered out to nothing, a couple of premises bombed down to their foundations by direct hits. Then, past a barren rural crossroads, snuggling behind a mini-escarpment, was a farmhouse complex where, in a little three-sided courtyard, men in fatigues hung around smoking.

Some of the outbuildings looked historic – thick walls swelled from the ground; foundations of the earth, almost. The farmhouse itself was from the eighties, optimistic and open. Then, running down one side, there were newer, airy, metal-framed barns and stores. More men sat in these, on iron stuff, old machinery and boxes of military materials.

'Wait? Waiting?' I asked our driver.

'*Attendu?*' Penny tried.

Our driver pointed for us to head into the house. We went up the couple of steps to the door, towards men who might or might not have been guards. I held the briefcase up in front of me like the Chancellor of the Exchequer before he goes to deliver the Budget.

'Hamdo Abdic? Babo? English. Peace?' I said. We smiled around us and a guy came out, nodded to our driver, and motioned for us to follow him into the farmhouse.

The structure of the place had been badly shaken. There were cracks in the plasterwork spidering out from every corner. Some farmer's wife would be crying at what they'd done to her place. The carpet was still fresh and cream-coloured along the skirting board, but down the central portion it had become as browned and beaten as an outdoor path.

In the big back kitchen, where I'd anticipated men sticking pins in maps, there was actually an air of lassitude. As soon as we entered the room, the small man sitting at the head of the table had taken us in, and was already looking at his colleagues to see what they made of us, and then back to us to ascertain what we thought of the scene he presided over – all in the time it took for us to settle at the doorway. He had a long earnest face and, while his adjunct or staff officer came to greet us, he stayed pointedly sitting in his chair, leg on table, smoking a cigarette.

'We bring this from Fikret Abdic – from Babo – for Hamdo Abdic,' I said.

The man at the head of the table extended a finger up his nose rather elegantly, picked away at something in there and then mumbled something which made all his staff laugh. Penny and I smiled too, though so far as we knew he might have been saying 'Take them to the limepit and shoot them in the eyes'.

'Thank you, Hamdo says thank you,' the adjunct said. He came over to take the case from me and laid it on the table. I felt I ought to say something, at this point. An address from the Peoples of the United Kingdom, or a soliloquy on the virtues of the fighting man. But I just nodded to Hamdo, whose long grey face stayed granite-still until he said something to the adjunct.

'You have brought supplies also?' the adjunct asked Penny.

'Yes – well, brought supplies but they were – requisitioned, taken, by guards in the Krajina and in Velika Kladusa. But we will be performing a play, to promote the peace. As soon as possible, and we hope you may be entertained by it.'

The adjunct translated.

'Porno?' Hamdo asked in English, to big laughs.

'No, it is not porno,' I said, forced to be the straight man.

'Thank you. I am joking. Tell Babo we have received what he sends,' Hamdo said via the translator and looked me in the eye.

'Good. Thank you,' I said.

'Good,' Hamdo said and opened his arm to the doorway.

As we were walking back to our car, I imagined the walls of the farmhouse blowing apart behind us as we left, scattering the yard with plaster and shredded skin, organ blast and bone. Then, my only defence against court martial, torture as a spy, would be my own insignificance. You can't hang a pawn – our necks are too shiny and slim. My head rushed and my ears filled with static; I put my hand on Penny's arm to halt her and turned round.

'I'm worried,' I said, heading back into the room. 'I apologise, but I am worried it might actually be a bomb.'

My reappearance and the word 'bomb', easily translatable,

pulled the tension taut and a couple of pistols twitched in my direction. There was a moment of consideration and then some low laughter after Hamdo said something. Then he looked at me, clicked the case open, and said, via the translator, 'It is not a bomb. You can go. It is good.'

I apologised again and Penny and I retreated, while he carried on picking his nose and began to pull stacks of big-denomination Deutschmarks out from the case and piled them onto a stool at his side.

Chapter 29

'I think it's good we mentioned it, anyway,' I said as we were driven back towards Bihac.

'Why is he sending money, do you think?' Penny said.

'I don't know. It's interesting, isn't it?'

Before she could answer the whole plain of earth before us jumped — the thin flesh of soil and rock leapt up before bouncing back down to the ground beneath.

My ears rang. The need for physical safety, for shelter, to ball up, felt violently pressing, unstoppable, but before we knew what had happened — *was* happening — our driver had pulled up sharply and, following his lead, we all ran fast from the jeep to shelter within the walls of a broken building.

'What the fuck was that?' I asked.

'Was that?' Penny said.

'Bomba,' said our driver.

'Artillery?' Penny said.

'Artillery,' I repeated.

I looked at the wobbly single skin of red brick around us. It was a derelict pumping station, all smashed up now. The walls looked laughably insubstantial, like children's building blocks, and I imagined a shell popping through, leaving a ragged circle, and then turning us all 'inside out'. There was another pop, a whistle, then the thud of impact and again that bounce of the land like we were huddled near the rim of a vast trampoline. My chest vibrated like an oil drum thumped with a lump hammer. The blast resonated deep and fearful, taking you at once back to Passchendaele and forward to death. It was horrible. And the second after it was somewhat over, it happened again and I realised that it was possible for this to go on for more than the minute — or maximum two — I thought my nerves could survive. Artillery bombardments. What did I know about artillery bombardments? I thought maybe I could remember TV historians talking of hours or days of firing. But when? Was that the exception? Or the rule? I desperately wanted facts. Was that possible — days? Was that continuous? At what rate of pause between the shells? How incredibly foolish not to have made a precise note of such information at any point in my life.

Penny's cheek was pressed to the earth and I watched intently as a woodlouse crawled up into the clean tangle of braids piled on top of her head, tied and intermingled with a scarf. I tried to blink it away, but couldn't help imagining for a second the woodlouse crawling on round the back — and I saw us both dead, her head falling away behind like wet cake as the grey beetle marched on.

But for now we were both intact and she looked into my eyes ardently, like there was something urgent we needed to communicate to one another that might save us.

'Are you OK?' I said, my voice muffled through a temporary deafness so that I seemed to be far from myself.

'Yes. Are you?'

There was another pop and whistle and I was grasping at

something I thought I knew, something clever. Was it that the sound of the shell was . . . would reach us after . . . the impact, or was that impossible? We would in fact, we couldn't be dead, or we'd be dead before we knew it, before we heard it. Therefore, if we were hearing them coming, that meant, we were – definitely not dead?

'It's OK. I think, if we can hear them . . . I think, if we can hear them. We're OK?' I explained to Penny.

'OK?' she said. 'What?'

The awesome thud came in again and made the whole horizon quiver.

I started again: shells must travel faster than sound – surely? And sound travels more slowly than light so . . . didn't that mean that it was always the previous shell I was hearing when the land shook? I was confused. It seemed suddenly a terrible indignity to die at the hands of a shell I didn't even understand.

There was a lull of a minute or two between explosions. I looked at my fingernails, ragged around the edges although I didn't remember biting them.

'Should we go?' Penny shouted to the driver, who was leaning with just the small of his back against a wall, his face bent between his knees. But then another of the awful booms pumped the earth.

I found myself praying to God.

And as I did, there was a second lull. It lasted a minute. Then another. Then the time since the last shell was longer than the interval between any previous two shells. The rhythm was broken, and after three or four minutes our driver got up and brushed himself down like this was nothing much at all and walked back towards the jeep, eventually looking back at us. We hurried not to be left behind.

'Fuck. Are you OK?' Penny asked.

My ears still rang and I'd drawn blood where I'd bitten at the inside of my lip, but . . . 'Yes.' Yes, I was basically OK.

When we reached the jeep and were about to climb in, I touched Penny's waist so she turned and I looked into her eyes and said: 'If I should die, think only this of me.' She smiled wanly and I paused for a beat and then said: 'That I was fucking amazing.' She laughed and I laughed too and we couldn't stop laughing as we took off again at speed.

I felt a mini-wave of elation and wondered if maybe I did in fact believe in God? Or was I just another of these pricks God must know so well who tend to turn up during an artillery attack? Well, officially, the headline was, for the purposes of discussion and inquiry, that I was an agnostic. But secretly, I reckoned I thought two things. First, that there definitely wasn't a God. That all the tomes of Victorian scriptural analysis, the volumes of sermons, the theological debates of a thousand years were all nothing but the memory of pub talk about a shaggy dog story — as bonfireable as all the Communist doctrinal disputes of the past hundred years. All chaff. Product of a mass delusion, lies too big to question for fear of what lay behind the curtain.

But the second thing I felt deeply, and so secretly I could hardly admit it to myself, was that there most certainly was a God. I mean, on no level did I 'think' this. It made no sense. But if you could X-ray my essence, nestling in my skull or breast or above my gut, there was the conviction that we didn't just move as atoms through air; there was something denser around us that made us more important than lottery balls bobbling on the under-blast. This thing, this wrap-around of importance, I didn't call God, and it had no intention, but it *noticed*. It noticed me in

261

particular. If I had to characterise it grossly it would be: somebody who was keeping score.

After all, humanism and atheism, so far as I had made out, posited that we could keep score ourselves. That in our bones we know the rules of the game. And I bought that. You don't have to be a pope to know not to kick a baby. But also, I knew that some of the human scorebooks kept false accounts. That sometimes wins were recorded that weren't wins. And I knew there was a truth beyond this and I felt that the power of that knowledge went beyond the subjective. Essentially, I think I believed there was a God because I knew that Oliver Stone's 1991 production *JFK* was bullshit and this knowledge could not be countermanded by claiming it was a subjective view. I knew it was an absolute truth. And if that was so, who was keeping the record? Well, I was afraid, it probably had to be some form of that whiskery old bastard, 'God'.

Our driver offered us a hipflask. I took a swig and coughed and so did Penny.

'Slivovitz?' Penny said.

The driver shrugged like we were in the right area. He drank and we drank and the flask kept on going round in a triangular circle till we had polished it off. The spirit rasped and I could feel in distinct increments the change in my physiology as the alcohol radiated out, unmediated by my empty tummy, forcing the blood tighter in its vessels, everything plumping and quickening around us as we began to chatter loudly like children.

'Artillery attack. This is exactly what my dad thought would happen to me!'

'Disappointingly, from his point of view, you made it through,' I said.

'Oh yeah. If I'd got killed he'd be a bit sad, but overall I think the satisfaction of being proved right would outweigh it.'

'At your funeral they could do an order of service with a picture of you on the front with "Our Stupid Daughter" underneath. In a sad, curly font.'

She laughed and I laughed and then we saw a tractor that had got turned over at a funny angle by a shell blast so that it teetered against a tree trunk and we laughed at that too. We were pretty close, sitting there on the back seat as we bounced back into town over the Una, deep blue-green, flushed with health and a powerful look of good about it.

'What are you going to do when we get back?' she asked.

'I don't know,' I said.

'You should come to London.'

'Yes,' I said. 'Maybe I should. But I wouldn't know what to do.'

'I don't know, someone like you would find something to do,' she said.

The driver stopped near a Swiss-cheesed tower block on the edge of the old town, where, shadowed by another, lower, residential block, there was a cafe with a Coca-Cola awning still open for business.

'OK?' he said and gave us half a glance of invitation. We followed him in, past the empty front bar and down a corridor.

In the back room the shy filament bulbs above the pool table were overwhelmed by the blare of the fluorescent tubes from the roof, drowning the soft light out with the hard. A man in an Adidas tracksuit played a man in jeans and a thin green V-neck with drips of oil down at the belly. The balls clacked like gunshots and then got swallowed by the wide accepting mouths of the pockets. You had the sense that at any moment a man might come in and announce that the player who pocketed the black would take the loser to the outside toilets and cut his throat and no one would raise an objection or a note of surprise.

We ordered beer for ourselves and our driver and he raised his heavy dimpled litre stein in thanks. Penny and I revelled in the ugliness of the place and talked about the artillery bombardment and Hamdo, while our driver retreated to sit in a corner with a couple of other men and smoke cigarettes with determined, almost professional, focus.

Penny was a little high on lager and survival and she started to tell me the story of how she had once got drunk at one of her father's lobbying receptions and ended up being sent to a pub across the way from the National Portrait Gallery to buy a gin and tonic for the prime minister, because that was what he actually preferred over the champagne on offer.

I laughed and said it sounded 'mad' and she said she'd dribbled a glob of saliva into his drink as she brought it back, as a protest about Bosnia and the Criminal Justice Act. I raised my eyebrows and we clinked glasses and I said, 'Good on you!' but I didn't believe her. It was, after all, a story she'd told me before, but without the spit. And the carelessness of the repetition made me sad. I'd never have told her the same story twice. I could remember every one of our interactions. I could have sketched on a graph, I reckoned, pretty much each one and whether it was a step forward or back, or what kind of sideways it took the dance I hoped we were engaged in.

Word must have leached out about where we were drinking because in the end Bev and the rest of the gang ended up there. I cheered each new arrival, it seeming magical and magnificent that we were reunited.

Penny and I were quite a few units of alcohol ahead of the others. And as the rounds mounted up, we raced further and further ahead until blinking caused me mini head spins and I preferred it when the conversation rolled around me without requiring any input. I was a hero in my own mind, back from the killing fields, with a shifted understanding of mortality. But when asked what had happened to us on our trip, it turned out the best expression I could find to describe my new understanding of the universe and our place within it was to say, 'It was so fucking scary I thought I was going to shit.'

'Uh-huh. Sounds scary,' Sara said and then announced to Penny and me: 'So — we have a performance space. It is not a beautiful space. It is not an ideal space, but we have a space.' Apparently, the head of the Bihac municipal council had kept Shannon and the others waiting for an hour and a half outside his office, but when he made time he was supportive enough of the 'Peace War' to find a space and accepted Shannon's invitation to attend the command performance.

He had asked when the first performance could be ready and Shannon, Sara said, had 'looked at me and said, "Tomorrow?" and I was about to say, "Fuck no!" when he said, "Very well, tomorrow." So it looks like it's tomorrow.'

We toasted the impossibility of it all with more tall beers and chasers. Not seeing that they were in part ironical, Bev clashed his big lager glass heartily for the toasts and then homed in on Penny and me and Christian, scraping a wooden chair from a distant table, like more incoming ordinance, and spilling out to Penny what was on his mind. 'You don't see many of your lot here, do you? Have you seen any others?'

'What, Ned's Atomic Dustbin fans?' she said.

Bev was bumped, but then got it and laughed heartily, and what Penny had intended as a roadblock appeared to Bev to be an invitation to enter into foreign country.

'Yeah. But — what's it actually like to be black then?' Bev said, and seeing Penny's reticence, continued encouragingly. 'I mean, I can see it, you can see it, it's right there in front of our faces, it's all right to say, isn't it?'

'Uh-huh,' Penny said. 'I've given up trying to hide it.'

Bev exploded with a laugh, his face all red. And I winced because I could see he now felt he was on the verge of a frank exchange on the topic of race relations such as had never been attempted in all history.

'But what's it actually like, being black and that?'

'I don't know, Bev. What's it like being white?'

'Fucking good question. Brilliant question. Yeah.' Bev considered. 'It's just normal.'

I smiled at Penny and tried to deflect Bev into talking about the quality of Bosnian beer. But he wasn't easily deterred. He was still worrying away at the brilliant question of what it was, like, actually like to be black?

Was Bev a racist? I wondered to myself as he pursued the question. He certainly had that thing that is not necessarily racism but also very much not the absence of racism, characterised by too much interest in race. Pre-racism: the classification, the bringing up, like a bad burp, of jokes about racial characteristics – old ones, imagined ones, ironised ones, non-ironised ones – to consider them anew. Racist words, what they meant, who could use them, why he couldn't? So you felt in the end that his violin only had one string and you started to wonder if he couldn't maybe play something else.

'Yeah, white is normal for me, black's normal for you, isn't it?' Bev was saying, with a satisfied sense he was heir to Dr King, before he then felt able to push the point. 'But some of the shit your lot get up to, fair dos, I'm only saying this because we're on a level, but it's fucking disgusting?'

'How do you mean?' Penny asked.

'Are these litres? I think they're litres,' I said. 'Is a litre more than a pint?'

'What some of these guys get up to? Gives you all a bad name.'

'Is a litre more than a pint?' I asked insistently.

'Yes. What specifically are you thinking of, Bev?' said Penny and drank down a swirling half-litre.

'Oh, don't give me that, mate, fucking, you know. Muggers, rapes, etc. You can't be up for all that is all I'm saying?'

'Oh fuck off,' Penny said.

'I thought we were on the level?'

'I don't know what the fuck you're talking about.'

'We were on the level,' Bev said, confused and menacing.

'What level?' Penny said.

'On the level.'

'I don't know what you mean!'

'All right, let's fucking have it out then!' Bev said.

As Penny got up, I stepped across in front of her and hustled her down the corridor and out of the bar.

'Let's get out of here,' I said.

*

'He's basically a good bloke, in a way — we all are, aren't we? — but he is all right,' I found myself saying towards the end of a long attack on Bev which accidentally turned into a hymn to common humanity.

'I don't think he is,' Penny said.

'No, you're right. You're right, he isn't,' I said. 'But he could have been? I mean, he's horrible and wrong, but he needn't have been.'

267

'What, if everything was different?'

'Yeah. I mean, I know up there, and he's just ended up like that, when really I bet he could have been, he sort of is, in a way, all right?'

'Why do you keep saying he's all right?' Penny asked.

'I don't know. He's a dickhead. I don't know.'

As we made it to the kerb outside the hotel, she tripped one of those violent drunken trips where you fly to the floor before you know it. I bent to help her but she just rolled over on her back before scrambling to her knees and then a squat and finally, shakily, up, like she was an alien entity surprised to find herself in human form, with no idea how these limbs she'd been equipped with worked.

I sat on the wall with her and we waved goodnight to Christian as he passed. There was a riled-up and unfinished air to the atmosphere between us. We were both very drunk and we kept returning to how scared we'd been when the shells were landing, and what the dead woman in the river had looked like.

At the hotel we took more beer from behind the bar and I lifted my blue M&S T-shirt up to pull some Deutschmarks out. My tummy flashed bare for a second. Penny flicked a slap at it with the back of her hand. I laughed, tried to catch her hand, and then, having stuffed not quite enough money into the box, it seemed the easiest thing in the world to slide towards our room and start kissing at the door and fall inside.

Penny pulled me onto her on one of the single metal beds. She kissed me hard, but I kept finding myself slipping away from the moment, back to the bar, or forward to tomorrow and how clearly I might be able to remember the current moment.

It seemed we had an unnaturally large number of layers of fabric to deal with, and getting them off or aside or out of the way was surprisingly complicated and irritating. I was twanging at a lot of elastic and shuffling socks off my own feet and maybe hers, while somehow the fibrous blanket over the rough sheet wedged itself up between us and scratched at my bare chest. Eventually, though, we got sufficient portions of ourselves naked that we could lock in and she rocked me between her legs.

My dream had come true. But like a child on their birthday morning who joylessly unwraps the present they have moithered for all year, it seemed I'd imagined the moment out of being. I wanted to be lost in the passion of it, but I needed to piss again.

My cock doinged off her thigh, a blunt instrument that then prodded to find the good groove and, failing to nuzzle any purchase, like a branch under tension, bounced up, and flopped onto her belly. Penny was lusty but abandoned, not at all focused on helping me. She left me to tackle the mechanics while she waited for the good stuff to happen. I felt like a man in the rain, struggling to get the jump leads set up right so the engine will fire, while the other car owner absolved themselves of responsibility, waiting in the warm.

'Simon?' she said.

'What!' I said.

'What?' she said.

'What. It's Andrew,' I said. 'Yeah?'

'Andy?'

'Did you say Simon?' I said, shrinking in my own hand like a burst lilo.

'Andy. Simon?' she said.

'Andy. It's Andy.'

'*I know*,' she said, quite pissed off all of a sudden.

'You – just – I think you said Simon?'

269

'No,' she said. 'You did.'

From there on in, we misfired. She came on strong, angry-horny and pressing hard, which got me going a bit, but after a while she faded strongly, like a marathon runner hitting the wall, and left me feeling I was being over-ardent. Then I worried again she didn't exactly know that I was me rather than my rival, so I said her name a lot to prompt her to respond with mine, which she did from time to time.

Slowly, like a once vibrant religion, whose believers end up tempted away by less demanding philosophies, the sex died out. Each of us kindling it again for a moment, but then forgetting what it was we believed in. As the last embers cooled I forced a bump of excitement and squirmed out a curlicue of wallpaper paste onto her belly before drifting into one of those tiny sleeps you jerk out of suddenly. At some point, Penny untacked our bellies and moved down to her bed.

I looked at the beautiful twist and bow of her side, where adolescent growth had stretched her long and lighter spangles of pulled-skin had opened up. I suddenly saw how disastrously things had gone and tried to make a clean start, going over and kissing the top of her head, but it felt dry and unresponsive and it was all wrong. She kissed me with a gentle pushing-off pressure that sent me to the bathroom to sit on the toilet and feel the room swing around me, slow and sad.

Chapter 30

She was gone when I woke up. As soon as I came to, I raised my head off the pillow and saw where she wasn't with an urgency that lit up the red-hot shovelful of wet cement that filled my head. I tried to stay totally still. Left my head cocked like a gun dog, to stop my poor liquid brain from slopping up against my skull, throbbing for release.

There's a special slab of dead meat that sits in your gut on the morning of a truly terrible hangover. While your head crackles with an unfriendly fizz, the slab pumps out a venom. And the venom transmits a message of terrible foreboding: something awful happened. Something dreadful, last night, and all is lost. Usually some Coca-Colas and the passing of the hours eats up the bad meat. But on especially horrible mornings you feel that something awful happened the previous evening not just because you are full of poison, but also because it did.

In the hotel buffet room Von and Cally sat together, him morosely squirting mustard and tomato ketchup sachets onto a paper plate, where Cally was mixing and using them to 'paint' another plate. But neither of them was able to soothe me or help reconstruct the evening. Penny, they said, had upped and

271

gone with the rest to start rehearsing. I tasted one sip of bitter coffee and placed a dry cut of baguette in my mouth. Unable to chew, I tried to suck some sustenance from it, but nothing came and I took the bread out of my mouth and left it on the wood-effect plastic tabletop. I followed Cally and Von out, stomach churning, limping with self-loathing.

Bihac was tired, huddled and shell-wrecked. Yet the main drag of the town still bustled. No vehicles came through, so the many peasant-farmer women in headscarves and men with trousers tucked into boots gathered in the road, all vibrating with a nervous listlessness. They intermingled everywhere with young folk, students in bad denim, band T-shirts and white trainer-boots. I walked by like a young lady at a finishing school, trying to keep a pile of books on her head. My cargo was more volatile; if I nudged my brain in its box I felt it would pull a rip cord in my stomach and I would throw myself up, throw myself inside out.

There was no electricity most places, gunshot splatter across every expanse of exterior plaster and render. Many buckets. Generators here and there. Huddles of people with nothing to huddle over. No products to seek. People had blankets laid out with a few wares to sell or exchange. Nothing really of value; there was no diesel or bread or booze on the blankets, just piles of stuff the owners could live without.

We headed into the complex of municipal buildings that was to host the play, built in a higgledy-piggledy modernist tumble in the centre of the old town. The clerks looked reproachful as we asked where to find our friends.

'Will you tell Clinton how we live?' one of them said, to which Von helpfully answered, numbly, 'Yes. Sorry.'

'I think it was a rhetorical question, Von,' I said.

'These poor fuckers,' he said. 'They're trapped. They just have to fucking take it and starve. What fun is that?'

'No fun. It's true. It's no fun.'

The room we were to rehearse and perform in had a high ceiling like a school assembly hall, a stage under a proscenium arch, and chairs stacked all around the walls. Several holes in the fabric of the building had been patched up with breeze blocks and mortar – from the inside, so the repairs were more like the patching of a sandcastle with handfuls of wet sand than proper building work.

Once Shannon saw the three of us arriving she called us down to the front and shuffled herself to sit on the stage at the centre of our troupe. She wanted to make a little speech. I looked over to Penny, but she was fixed on Shannon, lips parted as though she might mouth along to her address.

We should be proud, Shannon said, of getting to Bihac. Then she stood up and started to prowl the stage in full Colorado Rocky Mountain lion mode. 'We should be proud of ourselves for refusing to listen to the cynical voices of inertia.'

Penny, eyes fixed forward in admiration, smiled at her. I smiled too.

'We believe in peace and we have seen on our travels that peace can happen. Even here, even now, communities, Serb, Croat and Muslim, can still cooperate. Tonight, we perform to the people of this town. And we have reason to believe that our performance here could push things just a little, nudge them perhaps, towards peace.' She went on to say that she had had another idea, if we wanted to hear? That if peace did not arrive, perhaps then we should consider staying in Bihac? All of us, '*even*, perhaps *especially*, if the situation deteriorates?' Shannon imagined we might become what she called 'hostages to ourselves' – who, like cyclists on a motorway, might terrify the powerful with our vulnerability. 'If the world – if our parents – fails to see that real people are dying here perhaps they might care if it's their own sons and daughters? Intervention, decisive intervention, is what is needed, we all know that. But they are too cynical to come. But we can make them come. We will make them come!'

We all clapped the speech and went to find the scripts we were supposed to no longer need. Looking at the words numbly, I walked up behind Penny and touched a hand out to her waist, but the way she turned, outwards, away from the hand, suggested that there was no continuum from last night. We were starting afresh, with no base camp of intimacy.

'Are you feeling OK?' I asked.

'No. I feel like death,' she said.

'Me too, I'm sorry,' I said.

'What for?'

'Just a – a generalised apology for being – I don't know. I feel terrible, and I have a feeling it didn't, we didn't . . . It wasn't what – perhaps – I just think . . . I wasn't . . .?' This was actually a pretty lucid expression of my feelings.

'It's OK,' she said, 'we were so drunk.'

'Yeah,' I said and looked at my feet, wriggling my toes in my Dunlop Green Flash, feeling I was letting too much of the evening fall into the category of things which were to be written off as no good and broken.

'I mean, it was fun but – just I was a bit drunk,' I said.

'I was very, very, very drunk,' she said.

'Yeah.' I pretended to laugh and then turned away and did a tiny gulp's worth of sick into my mouth. I headed out quickly to find a toilet as prickles of sweat forced themselves out over my entire body – I could feel the dewy specks, viscous with the resin of self-loathing, coating me entirely. I made it into a room that looked right and threw up into a dry toilet bowl. No water came from any tap.

It wasn't much of an extra burden I was putting on the besieged enclave, but the fact that up to this point my net contribution to their difficult situation had been to drink a good deal of the beer that was presumably not easy to come by, and then throw it up in a government building with no water connection, did not feel great.

I snuck away from rehearsal and back to bed, telling Von I was off to finally nail my lines. I did try, lying on the metal bed at the hotel like it was my own personal torture rack, twisting and turning, looking in vain for a calm stretch of pillow until my restlessness itself tired out and I subsided into sleep.

*

I made it back just in time for the dress rehearsal. Shannon had decided that we should forget the stage and perform our play in the round. A set of chairs was arranged around the walls but most of the townspeople were to be invited to sit cross-legged in concentric circles on the floor.

The dress rehearsal was such a shambolic effort that the fact I hardly knew my words was entirely lost in the barrage of missed cues and recriminations. That I said anything at all, at roughly the right points, put me on the side of the angels, so I was able to sit on the stage in between my few scenes and smile supportively as Shannon marched around, her hair swinging wildly when she wasn't tugging on it in frustration.

'Do you want this war to succeed?' Sara, the assistant director, shouted at Christian at one point, when he left the stage area in the wrong direction. 'Do you want this play to fail? Do you *enjoy* people being killed?'

To which he answered, 'No.'

Simon had been appointed lighting director. There was still power in the building and with some extension cords and desk lamps, a few interior effects were being attempted and two shocking blackouts. He missed the cues for both. The poor guy was working from a handwritten version of the script, the photocopies being a suddenly valuable commodity. There was neither copier nor paper available in Bihac, or at least not to us. Once the dress rehearsal had ended – with Sara standing in front of Cally repeating the word 'no' many many times, staring at the top of her bowed head until Cally started softly crying – Shannon called everyone to order. There would be another dress rehearsal immediately, she announced.

But since the 'soldiers' had performed adequately I was given a small number of rewrites to complete while Penny discussed higher matters and 'performance notes' with Shannon and Sara. Von, our narrator, was also released to look for missing props: a replica gun, a candle, a child's teddy bear, and some stage blood or 'Kensington Gore', as Sara revelled in calling it, as though the term was common knowledge.

The style of the play, a kind of phoney minimalism, meant the few speeches which weren't composed in this style stuck out badly. I fixed them by changing things like 'The bread is fine and chewy this morning, Ivana. Is Mr Tomic using a new recipe?' to 'Good bread. Bread is good. [Satisfied tearing at the crusts].' I finished the changes in under five minutes and then strolled the building, noting that there was in fact a working photocopier in one office.

Outside, Bev and Von were smoking cigarettes with a man

and woman from the Bihac European Community Monitoring Mission – charged with observing and reporting compliance with the non-existent ceasefire. They invited the three of us in to their sandbagged bunker near the town council offices and made coffee as they asked about developments in the UK indie music scene. Yves, with fine sandy hair and red-rimmed eyelids, delicate and rabbit-gentle, was attuned enough to the pop and whizz of sniper bullets and the random sprays that raked into town that, even over a mixtape of jittery techno, he could hear enough to say, 'Two Deutschmarks, four Deutschmarks, six Deutschmarks,' counting off the cost of each incoming round, while Elsa, stubby and sparkly, with bright blue eyes, marked down the shots as bars on a tally. It was comforting that someone was keeping count.

'Why do the Serbs want this shithole anyway?' Von asked as he opened a fresh pack of Drinas and offered them around. Though nauseous, I took one. Everyone prized cigarettes so highly in the enclave it felt like a dishonour to the situation not to always want another.

'There is a railway line south of the Una,' Elsa said. 'If the Serbs take that they have a rail line that runs from Belgrade via Banja Luka to Knin, in Serb Krajina. It makes Greater Serbia real.'

Yves showed us the line the Serbs wanted to push to on a map.

'I think the 5th could push them back if it wasn't for the Autonomous Province,' Yves said. 'That guy, Abdic. Babo.'

'He's all right. He's a decent bloke,' Bev said.

'Babo was encouraged by Lord Owen to think he should be president. But when that didn't work, he's been made a little king,' Yves said. 'He's a whore. I think now, these little pockets, that's the idea. The big powers, they want it all over with.

277

Security. So they like leaving us in these places. These little spots that the Serbs can squeeze. They only like the big countries, the negotiators. The proper countries, ones who can march an army past a podium.'

'Yeah, well, he's keeping bread in their mouths,' Bev said.

Yves nodded, considering the international position deeply. 'Is it true that the Inspiral Carpets will split?' he asked me.

'Er – I don't know. That's a good question?'

Von exhaled heavily and sat on Elsa's chair, as she left to phone through the morning's conflict report. When she returned, Von pretended to offer her back her seat, though he didn't rise, and when she demurred, he stayed sitting there guiltlessly as Yves continued to count the bullets and I rested my back against the sandbags.

Von tipped back on the chair and wobbled smoothly at the apex, rolling his body back and forth to keep his balance. He always moved smoothly, I thought – all oiled up with the condensed sweat of the toil of men and women going generations back in breweries and brickworks, foundries and plantations. All that labour expended and gathered up, caught and banked, making him secure in the unconscious sense that everything would, basically, always be all right.

Through a slit in the sandbags of the bunker he watched the students who were gathering outside the other functioning cafe in town, a coffee and pizza place across the way.

'Look at them. Fucking look at them, Andrew,' said Von.

'I know.' There were a number of boys and young women. One girl pulled the scarf from her friend. They were both very beautiful with dark hair and a coltish wobble to them as they skirted their pack, laughing.

Von made a groan of physical pain and leaned into my ear.

278

'If I wanted one of them. If I really wanted to, I reckon I could do one, don't you?'

'I don't know . . .'

'Yeah,' he said. 'Money, London, jokes. I reckon I could probably get a sucker off any of them.' He watched for a while again. 'If I needed to.'

'It's a beautiful sentiment,' I said. But it made me sad in the stomach. If he focused all his social, financial and cultural capital on one Balkan girl, I reckoned he might be right.

Eventually, word came down that the second dress rehearsal had reassured everyone considerably – the hall was now being vacated to allow Onomatopoeic Bob to make adjustments to the performance space, while some of the cast ran lines. I said farewell to our new friends and went with Von to eat dry pastries and drink carbonated drinks in the hotel bar, until, slowly, I started to feel merely unwell.

Chapter 31

The room was full for our performance. There wasn't much in the way of entertainment in the Safe Area. Television output was mostly war news, propaganda from Belgrade, shaky stuff out of Sarajevo and the US soap opera *Santa Barbara*. *The Three Amigos* had been cancelled due to the increased artillery attacks.

Our show was an event, in a town where there were many dramatic events these days, but not so many you would want to attend. As the company assembled behind the curtain and peeked excitedly out, there must have been four or five hundred people by 8 p.m., sitting cross-legged on the floor around the circular stage Onomatopoeic Bob had laid out.

Nervous and jiggling, we regarded our audience like a primary-school class before a nativity play. They had dressed smartly for us. Not in jackets and ties or dresses, but in their modest best jumpers, fresh jeans, shirts. Many of the women in skirts sat side-saddle, both legs to one side. There were students too, and a few more countryish types, looking bored before we had even begun, examining the interesting facts of the room, its height, the fabrics of the curtains. Then there was the municipal bureaucracy, the mayor, his deputy and the clerks and officials from the town council building, and a large number, maybe fifty or so, from the French UN garrison plus the EU and UN monitors (including Yves and Elsa), UNICEF officials and some Red Cross folk.

We were impressed with ourselves, as we looked through the curtain; and I was impressed with Shannon. Whatever else might go wrong from here on in — and there was lots that could — at least the night wasn't going to be a damp squib or a wet fart. They were giving us their attention. I looked at Cally and Sara, both tense-lipped, scared that they would not let the brilliance they knew was within them burst forth. For myself, I feared more a disjuncture between expectation and quality. That the audience were prepared for a feast and we were about to roll out a single raisin. Penny clicked her fingers alternately, noiselessly, very fast.

'Do you think it'll be OK?' she asked me.

'Yeah. I mean, if we have a failure — it's going to be on quite a large scale, so that's — really — good?' She was too busy worrying to smile but she nodded at the joke. 'Do you think it'll be OK?' I asked her.

'Yeah. I do. I think it's a good play,' she said.

'It is a good play. It is a good play. It is,' I said. 'I hope.'

The deputy mayor appeared. He was a tall, pale, long tree trunk of a man, a paper birch whose two knots for eyes were surrounded by flaking eczema skin. He told Shannon and Sara that they were about to shut the doors and we could begin, but Sara had a point to raise. 'Excuse me, but why aren't there more soldiers here?' she asked.

'I'm sorry?' the deputy mayor said.

'We were expecting and hoping for more soldiers.'

'The soldiers are — fighting,' he said.

'Exactly,' Sara said. 'This is to stop them.'

'Well, not necessarily, simply —' Penny tried to interject.

'If they stop fighting, the Serbs will kill us,' the deputy mayor said.

'Well. We can't know that for sure,' Sara said. 'And, we'll do our play for them too. And – also, will they, do you know that *really*?'

'It's true, it's possible they might not,' the deputy mayor said generously.

'Well, there you go.'

'There are some soldiers here, some who are not at the front?' he offered.

'Oh, OK, there are some here. Well, that's good,' said Sara.

There was a disturbance nearby and the deputy mayor shifted to give due deference to the new centre of the room. He made a great fuss of introducing Shannon and then, for some reason, Von to Hamdo Abdic. Atif Dudakovic – the commander of the 5th Corps in Bihac, the supreme commander of the enclave – could not be there, Hamdo explained, but he was glad to represent him here and send his good wishes.

His long cliff of a face was hard to crack. His eyes moved from within it slow and penetrating, like search lights seeking out something he'd glimpsed in you. Tonight he wore full battledress and a green army beret with the blue Bosnian crest on the front. When he spotted me he strode over and hugged me tight, as though we'd held out for a week together against a regiment of Chetniks, with nothing but a box of matches and a Ghurkha knife.

'Good day,' I said, for some reason, as he gave me a wrist-clenching handshake.

He repeated 'Good day' back to me, meaningfully, like this was what the English said, and I went on to say I hoped he would like the play. Then Shannon started to try to say something, but Hamdo, with a politician's nose for commanding a room, raised his hand, thanked us for coming and said he hoped we would tell our families, our friends and our politicians what life was like in Bihac. Then he sent his long finger back up his nose on another of its exploratory missions and he and the deputy mayor retreated.

Shannon breathed in deeply, kissed her hands to her lips and threw her love out at us as we formed up behind the curtain. Then, just as we were about to walk out, six people carrying guitars came and sat on the stage.

A pulse of concern ran through the troupe. Had we got everything terribly wrong? Had we been hijacked? Who were they and what was going on? All our collective pre-play anxiety was funnelled into the possibility that we were somehow not expected in the way we understood.

Sara nipped out and came back with the news, whispered round, that we were invited to go out and stand on the stage. Unsure if we were audience or show, we filed out and took our places standing uncomfortably behind the group of guitar players, who sat smiling over their shoulders at us from the lip of the stage. They were amateurs, Sara hissed, who had been taught by a local music teacher in the long hours of the siege and would now perform a song of welcome for us.

They had been learning for many months, and when they started to strum it was evident right away that they were awful. Their teacher winced as they picked out the chords to the introduction to 'Perfect Day' by Lou Reed. The singer was a very serious small woman in her fifties with curly grey hair cropped tight around her head. To her side was a thin bald professorial figure in a brown, wide-lapelled early-eighties suit. Then a guy who might have been a groovy shop steward in T-shirt and jeans and beside him a young woman with long dark hair and glasses who smiled to herself and rolled her eyes appealingly at her own mistakes.

They did the lyrics in English, speak-singing them out phonet-ically. My eyes prickled with tears. Beautiful music poorly played, common endeavour, shared humanity, it was all too much for my lovelorn state: these were my people. The derided, unglam-orous provincial lower-middle classes. The good people who put bird feed on the bird table, and I bit my lip hard to try to stop tears from coming.

When their song was over, the guitarists nodded demurely at us and departed. From there we had to busk it, because we had expected to come out from behind the curtains in a line — 'the spear of truth', Christian had called it, not quite sarcastically.

After a good deal of whispering and shuffling and with eyeballed rebukes rebounding around, we formed our line, with Shannon at the head. Then, as we walked down the steps from the stage into the circle, along a path marked by Onomatopoeic Bob with the 'detritus of conflict' — scrunched tinfoil and old cola cans — unexpectedly Shannon began to intone a speech.

'We dedicate this play, the peace play, *The Summer House*, to the hope that one day the armies of the West, the great forces of the world, will shift their focus from shadow-boxing a Russian bear who only now exists in their minds, and become an army of light. An army of the powerless and the persecuted. An army that will chase from the stage the murderers and the dictators and the warmongers. And when these armies march for good, all will fall before them. Because the people of the world will spill their hearts in support!'

We made it to the centre of the stage circle and held hands and hummed and then, when we had created a sufficiently portentous atmosphere, Simon threw us into black.

*

When the lights came up again Shannon and Sara had become good peasant women making bread in the kitchen together and singing a made-up peasant song based on the tune to a caravan show-room advertisement I remembered from Central Television in the mid 1980s.

I guessed, as I looked around, that a lucky 50 per cent or so had no conception of what was going on. They seemed, however, not unhappy to see these youngsters perform for them. A quarter of the audience appeared intrigued, like they were just about following the simple words of the play. And then there was a dreaded final quarter, I reckoned, who could understand perfectly every single word.

The domestic pre-war scenes progressed without laughs or engagement, as I dug the nails into the palms of my hands and felt black bituminous horror push through my veins like bad mercury rising. Anything, anything would have been better than this. A Noël Coward, an Ayckbourn, a Shakespeare, *Hobson's Choice*, a selection of misremembered *Python* sketches – anything but this.

I had many least favourite bits. Every time anyone said 'Serb', 'Croat' or 'Muslim' I shivered away from myself and closed my eyes like a child who imagines if he can't see, then maybe he can't be seen. Urgh. The hideous, galumphing naming of things! The production suddenly appeared to me as a great combine harvester advancing slowly through a field where stalks of truth, or subtlety, were growing. And we were threshing them all, leaving a swathe of stubbly nothing behind.

Soon enough, it was time for me to make my entrance as a swaggering drunk 'Serb'. Since the first rehearsals, Penny and I had been working on a jaw-jutting Cro-Magnon look to imitate the savagery of the men we believed we were portraying. Our antics initially provoked generous laughs. It looked like we might be the comic relief. But then we started to smash up the pretend rooms. I tried not to catch the eye of any single audience member as I self-consciously lumbered about, sweeping things from tables, pretending to urinate on a bed, enacting to the people around me a thinly imagined version of their own nightmares. After a degree of pretend destruction, Penny and I high-fived (was that something the Serbs did? Who knew? Who cared?) and departed the scene to sit on the stage, in character, miming ruffian chat.

Von was now called upon to dump quite lengthy wedges of exposition as a 'professor' who teased out the subtleties of the current situation in Bosnia–Herzegovina. Then, with a rapid flickering at the light switches, the summer house was bombed. There was a great deal of weeping, and the womenfolk formed into two warring factions with their menfolk, as Penny and I, now joined by Von, harassed and attacked them in a display of general savagery. To show even-handedness Von wore the Croat flag on a shoulder flash, me the Serb, and Penny wore none. We had discussed for a while whether she should wear an Islamic or Bosnian state signifier, but that seemed too much – so she became an all-purpose receptacle for malevolence. Time moved on. Von and I performed more smashing actions, about which we laughed raucously. Ha ha ha ha ha!

It was felt unseemly for Von or me to pretend to do a sexual assault, so that was left to Penny, which caused a ripple of confused interest as she pushed Shannon down to the floor and hip-thrusted at her while swigging from a canteen.

Then, finally, the play began – like a small failed business – to come to its undramatic end. The dead, Shannon and Sara, were buried. Von marched around with his rifle over his shoulder (a real rifle since that was easier to come by than a replica), and we formed a circle to demonstrate how sustaining common humanity could be in the hour of need. 'We are a village, you shall not break us!' we shouted at the end. A conclusion not entirely demonstrated by the action that had preceded it.

Simon slightly mistimed the blackout, so for a second or two we all stood there, our eyes anxiously flicking over to him before we disappeared. It was not good. Still, it did at least provide a definitive end.

The applause was long and loud and we made six or seven bows before retreating up to the stage and back behind the curtain.

Pathetically, my dead certainty that this was the worst piece of theatre ever conceived began to ebb almost as soon as I was behind the curtain. Everyone circled round. Onomatopoeic Bob was sweaty and exuberant. Christian shook my hand. We back-slapped and hugged, laughing away the little mistakes we'd made, mistimed cues, paraphrases, ad libs. Had the audience not clapped? Was Penny not smiling broadly at me? Did it not feel pretty good? The first two or three times I said 'That was great, you were brilliant' I was certainly lying, seeking out from someone around me a hint that they, like me, had been so deeply embarrassed by the whole abomination that they could have cracked walnuts with the power of their clenching buttocks. But then there was a middle period, an interregnum, where I was acting, but buoyed, and the feeling like a toddler was sitting on my chest started to lift. By the time Shannon hugged me, holding me tight and swaying me and saying 'You did it, you did it', I wondered if perhaps I hadn't, in fact, to some extent, done it? After all, I did tend to be hard on myself. Maybe I was so self-critical I had mistaken gold for horseshit? That was possible. Perhaps Chekhov hated everything he wrote? That may well be. My standards were high. If everyone else said it was a triumph, who was I to say otherwise? Wasn't that a certain kind of vanity? To resist the praise?

Penny embraced me, saying that Simon himself had told her it was a minor masterpiece. And I noticed that my first reaction was to note the qualifier. I mean, if it was a *potential* masterpiece, which I doubted, but if it was, there was probably nothing *minor* about it . . . Onomatopoeic Bob was saying we should take it to Edinburgh and Shannon was talking about her friend in the theatre scene in Chicago and Penny and I embraced again and I shifted my hips back so my groin was far from hers and I could make sure this was a plain sweet hug of victory and friendship.

Penny whispered into my ear that, as he departed, she'd seen Hamdo pound a clenched fist against his heart. (Indigestion, the imp in me said.) But no, probably, as everyone else thought, once she told them too, the commander *had* been affected. Our message had been transmitted at the highest level! I smiled at her and nodded soulfully, and she smiled back and then she looked over at Shannon, who was talking to Simon, and walked off, leaving me with Sara, who was talking fast to an older gentleman who'd made it back to see us. He'd been a professor before the war in Belgrade, I learned, but had come home when the conflict started to look after his very own summer house.

'It works on different levels,' Sara was explaining.

'Yes?' he said.

'There's a level below what's happening. It's actually saying, take a look. Stop just for a moment and think about your common humanity.'

'I suppose for the people here – the message of peace . . . it's a little more complicated?' I said.

'Yes,' the professor said.

'Everything's always too fucking complicated,' Sara said.

'Yes,' the professor said and looked like he was willing to leave it at that.

'Peace? Yeah? You understand?' Sara said.

'Peace. Yes, very good, peace,' he said. 'Do not shoot today the man who wants to come kill you and your wife tomorrow?'

'Exactly,' Sara said, distracted, looking over at Shannon.

Von walked past us and did a clasping handshake with a smile and a wink which pressed into my palm a little white pill. He certainly knew timing. We were at the top of something and he had the hedonist's urge to push everything to the maximum. Most beautiful sunset ever? How about seeing it stoned! Breaking into the crypt at midnight? Why not trip while you go! Sara gobbled hers without hesitation, and after looking over at Penny and Shannon, so did I.

I peered over at Penny and Simon to check they were not 'sorting everything out', which was my great fear. But no, he had walked off to congratulate Christian on his performance. Penny talked fervently with Shannon, and when she glanced over at Simon there was no warmth, I reckoned. He gestured to her queryingly when Von gave him a pill, but she gave the shortest smile and glanced back to Shannon. It looked like my poetics had created a virtuously vicious circle, whereby she was reluctant to engage in the very conversations which would allow the details of my sabotage to be revealed.

I did fear, though, the effect that Ecstasy might have. After all, I thought, a hippy or BBC television had told me that it had started out as a relationship drug in some Swiss castle to help Hemingway types express their difficult feelings to their distant wives. But this worry was itself chased away by the first effects of the pill, the twinkle of moon dust popping candy drifting up my back.

I was pretty good at drugs. Rural provincial nothingy England doesn't offer you much, but if you want, it will teach you how to roll a very straight joint and say yes to any pill that comes to hand. That's the basic skill of drug taking. Saying yes. Not too much fucking around. I could see Cally was meandering around the question, holding her pill in her palm and talking to Christian, who was also looking for little clues on the surface of his pill, asking it the amateur's question: Will you kill me?

Von pushed out beyond the gang to offer his stash to local girls who'd stayed hanging around, and – where he had to – boys. Bob, meanwhile, wrestled with the audio leads to connect our Sanyo tape player to the hall's PA system. It came to life in a very loud burst of familiar magnetic-tape wobble we all knew from the van. Then, in a way that would have felt embarrassingly literal if I wasn't in the midst of getting all that kind of self-consciousness washed away, as the vocal came in, and Bobby Gillespie sang that he was moving on up, I started to come up on my pill.

*

The party never started very clearly. At first it was us standing around. There was a little white wine in thin plastic cups; Yves and Elsa from the bunker congratulated us; there were still many municipal folk in the room; adults, I think, at that point. Most of those people started to evaporate when the music kicked in and even if they didn't know what exactly was happening, they felt the atmosphere change as the first off-kilter smiles went round.

Then there was a bad road bump: I clocked that Von was being questioned by a municipal policeman at the hall's door. I went to hide from events by the tape player. But on my way, Simon intercepted and told me that the cop had become aware pills were being offered around and took me over to join the discussion. Von claimed he didn't know what the guy was talking about. Then the cop opened up his fist and held out one of the pills in his palm as evidence.

The night balanced on a cusp. Would the drug dealing and smuggling be waived, like a broken indicator during a bombing raid? Or would someone be summarily executed? We were in a war and wars are history, and you can get chewed in the cogs and come out a funny shape, or not at all, when you fuck with history. The cop was angry. He shouted something at Von. Yves and Elsa translated for Shannon, who tried to smooth things over. Then, presumably to prove its safety, Von plucked the pill out of the policeman's hand and just ate it.

'It's fine. It's nothing!' Von said, performing a kind of magic trick on the problem. Elsa said something soothing and with the disappearance of the offending item, and the fact that Von wasn't writhing on the floor, it was as though the offence had disappeared. The pill was the problem and the problem was gone.

'No body, no crime,' Von said confidently and waltzed off on his double dose.

The policeman's intervention came to be symbolic of all the fractured events of the night, as time sped in jags away from itself and the kaleidoscope shifted and threw us all together in different patterns. I was high. My stomach ground on itself and I felt the play of benign electric across my skin. I tried to remember all the fascinating things I was thinking but didn't really mind forgetting. Soon, Bev was dancing towards Christian, who did a military two-step in circles, ironising the thumbs ups that the mercenary was showing him, yet still not rejecting him.

Then Bev was suddenly a friendly chatterbox at my side. He said he'd apologised to Penny for whatever he'd got wrong in his inquiries about the souls of black folk and she'd told him he was just a big arsehole, but he was sure it had all been somehow very friendly and rather brilliant and he carried straight on, telling me the name of his primary school and his secondary school and recounting his whole life like repeated throws of a grappling hook, looking for a connection to pull us close. It started to become funny to us – hilarious – that whatever place or name he dug up, I never knew it, and then occasionally I would pretend that I did.

'Pete Broomwood?'

'Pete? Big lad?'

'Yeah!'

'Yeah, never heard of him.'

And we'd laugh, getting a connection out of our lack of connection, and like toddlers doing the same old joke over and over again as we leaned against a corner of wall away from the action and smoked his Drinas, which now slipped down like silvery chains as I tried to explain to him about race and culture and which things I thought you could look at straight on and which you couldn't.

'It's like . . . it's like, I don't know, I know you're all right, and you know I'm all right, but if I just came to you and said, "What's it like being . . .?" I dunno? What could I say that would be a bit . . .?'

'I dunno?'

'If I said, "What's it like being a meathead?" I mean, that's not the same, cos being a meathead is bad but being black isn't bad, but it – white people used to think, it was, so it's like –'

'Yeah,' Bev said. '. . . You think I'm a meathead?'

'No, I'm saying –'

'That's OK.'

'No, what I'm saying is, what could I say that would hurt your feelings?'

'But she is black and I'm not a meathead?'

292

'Yeah, I mean —' and I thought I could see in his eyes that I was allowed this —'you're a *bit* of a fucking meathead,' I said and we laughed.

'The thing is, I'm not always sure my sister makes as much use of it as she could?' Von interjected. He'd joined us in the delicious through-draught of the corridor. Just then it seemed the best place of all. Like when I'd been dancing: inconceivable that anyone would want to do anything else. Now it was clear that this spot was the centre of joy in the whole wide world.

'How do you mean?' Bev asked.

'I just think, I'm not criticising, but you know, I think I'd make a good black guy,' Von said.

'Yeah?'

'Yeah,' Von said. 'Oh yeah. Fuck yeah. I wouldn't take any shit.'

'I wouldn't take any shit if I was black,' Bev agreed.

'You see some black guys and you do think, sometimes, are they *wasting* it a bit? I'd be like — I'd wear a hat, like a top hat. But also trainers? And know all about the euro. I'd be into hip hop *and* classical. Yeah?'

'You'd get a fuck of a lot of fit girls,' Bev noted.

'I would,' Von said and nodded seriously.

On the dance floor an old man, forties at least, danced among the peace-play folk and the local kids and I joined the pack. I tried to ask some of the locals if they were on pills or just friendly, but my question seemed to get lost so I smiled and didn't want to know any longer and danced with three boys who stomped their rhythm hard into the floor and I thought I was a soldier marching with them somewhere to do something brave.

Then Sara was shouting in my ear, her breath hot, and I thought she looked so attractive, her torso wriggling to the music in a black elasticated leotard top. I told her I was sad about her and Shannon having a difficult time, because they were both so good. I explained I'd almost been sort of married to someone, or at least we had lived in a house, so I sort of knew what it was like, a big relationship, and I think she heard me and she said something indistinct and punched the air and danced off. But I felt proud of us all, of the whole gang, for coming.

'Even if nothing happens, even if we make things worse, I think it was worth us coming, don't you?' I said to Penny and she gave me a hug and nodded.

We must have played *Screamadelica* five times in a row until it was half a joke, half an addiction, then we put on a tape of Von's low-quality DJing, and though the execution of the mixing was very poor, the songs were good.

For a while, sometime after two, the lights went out totally and we danced in the dark and then by the flash of Bob's head torches. Through those minutes or hours of dancing in the black and flash, I imagined my solid middle was a fishy shimmer and my retreat-from-Moscow-steps were tap-dance quick. It was like a non-sexual orgy. Warm bodies in the dark, bumping without fear or favour – let the bearer pass without let or hindrance.

At four or so we were out in the warm air, still smoking cigarettes that came from somewhere, and Simon had an arm round me. His hair was wet but somehow his shirt was soft and dry. How was that?

'I didn't, you know. With Pen. In London?' he said.

'It's fine. It's all fine,' I said.

'I don't think she even likes me,' he said and I said that I thought she did, and though a flutter of guilt made its way through, I didn't feel the need to confess anything. The tidal surge of serotonin told me everything was for the best in this, the best of all possible worlds.

Chapter 32

When the lights flickered on and a caretaker cleared everyone out of the municipal hall, we reassembled in the bar of the hotel. It had a low ceiling and the smoke soon banked up in layers. We took possession of it comprehensively, Simon arranging for us to buy cases, boxes of beer. We asked permission from the night porter to rearrange the furniture, dragging one of the small slippery settees from another part of the room; and he neither assented nor disapproved, just walked his beat behind the front desk. For a while every time someone skinned up they did it in the toilet and we smoked the joints out of a big picture window that pivoted open horizontally from its middle. But in the end Von said, 'I'm making a herbal cigarette,' and Yves tried to translate, but the porter was uninterested, so joints were on the go all over by the time the armed men arrived to lock us all in.

The lead officer I recognised as Mr Miami Dolphins from the checkpoint, although a new cap suggested that maybe his real allegiance was to the Minnesota Vikings. He didn't wear a patch today, and where his eye was missing, the flesh puckered up like a tied balloon. His initial announcement was in English. We were, he said, to: 'Stay in hotel, for safety.'

We were full of an enlarged sense of humanity; our empathy glands throbbed. Was everything OK? Was everyone OK? we wanted to know. He strode in with two other guys who went about closing and padlocking the emergency exit doors. 'Not to worry, not to worry, all is good,' Minnesota Vikings announced, and was gone. We were left with a taciturn guy guarding the front entrance of the hotel, his rifle slung low like Peter Hook's bass guitar. We offered him cigarettes, we offered him booze, but his responses were terse. He emanated bad vibes.

Outside, the world was turning grey and real and when, in response, we turned the Sanyo up full blast, we chased the last of the night away even as we pursued it. One after another we tried to gauge what had happened and what this lock-in related to – the play, or the drugs, or the conflict – and one by one we went to see our guard with his gun, and tried to make a man or woman or human or food or drink connection.

Our huddle grew tighter and a rumour came through from Yves via the night porter that the French UN garrison was also confined to barracks.

'What does it mean?' Penny asked.

'Could be anything,' Bev said.

From the centre of town, we saw a couple of curls of smoke, and shortly after came the sounds of artillery rounds and then small arms fire.

'That is not – that is from – that is not coming from the normal positions, is it?' Elsa said and she looked at Yves.

Gunfire continued to pop and crackle, without rhythm or orchestration, no crescendo call or reply.

'Are the Serbs coming? Are the Serbs here?' Shannon asked.

'Could be. Could fucking be,' Bev said.

'I don't know,' Yves said. 'I don't think . . . that's coming from the area for it to be . . .'

'Is Babo coming? Has Babo's lot pushed south?' Simon said.

'Hmmm,' Bev said. 'Maybe.'

'It's possible but . . .' Elsa said.

'Could the Krajina Serbs be pushing in?' Christian said.

'Or NATO. Could it be NATO? Are NATO coming?' Shannon wondered.

'I really think that is not likely,' said Yves.

Tripping on MDMA through automatic gunfire was something I had never experienced before. But one of the effects of the drug is to declaw reality, so nothing seemed too scratchy. Sitting there through the war felt not unlike certain nights at bad clubs in Liverpool and Stoke and Manchester: Konspiracy and Quadrant Park, the Kitchen in flaking Hulme, where Helen and I had gone in shaky overloaded Fords.

'We'll be OK,' I said to Penny as I passed her a cigarette. 'We'll be all right. People survive. Laurie Lee, Orwell, that Mitford, they all came back from Spain.'

'Well, not the ones who died?' Penny said. 'The Julian Bells. They didn't write any books?'

It struck me forcefully that this was true. The dead don't write their books. And I suddenly felt strongly that those were actually the books I really wanted to read. The ones that didn't exist. The missing ones. It's so unfair, the tyranny of the living. The shouty beating ones making out the whole time that the survivor's story is the true story.

I blinked my stinging eyes in the fugged-up smoke. My throat was just starting to register a rasp from all the Drinas. The drugs were thinning out and my elastic spinal cord was beginning to suffer the first injection of crunchy calcium. Minnesota Vikings returned and spoke to the guard out front. Yves, Elsa and Shannon went to ask questions and soon returned with news.

'OK. Fuck,' Yves began and took a big breath. 'Well, if you want to know the situation, it seems it is this: we are in something. A local commander is leading, in a coup against this town authorities and the 5th Corps. These people, the coup people, this so-called Peace Force, including our guard, they want to join with Babo in Velika and make a pocket of peace.'

As we tried to take this in, Shannon, by Yves' side, clasped her hands together to make it clear that it was possible our mission had come to fruition in the most extraordinary and immediate way possible. The Forces of Peace were on the march!

Onomatopoeic Bob called it the Miracle of Bihac, playfully, but it only had to get said three or four times before the playfulness rubbed off.

'It's a little – civil war,' Yves said. But Shannon just shook her head in dumb wonder and went around kissing each of us in turn on both cheeks.

The gunfire started up again very close by, so that it echoed off the buildings. It made us huddle together in the bar. There was a bite now to the skitter – each burst followed by the shatter of glass, plaster getting cracked and hewn.

'What are they . . .?' I said to Bev.

'You don't fire a gun at nothing,' he said. People were probably dying nearby.

Our guard came in from outside to check on us and he didn't seem so comical in his reticence any more. What would the Bihac town forces do to collaborators if they managed to resist the coup? Everyone knew we were on the side of peace, that we had arrived in Bihac directly after visiting Babo. What would they do to us? I looked up at the ceiling that was bobbled with a sort of pebble-dash, sealed in a thick smooth plasticky gloss paint, and imagined the whole lot getting shattered and blood-spattered by a hand grenade rolled in on us.

The small arms fire ended, replaced by more artillery thuds. Yves made a call from the hotel payphone. Many numbers weren't working, but he came back with a report that apparently the 5th Corps central HQ was taking a pounding; that the battle in the centre of the town had subsided; some dead, many dead. But the town was definitely going Babo's way. That was the word.

'Good,' Penny said and looked at me seriously, as if our view of events was significant.

'Good,' I echoed. 'Good. Yes.'

'What the fuck?' Simon said and took a joint end from Onomatopoeic Bob.

'If Babo wins, there can be peace,' Penny said. 'People can get back to their lives. Supplies, school. We've seen it up there. Everything works."

'But Velika isn't free,' Simon said.

'Well, I don't know about that?' Penny said.

'It's safe. The people are safe,' I said.

'I don't know,' Simon said. I looked at the joint before him smouldering. 'Freedom, it – it doesn't do much except jam the door open to everything – but anything that shuts the door has to be mistrusted,' he said.

I looked at the floor with as much rueful scepticism as I could muster, wobbled my head and jutted my lip and tried to marshal my view into a paragraph. We had been there. We had seen the peace pocket: warm and dry and well cared for.

'People. Save the people. Don't hurt people. That's first. Just keep the human bodies, safe,' I said. Penny was listening, but she didn't look convinced.

'Maybe?' Simon said. And I looked to Penny again, for her to chip in, but she just shrugged. It was particularly dispiriting, not just because I was losing the argument, but because the views I was expressing were not mine at all, not mostly. They were a reimagined version of stuff she'd said in Manchester at our meetings. I was presenting them back to her like a cat delivering a dead mouse to the kitchen mat as trophy and expecting some reward. But it seemed she couldn't even be bothered to agree with herself.

'Who is POUM here?' she said eventually. 'Maybe Babo is POUM and Itzbegovic and the 5th are Stalin?'

'Or maybe Sarajevo is Barcelona and Velika is the Lubyanka?' Christian answered.

'How do you mean? What?' I asked and they both ignored me.

*

I loaded up with a fresh round of Coca-Colas. When I came back, Simon was seated next to Penny on the slippery sofa. I had to ignore their body language and accept at face value Penny's claim that I wasn't interrupting anything.

'But you did get it?' Simon asked.

'Yes,' she said, and no more.

'And did you like it?' he prompted.

'Er, sure. Sure.'

Wearing a face of frozen terror that I tried to thaw into something animated and lifelike, I handed them their drinks, hoping to break the moment. But Simon took his bottle without looking at me.

'I worked hard on it,' he said.

'Oh, I'm sure,' Penny said, smiling infuriatingly.

'I think it said everything I wanted it to say.' He knew it was a lovely little poem, the one I'd ripped up, and thought he knew she was clever enough to know this too. So why wouldn't she admit it?

'Sure,' she said.

'So is there any chance of . . .?' he began, glancing at me to fuck off.

'Of what – you pushing your "sea urchin" into my "clam"?' she said. To which Simon smiled quizzically, getting that there was a reference here to something but not quite able to summon what.

If Penny had read his face, rather than looking rather melodramatically straight ahead, she might have caught the truth: that he'd never heard this line before in his life, let alone written it.

'Er – well, of – of . . . how do you mean?'

My natural inclination is always to clear up a muddle, but I thanked God for this one.

'I'm not sure I'm ready to climb up, or down, to the sea with you, OK?' she said.

'All right. OK. Fine,' he said, tetchily. She was talking in riddles. And he sat back defeated, letting his aching jaw ride some circles now normal sensation was returning to his muscles after the chemical tremble of the night.

*

Once there had been no shooting for an hour or so, finally, sitting with my back against a wall, I slept. Or pretty much slept. It was that thin walking-on-frost sleep where half of you is being dragged under by deep physical tiredness but half is being tugged awake by pips and spurts of chemical still frazzling in the blood. Sara went to her room to sleep, but the rest of us stayed together.

301

Huddled like sheep, warm to each other from the night before, and sticking close in case we needed to dart from the wolf at the door.

I was woken from my dribbly slumber by Simon sitting down deliberately hard next to me. It was like waking to a nightmare. My head crackled. I was confused.

'I know what you did, you fucking shit,' he said.

'What?'

'You tried to fuck me.' My guts filled up with cold water drawn from a deep well.

'What?' I said, recalling where I was and that this was true.

'She showed me the poem. She doesn't want to believe you switched them. She doesn't think you're that kind of shit. But I think you are.'

'I'm not,' I said, then remembered, like in a crime drama, to add, 'I don't know what you're talking about.'

'Let's go and talk to her. If you say it wasn't you, maybe you can explain what happened? All right?'

I followed Simon's gaze beyond the bar, beyond the reception area, through into the plate glass of the refectory-restaurant, where I could see Von and Bev eating cereal from bowls. Penny sat on a nearby table massaging her temples. Simon offered me a hand to pull me upright and I was ready to follow him to my execution, to let the pain of the situation at least be anaesthetised by its drama, when across my line of vision came Hamdo Abdic, marching into the hotel past our grim-faced guard and followed by Miami Dolphins/Minnesota Vikings and a phalanx of foot soldiers.

After a word to the porter at reception, he came through and stood at the top of the short set of steps which led down into the bar and started to talk via his translator, Minnesota Vikings. Joints were still being extinguished. Von and Bev, Penny and

Christian were still making their way from the refectory, but he didn't wait. He gave no quarter. His authority had its own authority; it didn't need recognition.

'Good morning. I am here to inform you that through last evening and this morning a successful operation has taken place to remove the illegitimate command structure of the 5th Corps. They will no longer be holding Bihac pocket under their control. Atif Dudakovic has handed himself over to our forces. Members of the district assembly who were not willing to cooperate with the new town authority have been taken into custody.'

Shannon stood behind Sara and hugged her from behind. History was in the making! Von positioned himself to do the same to Cally, looping his arms over her shoulders and giving her breasts a very quick 'honk' on their way to clasping over her belly. She didn't seem to object.

'The Peace Force is now in full control. As soon as the necessary arrangements can be made, Bihac town, Cazin and the rest of the southern pocket will be reunited with the Autonomous Province of Western Bosnia,' Minnesota Vikings said, hurrying to keep up with Hamdo, as he yammered out the sentences. It seemed he had already delivered this speech a number of times and was growing bored of it. The relative proportion of admin to action is very high, even in a coup, I guess.

'We will be making a statement to the international agencies and representatives in the area such as yourselves throughout today,' he said. We looked at one another with not a little pride. Us, in our van, with our ghee and bleach, were international representatives!

'And reports as to the situation will be made on local media, which we, the Peace Force, are already in control of, as we are the rest of the town.' This repeated claim regarding the extent of the victory was the only thing to raise any doubt. Had Hamdo won? Or was this a premature declaration?

'And to cement our legitimacy of the announcement we are seeking representatives from among the international community to announce on Bihac Radio the current situation.'

And then, shockingly, like a shop mannequin speaking, Hamdo said in English, 'I want some to come now please. Come.'

He looked directly at me. I looked to Shannon. The gang huddled up while Bev, Yves and Elsa approached Hamdo and asked a number of questions.

'OK. We don't know what the fuck's going on. We stay here and sit tight. This guy showed up once before the play, we don't even know who he is,' Simon said quietly and quickly into the huddle.

'Well, we know him. Don't we, Andrew?' Penny said.

'Er, yes. Yes. We met him, we saw his HQ. When I took him something. When we went yesterday.'

'What? What did you take?' Simon asked.

'I don't know. From Babo. Maybe money. I don't know. We just took it.'

'For fuck's *sake*,' Simon said.

'I'm going to call for advice,' Von said, heading out towards the reception as Onomatopoeic Bob laughed after him:

'Good luck!'

'I think we go. Who should go? I should go,' Shannon said.

'Shannon. No. No. No no no no no no no no no,' Simon said.

'Very persuasive,' Christian said.

'Well argued,' I said.

'Well, who the fuck are these people?' Simon asked.

'They're the Peace Force. They actually call themselves the

Peace Force, Simon,' Onomatopoeic Bob said.

'Yeah, but if I called myself Dave the Egg you still couldn't dip your fucking toast in me.'

'No, but still,' Penny said.

'It would probably imply you at least liked omelettes?' I said, thinking it would sound more playful than it came out.

'They are bringing peace. Right?' Shannon said.

'They're fucking – collaborators,' Simon said. 'Collaborators paid by Andy.'

'Hey,' I said.

'I don't know if you have the right to use that word, Simon. Helper is, anyway, another name for a collaborator?' Christian said. 'Got to be careful of labels.'

'Helper *is* a nicer word,' Onomatopoeic Bob agreed.

'OK, they're helpers, of Babo, who are helpers of the Bosnian Serbs, who are helping people into shallow graves all over this country they're helping to pull to pieces.'

The truth was I had no idea what we should do. I tended to submit to men, especially with guns, who told me to do things. The room available for personal choice felt radically curtailed. I didn't really think I could be held to account for anything we did right now; we were just acting as required. They said to go to the radio station and report what was happening, and what was wrong with that? It was only Simon's presence that made any of us need to think about it at all.

Yves, Elsa and Bev were getting moved aside and Hamdo began to turn his attention to us, just as Von returned, bounding in like a red setter. 'I got through. I spoke to Dad, he says, to go. To get out of here. We can go.'

'OK,' Penny said.

'How did you even –'

'Satellite phone. There's a journalist staying here. He has a satellite phone,' Von said.

'OK, well, listen. All I will say is I think this is very unwise and we shouldn't help these guys,' Simon said.

'I'm going,' Shannon said.

'I'm going,' Penny said.

I looked at Simon.

'I'm going too,' I said.

'Von? Wanna come?' I asked.

I wanted another man with me. And he was big and strong and smiley and I just couldn't imagine anyone shooting him. It would be gratuitous, like shooting an inedible cow.

Von took my arm and pulled me aside. 'Sorry. This is it, matey. The big one. I'm gonna can it,' he said and nodded to Cally.

'Yeah . . .?' I said.

'Oh yeah, needs doing, and now,' he said and drew a finger across his throat, clarifying his intentions for the relationship. From the other side of the lobby Minnesota Vikings looked over at us. I feared a communications mix-up.

'Easy, Von,' I said and nodded at the watching soldiers. Helpfully, Von clarified things by putting a finger pistol in his mouth and blowing his head off.

'It's dead,' he said, then looked at the soldiers and asked me: 'Do you think we're all going to get killed?'

'Er . . .'

'I might give her one last waggle on the joystick?'

'I don't know,' I said. 'I can't really see why they'd shoot us, unless it's a mistake, or something?'

Hamdo gave me a hawkish nod and we headed out to join Minnesota Vikings. Penny and Shannon led the way out, joined at the last minute by Bob. Following them came me and Yves and Elsa. Finally, Bev caught up with us and said he thought it might be best to come too, 'as protection', although really I think it felt like getting left behind to stay.

*

We walked, surrounded by a buffer of soldiers, through empty streets. Penny's white T-shirt, which she'd worn under her khaki soldier's shirt for the performance, was hanging loose and as she walked she hitched it up to tuck into her fatigues. I saw for a second her back, lovely and shimmering with a little damp. I skipped a couple of paces to make up ground until I fell into step beside her. My legs quaked. I caught her eye and shook my head in general astonishment at the things that occur in the world, testing the water, but she just marched on.

Through the old town, there was a general curfew in place. The day was slack and hot. From many apartment windows people looked down and I had the curious sensation that I was onstage again. But without any lines. This was improv. When I whispered to Penny the words frothed and dribbled.

'Minnesota Vikings. Before it was – he was the guy from the checkpoint? Right?'

'Uh-huh,' she said. 'Minnesota Vikings, née Miami Dolphins.'

I laughed, a lot. Too much. Then stopped.

The sound of the soldiers' boots resounded off the walls of the main street. There were no corpses about. Either they had been pulled away to shallow graves or the hospital or perhaps the firefight had been relatively confined. Then, like it wasn't that big a thing, Penny asked me out flat: 'So, did you destroy a poem from Simon to me, Andrew?'

I stopped, and looked at her straight on, into her eyes, the tadpole pupils dilated from the night before, almost merging with the iris, and I went for something, a flanking manoeuvre, or the truth, a blurt of feeling, I can't really say what it was, if it was my 'heart' or trying to be clever, to cling on, but I met her stare full on and said: 'I love you.'

'Great, but what do I get out of it? Financially?' she said.

'I'm not joking.'

'Yeah?'

'I mean, we had sex,' I said.

'Yeah,' she said and turned to walk on — we were the last people in the group and Minnesota Vikings chivvied us to catch up with the others, who were passing beyond the municipal buildings where we had performed. 'But not really.'

'No, sure. But we did.'

Minnesota Vikings waved to two armed men outside the council offices who waved back.

'It didn't actually go in, did it?' she said airily, looking at some shell damage.

'Er — well, I don't know,' I said. 'Look, I don't want to —'

'I don't think it did,' she said.

'Sure, I mean, I guess that's not the point. I think for a bit it —'

'No, sure.'

We passed a mosque that had the shape of a church. I think it said in my guidebook that it had been a church. But outside were Muslim headstones — mini obelisks topped with a kind of poppy-head turban. We were close enough to the Una that we could hear the water rush.

'I mean, I love you,' I said.

'Yeah, you said. Look, did you throw away his poem?'

308

But then we arrived outside the radio station — and parked up outside, huge and hulking, like an elephant, was an actual, physical tank.

'That's a T-54,' Bev said, turning and breaking the moment between Penny and me.

'Right,' I said.

'That's Russian. Second World War.'

I looked at the big beast. It made me feel tired, as though I was revising for an A-level exam, just to look at its thick metal plate and great long ridiculous gun. Zhukov, Stalingrad, Hungary '56, Prague '68, the long boring seventies and eighties waiting on the German plain for nothing — and now here. The poor big bastard. What things we make things do.

*

Upstairs in the radio studio there were many civilians sitting on the floor around a producer's desk. In the presenter's booth a man and woman were playing fast folk pop music and frequently turning it down to read the same message from a typewritten sheet.

There wasn't any triumphant revolutionary fellow feeling in the radio studio. Our arrival and subsequent on-air appearance was more like an item to be crossed off from a checklist. All seven of us were ushered into the DJ area. There weren't any chairs for us so we huddled around a microphone that dangled from the end of a metal stand like an executed man. The room was beige and orange and in the corner there were three or four broken desk fans and an electric guitar without any strings. The song ended, then the host asked, 'Hi, you are EU monitoring representatives? What are you seeing on the streets of Bihac, can I ask?'

'It is peaceful. So far as we can tell,' Yves said.

The host gave a thumbs up and motioned with hands tumbling over one another that he could do with a little more.

'All seems to be peaceful. There is quiet,' Shannon said.

'You are also from the international theatre group nice work the Peace Force has defeated Dudakovic forces, correct, right?' the DJ asked me in particular.

I stepped forward and while maintaining eye contact with the host gently spoke up towards the microphone. 'That is what we can see from what our eyes tell us.'

I stepped back like a private on a parade ground, duty done.

'Thank you. Great to meet you guys. Good luck,' the DJ said and that was it. As we exited the booth the small heat around us dissipated entirely, and I felt like a sacked executive who, having been chauffeured in, is left to get the bus home. Hamdo and his entourage stayed behind talking quickly and laughing with folk in the radio station while we were escorted back to the hotel by just a single guy.

'What does it mean, though?' Penny asked me as we made our way back through the empty streets.

'What?' I said.

'"I love you." When you said that?'

'I love you? Well, it means – I really like you.'

'Does it mean – is that what it means?'

'Yeah.'

'Uh-huh? And where did it come from?'

'It means, I guess, it means I'll like you a lot, forever.'

'Yeah?'

'Well. I don't know. Maybe not.' I seemed to be talking my way into a break-up quite fast. 'What do you think it means . . .?'

'I don't know. I didn't say it.'

As we walked back through the main square, Onomatopoeic Bob broke away from the gang to look at some carvings on a lump of old stone preserved behind railings. 'A *stećci*! This is a *stećci*!' he shouted over.

'Amazing,' I said and Penny looked at me harshly.

We walked towards him as he knelt down and with a display of effortful wonder traced a finger around the worn-down spiralled carvings still evident. 'The Bosnians, back when everything was bullshit with the Catholics and Orthodoxes, they went their own way. The third way. Neither Washington nor Moscow. The Bogomils. Very mysterious. Very interesting actually,' he said.

'Yeah?' said Bev.

'Yeah, I think this is a headstone, or it may not be. Extraordinary beliefs,' Onomatopoeic Bob said.

Our guard didn't seem to mind the delay. He lit a cigarette and waved up to a girl; the apartment window she looked out of was surrounded by bullet marks, but the glass was still intact.

'Extraordinary beliefs,' Bob said again until Bev said, 'What did they believe?'

'Sort of — like a very spiritual sort of thing,' Onomatopoeic Bob said. 'Very anti the big guys. Very mysterious. Highly intriguing. They went their own way.'

Penny looked resolutely off into space, resistant to all my attempts to raise my eyebrows at her and gently mock Bob.

'That's why I swapped the poem,' I said. 'And it was a shitty thing to do, but I thought, I think, I'm in love and I'm sorry.'

'That *was* a shitty thing to do.'

'I know. But.' Her face was hardening against me. 'Have you never done something bad for a good reason? Is it always bad, to do the wrong thing? Is everything just what it seems? Probably,

311

knights had to kill dragons and even occasionally the wrong peasant on their way to a task? I mean, I know it's wrong, but, I think we'd really – have a great time, whereas I just think Simon is, he's not the real thing. He's – he doesn't get you. But I get you. And even if I don't, and I have totally the wrong idea about you, I honestly think that I do get you, so . . .?'

Penny looked like she'd received a long legal document and was going to have to consider it at length with her advisers.

'I mean, do you like me at all?' I asked.

'I don't know,' she said.

Chapter 33

At the hotel, back under curfew, our stern guard was letting people make use of the satellite phone to call people and tell them what was going on. The queue was long, but I quite wanted to call Helen and mention in passing, if she was interested, that I was far away, in a coup, travelling with girls who read long novels and drank dry white wine and lived in London and talked about the Spanish Civil War.

Now the party was really over. And not in the fun way when a party is first over but everyone still wants to be together and talk over the night; but instead the grotty time when everyone wants the grey taste out of their mouth and to be alone or with their one person in bed and to stop the static in their heads. So we all peeled off, me anxious that Simon would come a-knocking at our door, but resigned.

I said to Penny that I would stay in the bar while she showered. When I went up twenty minutes later the room was dark, the heavy brown curtain closed and Penny's breathing sad and slow, and I felt very lonely sitting on the side of the bed easing my clothes off as quietly as I could and then lying on my bed and taking shallow breaths. My heart beat in staccato trills. I worried that I would have a heart attack, and that Penny would think it was a ruse to get sympathy and leave me to jerk and spasm to death before she called a rough local doctor just a little too late. Again, I wished I could go back down to the satellite phone – but this time, so that I could tell Helen everything that had happened and about all these people who might or might not be my friends, but without hurting her, only for someone to know how far I had travelled. And as I shuddered and marvelled at myself, I guess I drifted off, finally, to sleep.

*

A few hours later, in the late afternoon, we were shaken awake by an insistent bang on the door. A fist thud repeated hard. I took a long time to swim up into the now. Too forceful to be Simon. I opened the door to a new soldier, under five foot and friendly and shuffling like a penguin. Everyone was being assembled in the bar.

Minnesota Vikings, né Dolphins (now totally capless), stood on a chair to speak to us, though we could all see him well enough anyway. Looking around, the troupe appeared empty and pliable, exhausted now.

'We want you to come out to a meet-up. Babo's sending some guys to a meet-up, a handover of some equipment to our forces and it would be good if you could come so, OK? We leave in twenty minutes, OK?'

Once Minnesota Vikings was down from his official position on the chair, we surrounded him and asked supplementaries.

'At the Izacic crossing to Croatia. Twenty or thirty kilometres from here. To the west. We have arrangements to make. Babo wants you to come, we want you to come. The UN won't come, so it would be nice for you to come,' he explained.

314

We discussed for some time whether to accept the offer or not while Minnesota Vikings and a group of auxiliaries, some in uniform, some not, formed a convoy in the hotel car park.

'If the UN aren't going? Should we go?' Christian asked.

'It may be safer to just stay here?' Sara pointed out.

But also, there was a pull, to be at the centre of things. And the rudeness of turning down an invitation.

But behind our discussion was a question I wasn't sure of the answer to: did we have freedom to refuse? It felt like we did. But it depended on the scale. On how wide you're looking. We had a certain amount of freedom. But like wasps in a nest with winter coming on, maybe we were free to fly and land on whichever windowpane we chose, but the big story was happening regardless?

'I just don't think we should be their — tools,' Simon said.

Hamdo's jeep skidded into the forecourt and though many wise things had been said about staying put and keeping our noses out and staying safe and taking a watching brief, we all looked at one another, collected some bags and bits and pieces, (Von a half-crate of beers) and headed out to our van.

Yves and Elsa felt constrained by their official role so stayed behind. But Bev was insistent that we might need his help. I felt he was a danger. A soldier in our midst who made us more complicated than we were. But I wasn't about to denounce him on the brink of the van. As we climbed aboard one by one, and touched our spray-painted 'Peace War' for luck, I still didn't know if we *had* to go.

The convoy drove fast ahead of us. From behind a big truck tucked right up our arse whenever Onomatopoeic Bob let his speed drop. He insisted on periodically looking at the fuel gauge, tapping it and tutting, making it quite clear that if we ground to a halt it was not going to be due to any lack of attention on his part.

'It's on zero. It can't go any lower, Bob,' Sara said eventually, 'and it's not going to go up.'

She had her head on Shannon's shoulder while Shannon worked on a speech or an article she wanted to put together to tell the world about the great good things we had done. She passed the draft back to Christian, who made amendments and then passed it back to Simon, who passed it to me. 'Can you pass this to Penny? Without making your own amendments, if possible?'

I smiled at him and nodded like we were both in on the same joke, while feeling a slab of granite force its way into my chest.

Penny read over the article and nodded, then passed it back to Simon, saying she thought it was good. But he looked at her and said, sadly, 'Yeah, I'm sorry, but I don't think I'm comfortable with my name being listed at the bottom. I don't think we should be supporting this action.'

'We don't even know what this is, yet,' Penny said and I nodded sagely.

'Our dad said go,' Von said.

'You're in the van. You are coming, Simon, in fact,' I said.

'Yeah, you can fuck off,' Simon said to me, and the others blanched a little, suggesting he hadn't told the story of how I'd betrayed him. 'I may be in the van, but I am not necessarily of the van.'

'Why do they even want us there?' Cally asked.

'We're stand-ins for the United Nations,' Sara said. 'I think it's in everyone's interests for an independent body to be there.'

'They were killing each other till yesterday?' Shannon said. 'Before the play.'

'And you think that's to do with us?' Simon said.

'We don't know. Maybe? Maybe not. Maybe we urged one single guy, the vital guy in one wavering platoon, to say let's

316

stop fighting our Muslim brothers? Let's go for peace and cheese. Maybe?'

I doubted it. We didn't seem important. But perhaps we were? I felt it was stupid to say the big things: 'Peace!' 'Love!' But maybe it was worth getting up and shouting them anyway, in case someone was listening, in case they weren't that obvious? Because, some fuckers do get up and shout 'War! Hate!'

We had started out under the last hot press of the day. Now the grey-white clouds blanked out the sun and the light was diffused over the gentle humps of the land on the way up and out of Bihac. At some point, Onomatopoeic Bob dropped quite a way behind the brake lights of the truck ahead and the elastic of the convoy snapped, so that we travelled on in the dark at the head of our own short column, with only the big truck behind us for company. I feared we might lose our companions and end up driving who knew where, straight into some hail-of-bullets roadblock. But Onomatopoeic Bob picked up the pace and soon we could see the brake lights of the lead vehicle again, idling, waiting for us. After another kilometre or two we made it to our destination.

We drove up a small hill and then fast into the forecourt of the meeting place – a big, freshly completed farmhouse property with steps up to the front door and a balcony above supported on square red-brick pillars. The property stood in a large rectangle of land, all enclosed by a wall topped with low iron fencing, and looked down on the border crossing point to Croatia below.

The atmosphere was confused. It was dark and as we climbed out and stood there, Hamdo and his two closest aides disembarked and passed us without a hello, spoke quickly with the six or seven soldiers from one of the lead trucks and then drove off again in a jeep. I had the sense we were like hamsters or guinea pigs to them, nice in theory but a huge pain in the arse to actually look after.

Shannon asked Minnesota Vikings when Babo's delegation would be arriving from Velika and he asked someone else and there was no reply. Our intrusion into these matters was not welcome. We were observers, not participants. After some more discussions, Minnesota Vikings led us to the back of the house. Round there, an outside light came on. It looked like building work had finished very recently, and where a garden might eventually be established, all was barren and rubble-strewn. A concrete patio area was built up around basement double doors that opened into a large open-plan kitchen with creamy marble flooring and a set of uncomfortably designed metal-framed chairs around a metal-and-glass dining table. Minnesota Vikings ushered us all down the steps to the kitchen. There was a slab of water bottles on the table and a single bottle of Bulgarian red wine, some Coca-Colas, and four big bags of crisps. Minnesota Vikings was explaining to us that we were to drink, relax and have a good time when out through the patio doors a group of armed men appeared.

I made out among the group Mohammed and Juso and some of the guys who had guarded Babo at our meetings with him. They looked in at us cautiously and waved a hello. We waved back, the zoo animals. Juso began to come down to us and Shannon responded, trying to get to him, then Sara too. I waved to Mohammed. But Minnesota Vikings went to the patio doors and ushered Babo's gang back while one of the Bihac soldiers blocked the doorway.

Several guys from Hamdo's security detail now appeared and between them and the Velika contingent there was a lot of fast hard talking.

'Why aren't they hugging?' Von asked. 'They're on the same side now, yes?'

'You don't automatically hug people, Von,' Penny explained.

Then Minnesota Vikings came back down and asked if a couple of us would step outside to join the Velika and Bihac factions. Mohammed caught my eye from the garden, so I volunteered to join Shannon and Penny and walked up to join the men. The arguments were going strong.

'We got shot at on our way here,' Mohammed told me when I looked at him. Then we remembered to embrace. There was his tang of cheap lemony soap.

'Who shot at you?' I asked.

'We don't know. It was a mistake. They say it was a mistake, so . . . But our lorries with the guns and money and ammunition are taking longer to make it through, they are back behind, and the Bihac guys are not pleased. They don't believe it's coming.'

'Is it OK?' I asked Mohammed.

'Yes,' he said.

'Yes?' I said.

Shannon was shaking hands with Juso, who did an elaborate courtly bow and kissed her hand. She looked back down to Sara in the basement kitchen. Sara tried to come up the steps to join them but again her way was barred by one of Hamdo's guys.

The two factions now walked round to the front entrance of the house. The three of us followed, shepherded by a guy carrying a Kalashnikov with its jaunty banana-shaped magazine and wearing a Leeds United top under his open khaki shirt.

We were guided upstairs into a sitting room as wide as the front of the farmhouse. The night was hot and the room smelt of the heavy sap of cypress trees, fresh plaster and spoiling food.

Snacks and soft drinks were laid out on a long table up there.

The place was half finished. A red rug covered only the central part of the floor, leaving the wide margins gritty with unfinished cement. Though the walls were painted – salmon pink, and the woodwork white – someone had proceeded too fast and there was now chasing chiselled into the paint and plaster and unfinished electrical sockets hung raw from the walls.

Mohammed, Juso and the rest of Babo's delegation were invited to tuck in to the bread, pastries and chicken on the table. It had been sitting there a while; a number of flies circles above the table. It was supposed to be a gesture of hospitality and camaraderie, I guess, but Minnesota Vikings and the others from the 5th Corps didn't join the feast; they watched from the sides of the room as their guests ripped little chunks of bread off and dipped them politely into beige-coloured dips in shallow white bowls. It was play-acting. No one was relaxed enough to eat. The bread stayed a long time in their mouths as they chewed and I saw one guy behind Mohammed touch a crisp with the tip of his tongue before he ate it, testing. Then, outside, Hamdo's jeep crunched the gravel and there was loud talk from the front of the property.

Mohammed smiled at me and nodded his head. He and his friend, a short fat young man with a long face that looked like it could not wait to get older, headed out onto the semicircular balcony that poked out over the front door.

'Does this feel OK to you?' I asked Shannon and Penny.

'How do you mean?' said Shannon.

'I don't know. It just – I mean, on one level, it's OK?' I said.

'Is it real?' said Penny.

Under the cool light of the single high-watt bulb above, there was not much sense of a reconciliation being effected.

It was the way the Bihac faction stood, showing only their backs to their new brothers from Velika, separate in a distinct and

320

impervious gang. It was the way they frowned and grimaced easily at one another and smiled hard and fast at their supposed new allies – and after a while stopped even doing that. The man in the Leeds shirt – who was actually more of a boy, only seventeen or so – was flicking at a little catch on the side of his weapon, the safety catch, I guess. And then he clicked something else by the front of the trigger guard and pulled the curved magazine off and flicked at the top bullet inside with his thumb, pressed down on something, blew in there and then clipped the magazine back on.

We looked over towards Mohammed out on the balcony. He was smoking a cigarette and shaking his puppet limbs out, like he was an actor before a show. Minnesota Vikings toyed absent-mindedly with the webbing of his belt. Soon he asked for Mohammed and his friend to come in, and for them and the others to head back downstairs.

Once Mohammed was inside, Minnesota Vikings came over to me, Penny and Shannon and said we needed to go back downstairs again now, that the 'party was over'. I caught Mohammed's eye as we were all escorted out, quite fast down the wide stairs, and then out through the entrance hall onto the forecourt.

I felt a bolt of certainty that something was wrong. That somebody was going to be hurt, very badly, and soon.

But what do you say? It was awkward. It would be, above all else, rude – to tell Mohammed and the others I thought they had fallen victim to a trap. Presumptuous, and hurtful. Especially as I had no idea what kind of trap it was, or if I was reading the signs right at all.

As Minnesota Vikings began to lead us back round to the garden area, two trucks driven by guys wearing Babo's insignia rumbled into the forecourt, blinding us momentarily with the dazzle of their headlights. There was a cheer from all the soldiers out front

– both Mohammed's Velika lot and the force from Bihac. Presumably, these were the vehicles carrying the promised arms and supplies and I wondered if I had been misreading what the tension in the room upstairs had meant. The drivers of the trucks were greeted with handshakes and then shepherded round with Mohammed and the rest of the Velika guys to stand in the unfinished garden space, smoking cigarettes, while Penny, Shannon and I were guided back into the basement.

In the kitchen, the big crisp packets were slit open along their sides for sharing and the gang were passing the bottles of water round. Sara hurried up to Shannon and asked after Juso. Was he OK, what had he said? But more than asking after him, she was asking after Shannon, trying to see if she was vibrating at all from the reunion.

Then there was a burst of gunfire.

It sounded horrible, the rattle sparking through the bare plastered walls and over the white-tiled floor like fat sizzling onto your skin. There were cries of shock and pain and horror then another hard clatter of shooting and everything shattered. We ran to the steps to get out, as men came down the internal stairs shouting and – not, I don't think, shooting, but holding their guns like they might. As we made it outside into the rough garden area everything split. Some men ran past us back into the house, somebody pulled at my arm. I could feel hot holes in human flesh nearby, or smell them, or see them – I didn't know what I knew except there were dark holes in people. Then I was down on my face eating the dirt of the garden, Penny was on my back and then her hand reached out and lifted me up and all the house lights were on and, sharply illuminated in the window, I saw a man dip a pistol almost elegantly so that it pointed out towards the garden. He shot a bullet through the

322

glass – which fell away beautifully, not like in any film – towards a target in the garden. There were all sorts of bodies around, some up and some down and all of us scrambling, and I wanted to make a headcount and to stop everything and sort it all out.

As I made it round to the front of the house, the main gate was being opened and a jeep drove out and it felt that maybe everything had stopped for a moment and I shouted for Mohammed and for Shannon, but then there was another shot and someone dropped or jumped or was pushed off the balcony and he fell like a person shouldn't fall, not putting his arms out when he hit the steps leading up to the front door, but instead flopping like a doll. That's what you do when you're dead, I thought: nothing.

Then I could hear a car revving harshly and stalling and revving outside the main gate and Penny shouted to us to get to the car. And I could make out Juso lifting his head up from the back seat and waving for us to climb over the perimeter wall and join him in a big Mercedes saloon. But Simon was beside us now, saying 'stay' to Penny, and to me that it wasn't safe to go.

At the same time, the Peace War van, right by me inside the forecourt, started up. The door opened by my side and I could see Christian crouching in the safety of the footwell as Bob, next to him, pumped the accelerator with his hand. Shannon climbed in. Simon shouted that he trusted the Bihac guys – we should stay. Von stood tall, looking alert and confused and blinking. The car out front with Juso inside began to pull away. There was another burst of gunfire round the back of the house and Mohammed's friend with the long young face ran to us and shouted for us to follow Juso's Mercedes. Then he carried on running, towards the gate, and he seemed to stumble and fall just when there was a pop from up on the balcony.

323

The side door of the van was still open. Cally said something sharp and Von and Bev dived in to join Shannon. Then me and Sara and Penny jumped aboard, and then we were gone, everyone except Simon, driving down the hill as people fired guns at or near us and we all lay on the floor and just hoped to stay safe for one second then two then three, till eventually we could start to think about a minute and begin to feel our bodies around us and think about what had just happened.

'Should we go back?' Penny asked. As soon, I felt, as it was clear that we wouldn't be going back. 'Did everyone come who wanted to come?'

'What the fuck happened?' Von said.

'I don't know,' I said.

'Someone started shooting,' Onomatopoeic Bob said.

'Was that — who was that who fell off the balcony?' Shannon asked.

'It was Mohammed,' I said, not really knowing for sure. But no one disagreed, so maybe it was. It looked like it was him. But I couldn't really believe it. 'It's confusing. What happened?'

'What did happen?' Von asked.

'They took them out,' Bev said.

'Who?' Onomatopoeic Bob asked. 'Who took who out?'

'The — I think the lads we came with, they took out Babo's lot? Did they?'

'We were downstairs, and it started, right? But were they shooting at us?' Onomatopoeic Bob said.

'Yes, they were shooting at us, of course! There were guys with guns,' Cally said.

'They weren't shooing at us. None of us was hit, were we?' Shannon said.

'Should we go back?' Penny asked.

324

'Everyone who wanted to come, came,' Von said. 'I think.'

'Simon wanted to stay, didn't he?' I said and suddenly my heart ratcheted up further – in case – in case it wasn't true and he'd said 'let me come' and I'd double-crossed him again somehow in the confusion, done something awful I was failing to admit to.

'Yes,' Bob said. 'I think. He wanted to stay. Right?'

'Yeah, that's right? Right?' Shannon agreed.

'Right. He was posturing,' Christian said.

'Yeah? I mean, he really did stay. That's quite a big posture,' I said and Christian shrugged while Penny looked back into the night.

'So they started shooting, and we went up, and then we left and I guess, the whole thing, was . . . was . . . what happened?' Shannon said.

We drove in silence for quite a while as we rattled along, trying to keep up with Juso in the Mercedes. They were gunning it fast, leading us north, travelling on back roads, like English country lanes but without the hedgerows. Soon the one we were on petered out into an untarmacked track.

We followed the Mercedes up a farm road to a hamlet, where Juso's car stopped. He got out and walked back towards the van illuminated in our headlights, a force field of mosquitoes and midges hissing around him. He told us to drive and not to stop, whatever happened to him or us when we went over the brow of the next hill, because we were about to cross the internal confrontation line back into Babo territory.

'What happened, Juso?' I said.

'Later,' he said.

'Are you OK?' Shannon asked.

'Later,' he said and started back towards the Merc.

'What about . . .' Onomatopoeic Bob had my guidebook on his

325

lap, open to the pages on the Pliva Lake district, just over in Croatia. 'I think there's another road, another way round . . . see?' He was bending the book hard so that the gluey white ribs of the spine were evident. I could just about see, at the tip of his hippy's hash-browned finger, a squiggle. 'That might be better . . . Juso!' Onomatopoeic Bob shouted. But the Mercedes was already going.

'Bob, is that where we are, is that even a road?' I asked, looking at the map.

But at that point he turned left and down a hard-topped side road.

'Fucking hell, Bob! For fuck's sake!' I said.

'Bob?' Cally said.

A little moonlight came through the gauze of cloud, enough only to make out an idea of the countryside. My anger and self-righteousness was all mixed up, to such an extent I didn't know if I wanted us to make it through, or for gunfire to blurt from the trees and pepper us with our just deserts.

'Are we not following the car?' Von said, insouciant and invul-nerable. 'I don't think that's a very good idea.'

'Bob. Seriously, man?'

'I think this will be good,' he said as the road bent to the left, south with the curve of a hillside. 'If they get into trouble, we'll be OK,' as if that related to anything or was even true.

'Penny. We should go back – let's go back,' I said. But then we curved up a hillside and straight along a little plateau until we could see lights ahead of us.

'Just go fucking slow. Do *not* get us shot,' I said.

The lights were the Mercedes idling in the road.

'Where did you go?' Juso asked through his window.

'Round the back,' Onomatopoeic Bob said, and Juso didn't admonish him.

'Good, we had to pass a checkpoint but they must be on patrol or back in their farms, but, good. OK. Twenty kilometres for Velika, OK? But we make some stops.'

Five or so more kilometres north beyond the internal confrontation line Juso stopped again in the centre of a little hamlet. This time he got out and we had time to ask him about the shooting at Izacic. We asked him what had happened so far as he could see.

'Double cross.'

'So – what, they weren't really part of the coup, our guys, Hamdo? The guys we came with?' Onomatopoeic Bob asked.

'I guess . . . I don't know? Was the coup even real, even? My driver says maybe it was a trick, to make out a coup for peace, but really they just wanted weapons. And to screw us?'

'Fuck,' Onomatopoeic Bob said, considering.

'We heard it? The coup. They locked us in,' I said.

'I don't buy it. The coup was for real. I'm sure,' Shannon said. But I could see certainty was a bulwark she was sending up, behind which she could contemplate the alternative.

'Why would they take us? Why did they bring us?' Onomatopoeic Bob asked.

'Babo was worried. He sent his guys south, and trucks of weapons. So he wanted UN there, or at least you guys. He thought it would make it more – official, more safe. He insisted,' Juso said.

'And why did you come?' Sara asked.

'Oh. Well. You know, I was invited and . . . I wanted to see you guys,' he said and looked at Shannon, then Sara.

'That was dangerous,' Shannon said.

'That was fucking stupid,' Sara said.

The driver of the Merc was leading an old woman and a young woman and a couple of other folk from a nearby house to our van. He motioned for us to make room and the old woman eased herself up and sat next to me, not smiling, not happy, her suitcase and an extra bundle of clothes pushed into the space at my feet.

'We think this is it, a big push north by the 5th Corps out of Bihac. With the weapons Babo sent. Mujahideen, bad guys, very fierce guys, will come, to take revenge now,' Juso explained. 'So, we want you to give as much space as you can. For refugees.'

We stocked up with five of the displaced folk from the hamlet and smiled at them benevolently, but then looked at one another discreetly and frowned, feeling compromised and invaded. We didn't sign up for this.

Then we started up again, driving north. Juso said this was dangerous territory, a no-man's-land. Though we were beyond the internal confrontation line, the moves and counter-moves away from the road made drawing a definitive front line impossible. We could easily run into some 5th Corps or local Bihac or Cazin militia hereabouts, so we were to make a straight run for Velika and not stop till we got there, every car for itself.

We were all quiet for a while, embarrassed of our youth and health and fear in front of our passengers. The old woman next to me drove her elbow hard into the seat back. It was a thick peasant arm that wasn't interested in subtle shifts or urban negotiations. It would take ordinance to move it out from where it pressed uncomfortably into my side. I tried another smile, but she was comprehensively wrapped up in herself. As we drove on, the aggressive accelerations and breaks at bends and dips in the road made me feel unwell.

But as well as the motion sickness, when I looked at the side of my neighbour's face, lit up enough by the dashboard instruments of the van to see her tightly wrinkled skin, spotted with a lifetime's abrasions and eruptions, I felt sick also at the unknowability of others. Even if I could find the foreign words to ask what her life had been — all the years, the whatever, the pre-war, the war, Tito, the farm, kids? and now this, another or a first evacuation — even if she could tell me a version of all that, what would I know about what it was actually like, from the story she pulled together?

My seat-mate made a loud burp, and for some reason I found myself saying, 'Excuse me.' Then Onomatopoeic Bob said from up front, 'Oh. OK. Yeah,' as the van slowed.

'Don't *fucking* stop,' I said. But the van continued to decelerate until it reached a gentle halt.

'Bob, you dickhead!' Von said. 'I am ordering you, Bob, no more bullshit, let's get out of here. Come on!'

'Thanks for the order. We're actually out of diesel.'

We looked at one another for bright ideas and the old woman made her first social contact, raising her eyebrows towards me as if to say, 'What's going on, dipshit?'

I said, 'Diesel, kaput, no diesel.' She looked at me blankly.

'What do we do?' Cally asked.

'Well . . .' said Shannon.

'Well, we can't stay here,' I said definitively.

But in fact there was very little else we could do. So, after talking it all through, we planned to rest until either Juso — whose brake lights had long disappeared — came back with a jerry can, or it grew light.

Chapter 34

I barely slept, staring avid and awake out of the window, seeing all kinds of commandos and ghosts, panthers and holy warriors stalking the van from the wood beyond the fence. The hours passed impossibly slowly. I was a resentful sentinel, pissy about being defaulted into responsibility as the one watchman who would have to raise the alarm when the attack came.

I looked at Penny. Lamenting the way things had gone and wondering if I shouldn't touch her gently on the shoulder and whisper my regrets. I was caught for a long time considering if that was a brilliant idea or a terrible one; my hand quivering on my leg waiting to hear from my brain what it was to do. I felt strongly that every action is a kind of tragedy. As soon as you act all the alternative worlds of possibility dissolve so they never existed, like castles of ash collapsing. Other futures, lives; love you might have known for a day or a lifetime, all of them are blasted in a furnace wind which scorches away everything but the black twig of you, faltering forward, doing whatever you stupidly choose to do.

I didn't touch her shoulder. I kept my hand on my leg. And thought that of course not acting is a kind of action too. My senses were skewed. I'd watched out of the window so long that I could hardly tell by the time I whispered to everyone to wake up whether it was still basically dark and I'd just wished it into comparative morning, or if it was in fact midday and I'd let them all sleep far too long.

'Penny? Hey? Do you think we should get up?'

The others roused too. We looked around at our exposed spot and the decision was made to get out and walk the road to Velika. Onomatopoeic Bob said it was about six kilometres. Some left their bags in the van but I strapped my blue aluminium-framed rucksack on. I liked to keep my stuff near me. We mimed to our refugee friends that we would be walking, and I took up my seat-mate's bundle of clothes tied in a rough sheet or tablecloth while she carried a very long and sagging black leather Puma holdall. Von tried to ignore her obvious need for aid, but when I'd nodded a few times at her struggling, he took her bag with elaborate courtesy, like he'd only just noticed her distress and couldn't bear it a second longer.

Shannon set the pace, taking Sara and Penny and Cally to the head of our column as the pathfinders. My old woman kept up a good lick. One leg was bad but she had a fast swivelling-jerk of a walk that took her tick-tocking beyond me as I shuffled, loaded up front and back. I had no real internal conception of what six kilometres might mean. I knew it wasn't much in a car. But on foot? Was that a hike to boast of, or just a walk from one edge of town to the other? Also, of course, to estimate the journey's length we were trusting a man I considered to be a congenital idiot. It was quite possible it was double or triple or half Onomatopoeic Bob's thumb-spanning measure.

'So, I put it in,' Von said, sidling up beside me.

'You did?'

331

'Yeah. After the party. When we all had a sleep.'

'OK. Right. And what did you think?'

'Yeah.'

'Yeah?'

'Yeah. Nice.'

'Nice, right?'

'Yeah. No, I liked it. I liked it a lot.'

The morning air was clear and the thin cloud fried off leaving us under a hot sun an hour into the walk. Von sped up to talk a while to Cally and then dropped back again.

'Just gave her a warning. For the old heave-ho,' he said merrily.

'Oh? Right?'

'She's a slut. Letting me put it right in?'

'Yeah?'

'Yeah. I'm gonna kick it in the head. Once we're safe.'

'OK,' I said. She looked round and blew a kiss to Von. He caught it in the air and sent one back, all like a stupid game they were too cool for. 'Is that what you really want to do?'

'Don't give me the fucking third degree, mate,' he said.

Bev trudged on my other side.

'It is nice country,' I said, looking across a meadow where a fat game bird squawked up into the sky.

'Yeah, that'll be all the fucking bodies under there, fertilising,' Bev said.

Onomatopoeic Bob, at our rear, picked grasses from the side of the road and chewed on a stalk.

'That good, mate?' Von asked.

'Mmm?' Bob said, discarding it and plucking another, like he knew one kind of hedge grass from another.

'Yeah, I just pissed on that,' Von said.

Ahead of us, Penny, Sara, Shannon and Cally were talking.

332

Sandwiched between our two groups were the refugees – my old woman, her daughter, another young woman and two boys of twelve or thirteen in nylon jogging bottoms, both carrying old-fashioned hard-sided suitcases. One case was heavier than the other and they swapped occasionally to keep things fair.

I walked a little faster, towards the women – away from the hard jokes of men, which always deflate. That's generally the main aim of male talk, to stop anything getting off the ground, above itself. To tug everything into the dirt, to make it stupid and dirty. Among the women, I felt, as I passed the refugees with a tight awkward smile, you could breathe. They let an idea go for a while, let it hover in the air to see what it might become, what was a good way to look at it. Things were allowed to be various – one thing and its opposite at once – and that's where I wanted to be: I touched Penny's elbow so she would break from the others.

'Penny, hey, Penny. Can I have a word a second?'

'Hey.'

She let her pace drop a little, so we were in step.

'Do you think Simon will be OK?' I said.

'I hope so,' she said and I nodded, trying to figure out how much she hoped so. To just a normal humane degree – or an extra amount on top? I felt that I had a difficult sale to make; pressing on a customer an unwanted piece of merchandise.

'Look, I know you might not want to hear this, but I'm in love with you. I am in love with you.' She walked on like she hadn't heard anything.

So I kept quiet until, after a while, she eventually said, 'Uh-huh?'

She seemed to be refusing to sign for the product.

'What?' I said.

'OK,' she said.

'Yeah. I mean — what do you think?' I said.

'It's just, I don't know if you are?' she said.

'Well, of course I am.'

'Yeah?'

'Well, I should know.' I wasn't an expert on much, I thought, but I was the leading authority on who I was in love with.

'It's just, yeah, it doesn't feel like that. I feel like you're throwing something at me when you say it, you know?'

'Right. Well. Sorry. I love you.'

'Like you're accusing me of something?'

'I think about you all the time.' I looked at a house we were passing. A child at an upstairs window looked out cautiously. A side door banged closed. 'What about trying to go out with me? For a bit?'

'Yeah?'

I knew it sounded foolish and callow. 'But think about it, how can you know until you give it a go? I feel like you don't take me seriously.'

'I do.'

'I mean, it's just a leap of thinking, isn't it?'

'Well . . .'

'Like, in some ways, it's like Yugoslavia. What is the imagined community? Do you want to be, and I don't really mean this, but for example, Croatia, saying, "I can't imagine being of the same state with you." Me, that is?'

'But aren't you being like Serbia, saying, "I insist you are a part of me, I won't listen to any alternative arguments"?'

'No, no. God, no. I'm being like the European Union. I'm making an imaginative leap of heroic community to — to — think of you and me together?'

'Yeah, but . . . I don't want to go out with you.'

'OK, now we get down to it,' I said. 'But isn't that in a way nationalistic, almost — fascistic?'

She looked at me and then she began to smile.

'OK. Listen. I mean, I quite like you,' she said. I wondered if I shouldn't stick on that. Maybe I should run away across a field right now? 'But, the thing is, there's Simon, and — and — I think, I — I'm going through something and I don't know what to call it but I definitely have feelings for Shannon.'

'Me too. That's fine,' I said. 'That's not a deal-breaker.'

'No, I have proper feelings about her.'

'Oh. Right,' I said. 'You're in love with Shannon?'

Penny looked over at her. Shannon was magnificent.

'I'm not in love with her, I don't think. I just have feelings. That I'd like to think about.'

'And what about Simon?'

'Yeah. What about him?' she said.

'Do you love him?'

'Andrew, I don't think I love anyone you're talking about. It's all more complicated.'

We walked in silence for a while, the road gritty and grey, and I wondered if perhaps I wasn't in love with Shannon. Maybe my love was fungible, available for replacement with a similar item?

'She is remarkable,' I said.

'She's — yeah — she's a very interesting person.'

'I don't know. God. I don't know Penny, I don't know if I love you or Shannon — or sometimes — Von, or even Cally or Helen. . .'

'Maybe you don't love anyone at the moment, is that possible?' She gave me a smile of infuriating equanimity.

'I'm just being honest, Penny,' I said. 'I'm trying to be.'

Then I dropped back to where Bev and Von were ripping the piss out of me.

'Back with the fucking numb-nuts, is it?' Bev said.

'No action, ah?' Von said.

I started an extended bout of laughter, even though there'd been no real joke, because I thought there was a chance I might start to cry and I hoped I could mess the faces up together if any tears did come.

Chapter 35

We arrived into the outskirts of Velika on a side track that abutted the bigger north–south road, and we slogged past the cement works and the big industrial plant with its thirties windows. It was once the houses and the shops started appearing that Juso and the Mercedes came into view. They'd assumed, he said, that we'd taken another one of our 'special routes', but finding us nowhere in town that morning they had got worried and driven back to the empty van. The back of the Merc was loaded up with the bags left behind and those who'd been wise enough to leave their bulky stuff in the unlocked vehicle looked at me with an air of self-regarding pity as I adjusted my rucksack straps.

Juso embraced Shannon, then Sara, and then loaded the car up – bags in the back, people in the front – and started running shuttles up to the hotel at the top of the town square.

The atmosphere in town had changed. For one thing, once we were on the main drag, the traffic was one way – all heading into Velika. And it was constant. Car after car, tractors and vans, horse-drawn carts and scooters too. The people heading into town were not just day visitors either. They were loaded up with bags and cases. One flatbed van had an aged woman lying in the back on a set of rugs. She looked like she hadn't seen the outside world since it was filmed in black and white and she bore the little jolts and jerks of her son or grandson's truck with a forbearance that said the worst was happening, the worst had happened, things now might get worse still or better, but she'd seen too much.

'Everyone's scared,' Juso said. 'After last night, the 5th Corps have guns and ammunition. They are coming.'

'Do we know what happened now?' I asked.

'No coup. For sure. There was no Peace Force. It was all lies to get ammunition and destabilise.'

'So – what, no coup and . . . Hamdo?'

'Hamdo is loyal to the 5th Corps. It was all bullshit. Firing into the air, the French UN, the EU, everyone was fooled. It was a bad trick.'

It was also, it had to be said, quite a good trick.

'What, so – it was – not real, none of it?' Von said.

'No, the battle was an act, they wanted, I guess, the reports to come out and everyone to believe it.'

I looked over at Shannon and she looked at the ground, unwilling to engage just yet. Juso had checked us in to the little hotel at the top of the town's dry-grass and tree-lined square, just beside the Agrokomerc and its tomato-red livery.

'What about the apartments?' Von asked. 'Our apartments? Can we look for that guy?'

'Not such a good idea. In case the people come back.'

'Might they come back?' I asked.

'I don't think they'll come back. But relatives.'

As we checked in to the small uncomfortable rooms at the hotel, we told the woman we didn't know how long we would be staying. She would only take a booking for a night anyway, since, she said, she would be leaving town tomorrow evening herself. It seemed that we should probably leave then too, or else be willing to take on by default the ownership of a provincial Balkan hotel.

We all went round the corner to the gloom of the unfriendly bar. The fat man behind the counter recognised us right away and was even more unfriendly than previously. The place was full – so that huddles of men occupied the place deep into its chilly white recesses. Shannon ordered and I looked around at Sara, Juso, Penny, and then Onomatopoeic Bob, and thought yes – possibly even in a way Von and Christian too – perhaps we were all to some degree in love with Shannon? Bev was probably the only one immune. After a very long wait she passed out the demi-measures of lager and smiled and we clinked and said, 'We made it!' and 'We fucking made it, guys!' and made a party of this terrible morning in a grim little town about to be overrun by its enemies.

As we drank, some militia guys came in and made an announcement calling for everyone in the bar to come out – there was something to be seen. Out on the street there was an air of unhappy carnival. People were being filtered along to the square by unofficial officials, serious self-important guys, and some actual soldiers and police. As we came out of our side street, to one of the square's broad flanks, we had to halt to let a posse of soldiers pass. In the centre of the pack was a guy in fatigues who looked tired beyond belief. His hands were tied behind him by a bit of the same sort of orange baler twine Onomatopoeic Bob had once used to stake out our rehearsal area. The man looked at me briefly and I smiled and raised my eyebrows supportively. I watched as he skipped a beat with his feet, so as not to trip on a big-lipped join in the pavement slabs as he was shepherded away.

We looked around for what the action was, sport or speech, pancake-flipping frying-pan race or carnival ride, but the focus, once it came, seemed to push after the tied man and towards the top of the square, where some building work was going on. There was a digger there, some piles of sand, a small cement mixer and bags of cement in a temporary dry store.

When I saw a length of rope come out I looked at the folk all around, trying to see if they knew what was coming. The townspeople appeared, I would say, interested. Interested and concerned. The crowd shuffled up on itself, making the space and the tension tighter, and though we wanted to edge back, away, it felt as though that would be bad-mannered, or worse.

A noose was made in the rope and they put that over the tired man's head.

'He's 5th Corps. Bihac. The uniform,' Onomatopoeic Bob said, and I wanted to tell him to fuck off for some reason; that no knowledge at this point was necessary, all context was redundant.

Then someone put a plastic bag – a shopping bag – over the soldier's head, and I thought, well, that's dangerous in itself. But another soldier, in a red beret, pulled the shopping bag off and started to wrap the other end of the rope round and round one of the prongs at the front of the digger's loading shovel, then tied it off. I tried to look at the face of the soldier with the noose around his neck, but though I could see his features, they had gone to another place – he had burrowed deep within himself and I felt bad for even looking. I looked at his whole body, head to toe, intently, because I felt that soon it would be dead and that if I tried to remember it exactly as it was alive, that at least would be something.

The guy in the beret near the shovel gave a thumbs up to the man who hung out of the cab and the engine came to life, blowing out hard a first chug of black smoke that then settled into grey with an easy throb.

Shannon shouted: 'No!'

I nodded encouragingly at her, but the townspeople who looked round at us shook their heads and muttered like everything was more complicated than that. And soon it was as if nothing had been said at all.

This was the moment for a pronouncement, or a denouncement, for the death sentence to be proclaimed by some official over by the digger. But I don't think there was anything that could have been said that would have framed the event. It was just savage. The soldiers who'd walked the victim up the square looked at one another to agree this was the time, then they backed away a little and nodded to the guy in the cab. The guy in the digger gave a nod back to them and moved his hands on the controls and the big shovel reacted – but instead of moving up, it dropped down half a metre and hit the ground with a resounding metal-on-concrete clang. The rope slipped off and there was something like a laugh from the crowd. That's comedy: subverting expectations.

The soldier in the beret pushed the loop of rope back down the prong, and the digger driver swivelled the shovel up a few degrees to make sure it was fast. The prisoner looked back at the arrangement of the rope, and as he was doing so the driver, who wasn't even looking at the man he was about to kill, let loose the hydraulics, bouncing the shovel up as high as it would go in one quick jerk. And with it, the body of the 5th Corps man went too. It was possible that his neck broke right away, because he didn't seem to move around much. It was hard to tell – the swing might have been from the movement of the digger, or it might have been his own. I suppose it didn't matter really, but it mattered to me and I asked people if he was dead. Bev said yes and I resented him for presuming to know about life or death or anything. Von was not looking – several people were not looking. I understood why, though later, when they tried, I thought, to make out that not looking was the more noble choice, I felt angry: I didn't think that not watching made you any better. I thought it was important to see what was happening as clearly as I could. Things matter, I think.

The crowd did not cheer or anything. But they did not dissent. Shannon shouted 'No!' again and then Penny did too and then, overcoming the fact I was a little afraid because the people in the crowd were now looking at us quite aggressively, I shouted it too, though my voice was hoarse and I knew it was too late.

The crowd didn't turn on us. They seemed to accept the heaving of something terrible onto their shoulders with resignation. They were witnesses, but also participants. It couldn't have happened without the crowd there. They were part of it and they knew it.

*

Afterwards, we didn't know what to do. Our beers were presumably still on the counter in the bar. So we walked back and, indeed, there they stood, heading towards room temperature, pathetic and oblivious, warming up. Cold beer warms, still blood cools, everything heads to the mean.

'What was it for?' Von asked, like a big kid.

'Everyone's on his side now. Babo's,' Onomatopoeic Bob said. For once on this whole trip finally correct, I guessed. 'They've had their hands dipped in blood. They're his. Everything's clear.'

It was true. Everything was becoming clear. Too clear – on

the big boring canvas of the war. All the shading of the world was getting blasted bland and around us everywhere grew this flatness. 'Yes, *but* . . .' you wanted to say the whole time − but you couldn't; hell was this, here, where the noise was so great only 'yes' or 'no' shouted loud could be heard, never the next bit, the qualification or the joke, or the question.

'Do you think, are we − did we come to the right side?' Von asked Shannon.

'We don't know what the 5th Corps do down there? They could be just as bad?' Juso said and looked at Shannon and Sara reasonably. But the hanging had snapped things for them, for us all.

'Yeah, fuck off, Juso,' Sara said.

'Yeah,' Shannon said.

'What if they hung two soldiers at the same time today?' he asked.

'Then, they'd be − I don't know − did they?' Christian asked.

'I don't know. But what if they did?'

'I suppose . . . but. No,' Shannon said. 'No. Fuck off.'

The bar was filling up with more and more men. Men in thin nylon tracksuit tops over white vests. Men with crew-neck jumpers of yellow and green over no T-shirt. Men with army uniforms, and guns. A municipal policeman. Then there was a little cheer and, immediately after, a hushing − Babo came in through the door.

The way to the bar parted as a small coffee was provided for him. He said a few words, the cadence of which followed a mumbling, a digression, a swelling, a shout of three or four short monosyllables, and then there was stamping on the floor and a brief rapid bit of applause like gunfire and he was out, to another bar or gathering.

After that, someone nudged Von and he spilled what was left of his drink. There was no apology. Like a band of superheroes, we started to direct the focus of our eyes only towards one another, as if we were going to muster a laser thunderbolt out of our concentrated attention. It felt like it was very, very important that we look at nobody at all in that bar right then, and I marvelled at how, just a little earlier, all had been well and near normal and how now I felt my life wobbled like a spinning top which a hand might at any moment stop dead.

I looked towards the door. A guy tapped an insistent finger on Penny's back, and when she turned a little, his big belly pushed in towards her insistently, like it was never going to stop.

'Right, let's go, follow me,' I said, and angled my shoulder like the prow of a tall ship through the crowd, giving no offence so far as I could, but not halting either. The gang snaked behind me and I tried to breathe as slowly and evenly as possible until we all made it out into the August air.

*

We didn't check out of the hotel. We just grabbed our stuff and left. Juso said the word all about town was that the border point to the north, the way we'd come in to Bosnia, was already choked and impassable.

'The main way out of town will be too dangerous for us,' Shannon said, as though Juso didn't exist. He puckered his pink lips in the middle of his beard.

Lumbering with our gear, we walked down towards the industrial part of town with the aim of heading across the border on a minor road. Juso tagged after, half the threadbare teddy, half the surly grizzly. The crowd around the square had dispersed quickly, just knots of folk here and there remained, turned in on themselves.

As we crossed the middle of the square, none of us looked up towards the hanged man, but he was there staring down at us, like a tough-nut in the pub, his dead eye the one we didn't want to catch. We stayed silent as we padded up the far side opposite him and turned off past a bar. I was grateful once the lane dipped and eventually I looked back to check that yes, he could no longer be seen.

'I guess. I suppose, we're going home? Are we?' Von asked.

Our direction of travel had been unspoken for a while.

'What do you think?' Shannon asked us.

'We could do the play again? Somewhere?' Sara said.

'Yeah?' Penny said.

I didn't want to think about the play, it made me feel unwell.

'I think we need to get out of here,' I said.

'What about Simon?' Penny asked.

'I thought he might . . . Do you think he'll be OK?' Christian said.

'I think he'll be OK. Bihac is winning,' Bev said.

We carried on walking. Penny increased her speed to catch up with Shannon and Sara, and then I walked faster too so I was by her side, then Juso upped his pace so that he was able to pass the line of us and walk a little in front. He did a little laugh, inviting someone to ask him what was funny. Then he shook his head noticeably. Sara and Shannon looked away. I caught his eye and he dropped back next to me. He wanted to say something.

'Why do you even care? About all this?' he said.

'I don't know. Maybe I don't. I don't know,' I said.

He looked weary and rubbed his eyes.

'Because of your Empire? Is it? The British Empire? You think you matter. You used to rule the world, so now you worry about it instead?'

Shannon wrinkled her nose and Penny, overhearing the odd word, looked at me.

'Juso. Not now, mate,' I said. The failure to have the unspoken argument was riling him.

'What's it got to do with you?'

'Nothing. It's true.'

'Do you think they worry about Bosnia in Mexico? No. They know it is not for them.'

I looked at Penny and shrugged and that pissed him off.

'Who are you to care about the whole world? Sending out blankets and your rice? Covering the world with your newspaper articles, like gunboats. Who the fuck do you think you are to care about me?'

'I'm sorry,' I said.

We passed a bakery and I went in with Penny as she bought up the few *burek* they had left. Cheese ones and meat ones too. It was when we left the bakery and walked on that Juso stopped. I wasn't sure if I had missed some further discussion. As we walked a little down the road, he fell further and further into the distance. A couple of hundred metres on Sara said, 'Shannon?' and they both looked back at him and he waved one strong stubby arm.

But Shannon didn't wave back. She took Sara's hand and on the other side Penny's and Penny reached out hers to me and I linked with Bev and he with Von, who said 'Don't gay me' but then took the hand, and with Cally and Christian and Bob we walked round a corner united in moral superiority against this man who had shown us nothing but kindness.

346

Once we were out of view, Penny made a tiny flinch of her palm to drop my hand out of hers, and spilling down the valley came the clatter of small arms fire. From the suburban street we walked, we could see the main road, a half-kilometre away. The flow of people into Velika was growing thicker, like a dirtied and knotted rope being wound in by the town.

Soon the tarmac grew broad and the houses at the roadside disappeared, replaced by plant-hire compounds and electrical-power substations and patches of grassy nothing. After a few more minutes' walk we joined the road that led down to the French UN compound. We could see over to the sandbagged and self-important entrance, where a jeep pulled out carrying three guys in soft blue berets, then a Land Cruiser, and a little later some blue-helmeted soldiers on foot bustled out, conferred, and retreated back inside, like uncertain honey bees at the edge of the hive. An assault was coming, a bit of war, and they were here to watch over it. A cluster of local boys stood near the gate asking for sweets and making a noise which was part cheering and part jeering as vehicles passed in and out.

What an odd demi-war it looked that morning. Half muted, but then all the more savage when it was set free behind the toilet block, out of sight; marshalled by Danes and Frenchmen and Jordanians, bored referees, inconstant parents, sometimes wildly protective, then unaccountably absent or found drunk, getting off with your girlfriend, finishing your plate of food.

But still it was worth it, this non-peacekeeping – that was what was hard to accept. It was still well worth it, to jam up the gears and meddle with the machine. The war machine was a fucking mess, but if you could add another fan belt, stick in some more ground-down gearing, some recording mechanisms, dials, gauges, crank in another round of rattling conveyer belt, to make the whole thing churn even less efficiently, gummed with documentation and negotiation, then that was all to the good. Because what the machine wanted to do was kill people, and stopping that, however clumsily, was all to the good.

The UN were all going south, towards the trouble, so as soon as we had passed the junction that led to their compound the road was quiet. There were shallow ditches to either side of the road, green in their soft, damp U-shaped bottoms, and beside them flowers like cow parsley, and many others – small ones in yellow and pink.

I felt anxious and unhappy. Lack of sleep and an execution will do that. Also love. I looked at Penny. And the others. They stirred something within me for sure. But when I tried to look into my heart, to X-ray it for my 'true feelings', it didn't show up as a good red throb with a name across it in curly font, nor even a complicatedly real four-chambered hunk. No, as I conceptualised a vessel which might contain my deepest feelings, the organ I imagined was a honeycomb, a black sponge – the chambers interconnected so multiply that the possibilities for a true reckoning of my loves and likings swam before my eyes, various as pomegranate seeds.

'Where will we go? What about the van?' Cally asked.

'I guess. I guess, we go back to London?' Penny said. 'If we can get to – to somewhere you can fly from? Zagreb?'

'There's a party in Dublin, in Cork,' Von said.

'It would be good to get the van,' Shannon said. After all, it did belong to the kayaking club. They were hoping to sell it.

'We really can't get back to the van, I don't think, can we?' Penny said.

'If we could get diesel, I would. It's just sitting there,' Sara said and waved her arm south.

'We could try to head to Sarajevo?' Onomatopoeic Bob said. I guess, like me, he didn't have much to go back to.

'I really would like to get to Ireland for this party.'

'Jesus, Von, haven't you been to enough parties?' Penny said.

'How many parties do you want? Parties are all the same,' I said and felt my attempted sophistication die in the heat of the road. Everyone was silent as we walked on; the only sound the tacky noise of our trainers, as with each step we peeled them off the road surface, where they'd bonded very slightly with the hot tarmac.

After thinking for a while, Shannon finally announced: 'OK. We've done what we intended. Now, we go back and tell people what's going on here. And get on with living our lives. We have a responsibility to do that too.'

Yes. Fuck. The whole of life lay open before me. Anything was possible, unfortunately.

Chapter 36

The road was dead flat until it headed up into the hills that marked the border. There was hardly any wind, so when we walked into a powerful acrid smell of chicken shit there was nothing to diffuse it. It felt like walking into a wall.

Just after the smell hit, a sandy track branched off the road. Barring access to the track was a red-and-white barrier pole resting in a Y of metal. Beyond the barrier a man sat on the ground with his back against one of the front wheels of a Toyota pickup.

The guard stood up as we approached and we clocked it was a face we knew. The ponytailed bar guy, who'd rented us the apartments – Mohammed's boss, or acquaintance. I couldn't remember the name, but Von, who had a public-school trick for picking up names like a magnet, waved a friendly arm and hailed him. 'Hasim!'

'Hasim?' Cally said.

He waved cautiously, and waited for us to draw nearer. 'Hello?' he said, with the air of someone who might deny all prior knowledge if we made a complaint about water pressure or electric shocks from the shower head at the apartments.

'Hey, Hasim?' Shannon said cautiously.

'What are you doing here?' he said and shook his head, flicking his threadbare ponytail flirtatiously.

'We're — we're walking,' Penny said. Beside his foot on the ground lay a baseball club and up from the front of his jeans, straight down from his naval, jutted the handle of a pistol.

'Where?' he said.

'Why?' Shannon said.

'Where?' he asked.

'Just tell him,' Sara said.

'We're actually walking to the border,' Shannon said,

'You're going? Where is your . . . big car?' he asked.

'The van? We left it — it's out of diesel,' Shannon said. 'How far is it to the border?'

He regarded the whole gang for a second, then told us, 'Near. For a car, near. For walking, too far.' And he waved his hand in several directions. 'Maybe tonight, very late, tomorrow, tomorrow night?'

'Seriously?'

'Where is your van?' he asked.

'Why?' Shannon asked.

'Why "why"?' he said.

'Why not "why"?' Shannon said.

'I want to help you. Maybe I have a little diesel.'

We broke out my guidebook and Onomatopoeic Bob guided Hasim's finger back over the junctions we had taken to walk into Velika.

'Hmm,' Hasim said, peering at the map. 'This is still OK. This morning this is still OK. Then, the 5th Corps will take it. Piss in it. In your van.'

'Hey, I've pissed in it, why shouldn't they?' Shannon said.

Hasim didn't laugh. 'How much money do you have?'

'How much to take us there and buy some diesel from you?'

'How much do you have?'

'How much is diesel?'

In the end Hasim agreed to make the trip, and supply six two-litre bottles of diesel. The price was three hundred Deutschmarks.

He led us to the back of the Toyota, where he imagined we would want to examine every fat green ex-mineral water bottle filled with diesel. He took the cap off each bottle in turn for us to smell and, if we wished, also taste the contents – his solicitous display of honesty revealing in its many parts how various were the deceptions to which he could imagine subjecting us. As Onomatopoeic Bob took the lead in the diesel tasting, Hasim explained there was one problem. He was manning, he said, a post, and it would be good for him, essential really, if one of us would stay behind with his cudgel.

Shannon looked around at us all. I said at once that I would wait. I thought it might look brave to offer, but actually I thought it was safer. They were driving back towards the battle. Plus, it's depressing going back: even when it's only retracing your steps to your flat to get your forgotten keys, you realise how blithely you once looked only ahead. Plus, I figured I'd done far too much hanging around Penny. Maybe a bit of getting blown about, all solitary, might burnish me in a way that rubbing up close had so clearly failed.

'Will you be all right?' Bev asked. I shrugged. Shannon climbed into the cab with Hasim while the others arranged themselves around the sides of the flatbed behind. I leaned on one end of the barrier to ease it up so the pickup could pass. Von dug deep into his daypack and pulled out a Nerf gun, which he handed to me reverentially as he passed.

'What's this for?' I asked.

'For protection,' he said and we both looked at the bright yellow-and-orange toy.

'Yeah?'

'Yeah. People might think it's a ray gun. Or something,' he said, starting to grow reproachful.

'You think?'

'They might. Round here? For a minute. They've probably never seen a ray gun,' he said.

'No. Right, Thank you, Von.'

Hasim wound down his window to say farewell. 'What do I do? What am I doing?' I asked him before he could drive off.

'Don't let anyone out, don't let anyone in. Tell them I will be back in thirty minutes.'

'In where? Out of where? Tell who?'

But they were gone.

I tucked the Nerf gun into my waistband and examined my post. There was a copse of good-size poplar trees at the top of a low hill across the road. Leading up to it a little path had been worn through the high dun-coloured grasses. There might be a nice dingly dell in there. A good place for a boozy picnic. On the far side of the barrier I was guarding, to the side of the track, was a drainage ditch and then a big wide field given over to pasture. Behind me, the track snaked to a low wire fence. Beyond that, the path swung round towards some grey agricultural buildings.

I walked my beat with my baseball bat on my shoulder. I was still in my play gear – a rough green military army surplus store shirt, and a pair of murky combat trousers which flapped around my trainers. The midday sun was hot and even though I knew it was way too soon, I felt the first spike of fear that my friends would leave me behind. That was a shame, because I guessed they wouldn't have even got halfway to the van yet. So if this was when I was starting to worry, I had a huge amount of anxiety to look forward to before they got back.

I sat on the dusty ground and watched the second hand on my watch tick round. It was an old-man watch that Helen had bought for me in Manchester from a place in Afflecks Palace where they sold second-hand jeans. On my arm it never recaptured the promise of another life it held in its glass case, but nor did it quite lose it. I leaned back against the bare zincky scaffold pole that hinged the barrier to nowhere.

After an hour or so, when I was growing certain that in the van they had forgotten or disregarded me, were maybe even laughing about me, I walked up the little drive towards the agricultural buildings in the distance and made some calculations. If Hasim claimed he'd be away half an hour, it was probably, what, maybe double that? Plus the unexpected hiccups. The difficulty filling the van with diesel, some wrong turns, and then the inexplicable additional 20 to 30 per cent of time above what seems reasonable that everything always takes when you are the one doing the waiting. So, what . . . I told myself it would be another hour really until I should actually feel anxious that they had hightailed it, leaving me to walk out of the war zone alone.

It was then that I saw the people. The farm buildings in the distance looked like poultry sheds. The end of one of them was open or hewn off, and inside it looked like there might be people – many, many people. Too many. Closer by, near the high fencing that surrounded the farm, a line of ten or twelve figures stood in front of two men in uniform with guns. You couldn't tell exactly what was happening, but the shapes were wrong. One of the people in the line would drop to the floor, not shot, but under their own power, and then stay there, crouched; then another one would go down; then the first one, after a long time, would pop up. It could almost have been an exercise regime, but the bodies of the people in the line were despondent, tired beyond resistance. Plus, when the ones who went down hit the floor in a crouch, one of the men with a gun went and stood over them and did something that might have been soft shuffling kicks or might have been something else. It was hard to see. But it wasn't friendly.

From the road I heard the sound of a vehicle changing down gears and I jogged fast back to my post. I felt a leap of hope. We were getting out. I didn't need to be the sole witness to this mistreatment. Just watching it made me complicit, but as soon as I could share it, as soon as I could speak about it to the others, then I could say it was wrong.

But when the road came into view, it wasn't the Peace War van idling by the sentry point. It was a French UN Land Cruiser.

In what sounded like Serbo-Croat, the officer in the passenger seat asked me something. Then he repeated it in French and I heard '*nom*', so I told him my name. The guy asking the questions must have been a linguist because he was able to tell I wasn't French or Yugoslav. He asked me in English who I was and I said my name again.

'Why are you here?' he asked and I said I was here by accident, for a friend, really an acquaintance. Less.

His face was something of a wedge. Not much chin, a sloping forehead and a long delicate nose, thin-skinned and pink like a pterodactyl wing. It poked far out and made me want to cover it with my hand. He asked if I was a mercenary and I said no, God no, and then he asked me what the fuck I was doing there at the gate. And I said again I was guarding it for someone I didn't really know.

The officer looked extremely sceptical. He glanced up and down at my fatigues and asked why I was working for Babo. 'I'm not. My friend just asked me to stay here while he went to get our van.'

The French officer spoke to his driver, a much more thickset man, who mumbled something back to his commanding officer, lit a cigarette and looked at me with frank disgust.

'You know what that place is?'

'I'm not to do with that,' I said. 'I'm just guarding this road to —'

'This is the other entrance,' he said.

'I don't know that. I didn't know that,' I said. 'Even if it is true.'

'It is true.'

'And what is it — there?'

'You know,' he said.

'I don't know,' I said and felt guilty, because I guess by then I did know. But it seemed too hard to explain that I had only just found out.

'This chicken farm is a camp for holding opponents in bad conditions.'

'Oh. My God,' I said, now committed to some bad acting. 'My God, I had no idea. I was just left holding this stick. For an acquaintance. This isn't a uniform, it's a costume.'

It sounded incredibly implausible, I could see that.

'Well, the 5th Corps are making rapid advances so we are here to watch for human rights infringements as they advance.'

'Oh, right. Good. That's a good idea. Good,' I said, and let the baseball bat drop as quietly as possible to the floor. Thunk!

'Will you give your full details to my colleague, please?'

'Of course. *Avec plaisir*,' I smiled ingratiatingly. If I was a war

356

criminal, I was going to be the nicest one in history. 'We did a play? Maybe you heard of it?' I said to the commanding officer and the thickset guy who was getting out several files and a legal pad. The Frenchman didn't look at me; instead he pointed at two subordinates to investigate the path opposite my post. As the privates disappeared up the path beaten through the high grass, the little stand of trees at the top looked much less inviting.

Now, right on cue, I saw the van approaching from a long way off. I felt angry as it chugged slowly towards me. My face grew hot. I had been seduced. This was what the posh got you to do. Guard concentration camps for them while they went to pick up the car.

The French officer waved them down to a halt.

'Where's he gone? Where's Hasim?' I asked Penny, who was at the passenger-side window.

'He stayed in town. What? What's going on?'

'It's a camp. He got me to guard his camp?'

'A camp? Like – camping?' Von said.

'No, not like camping. Like a fucking camp. For opponents.'

'Oh shit.'

At the driver's window Onomatopoeic Bob talked through the situation with the officer, who placed a pair of clear-framed round plastic glasses on his long nose as he examined our travel documents. They made him look a little like Andy Warhol and I felt they were out of keeping with the seriousness of the UN mission. There should be army-issue eyeglasses. Camouflage, or at least black.

'We can go,' Onomatopoeic Bob said a minute later to Shannon and the rest.

'But you, I need to talk with further,' the officer said to me sternly.

'For how long?'

'For as long as we say!' the thickset driver said, and squatted down, his automatic rifle beside him, so he could rest his file on his thigh as he wrote.

'Should we wait?' Shannon said.

But they hadn't even turned the engine off in the van.

'How long will you be? Do you think?'

I had no idea. Between three days and life was my private estimate.

'Look. It's OK. Go. I'll take what's coming. I'll explain,' I said and looked heroically at Penny.

'Can you safeguard us?' Shannon asked the Frenchman. 'If we wait for our friend?'

'No. We can safeguard nothing,' the officer said.

'Look. Go. You have to go, there's no option really,' I said.

'Will you be OK?' Penny said.

I did hope she would stay. Stay and sit with me. After all, so far any successes with Penny had come from getting as physically close to her as possible, while as drunk or tired as possible and waiting for us to essentially *fall* into one another. My best friends in terms of seduction were proximity and gravity. So maybe if she would wait with me . . .

'I'll be OK,' I said manfully. They took me at my word.

Bob revved the engine and Von rubber-stamped the decision, coming round from the sliding door of the van to shake my hand.

'This is a good number for me. Give me a ring,' he said and handed me a slip of paper. 'I won't be there for three months.'

'We will see you in Zagreb? Yeah?' Shannon said and I just nodded. 'Or in Manchester?'

Penny leaned out of the van and offered me her balled-up hand. I went to take it, to shake it or kiss it, but the centre was soft like a chocolate and from it fell a crumpled fifty-pound note.

As I unfurled it, it looked out of scale with my hand, so big I could have used it as a blanket.

'In case – you need to get back, and it's hard?'

'Right. Thank you,' I said and tried to look down not too coquettishly.

'Are you OK?'

'Absolutely.'

'You look – you look OK.'

My shirt was open. Somewhere along the way I'd started to copy how Von and Christian left their shirts open three or four top buttons and turned their collars up. I guess I'd lost a little baby fat from no longer eating late at night, stoned, from twenty-four-hour garages.

'Thank you. Some polish is gained with one's ruin, I guess,' I said.

'What?' she asked.

'I don't know. It's a poem. "Some polish is gained with one's ruin."'

'What's been ruined?'

I looked at the money meaningfully. 'I don't know.'

'You're not ruined.'

'Yeah. And I mean, you did make me leave Helen?'

'What?'

'It's fine but –'

'I did not.'

'Well, you did.'

'I absolutely did not.

'You did, you made that face.'

'I don't know what you're talking about?'

'We best rock,' Von interjected and Onomatopoeic Bob revved hard.

The French officer came and stood beside me like a gaoler.

'Look, Andy, at least we did something?' Penny said.

'Yeah,' I said. 'Yeah. No. Sorry. It is good to do something.'

I looked down at my feet as the van pulled away and then up and after them, reproachfully, as they rounded a corner out of sight. I should have just said, 'Yes stay. Definitely stay. Please stay.'

*

The thickset driver started on a series of questions, each of which was addressed to me first in French, then, when I shrugged in incomprehension, repeated in English.

I tried to be as honest as I could, but confusion and bad translation and the complexity of the situation meant that I kept on sounding like I was lying or contradicting myself and eventually the driver screwed up a whole sheet of answers and threw it to the ground.

He pulled out another sheet. I looked at that bend in the road, trying to summon a figure out of the mirage that quivered on the tarmac top.

As we started on the questions again, like in a dream, a figure did appear. My heart flipped with excitement even as I tried to damp it down and say it's not her, it's not her . . .

It wasn't her. Or Shannon.

It was Bev.

He marched back purposefully, looking at the ground, but then glancing up to me and waving an arm. What message was he bringing? Were they waiting further along? Had someone swooned for my absence?

'Couldn't leave you, mate,' he said.

'Are they waiting?' I said.

'Are they waiting? Nah, mate, they've gone.'

'Oh, yeah? I thought they'd go,' I said.

'Yeah, they need to go. The 5th Corps are coming. It's gonna be a shit show. But I thought you might need a hand.'

'Oh, Bev. Bev. You're a fucking sweetheart,' I said. I hadn't admitted to myself quite how scared I felt until he came back. But now I saw I wanted someone to be there for whatever interrogation I was to face, to confirm the stuff I said and help me phone the British Consulate and to begin the long haul of unravelling myself from this mess.

'Where will you take me? Can my friend come? Just one?' I asked the officer, who was back from a walk of the perimeter of the chicken farm.

'We are United Nations Protection Force. We cannot detain you. Only a national authority can detain you. We are monitors.'

'So you are not – you're not taking me anywhere?'

'No.'

'Oh. Right.'

'I'm asking you more questions,' the driver said, 'for a long time.'

'But if we want to go, mate?' Bev said to the commanding officer.

'No. We would like to ask you more questions,' the officer said, taking off his glasses and wiping his brow.

'Sure, but if we don't want to?'

'I don't mind,' I said and Bev looked at me like: don't be a prick. 'I mean, I'm happy to talk. But I would love to go?'

'I would like to talk to you,' the driver said.

'Right, you'd like to, but you can't make him?' Bev said. The driver and the officer looked at one another and I felt relief and anger flood me at once.

'You mean I could have gone – I could have gone with my friends?'

'Yes, you can go. Anyone can go. I would like to talk to you, but you can go.'

'Right. OK, then, I'm sorry, but I'm going to go,' I said, and hesitated before I started to walk, just to check that he wouldn't add, 'Of course if you go you are contravening section two of our rules of engagement and we may shoot you in the neck.'

He didn't say that. And he didn't say anything else. I said, 'Then we go. I'm sorry. For the confusion and for the inconvenience. And for the record, I think you are doing wonderful work, here. I am sorry I can't talk. It was a misunderstanding. Can you put on your report it was a misunderstanding? Thank you.'

They weren't about to thank a war criminal. So, as we began to walk off, the driver just tapped the paper where my details were recorded and nodded back towards town.

Chapter 37

Hasim had been lying, it turned out. The border wasn't far at all. Just after the main track up to the poultry farm, where two more Land Cruisers sat, their occupants off keeping watch at the main gates of the detention facility, the road slipped across a small valley and, with a couple of twists back on itself, into the borderland hills. We were accompanied by a family who joined the road from a countryside path, and also by a young man who pulled out of one of the few farmhouses along the way. He dragged a handcart with spoked bicycle wheels and a high-sided yellow inflatable paddling pool which sat almost perfectly on the square, flat piece of chipboard laid over the axle. Inside the pool were bundles of clothes neatly tied with string and in the centre one long MDF cabinet, the doors pushed open by plates and kitchenware and an ornate light fitting.

The border out of Babo's little bubble in Bosnia and into Croatia was guarded, but the atmosphere was relaxed. They weren't exactly giving out gold stars, yet the sense was that if you'd made it this far you deserved to be left alone, granted a hard sympathetic nod of appreciation as you passed through. After all, no one but a friend would be seeking to run away from the enemy who was coming from the south. Bev and I had our passports to show, but the guard, an older man with a moustache whose bristles were widely spaced and thick like cat's whiskers, waved us through, not wanting to get into the complicated questions. Perhaps he'd been alerted to our potential arrival by the occupants of the van that I hoped might be idling in a lay-by nearby? It wasn't.

We stayed that night in a farmer's spare back room. Overcharged, up front, for an uncomfortable eight hours between polyester sheets that felt like they sparked against my sweat as I swivelled for cool. In the morning our host called us a taxi which took us to the border of the Serb Krajina. With our UK passports, all the borders were much more permeable going out than coming in. This was a set of states and statelets that wanted outsiders out, to do their business unobserved. Via a provincial bus, which seemed to be a charter, not scheduled, we went through Karlovac and into Zagreb, resting our heads on the shaking window and barely bothering to look at the bullet marks on the buildings any more.

In the low grey bus station I exchanged my fifty-pound note at a brutalising exchange rate for tickets that would take us as far as Cologne. The route home was straight and boring. I sat with Bev as our mauve-and-turquoise liveried coach ate up the miles to central Germany. At Cologne I unzipped my last money-belt Deutschmarks to get us back into Calais on a luscious summer's day where we used up the last little bit of credit on Bev's card to board as foot passengers for Dover.

And then, there it was again – England, with its brazen white cliffs. Great Britain. What a funny little nub of gristle it was when you looked at it. Half finished and uppity and scared and doubting. Wounded, bust-up and bursting into the street looking for trouble, with a memory of self-righteousness whirring in its breast. Fractured, wonky, amenable to a certain humour but deep down serious. Serious and, for some reason, hurt.

We hitched out of Dover to London with a retired public-school master who, when we revealed we'd been in Bosnia, raised one corner of his mouth perhaps a millimetre and then asked no further questions. Instead he told us many details of his career in and around Salisbury and how a complicated piece of chicanery by a bad new head had swindled him, it would be no exaggeration to say, out of a fair final pension settlement.

I navigated us to the Calman house by memory and pressed the doorbell in a haze: a fug of hope and fear and excitement. The cleaner answered and I said a cheery 'Hello!' like a family friend and asked for Penny – she said Penny wasn't at home and, when I asked where she was, fetched Kenneth. I'm pretty sure he recognised me, but I introduced myself again to be sure. He left a brief pause and then said, 'Oh. Yes. Penny's on her way to France – she's driving from Yugoslavia, to stay in her grandma's house, with a whole pack of her pals.'

'Oh, right. Whereabouts in France?' I said.

He scrutinised me for a moment and then said, 'In France.'

'I'm her pal,' I said.

'Yes,' he said and looked at Bev in his ragged *It's a Kinda Magic* tour T-shirt on the pavement opposite, cleaning his teeth with a lolly stick.

'All right!' Bev shouted over, raising an arm and revealing a fresh sweat patch and the whitish concentric rings of several previous ones.

'Hello,' Kenneth said, starting to back away from the door ever so slightly.

'Can – can I have a glass of water?' I asked.

In the kitchen Kenneth let the tap run not at all before filling it and handing me the glass.

'Umm. Thirsty!' I said as I gulped the tepid, hard, London water.

He stood there 'patiently', as though I was detaining him from matters of national importance, with a brochure from a mail-order corduroy trouser company in his hand.

'Yes. Right. OK?' he said and showed me the way back out with an extended arm.

'I just wondered – about our trip?' I said. 'Whether you might have organised everything?'

'I'm sorry?'

I looked down at my scuffed Doc Martens as I steeled myself. 'Sent us via your friend in Croatia, Ronnie, at the embassy? Through the North Sector towards Bihac – instead of Sarajevo? And then – got a message through, to sort of, push us into Velika? Into Babo's town?'

'I'm sorry? *What?*' he said.

'And whether you think it's good there and that's what they should all do, shut up and get on with it, and the government, our government, and I just wanted to let you know, it doesn't work there. Velika. Maybe you thought we'd be safe there or something? Because we weren't.'

He looked at me and didn't say anything at all. I drank more water, my lip trembling. Some of it dribbled down my chin.

He turned, walked out and went back up the stairs without saying anything else to me, but mumbling what I think was 'Miss Marple with a hard-on' as he went.

I stayed on a half-minute or so alone in the kitchen, looking at a row of copper pans suspended in size order on hooks, like a rarely used item in the percussion section of an orchestra. Then I stole a tangerine from the overflowing fruit bowl and left the house, shutting the door quietly behind me, and walked back to Bev.

'All right?' Bev asked.

'Yeah. Bit of a cunt,' I said and he nodded.

'London,' he said.

'Yeah,' I said.

*

At Victoria Coach Station, I used a British cash card outside a branch of the Halifax to take money out. I said an audible 'thank you' to the machine as the cogs turned and the notes appeared. Bev and I climbed the three or four very steep steps up to the unfriendly Brummie driver and on into the coach's familiar scent of British cleaning products. We stopped short of the smoking section. That was where the adventures happened, and we were both full for the moment. Once into the green belt, the countryside went past thick and extraordinarily – Amazonianly – lush as we zoomed up to the borders.

I cracked open *War and Peace*. I'd had to go back and reread the section previous to the one I'd bookmarked so many times I was moving backwards through the text, and the Napoleonic invasion – that was making everything additionally confusing. After a while I skipped towards the end, to try to find out what happened, where I was headed, but found myself in quite a dense essay.

'What's it like, fucking Brainiac?' Bev asked.

'Oh – this? It's – this bit is quite – it's not so much story, it's his, um, sort of theory of history.'

'Oh, OK. What is it then?' Bev asked after a while.

'His theory?' I deliberated for a bit. By the time I had formulated my precis, Bev was looking out of the window. 'I think –

he'd say, what happens is, you know, it's not simple. It's fucking complicated.'

'OK,' Bev said, wobbling his head and jutting his lip, giving Tolstoy due consideration. 'Fair dos.' But he didn't look convinced.

'No?'

'Nah,' he said. 'Not really. I reckon, usually, if you're not a wanker, it's simple.'

*

Bev and I climbed down from our coach onto the pavement by the side of the A5, part outraged not to be met by fanfares, part so very pleased to be back on the rain-splattered summer tarmac of home, where we were just allowed to stand without papers or explanation or elaboration, and we knew how things would taste and how the vending machines worked and, mostly, what people meant when they looked at us.

He asked what I was going to do, and I didn't know, so we had two fast farewell pints in a pub on the main road. Across the way, on the road leading to Chirk Castle, there was building work in progress. We didn't talk about Bosnia at all, but just about the last few hours and our hitchhike. He called his brother, who came and revved a Ford Escort hard outside the pub until Bev finished off his pint and shook my hand.

'Well, fucking hell. Good on you, mate,' he said, as the lager curled round my brain, wrapping it up tight.

'Cheers then,' I said and waved a salute through the window to his brother, who didn't like the look of me and didn't give anything back.

I hoisted my rucksack on and started to walk, headed for a

certain house where I knew a gang of stoners had managed to catch a lease. They'd turned it into something of a hangout and I'd heard once that Helen sometimes went there now she'd moved back.

I was a little afraid as I walked across town that I'd hear she was dead. She had always been fragile and I worried that in letting things screw up so shittily I'd helped send her home to town. And in town, if you were clever, and nothing else happened, the most common career path was to become a smackhead.

The house was down on a bit of council estate where many tenants had bought their places. You could tell the privately owned houses because they had usually replaced the solid blue-painted council doors for plastic white ones with a three-section wobbly-glazed fan light. I knocked at the back door and a lad I knew answered and let me in without hesitation.

'Alright. Have you been away, Andy, or what?'

He led me into the front room, where two other lads and a girl called Yvette on early lunch break from a hairdresser's were smoking an incredibly long double-ended comedy joint. And there, sitting plum in the middle of the sofa, was Helen, smoking a cigarette. She looked sleek and clean and self-contained, like a cat wrapped up in its own warmth. I sat next to her and she said hello and asked me where I'd been and I said I'd been to Bosnia and she laughed and then so did everyone else, though I don't think the others knew why they were laughing.

Helen asked who I'd gone abroad with, was it 'that lot', and I said yes and she raised her eyebrows and I said they'd left me in the shit a bit and she smiled, not unkindly. I asked where she was living and I liked the way she told me about it: she was easy and calm and I felt like we were two scientists who were meeting up again after a period of contemplation who could now discuss objectively the rather disgusting sexual and emotional experiments we had conducted on one another in the past.

I said I didn't know what I was going to do with myself and she told me there were jobs going at a supermarket and not really knowing what else to do, after we'd listened to the Stone Roses for a while, and the cast of folk in the room started to revolve, I headed out and down to the job Centre.

*

I tried to explain my current situation to the lady down there. I came clean about my lack of degree; I think I came overly clean, probably. When she gave me an application form for Iceland, I told her everything.

'I don't know what to put here, about – "Anything I should tell them that might affect their decision"? The thing is, I might have been – sort of, I don't know, it's possible I've been recorded as a war criminal.' I explained that I wasn't really sure whether I was a war criminal or not. 'The UN took my name for a list, but I was never incarcerated,' I said.

'Oh, right,' the lady said. I tried to strip ten years or so off her – it was just possible I knew her from school, but I didn't think so.

'It's something of a grey area. A Frenchman said I was a war criminal, but it was unclear if he was joking.' I looked at the form hard. 'The thing about being charged as a war criminal,' I said, 'is that it has a lot of negative associations.'

'It does have a lot of negative associations,' the woman from the jobcentre admitted, leafing through her fact sheets. 'But we're . . . our role is to be here — to be here — to . . .' She was fumbling a little with her files. 'To — to help you through those,' she said, feeling, I think, increasingly uncertain a sheet could be located which applied to this particular client. 'You should probably explain just why — and how?'

'I mean, I'm not a . . . There are a lot of reasons I got listed as a war criminal,' I went on, my pen wavering over the application form. 'It's difficult to fit in this box. It's quite a — a — sort of complicated thing?'

Acknowledgements

Thanks to Jo Unwin, Alex Bowler, Dan Franklin, Milly Jenkins and Sam Bain.

Also to Josh Freedman Berthoud and Faisal A. Qureshi, Imogen O'Rorke, Charlie Morrissey and my fellow Oswestry State Theatre street performers. To Mohammed and everyone in Velika Kladusa, Bihac, Sarajevo and Zagreb who showed me kindness and hospitality.

Thanks to Cathy King, Georgia Garrett, Jon Elek, Matthew Broughton, Ruth Waldram, Rowan Routh, Carrie Plitt, and all at Jonathan Cape, RCW and Conville & Walsh.

Thanks to my very good friends Abe and Annie, and Hannah and Shane.

Thanks always to Ju, Jas, Mark, Rob, Will, Mungo and Sean.

Thanks to the authors whose books have informed this one (though of course all errors are my own): Misha Glenny, *The Fall of Yugoslavia*; Brendan Simms, *Unfinest Hour*; Anthony Lloyd, *My War Gone By, I Miss It So*; Brian Hall, *The Impossible Country*; Brendan O'Shea, *Bosnia's Forgotten Battlefield: Bihac*; Adam LeBor, *Milosevic*; David Rohde, *Endgame*; Steven L. Burg and Paul S. Shoup, *The War in Bosnia-Herzegovina*; Joe Sacco, *Safe Area Gorazde*;

Michael Ignatieff, *The Warrior's Honor*; David Leigh and Ed Vulliamy, *Sleaze: The Corruption of Parliament*; Keith Cory-Jones, *War Dogs*; Bill Carter, *Fools Rush In*; Andrew Mueller, *Rock and Hard Places*; Aubrey Verboven, *Border Crossings*; Celia Hawkesworth, *Colloquial Serbo-Croat*; David Owen, *Balkan Odyssey*; Douglas Hurd, *Ten Minutes to Turn the Devil*; Martin Dunford and Jack Holland, *The Rough Guide to Yugoslavia* (1990); Laura Silber and Allan Little, *The Death of Yugoslavia* (and the TV series it accompanied), and in particular Rebecca West, *Black Lamb and Grey Falcon*.